PRAISE FOR EILEEN WILKS'S LUPI NOVELS

NIGHT SEASON

"A captivating world." —*The Romance Reader*

"Filled with action and plenty of twists."
—*Midwest Book Review*

BLOOD LINES

"Another winner from Eileen Wilks."
—*Romance Reviews Today*

"Ms. Wilks is a true master of her craft." —*The Eternal Night*

"Fast-paced and nail-biting reading." —*Fresh Fiction*

"The magic seems plausible, the demons real, and the return of enigmatic Cynna, along with the sorcerer, hooks fans journeying the fantasy realm of Eileen Wilks." —*The Best Reviews*

"Intriguing . . . Surprises abound in *Blood Lines* . . . A masterful pen and sharp wit hone this third book in the Moon Children series into a work of art. Enjoy!" —*A Romance Review*

"Savor *Blood Lines* to the very last page." —*BookLoons*

"Quite enjoyable and sure to entertain . . . A fast-paced story with plenty of danger and intrigue." —*The Green Man Review*

"Those in search of paranormal tales that are rich and multifaceted will get exactly what they're looking for in the brilliant Wilks's exceptional supernatural stories." —*Romantic Times*

continued . . .

"I remember Eileen Wilks's characters
long after the last page is turned."
—*New York Times* bestselling author Kay Hooper

Books by Eileen Wilks

TEMPTING DANGER
MORTAL DANGER
BLOOD LINES
NIGHT SEASON
MORTAL SINS

Anthologies

CHARMED
(with Jayne Ann Krentz writing as Jayne Castle, Julie Beard,
and Lori Foster)

LOVER BEWARE
(with Christine Feehan, Katherine Sutcliffe, and Fiona Brand)

CRAVINGS
(with Laurell K. Hamilton, MaryJanice Davidson,
and Rebecca York)

ON THE PROWL
(with Patricia Briggs, Karen Chance, and Sunny)

MORTAL SINS

EILEEN WILKS

BERKLEY SENSATION, NEW YORK

THE BERKLEY PUBLISHING GROUP
Published by the Penguin Group
Penguin Group (USA) Inc.
375 Hudson Street, New York, New York 10014, USA
Penguin Group (Canada), 90 Eglinton Avenue East, Suite 700, Toronto, Ontario M4P 2Y3, Canada
(a division of Pearson Penguin Canada Inc.)
Penguin Books Ltd., 80 Strand, London WC2R 0RL, England
Penguin Group Ireland, 25 St. Stephen's Green, Dublin 2, Ireland (a division of Penguin Books Ltd.)
Penguin Group (Australia), 250 Camberwell Road, Camberwell, Victoria 3124, Australia
(a division of Pearson Australia Group Pty. Ltd.)
Penguin Books India Pvt. Ltd., 11 Community Centre, Panchsheel Park, New Delhi—110 017, India
Penguin Group (NZ), 67 Apollo Drive, Rosedale, North Shore 0632, New Zealand
(a division of Pearson New Zealand Ltd.)
Penguin Books (South Africa) (Pty.) Ltd., 24 Sturdee Avenue, Rosebank, Johannesburg 2196,
South Africa

Penguin Books Ltd., Registered Offices: 80 Strand, London WC2R 0RL, England

This is a work of fiction. Names, characters, places, and incidents either are the product of the author's imagination or are used fictitiously, and any resemblance to actual persons, living or dead, business establishments, events, or locales is entirely coincidental. The publisher does not have any control over and does not assume any responsibility for author or third-party websites or their content.

MORTAL SINS

A Berkley Sensation Book / published by arrangement with the author

PRINTING HISTORY
Berkley Sensation mass-market edition / February 2009

Copyright © 2009 by Eileen Wilks.
Excerpt from *Blood Magic* copyright © 2009 by Eileen Wilks.
Cover art by Don Sipley.
Cover design by George Long.
Interior text design by Kristin del Rosario.

ISBN: 978-0-425-22552-3

BERKLEY® SENSATION
Berkley Sensation Books are published by The Berkley Publishing Group,
a division of Penguin Group (USA) Inc.,
375 Hudson Street, New York, New York 10014.
BERKLEY® SENSATION and the "B" design are trademarks of Penguin Group (USA) Inc.

PRINTED IN THE UNITED STATES OF AMERICA

10 9 8 7 6 5 4 3 2 1

ONE

SOUTHERN air holds on to scent. Scent is vapor, after all, a chemical mist freed by heat to hang, trapped, in moist air. In his other form, Rule knew this.

In this form he knew only the richness. His world was more scent than sight as he raced through silver-shadowed woods, through air heavy with moisture and fragrance. Layers and layers of green overlaid the complex stew of water from a nearby stream with its notes of kudzu, rock, and fish. Rhododendron's subtle vanilla scent jumbled with moss, with dogwood and buckeye and the sugary scent of maple, punctuated by the cool tang of pine.

But it was the musk, blood, and fur scent of raccoon he chased.

A three-quarter moon hung high overhead as he leaped the stream, muscles reaching in an exhilarated approximation of flight. He landed almost on top of the prey—but his hind feet skidded in slick red clay. A second later, the raccoon shot up a tree.

He shook his head. Damned raccoons always climbed if they got a chance. He didn't begrudge the animal its escape, but wished he'd had more of a chase first.

Deer do not climb trees. He decided to course for that scent.

Coursing was as much excuse as action. He'd eaten well before Changing, so hunger was distant; the real delight was simply being in motion, reading the world through nose, ears, the pads of his feet.

The human part of him remained, a familiar slice of "I" that was not-wolf. He remembered his two-legged thoughts and experiences; they simply ceased to matter as much. Not when air slid through him like hot silk, pregnant with a thousand flavors. It was probably the human part that felt a pang for the wonders of these Southern woods, remembering the hotter, dryer land claimed by his clan in southern California. His grandfather had made the decision to buy land there for Nokolai's clanhome. In that place and time, the land had been cheap.

It had been a sound decision. The clan had prospered in California. But at Nokolai's clanhome, wolves ran on rocks scattered over hard-baked ground, not on a thick bed of pine needles and moss, through tree shadows surprised here and there by the tumble of a stream.

Rule had run as wolf in many places, yet there was something special about this night, these woods. Something new. He'd never run here as wolf before. Not with Leidolf's clanhome so near.

The spike of worry was real, but fleeting. Wolves understand fear. Worry is too mental, too predicated on the future, to hold their attention. The slice of him that remained man wanted to hold on to that worry, gnawing it like a bone that refused to crack. The wolf was more interested in the day-old spoor of an opossum.

This was why he ran tonight: too many worries, too much gnawing at problems that refused to crack open and release their marrow. He'd learned the hard way that the man needed the wolf at least as much as the wolf needed the man. These woods were sweet. He'd find no answers in them, but tonight he wasn't seeking answers.

Lily said they hadn't come up with the right questions yet.

Rule paused, head lifted. Thought of her was sweet to both man and wolf. If only she could . . .

He twitched his ear as if a fly had bitten it. Foolishness. Both his natures agreed on that. Things were as they were, not as he might wish them to be. Females did not Change.

An hour later he'd found no deer, though he'd crossed their trails often enough, along with many others—a pack of feral dogs, a copperhead, another raccoon. Perhaps he'd been more interested in the distractions than in the hunt when there were no clanmates to join the chase. He wished Benedict was here, or Cullen . . . wished, though he tried not to, for Lily. Who could never share this with him.

His son would. Not yet, but in a few years. His son, who slept in a nearby town tonight—a town that would not be Toby's home much longer. In a few days they would meet with the judge for the custody hearing, and as long as Toby's grandmother didn't change her mind . . .

She wouldn't. She *couldn't*.

Feelings thundered through him, a primal cacophony of bliss, fear, jubilation. Rule lifted his nose to the moon and joined in Her song. Then he flicked his tail and took off at a lope, tongue lolling in the heat.

At the base of a low hill he found another scent. The chemical message was old but unmistakable. At some point in the last few months, a Leidolf wolf had marked the spot with urine. Something more visceral than recognition stirred as the portion of new mantle he carried rose, *knowing* the scent. Welcoming it.

Briefly, he was confused. Always before, that scent had meant Enemy. But the message of the power curled within him was clear: this wolf was *his*.

The man understood this change, had expected it, and memory supplied the reasons, so the wolf acknowledged the change and moved on. He wound up the little hill, bathed in the aural ocean of cricket song, anticipating grass. His nose informed him of a grassy place nearby, a spot where some alteration in soil had discouraged trees.

He liked grass. Perhaps it would be tall and home to mice. Mice were small and tricky, but they crunched nicely.

A thought sifted through him, arising from both ways of being: a few months ago he wouldn't have noticed a scent trace as old as that left by the Leidolf wolf. Had the new mantle coiled in his belly made it possible to sort that scent? Or was it because there were two mantles now? Perhaps this night, these woods were unusually magic because he carried more magic within him.

He would consider that in his other form, which was better suited to thinking. For now . . . at the crest of the hill he checked the moon, aware of time passing and a woman who waited in the small town nearby . . . asleep? Probably. He'd told her he would be gone most of the night.

Part of him thought this was a poor way to spend the night when he could have been in her bed, but there was grass ahead, the chance of a mouse or three. He was here, not there, and it was impossible to regret the night.

It was growing late, though. The fireflies had turned off their glow-sticks and the moon was descending. He would investigate the tall grass, he decided. Then he'd return to the place he'd left his clothing and to the shape that fit those clothes.

The grass was indeed tall, and the pungent smell of mice greeted him as he approached the tiny meadow. Rabbits, too, but rabbits were for days, since they seldom venture out of their burrows in the dark.

A breeze rose, whispering in the grass and carrying a host of smells. He paused, curious, and tested the air.

Was that . . . ? Corruption, yes; the stench of rot was unmistakable, though faint and distant. It meant little. Animals died in the woods. Besides, the smell came from the general direction of the highway. Animals were hit by cars even more often than they died naturally. But was it an animal?

The mantles might help him find out.

They slept now. He wouldn't call them up, not even just the one he considered truly his—that portion of the Nokolai mantle his father had given him years ago. To call one meant both answered, and he'd been warned. Drawing strongly on the portion he held of the other clan's mantle could kill the mantle's true holder, who clung so narrowly to life.

Not that Rule objected to Victor Frey's death. In other circumstances he'd celebrate it, but he didn't want the clan that would come to him with Victor's dying. And neither he nor Nokolai needed the ruckus that would follow.

Could he use the mantles without actually calling them up?

The wolf thought so. The man, troubled by instinct or too much thinking, wanted to try.

With a wisp of attention, Rule woke the twin powers in his gut. He focused again on the trace of scent carried by the breeze, not so much using the mantles as including them in his intention.

That scent sharpened in his nostrils immediately. Not a dog hit by a car, no. Nor a deer brought down by disease. Though the rot-stench overpowered the rest, he was almost sure the body he smelled had never walked four-footed.

Go. The breeze might die, or this new acuity fade. *Go. Find out.*

He launched himself into a run.

Wolves are largely indifferent to death as long as it doesn't threaten them or theirs. The body he chased was certainly dead, so the wolf felt no urgency. But the man did. Rule ran for over a mile—not full-out, not over unfamiliar terrain with no immediate danger or prey. But he was fast in this form, faster than a born-wolf.

By the time he slowed, he knew he'd been right about the highway. He heard cars cruising perhaps half a mile ahead . . . not many. It wasn't a major highway.

But what he sought lay within the woods. The rankness made his lip curl back from his teeth as he approached. Some other scent hid beneath the stench, but even with the mantles' help he couldn't sort it clearly, smothered as it was by putrefaction. Whatever it was, it brought up his hackles and started a growl in his throat.

Unlike some predators, wolves don't sideline as scavengers; only one on the brink of starvation would consider eating meat this rotten. And Rule was too human, even now, to feel anything but a sad sort of horror at what lay in a shallow ditch between a pair of oaks.

Not all beasts are so picky, however. And he hadn't been the first to find them.

TWO

*

IN a small, upstairs room in a large frame house, Lily Yu was sleeping. She didn't know this.

She knew pain, grief, despair. A sky overhead that wasn't proper sky, but a storm-colored dome, dimly glowing. In that surreal sky, legend battled nightmare—a dragon, dark and immense, grappled with a flying worm-thing whose gaping jaws could have swallowed a small car. The ground Lily knelt on was stone and dirt without a trace of green.

In front of her, unconscious and bleeding, lay a huge silver and black wolf.

So much blood. She couldn't see how badly Rule was hurt, but it was bad. She knew it. The demon had ripped him open so thoroughly that even he couldn't heal in time. Rule needed a doctor, a hospital, but there were no hospitals in hell.

She knew what she had to do. It was a hard knowing, as hard as the stones of this place—and as certain as spring in that other place, the Earth she remembered. The Earth she would never see again.

Another woman knelt across the wolf's ripped and bloody body, a woman bound to Rule as she was bound because she, too, was Lily. Another Lily, the one who could take Rule home.

She looked up now and met her own eyes. "Leave now. You have to go right away and take him where he can heal. To a hospital. He'll die here."

The other-her swallowed. "The gate—"

"Sam told me how to fix it." That's what the dragon had told them to call him. Sam. Was that a bit of desert-dry dragon humor? She'd never know.

So much she'd never know. Never have the chance to learn.

Other-Lily's eyes widened, and Lily saw her own dread knowledge reflected at her—a certainty the other tried to deny. "There has to be another way."

"Funny." Her lips quirked up, but her eyes burned. "That's what I said." She reached up and ripped the chain with its dangling charm from her neck, the emblem of her bond with Rule. "There isn't, though. You're the gate."

Slowly the other-her held out a hand.

Lily dropped the toltoi charm into it. "Tell him . . ." Feelings smacked into her, a torrent too churned and powerful to sort. She looked down, blinking quickly, and stroked Rule's head. She didn't care that her voice shook. "Tell him how glad I was about him. How very glad."

Other-Lily's fingers closed around the necklace. She nodded, her expression stark.

Lily pushed to her feet. She tugged at the top of her sarong, and it came open. "Bind him with this. He's bleeding badly." She tossed it to her other self and took off running. Naked, barefoot, she ran full-out.

There were others nearby, too. Rule's friends—a sorcerer, a gnome, a woman he'd once cared for. And there were demons, the demons they fought. Not so many of them yet, but more were coming. Hundreds, maybe thousands more. And there was one demon, one small and insignificant demon, who was something like a friend. A little orange demon named Gan, who wasn't fighting as the others were, and so saw Lily race for the cliff. And understood.

"No!" Gan howled, and started after her. "No, Lily Yu! Lily Yu, I do like you! I do! Don't—"

She reached the edge of the cliff. And leaped.

And as the air rushed past, heavy with the scent of ocean, whistling of terror and death, the dragon who called himself Sam whispered in her mind, *Remember*.

The opening bars of Beethoven's Fifth cut through the whistling wind, snatching Lily away from the impact just in time. Her eyes popped open on darkness, her heart pounding in soul-sickening fear. Automatically her hand stretched out for her phone on the bedside table. And bumped into a wall.

That simple, unexpected collision with reality jolted her back the rest of the way, though it took her a second to figure out why her bedside table wasn't where it should be. No, why *she* wasn't where she should be.

Lily had slept in too many beds in too many places lately. Home was San Diego, but she'd recently spent several months in Washington, D.C., getting special training at Quantico . . . among other things. But she and Rule were back in San Diego now, staying at his place. Only this wasn't Rule's apartment.

She was in Halo, North Carolina. This was Toby's home, the house where Rule's son lived with his grandmother, Louise Asteglio. It was 3:42 A.M., and Beethoven's Fifth was Rule's ring tone. She crawled across tumbled sheets to retrieve her phone from atop the chest of drawers. "What's wrong?"

Rule's voice was steady, but grim. "I found bodies. Three of them. Humans. They're in a shallow grave, stacked on top of each other. The adult is on top."

"Shit. Shit. The adult? Then . . . you're sure? Stupid question," she corrected herself, juggling the phone so she could yank off the oversize tee she'd slept in. "I hate it when it's kids; that's all." She paused. Suitcase. Where was her . . . oh, yeah, in the closet. They'd arrived late enough that she hadn't unpacked, but tucked it in the closet.

Lily yanked the closet door open and dragged out her suitcase. "They're in the woods?"

"About half a mile east of Highway 159, north of town. I'll wait for you at the highway."

"I'll find you." That part would be easy. Just as a compass needle knows north, Lily knew where Rule was. That aspect of the mate bond came in handy.

Chosen, the lupi called her—and so did Rule, but not often. Mostly he called her *nadia*, which she'd learned came from a word meaning tie, girdle, or knot. But the lupi meant well when they called her Chosen, believing she'd been selected for Rule by their Lady—a being they insisted was neither mythical nor a goddess, though she seemed to play in that league.

Nine months ago Lily had met Rule's eyes, the two of them chosen for each other, knotted together by the mate bond. Nothing had been the same since.

Good thing she'd fallen in love with him.

Lily wedged the phone between her chin and her shoulder while Rule gave her more details as she dug out jeans, socks, a tee. Clothes to tramp the woods in. She'd want a jacket to hide the shoulder holster.

When he finished, she said, "Sounds like you've found the vics of that murder Mrs. Asteglio told us about. The local cops ought to be grateful, but I wouldn't count on it. Ah . . . it's okay for them to know you found them, isn't it?"

"I didn't call you instead of the local authorities to avoid involvement. I'd have kept you out of this if I could. No, don't argue," he said before she had a chance. "I know you've seen bodies. That's not the point. These bodies . . . there's a small pack of feral dogs in the area."

Oh, ugh. "The dogs dug them up."

"So it looks. Smells that way, too."

"You're sure it was dogs? I'll be asked," she added hastily. He knew she wouldn't accuse him of anything so vile, but others might. "And there are other carnivores around, aren't there? Bears?"

"Bears are unlikely at this elevation, and the scent is quite clear. Five distinct canine scents near the grave, though only three are actually on the uppermost body."

"Dogs, then." Lily frowned. Why *had* Rule called her? He could have phoned in a tip anonymously. "What haven't you told me? There's something important you aren't saying. What is it?"

"A smell. In addition to dogs and decay, there's a smell that . . . but I could be wrong. It's faint, and so smothered by normal putrefaction I can't be sure. You'll be able to tell."

Tell what? Not the nature of the scent, because she'd never notice it. Compared to lupi, humans were all but scent-blind.

All at once she keyed into the phrase he'd used: "normal putrefaction." "Shit. Oh, shit. Tell me the rest of it."

"Death magic. I'm not sure, but . . . I think the bodies smell of death magic."

JAY Deacon was thin, trim, under forty, and under six feet. With his gold-rimmed glasses and skin the color of wet tea leaves, he looked more like a Northern academic than a stereotypical Southern sheriff.

He sure acted like a small-town sheriff, though. "You're not listenin' to me, ma'am. Coroner's van'll be here any minute now. We don't need the FBI to work the scene, so once you take us to the bodies, you can go on back to bed."

Until a few months ago, Lily had been on the other side of the local–federal divide, working homicides in San Diego. She would have sympathized with the sheriff's desire to hang on to his case if he weren't virtually patting her on the head and telling her to toddle on home.

"Sheriff, I called you as a courtesy, not because there's any question of jurisdiction. My ERT will be here within the hour. Your people can hang around or go back to bed themselves— your choice. I am not conducting you to the bodies."

His people consisted of a pair of deputies, both male. No surprise there. They were also white, however, and didn't seem to have a problem working for a black boss, which might give her hope for the future of the nation . . . later. When she could think about something other than bodies tainted by death magic.

After showing Lily what he'd found, Rule had walked her to the highway to wait for the FBI's Emergency Response

Team, then gone back to the scene to make sure no more little forest creatures chowed down on the remains. Lily had left her headlights on to guide the ERT, but their illumination was partly blocked now by the three county cars pulled up on the shoulder behind her car.

Both deputies held flashlights. Sheriff Deacon wasn't carrying anything but an attitude.

"Your team can help, I suppose." He grudged the words, as if he were offering a major concession. "If they get here in time. But like I said, we've got the perp locked up, which makes this my scene."

"Murder by magical means is a federal crime."

He shook his head and sighed. "Roy Don Meacham didn't use magic to kill his family. Crazy sumbitch used his son Andrew's baseball bat. We've got the bat. Roy Don handed it to me himself. We've got a pattern of domestic violence—"

"How many calls?"

"Just one, but plenty of witnesses say Roy Don didn't mind using the back of his hand on the kids or Becky. We've got physical evidence—the murder weapon, and blood and other traces on his clothes and skin. Hell, we've got a witness. Bill Watkins has the postal route out that way. He heard screamin' when he pulled his truck up to the mailbox, so he went to help. Ended up with a plate in his skull where Roy Don whacked him, but he tried."

"He remembers what he saw at the house?" Severe head trauma usually meant some degree of amnesia covering the time of the injury.

"Oh, yeah. He went inside, saw Roy Don walloping on Becky with the bat. He doesn't remember anything after that, but he remembers that much, poor bastard. We've got all the evidence we need."

"Except a confession. Or the bodies."

"Which you've found. You got a tip," he added, his voice landing heavy on the last word. "One you haven't elected to tell me about."

"No, I haven't." Lily had to tilt her head back to meet his eyes. This wasn't uncommon; at almost five foot three, she looked up a lot. But Deacon was standing too close, making a point of the difference in their heights. That annoyed her. "However, I'd heard of the case, which is why—"

"Didn't know it had made any of the big city papers."

"I'm visiting a relative in the area." Sort of a relative. Rule's son didn't fit neatly into any of the labels people used for relationships. For that matter, neither did Rule. People looked at you funny if you spoke of your mate.

"Yeah? This relative have anything to do with that tip you won't tell me about?"

"You know, Sheriff, I'd be more likely to share information if you weren't such a pain in the ass. Step back."

Deacon scowled. "What the hell do you—"

"I want you to quit crowding me physically. It doesn't intimidate me. It just pisses me off."

Impossible to tell if he flushed. But the quick duck of his head suggested embarrassment, and he did move back a pace, yanking off his cap and running his forearm over his forehead as if he'd worked up a sweat.

Maybe he had. It wasn't as stinking hot at this hour as it had been yesterday when they arrived, but the moist air held on to heat. "You don't want me messing in your case. I get it. Problem is, you have no choice. Magic was involved in the deaths of three people. That makes this mine."

He reseated his cap and spoke with strained courtesy. "An' you know about this magic how?"

"I'm a touch sensitive." She waited to see if he knew what that meant. Most people did, or thought they did. As with many things magical, their assumptions were packed with old wives' tales, prejudice, and tabloid headlines. Kind of like the way people "knew" all about lupi.

His eyebrows climbed, then descended in a scowl. "Shit." He gave the word two syllables: *shee-it.* "You wouldn't happen to be that weer-lover, would you?"

Lily sighed. Pronounced like weird without the *D*, *weer* was Southern for werewolf, and she'd made the news a few times. Then there were the gossip mags, which were fascinated by her relationship with "the Nokolai prince," as they insisted on referring to Rule. "Maybe you haven't heard. We call them lupi these days."

"Yeah, well, I've heard about you. You and that Turner weer, the one who's some kind of prince."

Her hand tightened on the flashlight. "I doubt that whatever you've heard has any bearing on jurisdiction."

"Maybe not." His eyes were hard, dark walnuts, appraising her. "All right. I'll cooperate if you'll show me the bodies. I won't mess up your scene."

Temper urged her to give him the finger, but temper wasn't a good guide, and he had called it her scene. She was going to have to work with this man. He and his deputies had gathered the initial evidence; they knew the area and the people.

Wait, wait. She wasn't working with him because she'd be handing the case off. Assuming the Unit could get someone down here . . . well, they'd have to. She was here for Rule and Toby, not the FBI.

But for now, those bodies were her responsibility. "Deal. You'd better call your coroner, tell him to go back to bed."

Deacon didn't like that, but he was making an effort. He asked if she wanted his people to wait for the ERT. She thanked him, and he spoke to his deputies, then appropriated one of their flashlights. The batteries in his, he said, were dead. "How far is it?" he asked her.

"Less than a mile."

"Hope you know how to find your way around without street signs. Under a mile doesn't sound like much, but one tree looks a lot like another if you aren't used to woods. Especially at night."

Lily didn't have to know how to track the pathless primeval, not with Rule waiting for her. She just had to find him, and that was easy. "There's a deer trail, and I left someone on-scene who knows woods. If I have trouble finding the spot again, he'll assist."

He gave her a nod. She turned on her own flashlight and set off.

Near the highway the trees were new growth, young and dense and skinny. Teenage trees, she thought, but they were tall enough to spread an umbrella between her and the night sky. The moment she stepped under that canopy, the world turned godawful dark.

Crickets revved their motors like they were about to blast off. The ground was spongy, absorbing the sound of their footsteps as Deacon followed her. Lily kept her light trained on the piney carpet ahead. According to Rule, copperheads turned nocturnal in the hot months.

Trees had completely erased the highway behind them when Deacon spoke. "I guess you touched the bodies."

"The one on top. I didn't disturb the scene." Which was as ugly as any she'd ever been called out on. Lily wouldn't have known the body she'd touched was female if not for the bra tangled up with gnawed-on bones and scraps of stinking meat. "Why are you so determined to see the bodies, Sheriff?" She'd told him about the dogs. Did he think he had to prove how tough he was by seeing what they'd left?

He ignored her question. "When you touch things, you feel it if they've got magic in them."

"That's right. Magic is a texture to me."

"Hold up a minute."

Lily turned. With her flash pointed down, it was hard to make out his expression; his face was a dark blur in the greater darkness. But the pale skin on his outstretched palm showed up clearly.

Her eyebrows lifted. "Testing me?" Well, why not? She took his hand.

The prickle of magic was immediate. And confusing. She held his hand longer than she'd intended, frowning, trying to sort the sensation . . . slick, all slickness and surface, like a gumball. A faint pulsing, as if the magic within swayed to some distant tidal pull . . . "You're Gifted," she said at last, dropping his hand, "but damned if I can say what kind of Gift, though it's tied to water. There's some sort of worked magic overlaying it. Suppressing it, maybe."

After a moment he muttered, "Guess you know what you're doin'. No one's ever been able to tell. No one."

"You going to tell me about your Gift?"

He wasn't at all sure he would. That was obvious in his hesitation, if not his expression—she couldn't see clearly—but finally he said, "Empathy."

Her eyebrows rose. He wasn't talking about physical empathy. That was an Earth Gift, and rare. No, his Gift would be the emotional sort—more common and less welcome. With a minor empathic Gift, you could get by okay as long as you avoided crowds. A strong Gift like Deacon's could make life unlivable.

"That's a rough Gift for anyone," she said, "but for a cop . . . it seemed to be coated."

"I keep it spelled shut."

"I hadn't realized that was possible."

"My granny put up the block years ago. She, ah . . . she knows stuff. Her great-granddad was a shaman. Some stuff got passed down."

Lily nodded and turned to hunt her way through the trees. "I've got a friend trained in African traditions. She'd be interested in that spell, if you're willing to talk about it."

"Might be. Depends. I'd have to get a feel for her."

Even with his Gift coated by that spell, he probably picked up impressions about people. Lily's mouth twisted wryly. That didn't say much for her, considering how hostile he'd been. "You had any trouble with your block since the Turning? It's handling more magic now."

"I have to freshen the spell more often. That's about it. You were connected with that, weren't you? With the Turning and the dragons and all."

"With the dragons, anyway."

He stopped, staring at her. "So that part's true?"

THREE

THE Turning. The first person to call it that had been Lily's grandmother, and the name had somehow spread and stuck. It fit. The world had turned from one thing into another, leaving everyone scrambling to understand the new rules.

It happened just before Christmas last year. The realms had shifted and nodes all over the world had cracked open, spilling a tsunami of raw magic. Computers—and everything they controlled—had been scrambled for days. That initial, overwhelming surge hadn't been repeated, thank God, but power continued to leak into the world. Ambient magic levels were up and expected to keep rising.

One expert expected them to rise to levels not seen in roughly three thousand years.

For the moment, computers and related tech worked fine in places that lacked a major node. Unfortunately, people seemed attracted to nodes. All the big population centers had multiple nodes, which meant multiple problems . . . except for the cities that had dragons.

People used to think dragons were myth, like Cyclops or Baba Yaga. That's what Lily had believed until last November, when she ran into them in Dis . . . a realm better known as hell. The dragons had been ready to end their centuries-long exile; Lily had been more than ready to return to Earth. Together, they'd made that happen . . . for a price.

The price had been Lily. Part of her, anyway, a part that had been separately embodied at the time. But they'd brought Rule home; he'd had the surgery he needed, and he'd healed. And it turned out that the part of her that had been sacrificed wasn't entirely gone. Just mute. Mostly.

As for the dragons, they'd gone into hiding at first. Two months later, the Turning hit—and the dragons reappeared.

The world learned that dragons act as oversize sponges, soaking up magic. After serious negotiation culminating in the Dragon Accords, the dragons had agreed that each would overfly a prescribed territory, keeping the ambient magic level low. Problem was, there weren't enough dragons. Only the largest U.S. cities and a dozen overseas had a resident dragon. Rural areas like this had to make do with lesser protections— spelled collection crystals, silk coverings, and less proven barriers or receptors.

Then there were cell phones. Radios worked reliably everywhere, but cell phones were hit or miss—fine in some areas, chancy in others. This randomness offended scientists. Both radios and cell phones operated on broadcast radio waves, yet for some reason cell phones were more affected by magic. Worse, the interference seemed random.

So far, Lily's cell had worked fine here in Halo, North Carolina.

Deacon was staring at her as if she'd sprouted a second head. She sighed. "I don't know what you've heard. My involvement wasn't in the news."

"My cousin's with the Washington PD. He said you summoned the dragons."

Good grief. Lily wondered what other crazy stories were flying around, but for once left a question unasked. No point in it. As Grandmother said, rumors were like politics—inevitable whenever more than two people were around. "No one summons a dragon."

"What did you do, then?"

"It's complicated, large parts of the story are classified, and none of it relates to our problem tonight." She turned and started walking again, skirting a large fallen branch.

They'd left the mob of teenage trees behind. Here the trunks were thick and widely spaced, with little underbrush. Nothing looked like a path.

She aimed her light up into the trees. There. A scrap of white. When Rule was taking her back to the highway, he'd shredded a tissue from her purse, fixing the bits on branches here and there to mark a detour she needed to take around some low, wet ground. Lily hitched her purse more securely on her shoulder and followed the tiny white flags.

Deacon moved up beside her. "Nothing you learned by touch is admissible in court."

"Not as evidence, no. But it gives me reasonable grounds to believe magic was involved in the commission of a felony. According to the recent amendment to the Domestic Security and Magical Crimes Act—"

"Fuck that gobbledygook. Why are you here, huntin' up crimes? Don't you have anything better to do? Seems like I'm always hearing about how stretched you MCD folks are since the Turning, yet here you are, complicatin' a simple case."

MCD stood for Magical Crimes Division, the FBI division that, on paper, contained the unit Lily belonged to. And yes, they were stretched. Badly. "Sheer lust for power."

He didn't laugh.

Lily didn't roll her eyes. But she wanted to. "Joke, Sheriff. That was a joke. I'm not eager to complicate your life or mine. I'm supposed to be on vacation."

"Yeah? I don't see Disneyworld nearby."

"Personal leave, actually. Family stuff." And that's all she planned to say about it. Rule had given up a lot to protect his son from his own notoriety, and though the secret couldn't be kept much longer—not with Toby moving to San Diego to live with them—Lily wouldn't be the one to reveal it.

And she could not, of course, refer to the other reason they were in North Carolina. Rule's new tie to Leidolf was secret. "I understand the perp you've locked up—Meacham, right?— hasn't admitted anything."

"Claims he doesn't remember. Shit, half the time he refuses to believe his family's dead, says we're lying' to him. The DA thinks Roy Don's hopin' to cop an insanity plea."

"What do you think?"

"Oh, Roy Don's nuts, all right. I don't know if he matches up with the legal definition, but he's crazy as hell."

He sounded deeply sad, as if Meacham's insanity robbed him of something important. "Did you know him? Or the victims?"

"I met Roy Don a few times. Went to high school with his wife, Becky. Rebecca Nordstrom, back then. Didn't know her well—around here, kids mostly hang with their own in high school. Some of it's prejudice, but a lot is just social hang-ups. You know how, at a middle school dance, the boys bunch up together along one wall, the girls across from them? No one's sure what to say to the folks on the other side. That's how it is. Loosens up some if you go on to college, but Becky didn't— married Roy Don right out of high school." He was silent a moment. "Their youngest daughter was friends with my little girl. Pretty thing. Real sweet."

And now decaying under a tree. Lily thought she understood why he'd been such an ass about holding on to his case. "I used to work Homicide. It's hard when the victims are kids. And it's hell if you knew them."

"I don't let it interfere."

"I'm sure you don't." Lily didn't believe that, but he needed to. She knew how it was when the professional and the personal trampled all over each other. Most of the time, you could hold professionalism up like a shield to keep the horror at bay. Not entirely, maybe, but enough to do the job. When an investigation turned personal, you worked harder than ever at the shield. Knowing it wasn't enough.

She helped by turning the subject back to the job. "The killings happened quite recently, I understand."

"Four days. Four days," he repeated, his voice heavy with

skepticism. "You can be sure after so long that there was magic involved?"

"I'm sure. The traces are faint, but unmistakable." She didn't blame him for asking. Suspicion was a natural attitude for a cop—doubt edged sword-sharp by the knowledge that people lied. For big reasons, for small ones, for convenience, for the hell of it—people lied to cops all the time.

But, dammit, she was a cop, too. He might try to remember that. "I heard Meacham turned himself in, then denied he'd done it."

"Not exactly." He was silent a moment. "It was noon on Monday. I was fixing to head out for a bite to eat when Roy Don pulled up in his truck. Parked in a handicapped spot, which folks around here don't do, not right in front of my office, so I waited. Figured either he was drunk or somethin' was bad wrong. He got out." Another pause. "I never saw so much blood on a living person before."

"Did he have the bat?"

"No. No, he climbed out and just stood there, not talking, not moving, not seeing anything at all, from the look in his eyes. His eyes . . . I asked him, was he hurt. Where was he hurt. That's when he turned and got the bat from his front seat. He handed it to me. Didn't say a word, just handed it to me. It was another two hours before he spoke. He seemed to wake up all of a sudden. He was in a hospital gown—that's where we took him, to the hospital—but he still had blood on him. He saw that blood and thought he'd been in a wreck or somethin'. Didn't remember anything since breakfast."

"Did you go to the hospital with him?"

"No. No, I went out to his place to see if that's where the blood had come from, and found poor Bill Watkins out cold. Bingham—that's one of my deputies—took Roy Don to the hospital."

She nodded. "So you didn't actually see him when he, ah, came to."

"No, but Bingham told me about it. He's a good man. Pays attention."

"He's not an empath. Even with your Gift slicked over by

that spell, you probably pick up more than an unGifted could. Your hunches about people would be good." Which gave her an idea. "May not work with me, though. Maybe my Gift locks yours out." Maybe that's why he didn't like or trust her.

"I'm not used to talking about this stuff."

Tell me about it. Until her career change to the FBI, Lily never spoke of being a sensitive. Too often in the past, sensitives had been used to out the Gifted or those of the Blood, and she'd wanted no part of that. Being open about her ability had taken some getting used to. She figured she knew something of how a gay person felt, coming out of the closet. "Times are changing."

"I guess. Are you askin' me what I felt about Roy Don when he stepped out of the truck? When he handed me the bat?"

"What did you feel?"

"Nothin'. Like there was no one home."

"You get that feeling with me?"

"No, you're there. Like a closed door, but you're there. I've never had that feelin' with a person before. Not with a person. Bethany White's girl, now, she's mentally handicapped. Pretty severe—she wears diapers, can't feed herself, but she's *there.* Roy Don wasn't. He drove his truck into town, came to me, handed me that bat. And he wasn't there at all."

Shit. Lily didn't know what that meant, but it couldn't be good. She glanced at Deacon. "Is he still absent?"

"He's not what I'd call sane, but he's present. You got some idea what could do that to a man? I mean, you're sure there was magic involved, so, well. . . ." He hesitated, his voice dropping as if he were embarrassed. "Could Roy Don have been possessed? I know that's supposed to be an old wives' tale, but—"

"No, possession is real, and demons can cross if summoned, but it's extremely rare. Almost all summoning spells were lost during the Purge."

"Almost all?"

She waved that aside. "The point is, the magic I touched didn't come from a demon."

"You said it was faint."

But not orange. For some reason, demons tripped a synesthetic switch in her Gift. They felt like a color, not a texture. "Demon magic is unique. Nothing else feels anything like it. And it's been four days. If Meacham had been possessed and the demon left him for some reason, it would have found another host right away, or a series of hosts. And it would still be killing."

"If it couldn't find a new host—"

"It wouldn't have left Meacham without having one to slip into. A raised demon needs a host to anchor it here." It was more complicated than that, and Lily didn't know all the complications. But she knew a demon. Well, a former demon. And Gan had told her that only a demon who'd come through a gate, or one like her, who could cross unsummoned, could stay in this world without a host.

And Gan was, as she liked to point out, very, very special because of that ability. Lily's lips curved in the ghost of a smile. "I can't say it's impossible," she added. "But it's unlikely enough to not even make the list right now."

"Guess you've had experience with that sort of thing," Deacon said. "We nearly there?"

She nodded. Rule was close now.

"Who'd you leave on-scene? I don't see anyone."

"You won't see him unless he wants you to."

"Shit. You didn't bring that weer here, did you? He's here in my town?"

Just beyond the lance of her light, a shadow shifted. And growled.

Lily's right hand slid beneath her jacket. Her left hand raised the flashlight higher, searching. "Hold it," she snapped when Deacon didn't stop.

"You have to draw on your lover to make him behave?" he drawled.

She had her weapon out and aimed. "That's not—"

Two large dogs exploded from the underbrush—teeth bared, ears flat, moving fast. Lily didn't think. She fired. Fired again.

The first dog fell. The second faltered, but kept coming on three legs—a Rottweiler with a foaming muzzle and mad eyes. She fired again just as two gunshots, packed together, smacked her eardrums.

The second dog fell, blood spraying from its head. So did one she hadn't seen, a Doberman that had attacked from the right. Deacon's bullets had caught it in midleap.

Lily was breathing hard, as if she'd been running. Her hands shook—aftermath of the adrenaline that had wanted her to run. She swallowed bile.

Dogs. She'd shot dogs. "Good shooting," she managed.

"Shit." Deacon's voice shook slightly. "Did you see the way that one kept coming, even after you hit it? Sumbitches must've been rabid."

Rabid. Yeah, that might explain why they'd ventured here, where they must have been able to smell Rule, but . . . Rule. Where was Rule?

Deacon was shining his flashlight all over the place, wary now. "You reckon there's any more? Dogs don't attack that way. Not like that. These were rabid. I'll have to—hey!"

She'd taken off running.

Lily jumped a small log, skidded, then looped around a pair of scruffy pines. Rule was alive. She knew that as clearly as she knew the way the hot air felt as she sucked it in. If he'd been killed, the mate bond would have snapped.

But he hadn't come. He should have heard the dogs, the gunshots, and he hadn't come.

He wasn't far. That was the main reason her pell-mell race through the woods didn't put her on her butt, twist an ankle, or send her tumbling. She didn't have far to run before jerking to a stop, her stomach roiling at the smell. She fell to her knees, her fingers clenched tight on the flashlight.

Rule lay in a leaf and loam bed, curled up like Hansel lost in the woods. Ten feet away, an open grave poisoned the air, but she saw no signs of a fight or trauma on Rule—no blood, ripped clothing, scuffed ground. His breathing was even; his face, peaceful. The dark hair falling back from his face wasn't mussed.

She reached for his throat to reassure herself of a pulse. And jolted.

Magic. Thin and clammy, it coated his skin like pond scum . . . pond scum mixed with ground glass, for it held an abrasive wrongness she recognized. Even as her own heartbeat went crazy, her fingers found the steady beat in his carotid. And the ugly magic was fading. Evaporating like sweat on a hot, dry day.

His eyes opened slowly. He blinked. "Why am I lying on the ground?"

"I was hoping you could tell me. What's the last thing you remember?" She stroked his skin everywhere it showed—his cheek, his throat, his hand—reassuring herself. The scum of magic was gone.

"Waiting. An owl hooting, the crickets . . ." He frowned. "There's something else, but I can't . . . It's gone."

He started to sit up. Lily tried to push him back down—which made him smile gently and move her hands. "I'm fine, *nadia.*"

"You were out cold a second ago."

"Whatever caused it doesn't seem to have left any aftereffects."

"We don't know that."

"Lying on the ground won't help us find out." He stood, so Lily did, too. "Who's thrashing through the underbrush?"

"Sheriff Deacon, I suspect." Not that she could hear . . . No, wait, now that Rule had drawn her attention to it, she did hear movement, very faintly. "I think I lost him."

"You should probably recover him, then."

"I'll call him in a minute."

"I'm fine," he repeated, annoyed.

"Maybe. Rule, there was magic coating you when I arrived. Death magic."

He stilled. After a moment he said, "Whatever happened, I lived through it."

"The magic's gone now. Everywhere I've touched, it's gone. Which is good, but I don't understand it." But she hadn't touched everywhere, had she?

His shirt was loose. She ran both hands up under it, feeling his chest.

"Ah . . . Lily?"

"It could have localized, like the demon poison did." Not on his chest, though. She moved closer so she could reach beneath his shirt to feel his back. The skin was warm, slightly moist . . . and just skin. No pond-scum grit.

"Death magic either kills you or it doesn't. It didn't. Lily—"

"We don't know. We don't know what it can or can't do. You're going to need to take off your shirt."

"Christ." Deacon's voice came from behind her, thick with disgust. "You raced here to feel him up."

FOUR

HALO was tiny compared to San Diego, but it was no fly-speck. As the county seat, it held a four-story district court building, where Rule would learn if his son was coming home with him. And the two-story sheriff's department, where Rule was now. The Dawson County Sheriff's Department smelled of dust, disinfectant, tobacco, printer's ink, and mice. And people, of course. People who'd sweated and fretted, worked and eaten here for years

The most interesting thing about the smells, Rule thought, was the one that was absent: fear. That scent had been absent from the first, unfortunate moment he met Sheriff Deacon. The man didn't like Rule, but he didn't fear him. That was unusual enough to make Rule curious.

They were more or less alone. The sheriff's office was on the second floor of the cement block building, separated by a glass panel from a large, communal space crammed with desks. Most of those desks were empty at this hour, though a square-set woman in civilian clothes had grim possession of the desk in front of the door to Deacon's office.

It was 6:42 A.M. Rule sat on a hard wooden chair and longed for coffee. Lily might classify the liquid in his foam cup as that beverage, but Lily had drunk the sludge perpetrated by cop-house coffeepots too long. Her senses were permanently skewed by the experience.

"Okay." Deacon hit a button on his computer and the printer jumped into action. "I'll need you to sign your statement, then you're free to go. Don't leave town."

Rule considered pointing out that he'd been free to go all along—he was here voluntarily. Lily had wanted him to wait to give Deacon his statement until she was finished at the scene and could come with him. Rule had understood. He, too, knew the need to protect, though he still found it odd, even unsettling, to have that instinct trained on him.

Protection was unnecessary in this instance. He'd dealt with any number of suspicious or prejudiced police in his time. He'd chosen to cooperate with this one. So far, cooperation had earned him no points at all. "I'll wait here for Lily, if you've no objection."

Deacon shot him a hard glance. "Your lover may be a while, you know."

"Lover" was a fine word, yet in this man's mouth it sounded like "slut." Rule told himself he would not allow anger to make his choices for him, but it was just as well he didn't have Cullen's knack with fire. "It would be more respectful to refer to her as Agent Yu."

Deacon snorted. "Pull the other one. I know how your kind treats women, and respectful isn't the word for it." The printer spat out a sheet of paper and he leaned sideways to pluck it. "Here. Read and sign."

Rule accepted the page without looking at it. He couldn't tell Deacon he would be faithful to Lily unto death. She was his *nadia*, his Chosen. But while that was understood among his people, none outside the clans knew of the existence of the mate bond—which was the only form of fidelity that was acceptable for a lupus. But that was none of the human's business.

Yet the sheriff's attitude rankled. He didn't understand why. When had lupi cared what the out-clan thought? "It occurs to me you live in Leidolf's territory."

"In what?" Deacon shook his head. "You're from California, right? Maybe California schools don't teach kids about states and counties and such. Sheriffs are elected by the county, not some blamed territory."

"I'm aware of counties," Rule said dryly. "Leidolf is a lupus clan whose territory—which does not appear in your children's schoolbooks—includes much of North Carolina." In fact, the Leidolf clanhome was seventy miles south of Halo, but that was none of this man's business. "I'm wondering if your attitude comes from having known Leidolf lupi. Their treatment of women is not typical of my people."

"You gonna tell me you believe in marriage?"

"Is marriage the only way to demonstrate respect for a woman?"

"The only way that means anything."

"So you wouldn't object if your daughter grew up to marry one of us."

Rule thought the man would hit him. Deacon did, too, for a moment—which told Rule that Deacon's prejudice didn't involve any real knowledge of lupi. A man who knew much about Rule's people might, in a fit of temper, consider shooting. He didn't think of punching.

Deacon mastered the impulse. "Read and sign the statement."

This, of course, was the other reason, aside from cheap land, that Nokolai had settled in California so many years ago. The woods here were magnificent. The attitudes were not.

Rule read quickly. Barring a couple of typos, the statement was accurate enough. He smiled when he reached the last part . . . which described him disrobing so Lily could make sure no death magic clung to him. Anywhere.

Deacon's arrival hadn't fazed her. "Get your mind out of the sewer," she'd snapped, then gone on doing what she considered necessary. As she always did. Lily had offered Deacon a terse explanation once she finished, but it had been Rule who'd pointed out that it seemed wise to make sure he wasn't enspelled. It would be unfortunate if he went mad on them, wouldn't it?

Rule's smile faded. He hadn't known about the dogs when he said that. He looked up. "You have a pen?"

Deacon dug through the debris on his desk until he'd unearthed one. "You said you arrived in town yesterday. I need to know where you're staying."

"I have a room at the Comfort Inn." He wasn't staying in it, but he did have the room.

"What are you doing in Halo, anyway?"

"Personal business." Rule scrawled his signature and put the statement on Deacon's desk.

"What kind of personal? If there's another weer living in my town, I want to know about it."

"I realize you would consider that your business. I don't. As it happens, the law agrees with me." Not that he could hope to keep Toby a secret much longer, but damned if he'd turn belly-up to this man.

"Yu said she was here on family business."

"Yes."

"Would that be your family or hers?"

"That would be personal. As I've said. Do you have family, Sheriff?"

"We aren't talking about me."

"Perhaps we should. If you . . . Ah, here she is." Rule turned to look through the glass partition at a metal door on the far side of the large room. A moment later, it swung open, revealing a staircase and a slim, pissed-off woman.

The bulky woman seated at the desk directly in front of Deacon's office expressed a need to know what Lily wanted. Lily flashed her badge and spoke Deacon's name without breaking stride. The woman considered stopping her, shrugged, and went back to tapping at her keyboard.

Wise of her. Lily was not in a good mood.

She swung open the door to Deacon's office. "Deacon, you sent the damned vet to pick up those dogs."

"They've got to be checked for rabies."

"Believe it or not, the FBI lab is fully able to make that determination. The veterinarian wasn't happy about our presence or our refusal to allow him on the scene. He called the press. Not just your local rag—Durham and Raleigh."

Deacon shrugged. "I told Stan to wait a bit before he went out there. Sorry he didn't, but you should've told me your people were handling the dogs' bodies. Besides, what makes you think it was him tipped the press?"

"Dr. Stanfield informed me personally of his action and motives. He hoped to keep us from covering everything up—though he declined to say what, exactly, he thought might merit a cover-up. Possibly aliens. Or maybe he believes cover-up is the FBI's SOP in any investigation. As a result, we've got two television crews and a swarm of print reporters at the scene. Several of them followed me into town. They're downstairs now."

"They'll keep a bit."

Her lips stretched in a smile that should have made Deacon nervous. "You'll want to speak to them soon, Sheriff. I gave a brief statement at the scene. They know that the FBI received a tip about the location of three bodies, which have been tentatively identified by the sheriff of this county as those of your three vics. They are also aware we have reason to believe magic was involved in the deaths."

"You told 'em that? Shit! I'm going to have forty thousand scared people in this town! Why the hell did you—"

"Because I had to. Because my hand had been forced." She stepped up to his desk, set her palms on it, and leaned forward. "Because you were either too stupid to guess that Dr. Stanfield would freak at the presence of the FBI, or you called him, *knowing* good old Stan is a conspiracy nut and likely to call in the press. Knowing that and wanting it, because you're pissed. I would very much like to know which one it was."

Deacon scowled—but Rule caught the whiff of guilt-scent on him. "Why the hell would I want the press around?"

"You don't like bossy women. You don't like feds. And you really don't like bossy female feds who have a personal connection to a lupus, because you're a narrow-minded, self-righteous bigot." Lily straightened, glanced at Rule. "We'd better go before the vultures realize you're here."

"Bigot!" Deacon shot to his feet. "You're nuts, you know that? You notice that I'm black? Don't tell me about bigotry, you sorry little—"

"Sheriff." Rule stood. Anger slid into ice, setting its cold claws at his throat so that his voice dropped to what, in his other form, would have been a growl. "You don't want to finish that sentence."

Deacon stared at him, his Adam's apple bobbing as he swallowed. And didn't say a word.

Rule turned to Lily. "I'd rather not be on television this morning."

"My car's out front. Yours isn't. Back door?"

He nodded. The press would find him. He knew that. Halo was too small, and he was too well-known for his presence to remain secret. But he wanted a chance to talk to Toby first.

Lily opened the door, then paused to look over her shoulder. "By the way—the dogs weren't rabid. That will be confirmed by the appropriate tests, but I already know what the problem was."

"What?"

"Something they ate disagreed with them."

FIVE

RULE slid behind the wheel of his Mercedes. Lily shut the door on the passenger side with what, in a less perfectly engineered piece of equipment, would have been a slam. "Stupidity I can live with. God knows I have to, at times. But that sort of mean-spirited behavior . . . He did it on purpose, didn't he?"

Rule started the car. "Perhaps not consciously, but he knew the veterinarian would cause trouble for you." Not that Lily had taken that parting shot because of the trouble Deacon had caused her. To her way of thinking, she'd already dealt with that. She'd done it for Rule.

That protective instinct again. His lips curved up. Lily might never run four-footed in the moonlight with him, but in other ways she made a fine wolf.

"A couple of the reporters recognized me," she said. "They asked about you, of course. They'll find you pretty quickly here."

"I know. You've given me time to warn Toby and Mrs. Asteglio, at least. You touched the dogs' bodies?"

She nodded. "The magic felt different, I guess because of the way they, uh, encountered it—through ingestion. Slimy as hell. But it was there. I've warned the ERT to treat all the bodies as biohazards. Rule, Ruben wants me to work the case."

Ruben Brooks was the head of Unit 12, a formerly obscure section of the FBI's Magical Crimes Division that had risen to importance with the Turning because most of its agents were Gifted.

Rule was silent as he pulled out of the small parking lot onto an empty street. Dawn had cracked the horizon and light was bleeding back into the world, but no one seemed to be up yet, save themselves. "I suspect he didn't phrase it as a request."

"No. Not really."

"Good."

"What?" Her head swung toward him fast enough to send her hair flying. "I know you don't want me to work this case, not with the hearing so close. Then there's Leidolf and what you have to do there."

"I don't want it, no, which is why it's just as well Brooks didn't leave it up to you. You would have been torn by opposing obligations. I understand why Brooks wants you on it. No one else has your protection against death magic, for one thing." Lily's Gift gave her that. She could touch magic; she couldn't be touched by it. "For another, you want this one. It's already yours."

She reached for his right hand, curling hers around it. "Think you know me pretty well, don't you?"

"I wouldn't say that. You're like Russia."

"What?" This time he'd surprised a smile from her. "I'm guessing you don't mean I'm cold—too much evidence to the contrary. And as for any communist tendencies you think I'm harboring—"

"No, I was borrowing from Churchill. Like Russia, you're a 'riddle wrapped in a mystery inside an enigma.' But I've been studying the riddle, the mystery, and the enigma awhile. I know the obvious things. You'll let go of an investigation about as easily as a bulldog unclamps its jaws."

"So I'm an enigmatic bulldog."

"Of course."

"I don't know about the enigmatic part." Her smile faded.

"Speaking of dogs . . . it's stupid, but that got to me. Having to shoot those dogs got to me."

Rule didn't doubt that, though he suspected she was focusing on that horror because the other—the children—was too large to come at directly. He squeezed her hand. "I won't tell you it wasn't your fault, because you already know that. But maybe it hasn't occurred to you that death by bullet was cleaner than what they'd have endured otherwise."

"They'd been pets, you know? At least two of them had. They had collars. No tags, but collars. If you could have seen their ribs . . . They were starving to death. That's why they dug up the grave. They were starving."

"They were sinned against twice—by those who abandoned them, and by whoever left the tainted bodies for them to find. But not by you, Lily."

"I guess." Her eyebrows knitted. "I don't see why the magic transferred that way. Why they went mad. I wouldn't have thought that was possible."

"I don't know much about death magic."

"Well, neither do I, but I thought it took a big-deal ritual to work it. I'll ask Karonski about that."

"Ah. Will he be joining you? Or is Brooks sending you some other minions?"

"Minions. I like that." She smiled, but in the pale light of early morning, she looked tired. "For now, just the ERT. Karonski will be calling soon, though. Ruben's going to brief him. He's on a case in Wisconsin he can't leave—one involving a coven gone over to the dark side."

Surprised, he looked at her. "A Wiccan coven?"

"I'm afraid so. Magical theft. They found a way to persuade the Bank of America's computers they were millionaires. That's been done before, of course, but not effectively. Their spell was a lot more sophisticated than the typical lone practitioner's—it took months for the bank to become suspicious. The story's going to hit the media in a big way in another day or two, when Karonski makes the arrests. Ruben says Karonski plans to come out of the closet at the press conference."

"Out of the—oh. You mean he'll make his own Wiccan status public." Abel had avoided that in the past. "Damage control?"

"Yeah. If nothing else, people will see that they need the good witches to protect them from the bad ones." She shook her head. "There's always been some distrust of Wiccans, especially in rural areas, but it's worse since the Turning."

Rural areas, yes, and small towns like Halo.

"You didn't mention the AP earlier, or CNN. Are they here?"

"They will be."

Oh, yes. The prospect of a magical component to the murder of children would draw reporters in droves—reporters who would demand to know why Rule was in Halo. Reporters who would gleefully switch to report on a custody hearing involving the son of the Nokolai "prince," shoving their microphones at Toby, fighting for a chance to put the boy's face on the six o'clock news.

Rule wasn't too happy with the sheriff himself.

The sifted light of dawn had already strengthened as summer blew on the coals of yesterday's heat, ready to throw a new day onto the forge. Halo's streets remained quiet, but were no longer empty. Rule passed a shiny Ford pickup headed the other way, its driver sipping Coke from a cup the size of a bucket of popcorn. A gray Suburban was backing out of the cracked driveway leading to a small frame house surrounded by mounds of hydrangeas, their bright blue blooms floating in clouds of green like flakes from a dandruff sky.

The Suburban's movement startled an orange tabby, who streaked in front of Rule's car. He braked gently. "Looks like Harry."

"Hmm?" Lily had obviously been a thousand miles away, but she returned in time to see the cat attain the safety of the shrubbery on the other side of the street. "In coloring, maybe, but Harry wouldn't panic and run in front of a car that way."

"No, he'd park his ass in the street and dare me to keep coming." Dirty Harry was Lily's cat—or she was Harry's person, to phrase things from Harry's perspective. He was staying with Lily's grandmother while they were away. Not that Harry and Grandmother got along, but Grandmother's companion had a way with cats.

All sorts of cats. Rule smiled as he turned onto Sherwood Lane.

"I guess you were right about renting two cars," Lily said, "though at the moment mine's in front of the sheriff's office. Are you going to need this one?"

"I suppose you need it."

"Yes." She ran a hand through her hair, looked down at herself, and frowned. "How do I look?"

"Lickable."

Her eyes flicked to his, amusement swimming in their depths. No heat, but he heard the way her heartbeat kicked up. Her voice was dry. "Not the look I'm going for. I've got a meet with the DA—the one who's been planning to make a name with this case."

Rule understood the value of controlling the surface, creating a certain effect, so he gave her another once-over with that in mind. She was less correctly dressed than she liked, he supposed, having thrown on clothes for hiking through the woods: jeans, white T-shirt, black linen jacket, athletic shoes. No makeup.

Honey-and-cream skin. Black hair, shiny and smooth as if she'd just brushed it. Firm lips, unsmiling. Dark eyes that had pinned the sheriff in his chair when she stormed into his office.

What did she need with makeup? "Tidy," he said. "Casual, but professional. And gorgeous. Is this district attorney male?"

She snorted. "No. Not that it matters, since I'm not vamping my way into anyone's good graces. Even if I could, I wouldn't."

"Oh, you could. Why the DA first?"

"The arraignment's today. I need to see her before that. Plus she's arranging for me to see—uh, the suspect. The one they've locked up. I need an interview room, one where we aren't separated by glass."

"So you can touch him and tell if he's tainted by death magic."

"Yeah. Since it clung to the bodies this long, there must still be traces of it on him, too, but I have to check. Also . . ." She grimaced. "I'm going to have to talk to the veterinarian. The one who thinks I'm hiding an alien spaceship in the woods."

"Why?"

"People don't start working death magic out of the blue on humans. They practice on animals first, work their way up. I've got the office checking for reports of animal killings, but I'm not expecting much to come of it. Our practitioner would have to have been pretty obvious to tip his hand that way. But the vet's the head of the local SPCA. He might have heard about pets going missing, that sort of thing."

When Lily spoke of "the office," she meant FBI Head-quarters. "You'll be busy, then," Rule said, slowing. "Take this car and leave me your keys. If I need a vehicle before you get back, I'll pick up yours."

The house ahead on the right was a two-story frame struc-ture, the siding freshly painted white, the trim dark green to match the shingles on the roof. An enormous oak in the front yard discouraged grass, but made a nice home for an old-fashioned tire swing. The long, shaded front porch held a pair of wicker chairs, a porch swing, and a red bicycle.

The look of the place had often been a comfort to him. Halo might not have been Rule's choice for his son, but Toby's grandmother had done her best to make a home for him. Rule pulled into the drive.

"What's the plan?" Lily asked. "Are we going to stay here?"

"I don't know." Rule yanked the key out of the ignition, frustrated. He wasn't accustomed to indecision. "I don't know if it will do any good to move to the hotel. I need to talk to Toby and Mrs. Asteglio."

"Hmm. Well, you've been playing footsie with the media a long time now. You'll know how to handle them. Just let me know once you make a decision. Rule, when you nearly lost it with the sheriff back there—"

"I did not nearly lose it."

"All right, when you persuaded Deacon you *might* lose it. Was the new mantle . . . ah, active?"

He looked at her, startled. "I don't think so. I didn't notice it, at least. Why?"

"You were different."

"Different how?"

"If you'd told Deacon to go sit in the corner, he would have. He might not have stayed long, but he'd have gone."

He didn't enjoy having his mistakes pointed out. "I scared him, you mean. Until then he didn't fear me."

Lily huffed out a breath, impatient, as if he were being deliberately obtuse. "Rule, he's an empath. His Gift's blocked by a spell, but I suspect some stuff still leaks through. He didn't fear you at first because you weren't a danger. And I'm not sure it was fear that had him buckling under."

Dryly he said, "It was fear I had in mind when I suggested he be quiet."

"He's former military, you know. Military police."

"He told you that?"

"No, one of the pictures on his wall shows him in an MP uniform. Marine. What I'm saying is that I doubt he'd let fear freeze him that way."

Rule had been in that office much longer than she had, and he hadn't noticed the photo. But he was less visual than she was, and Lily had a cop's habits. She noticed everything. "I worried you."

"More like you turned me on, actually. But if the—"

Whatever else she'd meant to say was lost in his mouth. She tasted warm and welcoming, with hints of bad coffee and minty toothpaste. And what stirred in his belly and below had nothing to do with the mantles.

All too soon, she pulled away. Her well-kissed mouth curved in a smile. "Men are so opportunistic about sex."

He sighed. "Not in Mrs. Asteglio's driveway, I'm not."

"Good point. About the mantle—"

"I know better than to call up the new one, Lily."

"Okay. I have to go."

"Yes. I love you."

"Oh." Her eyes softened. She touched his lips with her fingertips. "Love you. Now I've got to go."

Moments later, Rule let himself into the silent house. Neither Toby nor his grandmother was awake yet, which wasn't surprising on a summer morning just brushing up on seven A.M. Rule had an urge to go upstairs where he could hear his son breathing, watch him sleep in the twin-size bed that had held Toby's dreaming self since he left his crib.

Watch him and worry, his wolf pointed out, about all manner of things he had no control over.

Well, wasn't worry a parent's prerogative? Still, he heeded the wolf this time, heading for the kitchen instead of the stairs. He'd brought some of his own coffee with him—already ground, which wasn't as savory, but Mrs. Asteglio didn't own a grinder, and Lily had rolled her eyes when he proposed bringing his.

The kitchen was a large, comfortable room at the back of the house, flanked by a den on one side and a formal dining room, seldom used, on the other. It was immaculate; Mrs. Asteglio was as uneasy with disorder as Lily, and more militant about it. Rule spotted the piece of paper on the counter right away.

A glance told him Lily had written it. She'd made sure that if she and Rule were delayed, Toby and his grandmother would know where they were and not worry. She thought of things like that.

He didn't, not always. He'd lived alone too long, grown accustomed to the autonomy of distance. Too, secrecy was a habit for most lupi, especially one in his position. He was learning new habits with Lily, but he had a ways to go. Lily would help, though—by pointing out when he screwed up, for one thing.

Rule grinned as he measured coffee and poured water, enjoying the smell and the habitual quality of the small ritual.

What about Toby's rituals? How were they going to change?

He knew some of them—the need for a book and tucking in at night; the way Toby brushed his teeth before washing his face; the proper order in which to build a peanut butter and jelly sandwich. Toby had spent part of his summers with his father, as well as a few rare weekends during the school year. But full-time fatherhood would be different from visits. He had much to learn.

He was eager, greedily eager, to begin those lessons.

While the coffee dripped, perfuming the house, Rule wandered into the little den, where the only television set in the house resided. He had a decision to make.

There seemed little chance of keeping the vultures of the press unaware of the hearing. Even if the judge and the various clerks with access to the court's schedule didn't spill the story, Mrs. Asteglio had probably spoken to her friends and neighbors about it. She wouldn't have told them who Toby's father was, but she would have spoken to them about the upcoming loss of her grandson.

The best way to deal with the press was usually to give them some portion of what they wanted. What if Rule told the reporters why he was here?

Not the main reason. Not about Toby. About Leidolf.

The human world knew little about lupus clans and nothing about the mantles that held them together. That was as it should be. The press insisted on calling Rule the Nokolai prince, but Rule's position, though partly hereditary, had little in common with human royalty. Rule was Lu Nuncio to Nokolai clan and had carried the heir's portion of the Nokolai mantle for many years now. His father held the main portion, of course, for it was the mantle that made him Rho, just as it made Nokolai a clan . . . and its members more than a hegemony broken into beast-lost packs.

Rule wouldn't speak of mantles to the press. But he could speak of clans—warring clans that were moving to mend their differences.

He smiled slowly. The press would eat it up.

His mind clicked over possibilities, complications, consequences . . . and the consequences could be large. But he could do it, yes, and in addition to possibly sparing Toby, it would be excellent press for his people.

Did he have the right? He'd be revealing Leidolf's existence to the press, and Leidolf's Rho had made it clear—back when Victor Frey was conscious and capable of clarity—that he did not want Leidolf to go public.

Rule paced to the sliding doors, staring out at the thousand shades of green in the tidy backyard. He'd have to decide quickly. If he chose this course, he needed to set things in motion right away. That meant calling Alex Thibideux, Lu Nuncio for Leidolf. He'd call his father, too, for he owed *his* Rho notice . . . notice, but not obedience. Not in this. The Nokolai Rho had no say in this decision, for it was Leidolf business.

Rule's mouth twisted, acknowledging the irony. Leidolf, the hereditary enemies of his clan, who'd tried to assassinate his father less than a year ago. Leidolf, whose Rho now lay comatose, slowly dying, having lost the treacherous toss of the dice he'd made when he tried to kill Rule last December.

Instead, he'd ended up making Rule his heir.

Traditionally, a clan's heir held little real authority—but traditionally, the heir was also Lu Nuncio. A Lu Nuncio enforced his Rho's will and could at times speak with the Rho's voice—because a Lu Nuncio did not act against his Rho's decisions. Ever.

But an heir who was not also Lu Nuncio . . .

Yes, Rule decided, he could act against Victor's avowed policies. He was not Leidolf's Lu Nuncio. Victor Frey was not his Rho, and he owed him no obedience.

The other mantle in his gut, the one forced on him six months ago, stirred. *Yes,* Leidolf's mantle seemed to whisper. *Yes, you must lead. You have the right.*

SIX

FBI agents tended to see themselves as the top of the law enforcement food chain, an attitude that did not endear them to
local law enforcement. Lily knew how annoying that attitude
could be, having been one of those locals until last November.
She also knew a number of ways the locals could make life
difficult for the big, bad feds if they wanted to, so she made a
point of getting along with locals whenever possible.

But cops, of whatever stripe, were more territorial than the
average lupus, so some clashes were unavoidable. She didn't
see any way she could have ducked the one with Deacon, but
she wasn't sure what to do now. She still had to work with
the man.

Maybe that was why she headed for those golden arches
before her meet with the DA: to remind herself of her law
enforcement roots.

She could have stayed at the house and eaten a much better
meal. Rule cooked, and he was good at it. But sometimes a
woman wanted junk. Junk was familiar. She'd eaten a lot of
fast food in her cop car.

Of course, her cop car hadn't been a Mercedes. She pulled

into the parking area and got in the drive-through line for the familiar foodlike products.

The car's interior was spotless. Rule was nowhere nearly as tidy as she was, but he kept his cars clean, even a rental like this one. He was so damned perfect—wealthy, sophisticated, sexy enough to wake a woman from a coma. It was reassuring to know that, under it all, he was still very much a guy. Never mind making the bed, but for God's sake don't get crumbs on the leather seats.

He was fussy about his appearance, too. Lily smiled as she inched forward another car length. A touch of vanity there. Maybe he saw a car as something he wore, the twenty-first-century equivalent of a knight's armor.

She'd eat carefully. Got to keep that armor shiny.

Three more cars ahead of her. Lily propped her laptop against the steering wheel and was filling out an online form when her phone buzzed like an electric razor—the ring tone she used for calls forwarded from her official number.

Turned out to be Deacon calling. He'd heard from the DA, who wanted to change their meet to eight thirty at the jail so she could be present when Lily interviewed Meacham. Lily told him it was no problem, though her interview was getting pretty damned crowded. Meacham's attorney from the public defender's office would be there, too.

She supposed she ought to be glad Halo's police chief wasn't attending. Meacham had lived—and killed—outside the city limits, so the case belonged to the sheriff's department.

Cities and states divvied up authority differently. Most FBI agents were attached to a local or regional office; they needed to know the chains of command for the various state, county, and city agencies in their areas. They didn't have to know how things were done in all fifty states.

Lily did. As a special agent attached to the Unit, she could be sent anywhere in the nation. Her boss had assured her he would assign her cases as near San Diego as possible whenever he could, because where she went, Rule had to go, too. That was the downside of the mate bond. It was currently allowing them a couple hundred miles of separation, but it was a capricious son of a bitch. She could wake up tomorrow and find she had to remain within fifty miles of him, maybe. Or ten. Or one.

Admittedly, one mile was unlikely. Rule said the bond was that rigid only when it first formed. But neither of them knew the rules, dammit. No one seemed to know the rules, or even if there were any. They didn't know when, why, or if the bond might suddenly constrict, so they generally stayed pretty close.

Rule shrugged it off. She didn't understand that—he wasn't exactly a laissez-faire kind of guy—but the mate bond's variable proximity clause didn't bug him the way it did her. "Why worry about it?" he'd said recently. "I don't get upset when gravity keeps me from floating off whenever I feel like it."

"But gravity's a constant! It doesn't suddenly drag me down twice as hard. I know what to expect with gravity."

"Maybe the mate bond is constant, too, and it's our experience of it that varies."

Since it was her unpredictable experience of the bond that drove her crazy, that didn't help much. At the moment, though, that aspect of the mate bond wasn't giving her trouble. It was another variable that fretted at her.

Memory.

It's normal to forget a name now and then, she assured herself as she accepted the sack and a lidded cup from the kid at the drive-up window. People forgot names all the time.

But to forget the name of the alleged perp? She'd never done that. "Meacham," she muttered as she pulled out of the parking area. "Roy Don Meacham. Now quit being paranoid."

She was downing coffee when her purse buzzed. She set her cup in the cup holder, dug her phone out of her purse, checked caller ID and the time, and flipped the phone open. "Hey, there. I didn't expect to hear from you for another hour or two, given the time difference."

Abel Karonski grunted. "Explain that to Ida. The woman doesn't sleep herself, so she's fuzzy on the concept."

Ida Rheinhart was Ruben's secretary and the terror of every

agent in the Unit. Lily grinned and looked for a spot to pull over. "Cynna swears that Ida lairs up beneath her desk at night."

"Lairs, yes. Sleeps, no. How else could she be at her desk calling me at five o'clock in the damned morning?"

"It's seven here. Hang on a sec—I need to park this thing, or my eggs will get cold while I juggle the phone."

"Eggs. You've got eggs."

"Well, the yellow stuff inside the muffin was purportedly once inside a chicken." She'd reached the sleepy peace of an elementary school set in a long sprawl of grass punctuated by swings and a slide. All empty, of course, this early on a summer morning. Parking spots were slanted along its length. She pulled into one and wondered if the dead children had gone to this school. "I've got coffee, too."

"I've got coffee. Hotels put coffeepots in the rooms these days, thank God. It's food I lack. Are you chewing? Do I hear chewing?"

Lily swallowed and grinned. She could picture Karonski sitting in a generic hotel room in his rumpled suit . . . No, he wouldn't be dressed yet. He probably slept in his shorts, but no way was she going to picture Karonski in his underwear, so she mentally provided him with brown Sansabelt slacks and a wrinkled shirt. Karonski's shirts were always wrinkled. "Who, me? That would be rude, even though I am in a hurry. I've got a meet in twenty minutes."

"Then you'd better tell me about these bodies you found."

Another image replaced the one of a wrinkled Karonski. This one had her putting the uneaten portion of her egg sandwich back in the bag it had come from. "Actually, Rule found them." She folded the bag down so no crumbs could escape, giving the task more attention than it warranted.

"A woman and two kids."

"Yeah. The locals locked up the father for it even though they didn't have the bodies, but they had cause. He showed up at the sheriff's office with the bloody baseball bat. There's supposed to be a witness, too, a postal worker who tried to help and got whacked."

"But you detected death magic on the bodies."

"Yes, and I don't understand it. Here's how it looks to me. Either the victims were killed by death magic, or they were killed creating it—as part of a ritual empowering the practitioner. The first one seems unlikely. Physical evidence on the bat marks it as the murder weapon, and there's a witness. It's barely possible the perp pounded the bodies afterward in an effort to hide their true manner of death, but that doesn't fit with his subsequent actions."

"Disposing of the bodies, then driving back into town so he could hand the sheriff the bat with all that great physical evidence."

"Yeah. The guy's nuts, but insanity usually has its own weird logic. I can't make that fit any kind of logic, no matter how twisted. As for the other scenario . . . evidence at the victims' home suggested that the kids were killed in their beds, but the mother was chased down. Death magic—the extraction of power through killing—has to be performed ritually, right? That doesn't sound like the kind of controlled situation a ritual requires."

"Could be the first kid was killed ritually and the others were taken out because they'd witnessed it."

"What kind of idiot sets up a ritual killing with others in the house?"

"He'd have to be loony tunes," Karonski agreed. "Probably a lousy practitioner, too. Maybe he thought he'd spelled the others asleep and got it wrong."

Lily tapped one finger against the steering wheel, frowning. It didn't feel right. "They all had it on them. I confirmed that on the scene. Death magic was smeared on all three of them. Would that be true if only one of them was killed ritually?"

Karonski had a deep, windy sigh like a weary hound. "No, you're right. I obviously need more coffee. Nothing I know makes that possible. Of course, there's a hell of a lot I don't know about death magic. What I keep having trouble with, though, is the bat. Blunt force trauma is not symbolically correct."

"Expand on that."

"Death magic involving human victims is extremely rare, but animal killings aren't, so we know a little about what's required. Every ritual I've heard of uses a knife or blade. The Aztecs didn't bash their sacrifices' heads in. Another thing . . . most Wiccans believe death magic operates the same as blood magic, that they're related. Blood magic requires a blade and control. You have to control what happens with the blood to use it. Hard to do that if you're smashing people with a baseball bat."

Lily shook her head. "I don't know. Blood magic doesn't feel the same to me. I know Wiccans believe it's tainted—"

"We're not the only ones."

"No, and you may be right, though the Catholics disagree. But that's not my point. The thing is, I don't personally know that blood magic is tainted. I don't pick up that sort of thing when I touch magic."

"Unless it's death magic."

"Yeah." Evil. That's what she touched when she touched death magic, and she did not understand. Power was power, and magic no more held a moral component than did electricity— or so she'd believed until the first time she'd touched a body slain by death magic. "I'm right about those bodies. I'm *sure*."

"Hey, I'm not doubting you. Just having a hard time coming up with an explanation. We may not know much about death magic, but what's happened there violates the little we do know. Have you talked to your pet sorcerer?"

"Not yet. It's still short of five A.M. in California. I texted him, but I texted Cynna, too, just to make sure."

Cynna was Lily's friend. She was also an FBI agent, Rule's former lover, and the only woman in the world married to a lupus—Cullen Seabourne, whom she was living with at Nokolai Clanhome while they awaited the birth of their child. Cullen was Rule's friend, a former lone wolf, a stripper . . . and a sorcerer. Sorcerers were supposed to have died out in the Purge; lone wolves were supposed to go crazy cut off from their clans; lupi were never Gifted—and they never, ever got married.

Cullen didn't so much break rules as explode them.

"How's she doing?' Karonski asked. "Is she getting fat yet?"

"You do know better than to use the word 'fat' around a pregnant woman, don't you? Especially Cynna. She's armed."

Karonski chuckled. "Good point. You figure she'll make sure Seabourne calls you back?"

"Yeah." Among Cullen's bad habits was ignoring phone calls if they weren't immediately interesting. Lily thought the mention of death magic would get his attention, but you never knew with Cullen, especially when he was hip-deep in some complicated arcane research. Which was usually. "Listen, I've got one hypothesis that might fit. I'd like to run it by you."

"Shoot."

"What if the whole family was involved? Maybe Meacham got them to participate, told them it was some other sort of ritual they were performing. Some spells require multiple practitioners, right? If they'd all been part of it, then when the boy was killed, they'd all be smeared by it."

He was silent a moment. "Theoretically possible, but you'd have a hell of a time proving it."

"I'm going to have a hell of a time proving anything. Especially if the Wiccan coven Ruben's sending can't confirm that death magic was involved." A limited number of Wiccan spells were the only form of magically acquired evidence admissible in court, but the coven might not pick up the traces Lily had. Cullen said that trying to get a spell to do what an innate Gift did was like programming a robot to walk. You could do it, but a toddler would outperform the robot.

In other words, there was a good chance the coven wouldn't be able to find anything.

"Is he having Sherry's bunch do the test?"

"Probably, and I know they're good, but it's been four days. The traces I felt were pretty faint. I . . ."

"What?"

She'd seen something move, or thought she had—at the edge of her vision, a flickering sort of movement. But when she looked in that direction, all she saw was a single swing swaying gently. The other swings weren't moving.

A pale bird—a dove, maybe—took off from the other end of the swing set and she shook her head, feeling foolish. Must have glimpsed another bird taking off from the swing, making it move. "Nothing. I'm distractable today." Maybe because she didn't like the next question she needed to ask. "Karonski . . . exactly what does a death magic ritual take from its victim?"

"You're asking about the soul."

She hadn't expected him to go there so fast. "I guess I am."

"Different systems, different faiths, have different takes on that. Most Christian churches teach that the soul is indestructible, but a few of the evangelical ones disagree. Of course, they're the ones who think a demon can steal your soul, so I don't put a lot of credence in their opinion. Still, many Wiccans believe that death magic can damage a soul, while Islam—"

"I'm not asking about religion. What do we *know*?"

"You asked about souls. Can't go there without talking religion, because we don't *know* a damned thing." He paused. "You said Turner was knocked out while he was guarding the bodies. He had death magic on him."

"It's gone now."

"Right, but how do you fit that in?"

"With a crowbar and a whole lot of maybes." She raked a hand through her hair. "If Meacham is the killer, then someone else wandering in the woods last night used death magic on Rule. That's not as far-fetched as it sounds. We don't know how many people were involved in the ritual. Maybe Meacham had one or more confederates. But it doesn't explain why . . ."

"Why he or she didn't kill Turner."

Lily swallowed. "Yeah. I'm thinking maybe he or she couldn't do it. Rule's not easy to kill, and our second perp might not have had enough juice to do the job. If the death magic was shared between a bunch of ritualists, maybe . . ." She broke off, sighed. "That's a lot of maybes." She needed to talk to Cullen, dammit, about what was or wasn't possible, but . . . she glanced at her watch. "Shit. I'm late."

"You go, then, and I can go get me some eggs."

Lily thanked him for the consult, put her phone away, tidied the take-out trash, and backed out of her spot in front of the school.

Religion. She hated the way it kept intruding on her cases. Not that she was opposed to religion, per se . . . *Oh, be honest,* she told herself. She had issues. Her father was Buddhist. Her mother was Christian. There'd been a discreet little war throughout her childhood on the subject. As a result, she was . . . well, not exactly prejudiced. Religion was fine for other people. She simply preferred not to think about it.

Lily pulled into the parking lot in back of the sheriff's office. Karonski was probably right about most of what he'd said, but they did know one thing about souls. At least, Lily did. Souls existed. That was more than she'd known for the first twenty-eight years of her life, so she counted it as an important datum.

Especially since she'd had to die to obtain it. Lily climbed out of the plush car, shut and locked the door. And did her best not to remember.

SEVEN

IN the fresh light of an early summer morning, something hovered on the wide front porch of the two-story house, waiting. It hung near the door, remembering walls and that doors need opening, but not how to manage the trick.

The man was inside the house. It knew that without having any idea how it knew, nor did it wonder at its knowledge. Questions, curiosity, thought . . . none endured long in the constant fracturing that was its reality.

Cold, cold. So cold. It knew how to gain warmth; dimly it remembered that lesson and the bliss, the sheer joy of heat. For a little while, it had thought it was fixed. Freed. For a little while, it had *remembered*.

Something had gone wrong. What? It didn't know, couldn't hold on to the thought or what passed for memory, not with bits of itself breaking up, always breaking up, like ice chips fracturing under pressure. But it knew—without knowing why—that to be warm again, it would have to leave this house.

It didn't want to go. The man was inside. The one who knew it. It wanted, needed, to wait here, wait for the man to come out the door. If it could be close to him again, maybe it would know . . .

It no longer remembered what was missing. What it needed to know.

The howl of anguish was silent, a shuddering despair too great for its shredded being. It quivered and lost track of doors and houses and whatever had held it in one place.

Deep in the darkness of its fractured self, it heard The Voice.

Maybe the calling had been there all along; maybe it was newly come. It only knew the loathing and fear and promise of The Voice.

The call would grow louder, until it could no longer resist. It had to escape. It had to get warm again. Once it was warm, it wouldn't hear The Voice, and then it could remember . . . surely warmth would let it remember enough. Then it could find the man who knew it. Maybe it could ask the man . . . whatever it was it needed so badly to know.

Once it was warm again. Yes.

It skittered away from the house, searching. Resisting the need to return to The Voice. Warmth would protect it, provide for it—yes, it remembered that much: when it was warm enough, The Voice went away.

Once it was warm again, all would be well. Yes.

It glided down the street—lost, fragmented, starved. Picking up speed as it went. Warmths were everywhere, but at first it found only the small warmths. Some of those would let it in, but the small warmths weren't enough. It remembered that. It needed more.

Come, said The Voice. *Come, come, come . . .*

No! Frantic now, it hunted. It had to find a warmth, the right kind of warmth, or return to The Voice. There were warmths nearby, large warmths in the houses it glided past, but they wouldn't work. It needed . . .

Ah, there! A door, a door in that warmth! Not a physical door—it had forgotten physicality again, so didn't note the distinction—but a door nonetheless. A way in.

Walls were barriers only when it noticed the physical. It slid through one now without being aware of the passage, focused on the warmth it tracked. It eased close, found the "door" it needed, and slipped through. And into the warmth.

The shock of heat, of *self*, was sweet beyond expression. Lost in the bliss of sensation—Arms, legs, skin! It had skin!—for some time it simply rode the physical without noticing the other things it had regained.

Memory, though not its own. And words.

Gun, it thought in surprise, remembering now what a gun was. Then, tenderly sharing the discovery with its warmth, it added more words: *Gun, yes. We will get the gun and kill and kill.*

EIGHT

AT 8:22 A.M. Lily walked back into Sheriff Deacon's office.

"Agent Yu." He didn't get up and his expression didn't tell her much, but he wasn't thrilled to see her. He nodded at the other person in the room, who had stood when Lily entered. "This is Meacham's attorney, Crystal Kessenblaum."

The PD was a tall, thin woman, thirtyish or more, with an explosion of red hair that had rained freckles all over her skin. She wore white linen slacks with a long, slitted tunic in spring green—a pretty outfit, but an odd choice for the situation. It all but screamed, "Don't think of me as a lawyer." She also wore glasses, little round Ben Franklins, and not a speck of makeup. She had a crisp nod for Lily, but didn't offer to shake hands.

So Lily did, extending one hand confidently. "Ms. Kessenblaum. I'm glad you could make it here so early."

Kessenblaum's nearly invisible eyebrows shot up. She stared at Lily's hand a second, then seemed to decide what the hell and took it. Her tone was belligerent. "Checking me out?"

She had a decent grip, damp palms, and a little lick of magic. Fire magic, mostly—one of the more common Gifts, and one that was relatively kind to its possessor. Most of those with a slight dose of Fire learned to control it fairly easily. A few never even knew it was there.

"Of course. I gather the sheriff told you I'm a sensitive?"

Kessenblaum shot the sheriff an aggravated glance. Maybe there was some history between the two of them; maybe Kessenblaum was always aggravated, annoyed, or otherwise aggrieved. "Yes, and I want to go on record that nothing you learn about my client through touch is admissible."

Why did everyone feel obliged to point that out? "So noted. Sheriff, have you heard from the DA?"

"Yeah, yeah. Twice. First time to say she was meeting you here. Second time to say she was running late. Her youngest came down with a stomach bug. Mark usually takes the kids to day care, but he's got the heaves, too, so she had to drop 'em off on her way here."

"How many children does she have?" Lily was newly interested in such things, in how women balanced careers and kids. Not that finding someone to pitch in when she and Rule had to be away would be a problem, not with his father right there at Clanhome and about a hundred other potential sitters standing by. Lupi were kind of communal about child care.

Not that she knew exactly what her place was in Toby's life. She wasn't a stepmom, wasn't sure she wanted to be one, but . . . but something ached inside her at the thought. Something she didn't understand.

"Three—two girls and a boy." Deacon shoved his chair back and stood. "We might as well head on down. Marcia will meet us there."

Kessenblaum headed out the door without another word. Lily started to follow. The sheriff's hand on her arm stopped her. "Listen, Agent Yu, I, uh . . ." He grimaced. "I had it coming. That's all I want to say."

Her eyebrows lifted in surprise. "Good enough."

THE jail occupied the basement and most of the first floor. Deacon took them to the admissions area, where he gave instructions for Meacham to be brought to a small interview room.

He'd just finished when Marcia Farquhar arrived, slightly breathless. "Sorry to keep you waiting."

"No problem," Lily said, holding out her hand. "The sheriff explained."

The DA looked like a mother. Not Lily's mother, heaven knows—Marcia Farquhar was plump and pink, with a drawl like raw honey—but someone's. Her hair was prematurely silver, worn long and pulled back in an old-fashioned bun from a soft, round face. She wore a good suit, dusky rose, with a crisp white shirt. Her handshake was brisk and businesslike.

No magic in Marcia Farquhar.

"You're messing with my case, Agent Yu."

Lily nodded. "You had every reason to believe this one was solid. Turns out it isn't. The arraignment's this afternoon, I understand. I'd like to discuss that, if you have a few minutes after the interview with Meacham. You delayed the arraignment the maximum allowed."

"We lacked bodies—which you have now provided, along with some complications. But that won't affect the arraignment."

It damned sure ought to. "We'll talk," Lily repeated.

Kessenblaum's eyes had been darting between the two of them. "You have information that affects my client, Agent Yu?"

"Nothing admissible." Lily took petty satisfaction in saying that.

"If you're planning to bring additional charges against Mr. Meacham—"

"I don't bring charges. I conduct investigations. Your client is a witness in an investigation into the use of magic in a multiple homicide."

"You won't learn anything here. Mr. Meacham is not competent to answer questions."

"He's competent enough to insist on your presence at all interviews."

"I'm glad he remembered to do that, but it doesn't indicate competency. More that he knows who to trust and who not to trust. He ought to be in a medical facility, not jail." The look she shot Marcia Farquhar sizzled with some prior argument.

"Crystal," Farquhar said in her honey-soft drawl, "you aren't going to do your client much good if you take everything so personally. Right now, you ought to be cozying up to Agent Yu, here. She's your new best friend, seein' that whatever screws up my case helps you."

Oh, yeah, plenty of history between these two. Normally a DA didn't give a wobbly young PD advice—not good advice, anyway. Lily wanted to know what the deal was with these two, but not now. She looked at Deacon. "Where's that interview room?"

The jail wasn't much different from a dozen others Lily had seen. Newer than some, which meant it ought to seem cleaner, but it didn't. The usual tang of disinfectant hovered over other scents, nothing her human nose could decipher precisely. Nothing pleasant, though. She was glad she lacked Rule's sense of smell, and even gladder she was wholly numb to whatever psychic effluvia clung to the place. How could even a blocked empath stand working directly over it?

Must be a damned good block, she decided.

The interview room was beige all over. It held one table, two chairs, two guards, and a man in an orange jumpsuit, handcuffs, and no shoes.

Lily knew from the file that Roy Don Meacham was five-six, one seventy, Caucasian, brown and brown, and had turned thirty-nine last December. The brown hair was thinning, the brown irises were surrounded by pink whites, and the 170 pounds was mostly muscle and mostly in the upper half of his body. His shoulders were disproportionately wide, his torso long and husky, his hips skinny, and his legs short.

He looked like a balding gorilla with really bad allergies.

The DA hadn't come in with them, electing to watch from behind the one-way mirror on the wall to the right of the door. Deacon had. He claimed that Meacham was unstable, subject to fits of violence, and he wasn't taking any chances. With two young, brawny guards—one Hispanic, the other as dark an African American as Lily had ever seen—the sheriff's caution seemed overdone, but understandable. It would be embarrassing as hell if a prisoner in his charge hurt a fed.

Kessenblaum amazed Lily by speaking gently. "Hey, Roy Don. They treating you okay?"

"Hey." Meacham's gaze jumped around before settling on Kessenblaum. He had a deep voice, appropriate for the barrel-shaped chest. It reminded her of Rule's father, Isen. "What the hell is it now? You finally convince these assholes to let me go home? I hope you brought me some cigarettes this time. A man needs a goddamned smoke in this place."

What he said was normal. The way he said it wasn't. The words skittered into each other abruptly or dragged in odd places, as if he'd forgotten the normal rhythms of human speech.

Kessenblaum shook her head. "Not getting out today, I'm afraid. This is Agent Yu of the FBI. She wants to talk to you."

The pink-and-brown eyes lighted on Lily, blinking fast, as if sending secret semaphores of distress. "FBI. Crap. I don't want to talk to no FBI . . . Why you here? You're too damned little. Don't look like no FBI agent."

Lily moved forward. "Are your eyes bothering you, Mr. Meacham?"

"My eyes?" He seemed puzzled. "You oughta arrest these assholes for locking me up. Got no reason. I need to go home. Becky's bound to be worried about me, gone so long." He frowned, still blinking. "How long I been gone, anyway?"

"Four days." Lily pulled out the only other chair in the room and sat across the table from Meacham. He'd been hand-cuffed with his hands in front, as she'd asked. Those hands rested on the table, the fingers restlessly twining and untwining. "Seems longer, I bet."

"Longer. Yeah." Blink, blink, blink. "Becky's good with the kids, but they need a man around. Got to get home, take care of them."

He'd been told. More than once, he'd been told that his wife and children were dead, that he was under arrest for killing them. Lily didn't think he was acting, though. People talk about the power of belief, but disbelief has power, too.

Meacham wasn't the first killer she'd seen wrecked by what he'd done, clinging to denial like a drowning man clings to a flimsy branch.

"Guess you'd like to have those taken off, huh?" She nodded at his hands, still busily wrapping and unwrapping themselves.

"Don't know what you're talkin' about." He didn't look down.

"Your handcuffs."

He stopped blinking. "Those ain't mine."

"I guess they belong to the sheriff's department, but they're on your hands." She tried a smile as she reached for one busy, busy hand. Her fingertips brushed one knuckle. "Mr. Meacham—"

"Not my hands!" he bellowed. And with that, he exploded.

The table shot up, propelled by Meacham's joined hands slamming it from underneath. He was roaring, on his feet, his face red and the cords in his neck standing out. Lily dived out of her chair, but wasn't quite quick enough. The table clipped her hip as she went down. Kessenblaum was screaming, a high, staccato counterpoint to Meacham's bass roar.

Lily scrambled to her feet. Both guards had jumped on Meacham, who bent, sending the Hispanic guard flying over his head to collide with the upturned table. The table blocked Lily, so she skidded around it and missed seeing the blow that crumpled the second guard, his hands clutching his crotch.

Deacon shot past her—going low, she realized, adjusting her own target.

The sheriff hit his prisoner at the knees, taking him down. Lily landed on Meacham's chest just as the man hit the floor. She leaned one forearm across his throat, ready to choke him as needed.

As abruptly as it had begun, the fight was over.

In the renewed quiet, Lily heard Kessenblaum panting, whispery little moans interspersed with the occasional "ohmygod." The guard who'd been kicked in the nuts was cursing steadily, but without much breath.

Deacon shifted to sit on Meacham's thighs while gripping

the man's wrists. He spoke calmly enough. "Anyone need a doctor?" When no one spoke, he said, "In that case, Corporal Sanchez, get your ass over here and take control of your prisoner."

"Yes, sir." Sanchez finished untangling himself from the table's legs just as the door swung open and two more guards entered, weapons drawn. "Holster 'em, boys," Deacon said without looking over. "Matheson, stand by. Hemmings, you and Sanchez secure the prisoner for return to his cell."

Sanchez limped over to them. "Miss—uh, I mean Agent Yu, I'll take him now."

"In a minute." She knew the man was deeply embarrassed. Bad enough to have a fed immobilizing his prisoner when he'd failed to control the man. Worse when that fed was female, five-two, and slim.

Tough. She looked down at the contorted face of the man who'd tried to take the room apart a moment ago. Meacham's cheeks were wet, his red eyes streaming. "You injured, Mr. Meacham?"

He looked up at her, blinking madly. "Got no hands," he whispered. "Not mine. They aren't mine."

She shifted so she could lay one hand along his wet, stubbled cheek without losing the ability to choke him if she needed to. She had to be sure . . . Oh, yes. Her touch confirmed the fleeting impression she'd received in the second between touching his hand and his going berserk.

Death magic, very faint, but unmistakable in its ground-glass foulness . . . and nothing else. Roy Don Meacham had not a shred of personal magic. Nothing he could have used to call up the death magic that still clung to his skin.

"That's right, Mr. Meacham," she agreed, hoarse and quiet. "Not your hands. It wasn't your hands that did it."

NINE

TOBY woke all at once, blinking at the buttery daylight on his ceiling and wondering why his stomach felt so excited. Then he remembered.

Dad was here. Right here in the house. He'd stayed here last night, which he never did because of not wanting reporters to come sniffing around. And when Dad left in about a week, Toby would be going with him.

Excitement bubbled up so fast it was a wonder he didn't just barf. Toby scrambled out of bed and into the hall. He peeked in the bedroom where Dad and Lily should have been, but the bed was empty. It wasn't made up and the suitcase was just sitting out on the floor, which surprised him because Lily was real neat, like Grammy. She even cleaned the top of the toothpaste tube. He knew that because he'd seen her doing it once when he was visiting Dad and her in Washington, and he'd asked why.

"So the cap will close properly," she'd said, "which is amazingly unimportant to many people."

Toby squinched up his nose. "But you think it matters?"

"I'm anal about this sort of thing."

"Anal" was a fancy word for asshole, which he wasn't allowed to say, and he didn't see why Lily would call herself that. She was pretty much okay, even if she was around Dad all the time, which was a big change. Dad's other women had been like Toby's mom—people Dad liked but didn't want to stay with. But the mate bond made things different.

Toby had warned Lily not to tell Grammy about cleaning the top of a toothpaste tube, not wanting that added to the list of things well-brought-up boys were supposed to do. But thinking about Grammy and lists and the unmade bed reminded him, so he dashed back to his room and yanked the covers up over his pillow real quick.

One of Grammy's big rules was to make the bed as soon as he got out of it. It was a sucky rule, but he wanted her to see that she'd raised him right, like she always said she was trying to do, and not worry that he'd be all uncivilized when he wasn't here with her anymore.

Thinking of Grammy made his stomach hurt in a different way. He hesitated, wondering if maybe he should get dressed before he went downstairs. But that was a school-time rule and it was summer, so she might not know he was doing it for her, and besides, he hated getting dressed before he even had breakfast.

At Clanhome, he could go around naked if he wanted. At least some of the time.

He grinned, then went to his bed and folded back the bedspread so he could fix the pillow the way Grammy liked, with the spread tucked in neatly. Now when she saw his bed, she'd know what he meant.

He hit the stairs at a run.

Dad and Grammy were in the kitchen, which smelled like coffee and bacon and eggs. Dad was sitting, but Grammy was on her feet by the stove. She claimed her leg was fine now, and besides, the muscles wouldn't get strong again if she babied it all the time. But he knew it still hurt sometimes. He had warned Dad not to fuss over her. She hated fussing unless she was the one doing it.

They were wearing grim faces, and stopped talking the moment he came in. Grammy made up a smile. "Good morning, bright eyes. You ready for some eggs?"

"Sure." He looked back and forth between them. "What's wrong?"

"Why, nothing." Grammy moved to the refrigerator to get the eggs, putting her back to him. "We left you some bacon. It's there on the table."

He hated it when she said nothing was wrong when something obviously was. "Dad?"

"When I went for my run last night, I found the bodies of—"

"Rule." Grammy turned, egg carton in one hand, her face tight the way it got when she was trying not to be mad. "I told you I didn't want him upset."

Dad nodded. He was always calm and respectful with Grammy, and Grammy was always polite with him, but Toby wasn't sure if they really liked each other. "Yes, and I understand your feelings. I disagree with your conclusion, however, as I said. Toby is already aware of the killings."

"Those kids?" Toby's feet got into the act along with his mouth, and he moved up to his dad. "You found the bodies of those kids who were killed with their mom?"

Rule laid his hands on Toby's shoulders. "I did. I told Lily, and she's investigating, as it seems there was magic involved. This creates some complications for us with the hearing so close."

"Why? I didn't know them." Toby immediately felt bad. "I mean, it's awful that they died and all, but what does that have to do with the hearing?" It was supposed to be a formality, Grammy said. That meant that they had to go do legal stuff, but no one was arguing, so the judge ought to just let him go with Dad.

"Reporters." Grammy whipped the fork through the eggs as if they'd talked back to her. "Some are already here, and your father thinks more will be coming." Her voice dropped, like she didn't really want them to hear the rest. "Bunch of busybodies, always poking their noses into other people's business."

Toby looked at her in surprise. He knew why he hated reporters: they interfered with *everything*. Because of reporters, he'd never been able to do a bunch of stuff with Dad, who'd wanted to keep the press from knowing about him. Of course, Mom was a reporter, and Toby used to blame her job for her never being around, but that was when he was too little to admit the truth. She didn't *want* to be around.

But Grammy never said bad stuff about reporters. Or about Mom, either. He was pretty sure she got mad at Mom sometimes, but she never said so. "How come you're mad at the reporters? Can they make the judge do things different than he's supposed to?"

Grammy gave him another of those tight smiles, the ones that meant she didn't feel like smiling, but she wanted him to know her mad wasn't about him. "She. The judge for our hearing is a she, not a he. And what reporters say ought not to make a difference, but there's a deal of space between 'ought not' and 'won't.' "

"A good judge won't let the presence of the press interfere," Dad said, "but she may take more care, go more slowly. More to the point, though, is that once the press knows about you, they'll bother your grandmother's friends and neighbors. They'll bother us, too, asking a great many questions, many of them insulting, and probably misquote us if we answer."

Toby nodded. He'd watched reporters asking his dad questions on TV, so he knew what kind of stupid questions they asked. "And you can't punch them or anything, 'cause that makes it worse."

"Exactly. They'll raise questions about my fitness to be a parent, of course. I'm expecting that. But since some of them are more interested in speculation and scandal than fact, they may also insinuate unpleasant things about your grandmother and your mother."

"But that's gonna happen anyway, isn't it?" Toby reached for a piece of bacon. "You told me they'd hear about the custody deal and we wouldn't like some of the stuff they said. It's just happening before the hearing instead of after."

Dad and Grammy shared one of those looks grown-ups give each other when they're not telling you something. Grammy turned to the stove and poured the eggs in the pan. "There's a plate for that bacon. Sit down to eat it, please."

Toby sighed and did as he was told, pulling out a chair.

His dad said, "After the hearing, you'll be at Clanhome. Reporters can't bother you there."

Toby chewed on that along with his bacon. "They can bother you and Grammy, though. And the neighbors and all."

"Dealing with reporters is part of my job," Rule said. "I wish I could offer your grandmother better protection from their harassment."

Grammy sniffed. "I can deal with a few nosy reporters if I have to. So can Connie. Eat your eggs, now." She brought the pan over and slid a bunch of eggs onto Toby's plate.

Connie was Mrs. Milligan, their next-door neighbor to the west, and she knew all about Toby being lupus. She and Grammy had been friends forever, since back when they were nurses together, before Grammy decided to retire and take care of him. Grammy had told her the truth when Toby's mom was expecting him, before he was even born. Mrs. Milligan had kept the secret for all the nine years since, and Toby figured Grammy was right. She and Mrs. Milligan could deal with nosy reporters just fine.

Probably they'd give those reporters cookies and coffee and make 'em wash their hands first and say, "Yes, ma'am" and "No, ma'am." Toby grinned.

"More coffee?" Grammy said, picking up the pot as Toby tucked into his eggs. Dad agreed that he'd like some, and thanked her.

Of course, Mrs. Milligan wasn't the only one who knew Toby's secret, but Justin was Toby's best friend in the whole world. He wouldn't tell the reporters anything. His sister wouldn't, either, because Talia had her own big secret, which Toby knew because it was only fair for Justin to tell him after she eavesdropped on them. She wouldn't want anyone telling her secret, so she'd be quiet, too.

But Toby thought old Mr. Hodge on the corner had his suspicions. After Grammy broke her leg, Dad and Lily had come here twice, making sure she was doing okay with the nurse Dad hired. Which she had, though at first Toby thought they wouldn't get along, because Grammy knew more about nursing than 'most anyone and didn't much like being a patient, but the hired nurse had let Grammy boss her around, so it had turned out okay. Ever since then, though, old Mr. Hodge had been looking at Toby funny. But he was one as kept to himself, like Grammy said, so he probably hadn't told anyone.

Dad was talking to Grammy. "Are you sure you don't want to go—"

"No. No, I'm not being run out of my home, but thank you for offering."

If a bunch of reporters came around bothering old Mr. Hodge, he'd probably chase them off with his shotgun. He didn't ever load it, but they wouldn't know that. Toby grinned around a mouthful of eggs. He'd like to see that.

"Very well, then. I'll get Lily's things together."

"Huh? Why?" Belatedly, Toby remembered to swallow.

"If I'm here, the reporters will be, too. So Lily will move to the hotel—she can't leave Halo with an investigation under way—and you and I will go to Leidolf's clanhome."

"Leidolf? But they—" He broke off, darting a glance at Grammy. He wasn't sure what he could say around her about clan stuff.

She sighed. "I can see you two need to discuss this privately. If you think Ms. Yu wouldn't mind, I'll go pack for her." Grammy's mouth twitched in the first real smile he'd seen on her face this morning. "I suspect she'd like my methods better than yours. She's a very tidy person."

Dad smiled slightly. "Thank you. I suspect you're right. Finish your eggs, Toby. We'll discuss this out back."

TEN

>≈≈

IN an old house on a quiet street, a fractured being was exploring its temporary structure. After the bliss at having skin and breath subsided, it had realized that its new warmth was different from the other one. Some of the parts didn't work well. It didn't understand the problem at first, for though the warmth's memories were available, the thoughts were not. Not exactly.

Finally it located the reason the knees and back ached: *Old knees, old back, old brain, old man. Jesus H. Christ, I hate being old.*

That was a thought, yes, but a thought played so often it had worn its own groove in the memories. Unfortunately, it made this discovery after telling its warmth to hurry. This had caused the warmth to rush too much, and fall.

That's when it rediscovered pain.

Bright and hot, pain absorbed it for a time, fascinating in its vividness, its familiarity. It had known pain before. Pain was not as welcome as breath and memories, but the familiarity was dear.

For a time it hoped it would truly *remember*.

That didn't happen, but being in the warmth stabilized it,

so despair didn't shake bits of it loose, and The Voice was silenced.

Fortunately, its warmth wasn't too damaged by the fall; once it woke from its contemplation of pain and told the warmth to stand up, he did so without great trouble. A few moments later, though, it noticed something disturbing. Something was wrong with the warmth. What?

It had the warmth touch his face. Wet. Blood? It remembered blood . . . no, not blood. The problem wasn't with the warmth's body. The warmth was sad, terribly sad. The wetness was tears.

It didn't want its warmth to be sad. It tried to comfort the *old man*, but telling him to feel better didn't work. It pondered that, wondering why one instruction was accepted and the other was not, as its warmth hunted through the chest of drawers, as ordered, for shotgun shells.

THIRTY minutes after the explosive interview with her witness, Lily had made one quick phone call, Deacon had his prisoner back in his cell, and the four of them—federal agent, public defender, district attorney, and sheriff—were once more in Deacon's office.

Kessenblaum had been embarrassed by her panicked reaction to her client's freak-out. Embarrassment, like so much else, turned the woman belligerent.

"You see?" Kessenblaum said, jabbing her finger in Farquhar's general direction. "You see he—Mr. Meacham—he's not stable. Not competent. You can't continue to hold him here. It's—"

"Give it a rest," Farquhar said wearily. "You aren't doing Meacham any favors by yelling at us."

"At least I'm on his side. At least I care. You just care about the media coverage, the election, and what—"

Lily was out of patience. "Ms. Kessenblaum, shut up."

After one second's startled silence, the woman sneered. "You're as bad as she is, determined to make your reputation on the backs of those without power, without voices. But I can tell you now, Mr. Meacham isn't alone. I won't let him be ground up by the system."

Oh, God, that was it. That explained the inappropriate clothes. Kessenblaum wanted to be a hippie, but had been born a generation too late. "You want to stage a sit-in or you want to help your client?" Lily asked.

Kessenblaum rolled her eyes. "Oh, isn't that just like a cop? Shove me into a comfortable little cliché so you can ignore what I'm saying!"

"Talk's cheap. What have you done other than bitch? Why hasn't Meacham been seen by someone with plenty of alphabet soup after his name who could put some weight behind your claims?"

"I don't have money for that! If you knew what a joke the budget for the public defender's office is around here—"

"Get it pro bono," she snapped. "Quit whining and start calling around. But do it elsewhere. The grown-ups need to get some work done."

Kessenblaum's face went white, then red. "You don't—you can't talk to me that way."

"Think she just did," Deacon said. His eyes held a glint of humor. "Come on, Crystal. You must have better things to do than badger your godmother, and God knows I've got better things to do than supervise the fireworks. Besides," he added, moving to hold the door for her in a broad hint, "you don't want to make the FBI agent mad. She'll clean your clock."

After one fuming, frustrated moment, Kessenblaum stomped out. Deacon closed the door gently behind her.

Lily looked at Farquhar, one eyebrow lifted. "Godmother?"

Farquhar's eyes twinkled. "I hope you're shocked that a woman my age could have a goddaughter Crystal's age."

"I am. She's what—thirty or so? And you can't be much more than forty." With children young enough to need to be driven to school, Lily remembered.

Marcia Farquhar patted Lily's hand. "Bless you. Crystal's thirty-three, and I've a bit more mileage than those forty years you tactfully mentioned. I started my family quite late—scandalously so, according to some, who were more upset at my delaying pregnancy so long than at Crystal's mother giving birth when she was sixteen." She exchanged a wry look with Deacon. "Her mother and I were close growing up, being among the few Catholics in Halo. As a result, I might have become a mother late in life, but I became a godmother quite young."

"Hmm." Lily had noticed that people in the South often found a way to let you know their religious affiliation, pretty much the same way they'd bring up their favorite football team. It disconcerted her.

Farquhar shrugged. "Her mother and I have drifted apart over the years, but I still have a soft spot for Crystal, which results in giving her advice. Which, as you've noticed, she does not appreciate."

"She's like a puppy," Deacon said. "Chews up your shoes, gets underfoot, then doesn't understand why you're mad. Means well, I guess. Never saw an underdog she didn't want to champion." He gave Lily a smile that held a hint of a taunt. "Poor Crystal's probably got the same problem with you she does with me. I'm black, which oughta make me an underdog, but this badge makes me one of the oppressors."

Lily's eyebrows lifted. "I can't imagine why someone would mistake me for an underdog." Underdog, to Lily, meant *victim*. She'd been one once, when she was nine. Not since.

"Not you so much, maybe. That weer you're hooked up with. Crystal's big cause these days is werewolf rights."

To Lily's surprise, it was Farquhar who corrected him. "Lupus, Jay. We don't call them werewolves now. Agent Yu." She flicked a glance at her wrist, where a dainty gold watch rested. "I've got a great deal to do before the arraignment."

And Lily had allowed herself to be distracted, taking out some of her feelings on the ineffectual Kessenblaum. Maybe that was just as well. She'd been pretty pissed. "There won't be an arraignment."

Farquhar's eyebrows shot up. "I beg your pardon."

"Kessenblaum is annoying, but she's right. Meacham isn't competent. He doesn't belong in a jail cell, and he isn't guilty."

Farquhar's voice dropped into the freezer. "I've got more than enough evidence to prove that he is."

"He hasn't got a Gift, not the tiniest trace of one. He can't use magic. Magic was used in the deaths of Becky Meacham and her children. *He* was used."

"Oh, come on, now. You aren't claiming he was possessed."

Deacon scowled. "You said he wasn't. When I asked, you said there were no traces of demon on the bodies."

"I don't know what was done to Meacham. I don't know who did it or how. But Roy Don Meacham, like his wife and children, has traces of death magic clinging to him, and there's no way he could have put it there. Someone else did, and that's our perp."

"You're babbling," Farquhar snapped as she started for the door. "If that's all you wanted to discuss—"

"Not quite everything." Lily had hoped they could work this out without her pulling out the big guns. Wasn't going to happen. "I also need to notify you that the FBI will be taking custody of Roy Don Meacham today. The marshals should be here in a couple hours."

Farquhar stopped. Turned. "Oh, no, you're not. If you think I'm going to roll over because you've got some crazy idea that a man who clubbed his wife and children to death is a *victim*—"

"I realize that you've only my word about the magic. However, his lack of magic makes it—"

"I don't give a good damn whether Roy Don Meacham has magic or not. He killed those kids."

Lily heard that broken voice again: *Not my hand. Got no hands.* "His hands killed those children and their mother. Roy Don wasn't in charge of them at the time. Someone or something used Meacham, and somewhere in his head is information about that. I'm not taking chances with him. He'll be examined by competent experts, both medical and magical, and placed on suicide watch."

Farquhar sniffed. "I *might* let your experts see him—after the arraignment. But—"

"Marcia," Deacon said.

"But there is no way I'm going to let you—"

"Marcia," Deacon repeated, louder. "She's Unit Twelve and she's claimed jurisdiction. How you gonna stop her?"

Silence. Then Farquhar flung one furious glance at Lily and left. She didn't slam the door behind her. She closed it carefully, as if she were too angry to let even a little steam out that way.

Lily sighed. She was making friends all over the place today. "I guess it would be awkward for you to storm out, too, seeing as this is your office."

Deacon resumed his seat. "Guess it would. You going to need some work space here?"

He'd surprised her again. "Probably. This didn't seem like the best time to mention it."

He shrugged. "You burst Marcia's bubble. I'm not Marcia. She doesn't have a whiff of a Gift, does she?"

"If Ms. Farquhar asks what I felt when I touched her hand, I'll tell her." She paused. "Just as I told you what I felt when we shook hands." The implication being that she considered such information private.

He nodded. "You've got a careful way of putting things. I appreciate caution. Marcia does, too, but she doesn't appreciate magic. She thinks you're grandstanding. I've got a little edge on her there. I can tell you believe what you're saying, and I've got reason to think you know what you're talking about. Now." He leaned back in his chair. "About that work space— best I can offer you is the conference room."

"I'll take it. Ah . . . I've put in for some backup, but I'm not sure when I'll get them. Noon, maybe later."

"Conference room should hold more'n one person. Who's coming to pick up Meacham?"

"A pair of federal marshals and a medevac unit."

His eyebrows shot up. "Medevac?"

"He needs medical attention. Possession tends to screw up the host's mind. Sometimes the body, too. We don't know that he was possessed, exactly, but something sure screwed with him. And I think he'll travel better sedated."

"Your marshals will have an easier time if he is," Deacon said dryly. "Where will you put him?"

"Georgetown in D.C." There was no such thing as true magical shielding, not in their realm, anyway. But Georgetown University Hospital had a couple of rooms that were circled and heavily warded. It was the best they could do.

Deacon leaned forward, pressed a button on his phone. "Edna? Could you come in here a minute?" He leaned back. "I've got a few things to do that don't have a blame thing to do with Roy Don Meacham, so I'm going to let Edna get you settled. She's been copying the case file for you. I hope you'll be able to bring in your own office supplies and such. The budget's tight."

"SOP is for me to order in what I need, then donate to the host jurisdiction whatever's left when I leave. Which means you'll probably come out ahead by a fax machine, copier, and whiteboard."

He smiled, satisfied. "Sometimes it pays to be the nice guy."

"Sometimes it does. Here's another chance to play nice. I'm going to need to look at the crime scene—Meacham's home. I also need to talk to your witness, the mailman with the broken skull." This time the name was there, waiting, like it was supposed to be. "Watkins, right?"

"Bill Watkins. He's still hospitalized, but stable. Shouldn't be any problem seeing him. The key to Meacham's place is in Evidence. Edna'll get it for you."

"Great. Quick question. You said the physical evidence at the scene suggested the two kids were killed in bed. How far apart are their rooms?"

He frowned suspiciously, as if it were a trick question. "They're right next to each other."

"And the mother, Becky Meacham. Where was she killed?"

"From the look of the blood, all over the damned place."

She sighed, nodded, and reached for the door.

"Ah . . ."

Lily paused with her hand on the doorknob. Deacon was fiddling with a pen. He spoke without looking at her. "I'm going to ask you something that's none of my business."

Her eyebrows shot up as curiosity fought with common sense. Whatever he wanted to ask, it would probably annoy her and possibly make it hard to work with the man.

But with Lily, curiosity almost always won. "What's that?"

"It doesn't bother you, the way Turner is?"

"Lupi aren't the bestial killers that popular culture makes them out to be."

"I don't mean that. I've seen him. He holds it together okay, even when you push at him some." Deacon put the pen down. "I mean the way he is with women. Weers—I mean lupi—they don't believe in marriage."

A dozen things jostled through her brain, trying to make it into speech. Explanations, justifications . . . reasons. Lupi had reasons for their ways. They were nearly infertile, and their very survival had long depended on scattering their seed as widely as possible.

That secret could not be spoken, of course. Neither could she explain that Rule *was* faithful to her. The mate bond that tied them together made it unthinkable for him to stray, even though she could. She wouldn't, but according to his beliefs, it was acceptable for her to dabble on the side.

Lily wasn't sure how much he truly believed that. She wasn't sure she wanted to know. But in fact, she had a guarantee of faithfulness perhaps no other woman could claim . . . and no chance of claiming it aloud. "No," she said after a brief pause. "It doesn't bother me, Sheriff."

She closed the door quietly behind her.

ELEVEN

EDNA was a six-footer with a linebacker's shoulders, a sun worshipper's wrinkles, and a ship's prow of a bosom. Her hair was short, gray, and straight. She wore a wholly unflattering white oxford shirt tucked into belted khakis. No weapon.

"Crime scene photos," Edna said, slapping a folder on the conference table. "Rest of it's in here." A second, thicker folder landed on top of the first. "Coffee's in the break room, west end of the building, between the restrooms. Like we all want to hang out at break next to the piss pots, right?"

Lily agreed that those who did space planning for public buildings were idiots, and Edna went to get the key from Evidence.

Like almost everyone in the Unit, Lily had been sent all over the place in the seven months since the Turning, so she was used to quickly setting up a field office. She called a local office supply store, then sat down with the files. First she'd go through the reports, get a picture of what had happened at Meacham's house four days ago. So far all she had was Deacon's version.

She'd studied the photos and was halfway through the thicker folder when a muffled drumroll sounded in her purse.

That was Cullen. She frowned, glancing at her watch as she retrieved the toy Rule had given her for her birthday in April—an iPhone. "It's six forty in the morning in California. What's wrong?"

"Wrong?" Cullen asked. "What could be wrong? You texted me. I called." The next part came out louder, but muffled, as if he'd turned his head. "How would I know? I'm not the Finder here. All right, all right, I'll look for it. Just get your beautifully gravid body in and out of that shower fast. The plane leaves in seventy minutes."

"Plane?" Lily repeated. "Where are you going?"

"Washington—the state, not D. of C. Kidnapping. A little boy this time, four years old. She just got the call."

Cynna was on limited duty due to her pregnancy, which meant that, unlike other Unit agents, she wasn't flying all over the U.S. these days. Except in special cases, that was. Cases like this, when a child's life was at stake. Cynna was the top Finder in the country.

"You're going with her again?"

"Of course I'm going with her. I'm not about to . . . Lily," he snapped, and it took her a second to realize he was speaking to Cynna, not her. "I'm talking to Lily, who's allowed to know about kidnappings and such, right? Since she's FBI, too, and not likely to give interviews on the subject. Now, are you going to take a shower or not?"

This time Lily caught Cynna's raised voice. And the slam of a door. "Maybe you shouldn't yell at the pregnant woman."

"If I don't nip back when she nips at me, she'll think something's wrong. Tell me about the death magic Rule found."

She did. Lily was good at condensing a report to the key points, having given plenty of them in her days as a beat cop, then in Homicide. But she didn't believe in skimping on the details when consulting an expert—she couldn't know which details Cullen needed. So it took several minutes.

When she finished, Cullen proved once again that he was as bright as he was irritating. "You're wanting to know just how shaky the limb is you've crawled out on, yanking Meacham away from the locals. Was he responsible for what he did, or not? Sorry, love. Can't say for damned certain sure."

"You can tell me for certain sure if Meacham needed a Gift to use death magic."

"To invoke it, yes. To use it? That's where things turn iffy. There've been reports going back to pre-Purge days of . . . Yes, it's still Lily." Cullen's voice took on a different tone. Husky. "Have I mentioned how great you look wet, naked, and knocked up? There's probably another flight we could catch. . . ."

The next part was muffled, but suggested a moment that should have been more private than it was. Then Cullen's voice came back, sounding absurdly cheerful, considering he couldn't have done much in that brief time. "Cynna says hi. Now, where was I?"

"Explaining the difference between invoking death magic and using it."

"Oh, yeah. I'll give you the short version, because we're leaving as soon as that luscious body I get to touch whenever I want to is covered—hey, no throwing things!" Lily assumed that bit wasn't directed at her. "Full disclosure: I don't know much about death magic."

Lily paused a beat. "Inconvenient, yet reassuring."

She could hear the grin in his voice. "That said, I'm eighty or ninety percent sure no one in this realm could perform the invocation ritual solo. And ritual is required—there's no way of just slurping up power by killing people at random. Meacham couldn't perform any part of that ritual, but it might—just might—be possible for him to do the killing. The power released by the deaths would be contained within a circle and absorbed by whoever created the circle."

"The three victims were killed at some distance from each other, separated by walls. Doesn't sound like there was a circle."

"No. Bludgeoning with a baseball bat doesn't fit what I

know, either. But again, on this particular area of magical practices I am not an expert."

"Get to the part about how using death magic is different from invoking it."

"It's possible to create a charm or talisman even a null could use. Hellish hard, but it can be done. So technically, it's possible for someone like Meacham, someone without magic, to have used a talisman."

"Talisman?" Her heart gave a sudden, scared jump in her chest. "Is that another way of saying artifact?"

"Not exactly, but you probably aren't interested in the precise definitions."

"No, I'm not." Absently, Lily rubbed the place on her stomach where the skin was shiny-smooth . . . a burn scar. Cullen had given it to her last year, but she didn't hold it against him. Not considering the alternative—an ancient staff powered by death magic in the hands of the man it had driven mad. The staff had been used to control others.

It had also sent Rule to hell, along with part of Lily. The part that ended up dying there.

"Déjà vu all over again?" Cullen said gently. "I don't know what's going on in Halo, but it's not the staff. I burned it, Lily. Mage fire doesn't leave any remnants behind, not even ash. That staff is gone."

"Okay." She grabbed a good breath and let it out. "Okay, that's not it, but I hope you've got some ideas to offer in its place."

"Three possibilities." She heard what sounded like the trunk of a car slamming, followed by Cynna's voice, indistinct in the background. "One: someone discovered yet another powerful ancient artifact and is feeding it. Two: your perp or perps discovered or invented a kick-ass coercion spell and forced Meacham to kill his family, somehow using those deaths to gain power themselves. Three: your victims were killed, and Meacham coerced, through some unknown but innate magical ability."

Lily didn't like any of those possibilities, but . . . "Number one's the simplest."

"Not really. Hold on a minute."

Cullen told Cynna to chill, that he could drive and talk at the same time, at least until they hit the highway. That last was a concession to Cynna's condition, Lily figured. All lupi had fast reflexes, but Cullen's were off the charts. He could probably drive, talk, and play with fire—literally—and still react quicker to traffic than most people.

She heard a car door close. "You still there?" he asked.

"Oh, yeah. You don't like Door Number One?"

"I included it only to be thorough. Even if we ignore the fleetingly small chance of yet another ancient artifact turning up—and recent experience to the contrary, they remain more legend than reality—power like that tends to draw attention. Earth isn't interdicted anymore. If an ancient artifact turned up here, maybe blown in by the power winds, all sorts of bad-asses would have hoofed it to our humble little realm and be duking it out now for possession. Hard to miss that sort of thing."

That made sense. "And Door Number Two? Coercion spells aren't supposed to work."

"Yeah, but if someone invented one that almost worked . . . maybe that's why Meacham's nuts and his family's dead. The spell sent him into a homicidal frenzy instead of making him do . . . whatever. Not that I really think that's what happened—it doesn't explain the death magic—but I can't rule it out."

Meacham didn't seem a likely target for some hotshot co-ercion spell. What could he have had that anyone wanted? "You're going for Door Number Three—an innate magical ability. But it wasn't a demon, Cullen."

"Maybe the traces of demon magic faded before you touched the bodies."

She rubbed her temple. "Possible, I guess, but I've found traces lingering more than two weeks after someone made a demonic pact. That's not the same as possession, but . . . shit, I need to know more. Do demons use or, ah, invoke death magic?"

"You can consult about that possibility with my resident demon expert here, after I get off the phone. Which will be in

a couple minutes. We don't know much about out-realm beings, do we?"

"You think something crossed during the power winds.
Not an artifact, but a—a being or a creature."

"I hate to say yes. It's here-there-be-dragons thinking—we
don't know what's out there, so we draw whatever shapes suit
us. But that does seem the most possible of the possibilities."

"This creature would—well, feed, I guess. That's what you
mean. That it uses the energy generated by death magic."

"I don't know. I could draw some pretty shapes for you,
but I do not know." And ignorance pissed Cullen off. "And
even my best possibility doesn't really fit, dammit. It doesn't
fit all the facts."

"What do you mean?"

"Lily, you aren't thinking. Death magic clung to your
corpses and to Meacham for four days, but it didn't cling to
Rule for more than moments. It knocked him out, then just
went away. And there is nothing I know of to explain that."

Shit. Double shit. That should have jumped out at her, the
one variation in a solid pattern.

"Somehow he shed death magic like a duck sheds water,"
Cullen was saying. "And no, that doesn't sound like any natural lupus ability I ever heard of. Unless there's something
about being two-mantled . . . I don't see what, but there's a
helluva lot I don't know about mantles."

"You must know more than I do. You're affected by one."

"You can be affected by sunlight without knowing shit
about photons, frequencies, or nuclear decay. You need to talk
to Rule, maybe Isen. Someone who's carried a mantle or part
of one."

"I'll do that. You have any other ideas?"

He didn't. He made a vague promise to see what he could
turn up. The vagueness meant he didn't want to tell her what
kind of stones he'd be looking under, but she had no problem
with that. He passed the phone to Cynna, who snorted at the
notion of a demon using death magic.

"But they eat something other than flesh when they eat an
animal," Lily said. "Or each other."

"Well, yeah, but . . . look, it isn't the same. Most of us—people who've, uh, studied this—think demons eat the life energy of whatever they consume, but it's a biological energy. Material. Probably magical, too, since they get the memories of whatever they eat. But death magic involves spiritual shit. Demons can't touch the spiritual shit."

"By spiritual shit, do you mean souls? Karonski wasn't at all sure souls were affected by death magic."

"Yeah, but Abel is Wiccan. Wiccans focus on this life, not what comes after. They don't talk much about souls. They don't really have a theory or dogma about what souls are."

"I suppose you do?"

"Sure. Your soul is the part of you that loves. Say, what do you think about Daniel Abel?"

The part of you that loves. It couldn't be that simple . . .

"Lily?"

She tried to remember what Cynna had just said. "What about Abel?"

"Daniel Abel. For the baby's names. His middle names, that is, because I think kids should have their own first names, but the middle one, that's a good place to connect him to people who matter. So I was trying to decide between Daniel and Abel, because I'd like him to be connected to my dad, but . . . well, I wouldn't have gotten straightened out without Abel, you know? Cullen thinks we could give him two middle names. Do you think that's too much?"

"Two's okay. You probably don't want to go for three. What about his first name?"

"Still stuck there."

"Well, if you do name your baby for Karonski, I want to see his face when he finds out. He'll melt right down to goo. Listen, I'd better go."

When Lily put her phone down, she was smiling in spite of the ache that had set up residence at the back of her skull. She glanced at the files, grimaced, and decided to retrieve her laptop before diving in. It was in the trunk of her car.

She needed to make some notes about her discussion with Cullen anyway, so this wasn't entirely an excuse to get up and move. But it felt good to move, to hurry down the stairs and get a breath of muggy, unprocessed air when she left the building. It would have felt even better to just keep going. She needed a run.

That wasn't happening anytime soon. In the morning, maybe.

She got her laptop and had just closed the trunk when she heard her name called. Turning, she saw a tall, thin man striding toward her from the far end of the building, his head thrust forward and long, skinny legs covering ground fast, like a stork in a hurry.

Lily sighed. Ed Eames was a reporter with the AP. She'd had some interaction with him in D.C., and he wasn't a bad sort—the dim, amiable exterior hid a sharp mind and a bulldog's tenaciousness, but he played fair.

"Can't give you anything, Ed," she said when he reached her, and almost managed to sound regretful. "Not even an off-the-record hint. It's too early in the investigation."

"Oh, well. Maybe later." He smiled in that vague way he had. "That wasn't why I stopped you, though. I'm the one with something to say off the record . . . about Alicia Asteglio."

TWELVE

WINTER or summer, the backyard was Toby's favorite place. He loved everything about it—the gazebo, the grass and flowers, the trees. Even when it was real hot, there was lots of shade.

Not that Toby really minded hot weather. Or cold weather, either, from what he could tell, though he hadn't seen much really cold stuff, not in Halo. Dad said most lupi were like that, not much affected by hot and cold. The magic in Toby was mostly asleep still, but it was there and it had a pattern for him. He sort of leaned toward that pattern even now, years before he could run on four feet instead of two.

Dad started walking along the fence, moving slowly. It felt weird, walking around his yard like this with his dad. Soon this place would be for visits, not really his anymore.

Dad seemed to know that. "There's a lot here you're going to miss."

"Yeah."

"Make you mad?"

Toby stopped and stared. Sometimes Dad pulled the thoughts right out of his head, like there was a string attached to them he could tug on. "It doesn't make *sense* for me to be mad. I want to go. I know it's right for me to go. So how come it makes me mad when I think about not being here in my yard anymore?"

Dad smiled. "You've a strong sense of territory. Most of us do, but it's stronger in some than others. You've been the only wolf here, so this yard is completely yours. It doesn't matter to your wolf that your grammy is in charge—to him, she's only in charge of your human self. So this place is yours in a way Clanhome isn't. Clanhome is your grandfather's territory—shared with all who are Nokolai, yes, but *his*. No matter how much you want to be there, you don't want to surrender what's yours."

"Yeah! Yeah, that's what it's like. I want to be at Clanhome, but this . . . this is mine. Only how come I feel that way when my wolf's still asleep?"

"Asleep or not, he's there. Also, humans are almost as territorial as wolves, so the two instincts strengthen each other rather than competing. Though your wolf's sense of territory may be somewhat different from your human understanding of it."

They'd reached the back fence, where Grammy's azaleas were thick and bushy and smelled so good. "I don't think I can sort out what's the wolf and what isn't. It all feels like me."

"It is all you. What did you dream last night?"

"Huh?" It took a moment to remember. "I was playing baseball, but there weren't enough of us on the team and we were losing. The TV people were there 'cause it was a big game, and one of them had a lot of dogs and the dogs wanted to play, too. Grammy said dogs couldn't play baseball 'cause it wasn't in the rules, and how would they hit the ball? But you said it was okay, so then the dogs got to be on my team. And then we started winning."

Dad's mouth crooked up and his eyes went all pleased, as if that silly dream meant something to him. "The Toby who dreamed about baseball isn't exactly the same Toby who plays baseball, is he?"

"Oh." He thought that over. "I see what you mean. When I'm asleep, things seem different from when I'm awake, and I know different things and all. But it's all me."

Dad nodded. "For now, your wolf is sleeping so deeply that the awake Toby doesn't know what the sleeping part knows. It's like when we can't remember our dreams—that doesn't mean we didn't dream. Just that our dream self is too distant from our awake self for us to claim the memories. After the wolf wakes and you take that form, you'll remember that part of you all the time. You'll see many things differently. Some of those differences will be confusing."

"I know that," Toby said, impatient. It wasn't like they'd never talked about this before. "Confusing" meant that when First Change hit, his wolf would be real strong and people would smell like food, so when he was twelve he'd go to *terra tradis*, where everyone was lupus, so he didn't hurt anyone. He'd have to stay at *tradis* after the Change, too, and be home-schooled there, but he'd probably be able to go to a regular high school.

That's what he planned, anyway. Uncle Benedict said not to count on that. Most new wolves weren't ready to be around humans all the time, not until they were real old—maybe eighteen. But some of them managed it younger. Dad had. Toby figured he would, too.

They'd finished their circuit of the yard, ending up near the patio. Dad stopped and turned to him. "I told you last night I had some clan business to take care of while I'm here. Because your grammy was present, I didn't say which clan."

"Oh. Oh! You mean you have to do Leidolf business? That's why we're going there?" Toby's nose wrinkled. He didn't like that Dad was connected to the other clan, who had been Nokolai's enemies forever. Unless . . . He brightened. "Hey! Have you figured out how you can give the new mantle to someone else?"

Dad shook his head. "That won't happen until the All-Clan."

Toby didn't exactly understand mantles yet, but they were

sort of like magic blankets covering the clans, keeping everyone steady. It was supposed to be impossible for anyone to carry parts of two mantles, just like it was impossible to belong to two clans. But Dad was doing it.

According to Grandpa, that was the Lady's doing, and maybe the reason for the mate bond between Dad and Lily. Grandpa thought the Lady used the mate bond—which came from her, after all—to help Dad because she wanted the two clans to be friends again. When Toby had asked Dad about that, he'd shrugged and said perhaps. That was one of Dad's words—perhaps. He used it a lot.

But the Leidolf Rho was real sick and could die, and if he did, the whole mantle would go to Dad. Toby wasn't sure what would happen then, but it must be pretty bad. No one wanted the whole mantle to go to Dad. Not even Grandpa. That's why the Rhejes were going to shift it, but they had to all get together to do it, and that wouldn't happen until the All-Clan, which was months and months away.

"Hey." Dad ruffled Toby's hair, then cupped the side of his head. "Don't look so worried."

"But if the Leidolf Rho dies and you have to take it all—"

"It will be okay. I'll be okay, Toby. The Leidolf Rhej is a skilled healer. She's keeping Victor alive, and I'm careful not to call on that mantle."

Dad wanted him to feel better, so Toby tried. After all, even if the old Rho died right this minute, Dad had the mate bond, so the Lady could still help him. "You'll be okay," he echoed. "But I wish you didn't have to do Leidolf stuff right now."

"But right now I do have the heir's portion, so in all honor I need to fulfill those duties their comatose Rho cannot. Two of Leidolf's youngsters are ready for the *gens compleo*."

Toby didn't know much about the *gens compleo*, just that it was when a lupus was accepted into the clan as a full adult. But he knew it involved the clan's mantle. "They—those youngsters—they're already in the mantle, though, right? They're already clan."

"They're clan and past First Change, so the mantle knows them, but they aren't *of* the mantle yet. That's what the *gens compleo* is for."

That didn't really explain anything, but Dad said that talking about mantles was like trying to wrap up color in words. No matter how good your words were, they ended up pointing in the wrong direction. He also said that, for lupi, talking about the mantles was like talking about sex used to be for humans—something you did kind of hushed, where others wouldn't hear.

That had made Toby snort. The grown-ups he knew here in Halo still talked about sex like that. "Hey—you made sure no one was listening, didn't you? That's why we went outside and walked around. So you could be sure nobody would hear us, because the mantles are the Lady's secret."

"That's right. We keep many secrets from the humans around us, but only one at the Lady's behest—the clan mantles."

Toby nodded. The Lady wasn't like Santa Claus. She wasn't like God, either, who you had to believe in, but not everybody did, and even people who did believe argued about Him. But the Lady was real, one hundred percent, and the clans didn't argue about her because the Rhejes had the memories of what she'd said, only mostly she didn't talk to them or do much. But sometimes she did. "Lily's human, but she knows about mantles, doesn't she?"

"She's both Chosen and clan. She knows."

"So the Lady didn't say humans couldn't know. Just the out-clan."

"That's right." Dad touched his shoulder, smiling. "You're full of questions this morning. If I . . . That's Lily," he said, and headed for the house.

Toby followed. He hadn't heard anything. Maybe Dad just picked up that Lily was here? The mate bond let him know where she was, so . . . But it was a more ordinary connection this time, he saw. Dad had his phone up to his ear and was talking, then listening.

It didn't sound like it was good news. "Shit. Yes, I see. Tell your reporter friend I appreciate the notice . . . No, that won't be necessary."

"What is it?" Toby asked as soon as Dad set the phone down.

"I'm afraid reporters are on their way here. They were tipped off about the hearing. I'll have to talk to them, but you and your grandmother don't."

Toby's heart sped up. "I think I should."

"No." Dad headed for the stairs. "Mrs. Asteglio?"

Grammy called back, "Almost finished. I'll be right down."

Toby figured he'd better talk fast, 'cause he knew what Grammy would say. "Listen to me! Listen. People like kids. I mean . . ." It sounded dumb when he tried to put words to it, but Toby pushed on. "You're sort of the image for lupi, right? That's why you went public and why you do a bunch of stuff, letting people see that lupi are okay. Wouldn't I make a good image, too? I'm just a kid, but I'll be a wolf one day, only I don't look scary or anything."

Dad stopped at the foot of the stairs. "You're suggesting you would be good PR for our people?"

Toby nodded. "Humans need to stop being scared of us, right? Well, no one's gonna be scared of me." He grimaced. "Old ladies think I'm cute."

"You've a good point, and I'm proud that you're thinking of our people. However—"

"It's not the paparazzi, is it? Just regular reporters?"

Dad's eyebrows lifted. "What do you know about paparazzi?"

"Well, they hounded that poor princess to her death. That's what Mrs. Milligan says, anyway. And they make up stupid stuff, like that dumb story about your love slaves that was in one magazine next to the alien baby pictures. And they try to take pictures of people when they're naked."

Dad's lips twitched. "Not a bad description. Paparazzi are photographers who . . . you might think of them as lone wolves. A problem on their own, and dangerous when they travel in packs."

"Rule, a van just pulled up out front. A television van."
Grammy stood at the top of the stairs, looking like she'd bit-
ten into a rotten apple—and meant to spit it out on someone.
"How did they find out?"

"That . . . is something I need to explain. Toby." Dad knelt,
putting his hands on Toby's shoulders. Which made him feel
queasy, because it meant he wasn't going to like what Dad
had to say. "I've some news that may be upsetting. Lily learned
of it from an acquaintance of hers who works for the AP."

Toby swallowed hard and didn't say a word, because he
knew. The moment his dad said "the AP," he knew.

Dad's eyes were angry, but he kept it out of his voice.
"Your mother is in town. She's told the other reporters about
the hearing."

THIRTEEN

THE sharks were circling when Lily pulled to a stop three doors down from the Asteglio house. The press had taken all the closer parking.

But reporters weren't the only ones on Mrs. Asteglio's grass. A gaggle of teenagers, several women, a young man holding a toddler on one hip, and assorted sizes of children filled any gaps between cameras, microphone wielders, and the rumpled suits of the print press.

Lily kept her "no comment's" polite as she threaded her way past outthrust microphones to the semi-safety of the porch. Someone must have threatened them, or they'd have been banging on the door.

The door opened before she could touch the knob. She slid inside, and Rule closed it on the shouted questions.

He was looking especially magnificent. He'd changed into his usual black—black dress slacks, black silk-blend shirt. He wore a pretty dark expression, too, though his voice was mild. "I did say you weren't to come."

"I don't mind well, do I? How'd you get the sharks to stay away from the door?"

"Anyone who comes up on the porch will be asked to leave

the property entirely—and so will not be included in the interview I grant the rest."

"You're mean. I like that."

"On the phone you mentioned a problem with the investigation."

"I'll fill you in later." She glanced around.

The foyer opened on the left to the stairs; at the rear to the kitchen; and on the right to a living room that held two sofas and an upright piano. Mrs. Asteglio stood beside the large picture window backing one of the sofas, glaring out at the invaders on her lawn. She was a lanky woman a little over Lily's height with gray hair cropped no-nonsense short and pampered skin. Lily had never seen her without makeup and pretty pink fingernails. Today she wore robin's egg blue slacks with a button-down shirt in a gingham check.

Toby stood a few steps behind Rule, his chin held at a stubborn angle that reminded her of his grandfather, Isen. His eyes were very much Rule's, though—dark, liquid, hinting at secrets, with the same dramatic eyebrows.

She smiled at him. "Hey, there."

"Hi, Lily. Tell Dad this is my business, too."

Lily glanced at Rule, eyebrows lifted, but before he could respond, Mrs. Asteglio announced, "I'm going to go out there and tell them all to go away. They can't come on private property. Those *journalists*"—she made the word sound like a curse—"and my neighbors, too, who ought to be ashamed of themselves."

Rule shook his head. "Your neighbors might leave, but the press will just camp out on the sidewalk and street. The best way to be rid of them is to give them a little of what they want. I'm not the biggest story here, so if I give them a few sound bites, they'll go back to pestering Lily and the sheriff."

"And me," Toby said. "I've got sound bites, too."

"You can just forget that notion, young man," Mrs. Asteglio told him firmly.

"I need to," he insisted. "It's clan business."

The older woman huffed out a breath. "It's my grass they're

trampling, my family they want to gossip about, and my daughter who told them about—oh, about your father, and the hearing. Things that should be private. That makes it my business."

"But Grammy—"

"You want to see yourself on television, but you don't realize what it would be like, so it's up to the adults in your life to do what's right for you. If . . . Rats!"

"Rats" was the strongest expletive Lily had ever heard from the older woman. This time it came in response to the trill of a phone. At least Lily supposed that's what it was—it sounded like an electronic bird.

"Don't answer it," Rule said.

Mrs. Asteglio's lips tightened to near invisibility as she turned away to delve into her purse, which sat in its usual place beside the couch. "Oh, I'll answer. That's my daughter's ring tone, and she has some explaining to do."

Lily wanted to grab the phone and ask her own questions, but throttled back that unhelpful impulse. She turned to Toby. "So you want to go talk to the reporters."

"Lily." Rule's voice was as slick and hard as ice. "Don't meddle."

Her head jerked back. Where the hell did that come from? "You'd better take a deep breath and shove that attitude back down."

The hardness dropped away, leaving his face oddly blank. "You're right. You're right. I don't know . . ." He scrubbed a hand over his face. "Hell, I've got to do better."

She didn't know what he meant. Better at sharing the parenting of his son? He'd been doing that all along, though with Toby's grandmother, not with Lily. But this wasn't the time to ask.

It *was* the time for another question. She looked at Toby. "Toby, why do you want to talk to the reporters? If you do it because you're mad at your mom and want to get back at her, that's likely to backfire."

"That's not it! Well, not . . ." He hit that word and stumbled, picking up again more slowly. "Not much of it, anyway.

I am mad. Why'd she have to tell her reporter friends and not even let us know she told them?"

"I don't know."

He gave a little shrug, denying that it mattered when it obviously did. "Well, anyway, even before you called, I was telling Dad I ought to talk to the reporters, too. Or trying to tell him." He shot Rule a look chock-full of early-onset pre-teen resentment. "People don't think about us lupi being kids because the clans' kids have always been hidden away to keep us safe. Maybe that's how things used to have to be, but everything's changing now. And—and I don't want them making stuff up about me. I want to tell them the truth so they can't do that."

The twin slashes of Rule's eyebrows drew down. "Unfortunately, telling the truth doesn't stop others from making stuff up and reporters from repeating it. It's my responsibility to represent us to the press, not yours. And I think that's enough discussion of the subject."

Toby tilted his head back to stare up at his father. "Are you being my dad or my Lu Nuncio? 'Cause it feels like you're pushing at me to agree, and that's . . ." He stopped, darting a glance at his grandmother.

Rule looked taken aback. "Either role requires your obedience."

"Rule." Lily put a hand on his arm. "Talk to me a minute, okay? In the other room."

His eyes met hers, and an echo of the first time their gazes locked rippled through her—the click, the falling, the sensation of utter change when the mate bond had dropped into place. She blinked, and once more they were just eyes. Beautiful and familiar eyes the color of bitter chocolate, filled now with a mix of exasperation and rue.

"If you wish," he said, "but let's make it quick."

She hoped it would be quick. She had multiple murders to investigate and was fresh out of suspects—unless you counted Cullen's hypothetical out-realm being.

Here there be dragons, indeed. Problem was, dragons had turned out to be real.

Rule headed for the kitchen. Lily followed, trying to sort impressions and puzzlement into sense, into words. Something was eating at Rule. Of course, he had the whole alpha, prince-of-his-people thing going, which made him a tad autocratic at times. But now . . . what, exactly, was bothering her about his reaction?

He went straight to the coffeepot. "Want a cup?"

"Did you make it?" At his nod she said, "Sure. I didn't get any of the good stuff earlier."

He poured for her first and handed her the mug. "I take it you disagree with my decision."

"I don't understand it." She brought the mug up to her face and breathed in the aroma, her eyes closing briefly. When she opened them and sipped, she saw a familiar expression on his face. "Hey. Not now."

"Can I help it if watching you enjoy coffee turns me on?" His smile turned wry as he brought his own mug up to sip and leaned back against the counter. "I apologize for my comment earlier. It was uncalled for, but . . . I thought we were agreed about protecting Toby from the press. Your question to him took me by surprise, and I responded poorly."

That was it. That's what was bothering her. Rule never objected to questions. He didn't always answer them, but he didn't object to them. "We were agreed, but that was before the press found out about him. It was also before we knew Toby wanted a chance to tell his side of things. The situation's changed, but your decision hasn't. Why not?"

"Dammit, Lily, I'm not using my son for PR! He's too young. Someday he'll have to . . . but that's years away. I'll not have him used."

"Yet he wants to do this," she said mildly. "Is it using him if it's his idea?"

"Is it his idea?" Rule's expression darkened. "My father wanted this all along. He wanted Toby in front of the cameras, talking about how much he wants to live with me. Great publicity for us, paves the way for other lupi who want the courts to recognize their rights. I'll bet he's been talking to Toby. I should have seen that. He put this idea in Toby's head."

Ah, now she understood. "Grandmother says that parents are always trying to raise themselves all over again, repair the things their own parents did wrong." Grandmother said it in Chinese, and more eloquently. But that's what she meant.

"Your grandmother is a remarkable woman." Rule was polite. He was always polite with Grandmother, whether she was present or not. "But does that have anything to do with the subject?"

"Maybe you're doing what you wish someone could have done for you when you were small. But Toby isn't you."

Rule's gaze shifted away. He sipped his coffee, hooded eyes holding his thoughts in. After a long silence he sighed. "What do you suggest?"

"If Mrs. Asteglio is willing, why don't we all go out together? You make a brief statement and control the flow of questions, pick what Toby responds to."

"I dislike it when I'm wrong."

"Yeah. I know what you mean."

He put his mug down and just stood there, looking at it as if the pretty yellow flowers circling the rim carried an important message. "Why do you think Toby wants to do this so badly? Altruism aside," he added dryly. "My son is certainly capable of that, but I don't think it's his only motive."

"Why don't you ask him?"

"More common sense. Yes, but he may prefer privacy for the discussion. Ask him to come in here, please."

LILY saw with disturbing clarity at times, Rule thought as he sipped his coffee and waited. He had good reasons for wanting to shield his son, but on a deep and foolish level she was right. He'd been trying to shield the boy he once was, as well.

Not that he had been thrust in front of the press at Toby's age. Lupi were still very much in hiding then, passing as human. But his father's goal had been clear years before anyone believed it would be possible for a lupus to live openly as what he was. From an early age, Rule had known he would someday be the public face for his people. If the Supreme Court hadn't ruled that lupi in human form were "entitled to and compelled by all the rights and responsibilities of citizenship," Isen would still have had Rule proclaim himself publicly.

And Rule had been ready to do so. He'd always challenged himself by riding in elevators, on trains and airplanes, teaching himself to handle the fear of small, enclosed places common to most lupi . . . and, he admitted, especially strong in him. He'd done that because he expected to be locked up someday. And he would have been, had the Supreme Court ruling gone against them. He would still have gone public, just as he had, but with the goal of eliciting as much sympathy and airtime as possible when federal agents apprehended him, imprisoned him, and injected him with one of the very few drugs his system couldn't override: the one that robbed lupi of the Change.

He would have done it because his Rho told him to—and because Isen was right. Lupi could no longer hide themselves from the rest of the world; technology and the sheer press of population growth made that impossible. They had to find a way to live openly and peaceably with humans. For that, they needed to replace fear with sympathy and support.

But it's one thing for an adult to understand and accept such a necessity. Rule hadn't wanted his son to grow up feeling shaped for sacrifice.

He grimaced and put down his mug as Toby entered the kitchen, just over four feet of wary defiance cast in a familiar mold. Rule had sometimes wondered if Alicia's indifference to the child they'd made rose from her inability to see herself in the boy's face or future. Toby would grow up to assume a second form, one forever denied his mother, and his present form looked nothing like Alicia. Hair, eyes, mouth—all mirrored his father, not his mother. His build was much like Rule's had been at that age, too, though something in the way he moved—the quick certainty of it, perhaps—reminded Rule of his brother Mick.

The reminder was bittersweet. He and Mick had not been

close, being separated by age, experience, and ambition. In the end, Mick had betrayed Rule . . . then died saving him.

The way Toby's long eyelashes flickered as he swept his gaze around the room was familiar, too, but that trait wasn't Rule's alone. Lupi habitually checked out a space when they entered it. They were like cops that way, though their instinct was innate, not acquired.

Toby squared up in front of Rule. "Lily said you wanted to talk to me."

What he truly wanted was to grab the boy up and swing him around and make him laugh. Toby had a laugh that could lift the world. But this wasn't the time. "Lily persuaded me to reconsider. As your father, I still believe allowing you to speak to the reporters is a mistake. If it is, however, it's one you'll survive and should be allowed to make if you wish."

Toby's face lit up. "Then—then you've changed your mind?"

"Your father has. Your Lu Nuncio remains undecided, which is why I wished to speak with you privately."

Understanding touched with hurt flashed through Toby's eyes, but he didn't whine, didn't make his feelings more important than his duty. Rule felt a surge of pride in the boy . . . and wondered if his own father had felt a similar pride when Rule was learning these hard, early lessons. And did that make Isen right in retrospect, or Rule wrong in the present?

Toby swallowed. "You aren't sure I can represent us right?"

"I don't know. I need more information. Why do you want this so badly?"

"I told you!"

"You told me one reason. I don't doubt that it's true—that you want to do this for our people—yet I believe there's a more personal reason as well. I need to know that reason. It might affect the way you represent us to the human world."

Toby looked down and shuffled his feet as if wanting to be somewhere else. "I guess I got to tell you, then. See, it's like . . . I've got friends here, you know? And lots of people I just know, like Mr. Peters that teaches math and Coach Tom in

Sunday school, and—and when they hear about me being lupus . . . I thought maybe if they see me on TV, see that I'm still just me, they won't think I'm a freak or something."

"Toby." Rule's throat burned, making it hard to speak.

"I know," Toby said earnestly, hopefully. "I know I'm not going to live here anymore, so maybe it shouldn't matter, but I'll still *visit* sometimes, and it's kind of cool to be on TV. Maybe that will make up for—well, for me being lupus."

This was the real danger he'd wanted to protect Toby from—the hurt of being different. Of turned backs and threats, insults and closed minds . . . He'd yearned to keep all that from touching his son. And couldn't.

Rule thought of dozens of things to say—advice about how real friends stand by you, warnings about how little control anyone has over what others think. But what boy listens to such cautions? He settled for ruffling Toby's hair. "Maybe it will make a difference for some. Maybe not. Either way, your hope for acceptance will do your people no harm."

He held out his hand. Toby took it. Together they walked back to the living room.

Toby's grandmother was talking with Lily. She broke off, her gaze going to Rule's face, then Toby's. Rule noticed that she'd freshened her lipstick.

She grimaced. "You're going to let him do it, then. I can't say I approve, but I suppose I'd best get used to not having the final say."

"You will always have a say where Toby's concerned," Rule said quietly. "Always. I've given permission, but if you are adamantly opposed—"

"No. No, it's not . . ." She sighed. Her eyes held an old ache. "I've got too many things poking at me, I guess. Alicia said she didn't tip the other reporters. She told one man, a friend and coworker, in confidence. He turned out to be less than a friend ought to be."

Toby's hand tightened in Rule's. Rule made himself keep his voice calm. "Did she also explain why she's here? I understood her lawyer was handling everything for her. Why did she come without letting you know?"

"She said . . . she wants us to meet with her and her lawyer before the hearing. She wouldn't tell me why."

Dammit. Dammit all to hell. If Alicia planned to contest his claim now—

Lily touched his arm. "We can discuss that later. Mrs. Asteglio is willing to be part of our little show. Should we all go out together?"

Rule took a breath, let it out slowly. Anger would only trip him up. "I'll go out first and arrange things. I thought we'd take questions on the porch. The sun's nearly overhead, which is less than ideal lighting, but the porch is a reassuring setting. It looks like exactly what it is—a comfortable place for a family to relax in a small Southern town."

Mrs. Asteglio looked sour. She disliked what she considered artifice, he knew, the planned impressions essential to PR. Yet she'd freshened her lipstick, hadn't she?

"All right, " Lily said. "Let's do it. Ah . . . the AP reporter. Ed Eames. If you can throw him anything, that would be good. He's the one who tipped me."

"If I throw him something now, everyone gets it. But I'll keep him in mind."

"Okay. If you need me to, I can take over at the end, switch them back to the story they came here for, so the rest of you can escape."

Rule smiled and reached for her hand. "Now there's real self-sacrifice."

"You better believe it."

FOURTEEN

RULE went out on the porch with his body loose and his face relaxed, ready to smile as if he were greeting old friends who'd dropped in at an inopportune time yet were always welcome.

Flashes went off. Lupus eyes react to light like human eyes, but recover faster. He was blinded for a second but ignored it, walking to the edge of the porch as if he could see perfectly. By the time he reached it, he could.

Quite a crowd. He didn't know any of the television people, but three faces from the print press were familiar—Ed Eames from the AP, a woman named Miriam from the *Washington Post*, and a sad-faced fellow who worked for one of the scandal rags. Rule couldn't summon the man's name, but he knew the face.

Rule kept his smile easy as the shouted questions flowed over him. He raised his voice slightly. "Ed, Miriam, good to see you again. This isn't your usual beat, is it? And, ah . . ." He aimed his smile at the man from the scandal rag, who stood near the rear of the crowd. "I should know your name, shouldn't I?"

"Jimmy Bassinger with *Global*. Is it true you—"

"Jimmy. Of course. But—no, no. Wait." Rule held up a hand, speaking over the pushy tabloid reporter. "No questions yet. Was it Dan Rather who said that a good interview is ninety percent listening? Please listen a moment." He swept his gaze over the lot of them, cocking an eyebrow quizzically. "I understand you—all of you—would like a few moments of my time."

A couple of them laughed. Another flash went off. Good. Rule spoke simply. "You are here because of my son. So am I." And that quickly, the damned lump was back in his throat. He swallowed. Should he have known how strongly it would affect him to declare Toby's existence to the world?

Naturally, his statement set off another round of questions. He didn't allow himself to feel the insult implicit in some of them, but held up his hand again. "I'll give you a statement, answer some questions, but I thought you might like to speak with Toby, too. And with his grandmother, Mrs. Louise Asteglio, who has loved and cared for him since birth. And, of course, with my beloved, whom you already know—you've been besieging her regarding quite a different story."

With that enticement, it was easy to arrange a few ground rules. He expected those rules to be bent or broken by some, but the agreement gave him some leverage.

He opened the front door and gestured for the others to come out. "They aren't supposed to ask questions until I give the go-ahead, but one or two probably will, as soon as you appear," he said. "Ignore them."

"Oh, I can do that." Lily gave him a small smile and brushed his hand with hers as she passed.

Mrs. Asteglio touched her hair, took a deep breath, and followed.

Toby hung back.

"If you've changed your mind," Rule began gently.

"No, but it went all empty! My mind did, I mean. All of a sudden there's nothing there, and I don't know what to say!"

"Ah. Tell the truth. Keep your answers short. You don't have to answer questions you don't like. If you don't want to answer, squeeze my hand and I'll deal with it." He held out his hand.

Toby bit his lip. "Mostly boys my age don't hold their dad's hand."

"Mostly boys your age aren't lupus. We require more touch than humans seem to. And you're presenting yourself as lupus today."

Toby slipped his hand into Rule's and nodded once. "Okay. I'm ready."

RULE arranged them on the porch swing—Toby on his right side, Lily on his left, and Mrs. Asteglio on Toby's far side. One of the television vans had brought portable spots; the tech was setting them up on either side of the swing, which faced the yard. The porch's elevation would put them approximately on a level with their interrogators, even while seated.

"Good grief," Mrs. Asteglio muttered, smoothing her shirt. "I don't even know half those people."

He assumed she meant the crowd gathered to watch the press uphold their right to be informed. "The bystanders will leave when the TV vans do," he told her quietly, then raised his voice. "If you're ready, I'll give a brief statement first, then we will accept questions."

"Give us another sec, here," the brunette anchor from one of the TV stations said. "Let them get the lights fixed. Joe," she said, turning to her cameraman, "you still getting that shadow?"

"Mrs. Asteglio," the scandal-rag reporter called from the rear of the crowd, "is it true that Turner seduced and abandoned your daughter? And that you've been raising her love child?"

Rule just smiled and waited.

"Love child," Mrs. Asteglio sputtered. "Love child? Why, I—"

"Shh," Lily said. "He wants a reaction. Don't give him one."

If Toby objected to being called a love child, it didn't show. "Look," he piped up, "here comes Mr. Hodge. Bet he's going to make them all go away. You think they will? Maybe he brought his shotgun to scare them."

"His shotgun?" Lily exclaimed. "Where? Where is he?"

Rule was on his feet. Without intention, without knowing he would do it, he'd stood, his nape cold and bristling. *There.* There, at the back of the crowd, stood an older man, dark-skinned, nearly hidden by people and by the large oak tree—stepping forward now, holding something, bringing it up—

"It's okay," Toby said, reassuring. "He never loads it, right, Grammy? He just likes to—"

Time slowed as Earth magic surged up through Rule to join, with a sudden snap, with the moonsong always present—join and *pull.* Between one second and the next he fell into *certa*, a place of ice and clarity, where sensation is sharp enough to cut and action flows too swiftly for thought.

And held himself back, by sheer will, from the rest of the fall.

"—make out like he's all mean, but he really—"

Rule used one arm to sweep Toby and his grandmother off the swing, onto the porch floor. He was aware of everything—the reporters just starting to react, not to the threat behind them, but to Rule. Toby squawking. Lily on her feet, reaching under her jacket, shouting, "Down!" at the crowd.

But he was already in the air, sailing in one leap over the head of the brunette reporter, letting the vicious pull have him as Earth and moon finished their dance and dragged him through the twist they'd made in reality. The blast from the shotgun smacked his human ears—

—and echoed in the much better ears he landed with, the incandescent pain of the Change already gone. Landed amid screams and blood-scent, steady on all four feet, ready to launch himself forward—but people were in the way. People scrambling, falling, yelling, standing frozen. Too bloody many people between him and the threat to his mate and son.

Another concussion of sound—the shotgun's second barrel. It tipped him out of *certa* and close to frenzy, but he held on, held back, gathering himself on his haunches—and leaped again.

Over the people.

He lacked the elevation of the porch this time, but he was a very large wolf. He couldn't high-jump the whole crowd, but he leaped over the two people immediately impeding him and darted through the rest—who would doubtless have given way for him if they'd had time, but he moved too fast for their human reactions.

There. The enemy. Senses merged into a single data flow as Rule saw/scented the man, the gun, and something else. Something unutterably foul.

The man saw him, too—the gun's barrel swung toward Rule as the man's eyes widened, his face contorting. "I didn't know!" he cried, dropping the gun, stumbling back. "I didn't know!"

In his backward retreat, he tripped. Fell.

The enemy was down. Rule leaped on him, snarling, teeth reaching—

The man tipped his head back, sobbing as he bared his throat.

Rule froze. Need strove with need, clashing instincts mounting an explosion barely capped by will. *Blood!* screamed the loudest part of him—he needed blood, needed to finish the enemy.

An enemy who reeked of perversion. Of death magic. Dimly, Rule recalled the name for the stink coating his nostrils, but the wolf was more interested in destroying such foulness than naming it. But the man's action had tripped another switch.

Rule's enemy had acknowledged him, subordinating himself.

The immediacy of bloodlust faded. The man was his now, his to kill or to spare. Killing made sense. It would eliminate any future threats, and anything that stank of such perversion deserved death. Besides, what would he do with the man if he let him live? Rule couldn't keep him. He was human, not clan.

And yet there was some reason, some important reason, for sparing him. Only he couldn't quite . . .

I know him.

No, he didn't. Beneath the reek of death magic, the man's smell was unfamiliar. Confused, the wolf hesitated.

"Rule!" Dimly through the clamor he heard and felt her coming. His mate. Lily. "Don't, Rule—I need him alive."

He would wait. She knew . . . knew *both* of him, he remembered, and suddenly Rule-the-man was present again. Not in charge, but present, and echoing Lily's command to spare the man.

Lily reached him, put a hand on his back, and her scent calmed him in spite of the traces of fear-stink that clung to her skin like a burr caught in fur. Her fear didn't worry him. Lily was warrior. She could both fear and act.

"He's down," she told him, low-voiced. "I need you to keep him down while I—oh, shit."

The enemy beneath him was convulsing.

Lily shoved at Rule, who stepped off. She touched the man's throat, then ripped open his shirt and started CPR.

FIFTEEN

IT takes time to clear away the detritus of violent death. The patrol cars arrived first, then the ambulances, followed eventually by the same ERT Lily had summoned to another death scene early that morning.

An hour and twenty minutes after turning wolf, Rule was back in his human form, back in his clothes, and back in the house where his son had grown up.

Toby's grandmother was upstairs, showering off other people's blood. There had been two wounded—one with relatively minor injuries, one critical. Mrs. Asteglio might not have worked as a nurse in years, but she hadn't forgotten much. As soon as the shooting stopped, she'd hugged Toby, then sent him to get a sheet for bandages.

Hodge hadn't died, thanks to Lily's quick action. Two others had. A boy, perhaps sixteen, with three silver rings in one ear, had taken a shotgun blast to the back of his head. He'd died instantly. Jimmy Bassinger, who'd asked about Rule's "love child," had been hit in the chest and throat. He'd bled out.

Lily was still outside, interviewing witnesses or directing her people or perhaps bossing around the city cops who'd shown up. Rule wanted to be with her. He also wanted to be exactly where he was—sitting on the couch in the den with Toby snuggled up against him, savoring the little-boy warmth against his side. The radio was on. The orderly beauty of a Mozart piano concerto soothed both wolf and man.

Classical music was one of the pleasures he'd shared with Alicia in their infrequent liaisons. He wondered if she still listened to Bach when she was on deadline. He wondered why she was in Halo, what she meant to do.

Mrs. Asteglio had called Alicia before heading upstairs to shower, letting her know Toby had survived the shooting. Rule had heard Alicia burst into tears on the other end of the phone. She'd sobbed out her relief.

He didn't understand her. He supposed he never would. How could anyone give up this sweetness?

Rule inhaled deeply. *Copper, earth, and mint,* he thought. That's what Toby's scent reminded him of, or maybe those scents reminded him of Toby . . . who had been glued to him ever since he Changed back. The boy needed this closeness, the physical contact.

That was all right. So did Rule.

He could have lost them. Toby, Lily—one of them or both of them. He could have lost them.

Toby stirred. "Dad? How did you know? About—about Mr. Hodge. Was it just 'cause he had the shotgun?"

"Instinct," Rule said, sifting his hand through Toby's hair. "Though I suppose that's not a very satisfactory answer, is it?" He felt Toby shake his head. "Let's say, then, that my human part reacted to the sight of a gun, but the wolf had already recognized wrongness. I can piece that recognition together logically now, but I didn't at the time."

"Tell me about the logical part, 'cause I don't get the instinct part."

"Franklin Hodge was hiding behind a tree. A man who intends to bluster and threaten doesn't hide himself. He'd brought his shotgun. A man in his right mind doesn't bring a gun to his neighbor's house to make a point."

Toby picked at a loose thread in the seam of Rule's slacks.

His voice was small. "Mr. Hodge wasn't in his right mind, was he?"

"No. We don't know what happened to him, but he was certainly not in his right mind."

"Dad, when you . . ." Toby's voice trailed off. "You were going to kill him, weren't you?"

Rule stilled. But there was only one answer possible. "Yes."

"I'm glad Lily stopped you."

"So am I." Glad, very glad, that Toby hadn't had to see his father kill an old man, however murderous. Yet on another level, it was as well the boy knew that Rule's wolf was capable of such an act. Toby was tired of hearing warnings about First Change. He thought he understood what it would be like for the human to be swallowed by the wolf. He didn't. Couldn't. Yet. "Although I stopped needing his death before she arrived."

"Yeah?" Toby turned his face up. "How come?"

Rule picked words as carefully as a rock climber chooses handholds. "I was wholly wolf for a brief time. Somewhere between leaping from the porch and spotting my enemy, I lost the man. It was a combination of factors, I believe, that tipped me over. The threat to you and Lily, of course. But there was also the stink of him . . . death magic reeks."

Toby looked scared. "I don't know that that is."

"Cullen calls it power sourced by death."

"Mr. Hodge wouldn't *do* that. He wouldn't."

"I don't know that he caused it. Just that he stank of it."

The creak of the wooden floor turned Rule's attention from his son to his son's grandmother, entering from the foyer. She moved slowly. Her face was taut, the lines around her eyes and bracketing her mouth deeper than usual, but her makeup was freshly applied.

She smelled of soap. She sounded pissed. "I suppose they're all still out there."

"The police and FBI are, yes. Most of the reporters are probably gone." One to the hospital, one to the morgue, the rest to file their stories—unless they hadn't yet been interviewed by whichever officers were handling that.

"I am *not* going to feed them."

Rule understood this for the radical statement it was. "You aren't expected to," he assured her.

"Well, it seems very strange to have people on my property and not . . ." She hesitated, shrugged, and continued into the kitchen. "I don't suppose any of us are hungry, but we'd better eat something. I've got plenty of roast from last night. Toby, you can help me put together some sandwiches."

He bounced up. "Okay. Dad needs extra meat on his, and prob'ly extra sandwiches, too. Right, Dad?" He gave Rule a look half searching, half stern. "After a Change you're supposed to eat. Especially meat."

Toby didn't see the fear that flickered through his grandmother's eyes, but Rule did. The woman had never seen him as wolf before. This had not been a good introduction to his other form. "That's right."

Mrs. Asteglio gave one short jerk of a nod and opened the refrigerator. Rule heard another door open, and stood. Toby heard it, too. "Is that Lily? Lily!" he called as he raced for the foyer. "Is Mr. Hodge going to be okay? Do they know what went wrong with him to make him go crazy?"

Lily looked startled when Toby careened into her, but she bent and hugged him. "He's at the hospital. We don't know yet what went wrong with him, but evidence indicates it wasn't really *him* who shot those people. Something or someone made him do that."

Toby pulled back, frowning hard. "They took him away in an ambulance, not a police car."

"According to his Medic Alert bracelet, he has a pacemaker. What happened seems to have disrupted it—magic can do that—which made his heart act up. That's serious, but he's getting good care."

"Did someone do death magic on him?"

Her eyebrows went up. She glanced at Rule. "Death magic is involved, but we don't know how."

"How could that make him crazy? Why would someone want to make him crazy?"

"I don't know yet. It's my job to find out."

He was silent a moment. "That's a big job."

"Yes, it is. Good thing I have plenty of help."

"And a sandwich. You should have one. Grammy and me are gonna make some." Toby gave her a firm nod. "You like pickles, right?"

"Right." Lily watched him scoot back into the kitchen, her expression baffled, as if she'd tripped over love unexpectedly and wasn't sure what to do about it.

Rule felt himself smiling. It came as a surprise amid the day's shocks. He went to her, slid an arm around her waist. "Children have a way of making parents feel helpless at times."

She tilted her face up, perplexed. "I'm not . . . well, not exactly. There isn't a word for my relationship with Toby."

The lack of a word for her role bothered her. Possibly it struck her as untidy. He smiled and tucked her hair behind her ear. "Parent will do. Parenthood isn't always biological."

"I guess not. As parents, then, shouldn't we be feeding him instead of the other way around?"

"He needs to contribute."

He could see that click in place. Lily would understand such a need. "I'll have to eat fast. My backup's here—four agents from the Charlotte office. That's good, but they're regular FBI. No experience with magic, no background or training in this sort of thing. One guy's pretty senior." She paused, frowning. "I had them start interviewing the neighbors. I'll interview Toby and Mrs. Asteglio myself—that's half the reason I came in now."

"And the other half?"

"I could use your nose."

"It's at your service, but what do you want me to sniff for?"

"I need to check out Hodge's house before the ERT does. I need to know if he's had company in the last day or two. We're asking the neighbors about that, but you should be able to smell it if he's had visitors recently, right?"

"As long as he hasn't scrubbed with one of those ghastly pine-scented cleaners."

"If you do pick up a scent, you'll know if they were human or not."

Rule's eyebrows lifted. "You think you're looking for an inhuman agent?"

"Maybe. Cullen called this morning, gave me some possibilities. One is that we're dealing with someone or something from out-realm. Some kind of death magic creature. Will you do your sniffing on two legs?"

Death magic creature? Far be it for him to argue with the expert, but that sounded . . . just barely possible, he decided. "The wolf's nose is much better than the man's. I'll Change again, though I should eat first, if there's time."

"Sure. Try not to shed in his house, okay?"

"I'll do my best. Lily . . ." His voice dropped as his heartbeat picked up, a quiet drumbeat of unease.

"Yes?"

"I would have killed him. Hodge. He stopped me. It doesn't make sense, but he did."

"I guessed the first," she said dryly. "As for the second . . . how could he stop you?"

"He tipped his head back, exposing his throat. He said—called out—that he didn't know. I have no idea what he meant, but then he submitted to me. He's not lupus, Lily. Beneath the smear of death magic, his smell was wholly human."

She frowned. "So how could he know that baring his throat to you would work? I guess the information could be in an article he read, but . . . no." She shook her head. "That's not enough."

"No, it isn't. Human instinct is to protect the throat. I've a hard time believing a man in the grip of whatever had him pumping shotgun pellets into strangers could remember some article he once read and act accordingly with a wolf about to rip out his throat."

She winced. "Getting a little graphic there. Why were you going to kill him instead of stopping him, Rule? I've seen you in bad situations before. You didn't stop thinking, didn't lose control."

"I've never had both you and Toby at risk. And there was

the stink, the smell of death magic . . ." But this time the explanation tasted false in his mouth. He shook his head. "I don't know, exactly."

"Could it have something to do with the mantles?"

"I don't see how. If anything, the presence of two heir's portions should give me better control, not worsen it."

"But the new one, the Leidolf portion . . . you said mantles take on some of the qualities of their holders, and that one has belonged to a ripe old bastard for a very long time." Her eyes widened. "Rule—if Victor Frey can somehow influence you—"

"No. No, that isn't possible. The mantles . . ." He ran a hand over his hair, frustrated. Lily kept blaming the mantles for every oddity or irritation. True, the new mantle had influenced him a couple of times . . . *When I snapped at her about Toby*, he thought with a flash of guilt. But that was a different situation entirely. "There isn't time to explain, and possibly not words, but Victor can't influence me that way, and I can't influence him."

"All right. I'll ask again later, though, for that explanation. This reminds me that I need to ask you something else. Cullen said—"

"Here you go," Toby said, hurrying toward them with a plate in each hand. One plate held a single sandwich; the other, three. Three very fat sandwiches. "I'll get you some Cokes, too."

"I'll just take a swig of your dad's drink," Lily said, accepting her single-sandwich plate.

Toby frowned sternly. "You don't want to get dehydrated."

"Oh," she said meekly. "Right."

"Here." Toby thrust the other plate at Rule. "You know when you Changed like that, in midair? I didn't know you could do that. It was awesome."

Surprised, Rule smiled. "Thank you."

"So is that why I felt it this time? Because you did it so fast?"

Shock hollowed out Rule's skull.

When he didn't respond, Toby looked worried. "Dad?"

Lily stepped in as casually as if they were still discussing sandwiches and soft drinks. "I take it you don't usually feel it when your dad Changes?"

Of course she asked a question. Lily always had questions, which was just as well, because all Rule had were echoes in the empty place between his ears. Increasingly noisy echoes.

"Huh-uh. I thought I wasn't supposed to until after First Change." He brightened. "Maybe I'm getting close, and that's why?"

He was nine. Only nine. A young lupus shouldn't feel the tug from an adult Changing until he was very near First Change himself. And Toby wasn't.

"I don't think so," Rule said at last, and blessed years of training because he sounded as calm as Lily—who had little idea what might be wrong. "We generally reach puberty slightly later than humans, and you don't have the scent of one crossing into that territory. Your body may have stepped up production of some of the hormones that trigger puberty, but . . ." Rule paused, shook his head. "No. That shouldn't cause you to respond to an adult's Change, even one as emphatic as mine was."

"But I did feel it," Toby insisted.

"What did it feel like?" Lily asked.

"Like . . . like I was piano wires and someone plucked all of me at the same time."

Nausea gripped Rule's gut. "I see." He could make sure his fear didn't show, but it was just as well Toby's nose still functioned at human levels. "Well, the Leidolf Rhej is a healer."

"Like Nettie?"

"Yes, though trained in a different tradition. We'll have her take a look at you, see if you're closer than I think."

Lily looked at him sharply. "You're still planning to go?"

"Yes." God, yes—though he'd be calling Nettie, too. He trusted the Leidolf Rhej, but wanted his own clan's healer to look at his son. "Today, I think. All else aside, it would be best to have Toby away from whatever or whoever is turning random people into killers."

Her reaction was a sigh so faint even his hearing barely picked it up. She looked at Toby. "Then I'd better talk to you now, if it's okay with your grandmother. I'd like to hear what you know about Franklin Hodge." She glanced up at the woman still in the kitchen. "You, too, Mrs. Asteglio."

SIXTEEN

RANDOM killers. That's what Rule had called them, but Lily wasn't convinced Meacham and Hodge were truly random. There must be something connecting them, some commonality.

Probably some *person*. She wasn't discounting Cullen's theory about an out-realm creature being responsible, but that seemed more of a stretch than a human agent who'd stumbled across a previously unknown ability or ritual.

As she stepped out on the porch, she was hoping hard that Rule's nose would turn up that connection, human or otherwise.

"I need to talk to Brown a minute," she said to Rule as he closed the door behind them. The ERT techs were busy combing through Mrs. Asteglio's grass, but almost everyone else had left. Nathan Brown stood in the next-door neighbor's driveway, talking to a city cop. "He's the most senior agent. Before I do, though, what's worrying you about Toby?"

"Not now. Not here."

She considered him. His eyes were hard, heavy-lidded—which meant he intended to shut her out. Or maybe he was shutting something else out. But what? Worry squeezed her like a boa softening up dinner, only she didn't know what she needed to worry about. "All right. But I know something's wrong."

"Possibly wrong. Maybe. And I can't discuss it here."

Here, with all these pesky humans around . . . Well, she could understand that. "Okay. Meet me at Hodge's place?"

His smile was small. "Certainly. I'll Change into something more furry for the occasion."

She headed for the neighbor's drive. Nathan Brown was short, chubby, and pale, a Pillsbury Doughboy of a man with luxuriant hair the color of pecans and an oversize mustache. He had twenty-two years on the job, and he didn't like her.

Lily didn't assume his dislike arose from prejudice. It might, but she suspected his resentment was more generic. He was regular FBI; she was Unit. The Turning had led Congress to put a lot of authority into the hands of Unit agents. People like Brown, with all the experience and seniority Lily lacked, didn't always appreciate being seconded to a newcomer. Especially one as young as Lily.

Tough. She motioned for him to step aside from the young officer he'd been talking with. He scowled, but did, joining her near the street. "You've got the city cops doing the knock-on-doors?"

"Partnered with our people, yeah. You got a problem with that?"

"No, it's a good idea. People might be more comfortable, more forthcoming, with those they see as their own. I'm going to check out Hodge's house before I let the ERT in. Anything I need to know before I do that?"

"Guess you don't worry much about contaminating a scene."

"I'll take precautions. I need to know if there are magical traces in his house. He wasn't Gifted himself, so anything I find along those lines could be meaningful." She paused a beat. "Rule will be checking the place for scents, too."

Brown's gaze flickered to Rule, who was headed down the street for the single-story house on the corner. "You're kidding me, right? You don't really plan to walk your doggie around the house."

"The attorney general will be formally issuing a new policy on scent next week. I'm anticipating it."

His eyebrows lifted in exaggerated surprise. "Friend of yours, the AG? He keeps you posted on things?"

"No. He is friendly with my boss, and Ruben keeps me posted. As I was saying, the new policy will specifically allow the use of witnesses who are able to distinguish scents with great acuity."

"Great acuity. Huh." He reached inside his suit jacket and pulled out an opened package of gum. "Guess you are going to walk your doggie around the house."

Lily drummed her fingers on her thigh. "Okay. I don't need to know if you dislike me because I'm Unit, or because I'm Gifted, or if I just look like your ex-girlfriend. I do need to know if that dislike will interfere with you doing the job."

Something flashed in his eyes—anger, maybe, or surprise. Hard to say when his scowl didn't change. "I always do the job, ma'am. You don't have to worry about that." He held out the gum. "Want some? No? You're probably wondering why the office sent you a son of a bitch with a lousy attitude who doesn't know shit about magic, and doesn't much care for those who do."

"I'm hoping you do know shit about investigating."

"I do." He nodded. "I do. But what you really need me for is all these goddamned cops littering the landscape. We've got county cops from the previous case, city cops with this one, and no goddamn guarantee any of them will tell us one word more than they have to. But you lucked out. I'm a goddamned genius at keeping things straight with the goddammed locals."

"Must be your inherent charm and charisma."

"That'd be it. Now, I've got work to do, so unless you need me to hold your hand—"

"Go. Please." She did, too.

Hodge's house was a small, single-story frame structure set on a large, unfenced corner lot. There was a lovely mix of annuals, perennials, and small shrubs in the beds flanking the sidewalk that bisected the front yard; the grass was lush. She didn't see Rule.

He must have decided to check out the yard. She headed for the side of the house, where a large, bushy cedar blocked the view.

His clothes were there, left in the dirt. Automatically she picked them up and folded them, then kept going to the back of the house. As soon as she rounded the corner, she saw him wiggling under the partly closed door of a detached garage. He stood, shook himself, and trotted toward her.

Rule made a very large, very beautiful wolf. His fur was a black and silver mix, heavy on the silver and palest on his face, where his eyes were rimmed in black like an Egyptian houri.

Good, so good, to see you like this.

The thought fluttered across her mind like a breath of smoke tattered by the air it rode—there; then wisp; then gone. But the place it came from wasn't gone. Mostly she couldn't touch those memories, but the part of her that had been through hell with Rule, knowing him only as wolf, was still there. Still her.

Lily stopped moving and found that a smile had settled on her face. Rule came to her and pushed his nose against her hand. She grinned.

He wasn't much like a dog—too big, too smart, too wild— but he did love a good pet. She rubbed him briefly behind the ears. "Did you find anything interesting out here?"

He gave his head a single shake.

"Come on, then. I'll bag your feet on the porch."

They'd done this at a couple of other scenes, so had the routine down. Lily put plastic bags on Rule's feet, securing them with covered rubber bands. Then she took off her shoes, cleaned her feet with an alcohol wipe, and pulled on her gloves.

Bare feet weren't the preferred way to enter a scene you didn't want contaminated, but they were the fastest way of picking up any magical traces inside. Lily checked the door, ready with the key she'd taken from Hodge's pocket. But he hadn't locked it before leaving home to kill people.

The door opened directly into the living room. It was small, cluttered, and dusty. The sofa was floral and faded; the La-Z-Boy recliner, newer and facing the television. Shelves along one wall held framed photos, books, a hodgepodge of inexpensive collectibles in glass and ceramic.

"He's been a widower about ten years, according to Mrs. Asteglio. Looks like he kept things the way his wife had them." Lily moved farther into the room. Here, yes—a prickly foulness on the soles of her feet, faint but unmistakable. "Check along here, where I'm standing. Traces of death magic."

Rule sniffed. His lip curled back. He looked at her and waited.

The trick was to ask only yes-or-no questions. "You smell anything nonhuman?" He shook his head. "Human, then?" A nod. "Someone other than Hodge?" Negative. "Damn. Well, let's keep looking."

But twenty minutes later, the only magical traces Lily had found were the fading touches of death magic here and there, apparently left by Hodge himself after being possessed or constrained by something wielding death magic. That and a dim, indeterminate tingle on the old Bible on the table next to Hodge's double bed.

It wasn't the first time she'd run across a nondescript magical residue on objects of faith. You'd expect it with Wiccan holy symbols, given that religion's connection with magic, but she'd found it on Bibles, Torahs, once on a small statue of Buddha. Magic sometimes built up in them over time, a slow, sedimentary accumulation, even when the individual who owned the object had no magic at all to confer upon it. She didn't understand that, but it wasn't unusual.

It was damned discouraging, though, in this case. Hodge was a man of faith, but his faith hadn't protected him.

Still, it was confirmation that whatever they were dealing with, it wasn't demonic. Those of strong faith couldn't be possessed by demons.

"You find anything?" she asked Rule. He shook his head. She sighed. "Okay, let's go. I'll bring your clothes."

They went to the old cedar so Rule could return to his

usual form without giving the neighbors a thrill. The Change came more easily, she knew, when he had his feet planted literally on the ground. She held his clothes and waited.

Lily held a secret conviction that one day, if she watched carefully enough, she'd be able to make sense of what she saw when Rule Changed. Did his eyes alter first? Was his fur swallowed up by spreading skin? Did the bones melt before re-forming?

This wasn't the day. If there was order in the process, her eyes refused to find it, reporting only unsynchronized snatches.

First he stood there on four feet; then the universe bent, folded, and folded again in directions that didn't exist. Feet were two, four, and two again. Fur both was and wasn't, but the "wasn't" stuck. Prickles danced across her eyeballs as if the air were playing a tune on them.

Then he was a man, naked and magnificent. She handed him his underwear, not allowing herself to regret the necessity. She would see him naked again soon, she hoped. Not as soon as she'd like, with him heading for Leidolf Clanhome. But soon.

"I didn't find any magical traces, except the nasty stuff. You?"

"Nothing." He stepped into the shorts and accepted his pants. "I could swear no one has been in that house except Hodge himself for at least a week."

"Then he was contaminated elsewhere." A sigh sneaked out. It would be hard, maybe impossible, to learn who all Hodge had been in contact with away from his house. At least they had a limited time frame to work with—the four days since the other killings.

Or did they? Could the whatever-it-was have infected two people at the same time? More than two? "Maybe I'll luck out and he'll be able to tell me what happened to him." If he lived. If he hadn't been driven insane like Meacham. "I'm going to head for the hospital next, see if he made it. See if I can talk to him."

"I'll be gone when you return, then." Half-dressed, Rule

lost interest in completing the job, putting his hands on her shoulders. "I wish I could be in two places. I don't like leaving you to deal with this alone."

"I won't be handling it alone." But she didn't want him to go. It was selfish, it was stupid, but she didn't want him to go. She told herself to ignore that. "Rule . . . can you tell me about Toby now? Why you're worried?"

He was silent, unmoving, for several heartbeats. When he spoke, his voice was carefully even. "A boy nearing First Change is kept segregated at the *terra tradis*. This is for the safety of the human members of the clan, of course, but also so that he'll be surrounded by clan lupi at First Change, so the mantle will know him. Toby should not respond to either my Changing or the mantles this young. Do you remember when Cullen explained the type of cancer that sometimes afflicts us in old age?"

"Sure. That's what the Leidolf Rho has. The magic in his system has separated from the pattern that should hold him to his proper shape. Cullen said . . . Oh. Oh, *shit*." She'd just remembered the rest of it—the other time, aside from extreme old age, when a lupus might be struck down by this wild cancer.

"Yes." Rule's voice was soft now, almost a whisper. "Sometimes—rarely—it strikes in early adolescence, at or soon after First Change. We don't know what goes wrong for those few, but some say . . . There are reports, anecdotal evidence . . ." He stopped. His jaw tightened.

Lily knew he was fighting for control—and that he needed it. Right now he needed the flat force of logic to keep the monsters at bay. So she waited, holding back her questions and fears to give him time.

Finally he swallowed and finished. "When a boy feels the tug of Change too young—when it pulls at him before he's heard the moonsong—it may be a sign that First Change will trigger the cancer."

SEVENTEEN

LILY hated hospitals. Just pulling into the parking lot of one made her jaw set, kind of like lowering her butt into the dentist's chair. She was a reasonable woman, she thought as she locked her car and strode toward the entrance. She was glad some people didn't share her aversion. It would be hard to staff the places if everyone shuddered at the thought of walking into one.

Though she didn't see why anyone would want to work in a hospital. Maybe it was like coffee—you started drinking it, despite the taste, because you needed something to pry your eyes open, and before you knew it, you were grinding beans or paying five bucks for fancy caffeinated froth.

Pritchard Memorial was midsize. She'd been assured it had good doctors, good tech, and at least some shielding for that tech. They didn't have a separate cardiac unit, though, so Hodge was in ICU awaiting surgery tomorrow, when his pacemaker would be replaced.

She stopped in the ER first, where she found that Ed Eames was about to be released. "I'm one of those 'treated and released' victims," he told her with a smile that missed the cockiness she thought he was aiming for. "The kind who don't get mentioned in the story by name. You heard anything about that woman? The young mother?"

"She's out of surgery," Lily told him. "They're sounding hopeful about her chances."

"Helluva thing." He shook his head and repeated himself. "Helluva thing. Guess people are saying Hodge was quiet, kept to himself?"

"More that he was an old grouch."

"Huh. I've covered this sort of story before. Never been part of it."

He was wrong about that. He'd never covered anything like this, but Lily didn't tell him that.

She made her way to the second floor and, after speaking with a nurse, a small waiting room near the ICU. For company she had a television tuned to an all-news channel and an elderly man with skin the color of old teak who never took his eyes off the TV.

While she waited for Hodge's doctor, she composed an informal report. She didn't object to the brief wait; organizing her data and theories for Ruben clarified her thinking. She did object to the seating.

Whoever thought that molding plastic to fit a so-called average shape was a good idea? No one, Lily decided as she shifted yet again, was really average, which meant the seats were uncomfortable for everyone. Democracy was great for many things, but furniture wasn't one of them.

She'd just sent the report off—she had a USB GPRS modem on her laptop—when her phone vibrated. She pulled it out of her pocket and slid her laptop into its silk-lined pocket in her tote. "Yes?"

It was Brown. The neighbors had confirmed that Hodge apparently hadn't had any recent visitors. She told him to let everyone grab something to eat; she'd call him back with instructions after speaking with Hodge.

"All right. You want some advice?"

"Sure."

He was silent a second, as if she'd surprised him. "You're

young, you've got a major goddamned investigation on your hands, and you're a control freak. Don't ask how I know. I know because everyone in law enforcement's a control freak—that's how we get off. You're going to try to do everything yourself. Don't."

"That's your advice? Delegate?"

"That's it. You won't do it," he said glumly. "But I'm such a goddamned optimist I had to say it anyway."

He disconnected. She started to put her phone up, but saw that she had a text message from Rule. When she opened it, she sighed. He was leaving now, heading for Leidolf Clanhome with Toby. He wanted her to call tonight.

"Some people!"

Lily looked up. The pair of women who stood in the doorway were twins. Had to be. They wore matching helmet-heads of iron gray curls and matching floral smocks with pink stretch pants. It was an unfortunate fashion choice, since each woman was at least a hundred pounds overweight—with about fifty percent of that in their boobs.

They had identical glares, too. The one on the left spoke. "Cell phones are not allowed in the hospital. Do you want to make all those machines quit working?"

"That's unlikely," Lily said patiently, "according the Mayo Clinic, which found no problems when cell phones were used near hospital equipment. Admittedly, Dutch researchers did find some interference, but that was at distances of five centimeters or so."

The other sister snorted. "I suppose you know better than the doctors who make the rules, missy!"

Guilt twinged. It was never easy for Lily to ignore a rule, even one that was based on faulty assumptions. "My job requires me to stay in touch, ma'am." She glanced at her watch. If that doctor didn't show up soon—

"*Some* people think they're too *important* to follow the rules everyone *else* has to follow, don't they, Bessie?" Pink Pants on the left moved ponderously into the room.

Bessie? Oh, my. Lily managed not to grin.

"Ladies?" said a man's voice with a hint of an accent. "Excuse me, please, ladies . . ." A second later the owner of the voice emerged from behind the women. He wore scrubs.

Lily rose. "Dr. Patel?"

"Yes, yes." He came forward, beaming as if she were a long-lost cousin, one hand outstretched. He had teeth of news-anchor brilliance, a square face, and skin a rich, coppery brown that made her think of Rule's older brother Benedict, though he came from the other side of the world.

What she immediately liked about him, though, was his height—maybe one inch above her own. It was a rare and admirable trait.

"You are Lily Yu?" he said.

"I am." Dr. Patel, she discovered as she shook his hand, had a minor Finding Gift. This wasn't a big surprise, as a disproportionately large number of physicians had some trace of magic, and not necessarily one connected with healing. Finding could be a handy diagnostic tool, she supposed, though given the meager nature of his Gift, he might just think he had excellent hunches.

"I am sorry for the delay," he said, and looked truly apologetic. "I am the only cardiologist in Halo, you see."

"Doctor," one of the twins said, "I wish to make a complaint. This woman *insisted* on using her cell phone."

Dr. Patel smiled gently. "Ladies, I hope you will do me the courtesy of sitting down and resting yourselves while you wait to speak with your own doctor, with whom you may register all the complaints you wish. Agent Yu . . . ?" He gestured at the doorway.

"Agent?" one of the twins gasped.

Lily slung her tote on her shoulder and preceded the doctor into the hall.

"Nicely done," she told him. "You remind me of my grandmother." Actually he was much nicer, but Grandmother could—when she wanted—cut someone off at the knees with such exquisite courtesy that he'd be thanking her even as he bled out. She didn't usually bother, but she could.

Dr. Patel smiled. "I believe this is a compliment? Then

thank you. Now, about Mr. Hodge . . . I believe you administered CPR at the scene? That was well-done. However, I must ask you to keep your questioning brief. His condition is good, under the circumstances, but his mental state is not."

"About his mental state—is he rational? Does he remember what happened?"

"Rational? Yes, to the extent that he understands where he is and who he is, and can give permission for treatment. I don't know what he remembers of recent events. He certainly remembers me, and the last time he was here."

"When you implanted his pacemaker."

"Yes. He had a major myocardial infarction. In fact, he died on the way to the operating room. Quite dramatic. I was most pleased to be able to bring him back, offer him perhaps many more years of life."

Dr. Patel didn't look pleased. He looked grieved and guilty, regretting what his patient had done. "This is not for broadcast, Doctor, but in a very real sense I don't believe Hodge killed those people. I don't think he was in charge of his body when the trigger was pulled."

He stopped, staring at her. "But what, then—"

"I'm sorry. I can't tell you more."

"If he is possessed . . . Agent Yu, we cannot have someone here who might harm other patients or staff. Unless he's been exorcised—"

"There's no demon in him now. I can be sure of that. I don't believe he's a danger to others at this time, but I've asked the chief of police to keep officers stationed at his room."

"Yes, they're here. I thought . . . I assumed Mr. Hodge was under arrest."

"At this time, I consider him a key witness. I don't know if he was complicit in what was done to him, or if he is every bit as much a victim as those who were shot. I intend to find out."

"I see." His expression said he didn't see, not at all, but mixed with the puzzlement was relief. "I must say I did not see any signs in him earlier of the sort of disturbance that could have led to today's actions. No symptoms of mania or schizophrenia, no rage, no terrible grievance that might erupt in indiscriminate violence. I had wondered at my lack of perception."

"You weren't responsible in any way for what happened today. Not even in the vague 'I should have known' sort of way."

He looked down as if embarrassed. After a moment he nodded slightly. "Yes. Thank you. I must still ask you to keep your questions brief. Ten minutes at most, and I will be present to monitor his condition."

"I'd assumed you would be." That's why she'd felt free to tell him as much as she had. He was going to hear it anyway.

He started moving again, headed for the door at the end of the hall. "Perhaps your visit will not be as stressful for him as I had thought, however."

Lily couldn't assure him of that. She needed Hodge to remember, and remembering had pushed Meacham over his personal edge. "We'll see. I will have to . . ." She stopped, staring at the neatly lettered sign taped to the door leading to ICU: NO GIFTED PERSONS ALLOWED BEYOND THIS POINT. "What the hell?"

"The sign? It's a new policy. The hospital board fears the disruption that magic might bring to delicate equipment."

Lily reached out, ripped the sign off, and handed it to Patel. "Tell them they'd do better to fear the lawsuits that prejudice might bring to their delicate hospital."

He blinked. "But this isn't a matter of prejudice. Magic can affect some of our instruments. We lost several patients at the Turning. Mr. Hodge's malfunctioning pacemaker proves that magic and technology do not mix well."

"There's a problem with raw magic, loose magic. The magic in someone with a Gift isn't loose, dammit. And we don't know what Hodge is an example of, but his pacemaker quit because of death magic, not because someone's Gift leaked on him."

"Unless we can guarantee that Gifted persons will not accidentally expose our patients to risk—"

"Guess what. You've probably got Gifted people in there

right now, as patients or staff or both. You do still treat the Gifted, don't you? Had any problems with your tech? We can find out for sure in a few seconds—as soon as you step through that door. We'll see if you make the equipment turn wonky."

"Me?" His voice rose. "I'm not—you're mistaken."

"You. A minor Gift, admittedly, but I bet you never lose your car keys." She shoved the door open and stepped through.

How about that? Turned out some rules were real easy for her to break.

IT was a good thing Dr. Patel had told her Hodge was doing okay. She wouldn't have guessed it to look at him.

Franklin Hodge had a long face, deeply grooved, with short salt-and-pepper hair curled tightly against his skull. His skin was that rare shade that looks almost black, unlike most people of African descent, who come in so many hues of brown. At the moment he was ashy, grayed out by a tricky heartbeat.

Or by memory. "Mr. Hodge," Lily said softly, "I'm Agent Lily Yu with the FBI. I need to ask you some questions. I'm going to record our conversation." She set the recorder on his bedside table.

He turned his head away without speaking.

"I need to know what happened to you. I need to keep it from happening to anyone else."

Slowly his head turned back toward her. His eyes were dull. "What do you mean?"

"Did it happen today? Or yesterday, or the day before?"

His throat moved as he swallowed. "You know. You know what it is, what did that to me." One large, pink-palmed hand groped toward her.

Lily had to force herself to take that reaching hand. The slimy prickle of death magic was much less than it had been earlier—fading, but still present. "I need you to describe it for me."

"I was tidying up the kitchen. I like things tidy. I was washing the coffeepot and then all at once . . . it was like winter came inside me and froze me and I was just watching. Watching myself holding that pot, and the water still running. I was so cold. I couldn't move." He licked his lips. "For the longest time all I could do was stand there and see that coffeepot. I couldn't blink or look away. I couldn't do one thing. Then I saw my hand stretch out and shut off the water." He shuddered. "I saw it, but I didn't do it."

"That must have been terrifying."

"Yes, ma'am. Yes, ma'am, it was. I . . . for a bit I just moved around the house, or my body moved and my mind went along. I had no choice in that. Then I started thinking about my gun." The hand Lily held trembled. "Only it didn't really feel like me thinking. More like something goosed me somehow and made me think about it, where it was and all. And once I did . . . once I did . . ."

"What happened?"

"My body turned itself around and tried to hurry. Stupid of it. I've got a bum knee. It gave out and I fell and banged it. Hurt like blazes, but that was okay, that would have been fine, if I could've just made myself blink. But all I could do was lie there, and for a second, just a second, it seemed like I heard someone. Like someone felt sorry for me, being old and hurting. I thought maybe God wanted to help me. I prayed so hard . . ." His eyes sheened with moisture. He blinked. "So hard, but it didn't help. After a bit my body stood itself back up a bit and went . . . went to get my gun."

"What time did you wash out your coffeepot, Mr. Hodge?"

"'Bout nine thirty. The doctor here doesn't want me to drink coffee anymore, but I like a couple cups in the morning. I don't have but two cups, though."

Lily took him through the rest of the morning's events, circling away when he grew agitated, asking about his contacts in the last four days, his knowledge of magic, any connection to Roy Don Meacham. He blinked a lot, she noticed. Not as much as Meacham, but more than was normal.

She circled back again to that morning, what he remembered, what he'd experienced. "You didn't hear a voice telling you what to do? Or have thoughts in your head that didn't seem to come from you?"

"No. No, it wasn't like that. I just watched while my body did what it did. I couldn't make it stop." His eyes watered again and his voice shook. "Couldn't make it stop."

"Agent Yu," Doctor Patel said, "I'm afraid your ten minutes are over."

"Did you feel anything different? Were your sensations the same?"

Patel moved closer, to stand on the other side of the bed from Lily. "I must ask you to leave now."

"S'okay, Doctor," Hodge said, but his voice was growing weak. "I want to tell her . . . just the cold."

"When?"

"The whole time. I got chilled right away, but not bad, and it kept getting colder, right up until . . ."

"Yes?"

A tear spilled down one grooved cheek. "Right up till my body started killing people. Then the cold went away. Then I was warm."

"Thank you, Mr. Hodge." She shut off the recorder. "Ah—are your eyes bothering you?"

"Didn't blink enough," he said softly. "When my body was running things, it didn't blink enough. Left my eyes sore."

Dr. Patel's eyebrows lifted slightly. "You must tell me these things, Mr. Hodge. I will see you get some drops."

Lily slid the recorder back in her tote and took something else out. "I brought something from your house. I hoped it might bring you some comfort."

When he saw what she held, he smiled—a small, weary smile, maybe, but there was an easing around his eyes and in the worn lines of his face. "My Maisie's Bible. Yes, ma'am, that is a comfort. Thank you. Ma'am?"

"Yes?" His hands were shaky. She slid the Bible under one.

"Do you know what did that to me? What made my body do those terrible things?"

"Not yet. I will."

He studied her a moment with weary eyes. "I 'spect you will. Yes, ma'am, I 'spect you will." His eyes drifted closed.

Once again, Dr. Patel indicated that Lily should precede him out of the room. And when he closed the door on Hodge's room, he said, "That was nicely done. Although I can't say you remind me of my grandmother, not when—Agent Yu?" He reached for her.

Lily didn't quite fall. The dizziness had hit so suddenly, between one breath and the next, that her legs buckled, but she didn't fall. Dr. Patel's arm helped. "Give me a minute."

"You must sit."

"No, I have to . . ." Had to get her breath, which was being squeezed out of her, making her so weak it was an effort to get words out.

She knew what was wrong. Dammit to hell. She knew.

After months of quiescence, the mate bond had picked *now* to act up. Now, when Rule was in a car with Toby . . . "I need to go that way," she said, nodding to the south. That's where Rule was, and she had to close some of the distance between them. Fast.

She needed the doctor's help. He didn't want her moving, but she wasn't going to do what he wanted, so he gave in and helped. She shuffled back out of the ICU, all the way down the hall, past the entrance to the waiting room . . . and finally, just as she reached the elevators, it eased.

She drew a deep breath. "Okay. I'm okay now."

"You most certainly are not." The doctor was angry. "I don't know what is wrong, but you certainly must be examined."

She dug her phone out of her pocket. "My condition is . . . unusual, nothing you would have heard of. Trust me. I'm all right now." She hit speed dial, her heart pounding and her mouth dry, and remembered to add, "Thank you for helping me."

"Whether you wish it or not, I am not finished helping you." He grabbed the hand that wasn't holding the phone and took her pulse.

And then, thank God, she heard Rule's voice. "We're fine.

I pulled over in time and am turning around now. The dizziness eased enough for me to do that, which I assume means you're mobile? Unhurt?"

"I'm fine. You're coming back."

"I have to, don't I?"

EIGHTEEN

IT was ten o'clock and full dark when Lily pulled into the driveway at Toby's home.

The yard was empty once more. Rule would still be able to smell the blood, she thought as she climbed out of the car. She couldn't. In the yellow glow from the porch light, the grass looked trampled and weary.

About the way she felt. Lily dragged her tote out of the car, closed the door, and clicked it to lock.

The front door opened before she could knock—but it wasn't Rule who stood there.

"I saw the headlights," Toby's grandmother said. She wore a long cotton robe in cheerful green stripes. "Come on in. You must be exhausted."

"It's been a long day," Lily agreed. And not just for her. She stopped in the foyer, studying a face that seemed to have aged ten years in a day. Oh—Mrs. Asteglio wasn't wearing makeup. Lily had never seen her without it. "Are you all right, Mrs. Asteglio?"

"Not yet, but I will be. And do call me Louise. It's time, past time . . ." She glanced behind her. The kitchen lights were on; in the den the television was on. She sighed. "I've never asked him to use my first name. I wanted to keep him at a distance, but it hasn't helped, has it?"

It took Lily a second to realize what she meant. "This is happening sooner than you'd expected, but you knew Toby would have to go to his father eventually."

"I know. That's why I wanted his father on a last-name basis. Foolish, but I'm not in the mood to be reasonable now, dear. I will be later, but not tonight. Have you eaten? I saved you a plate. Chicken and rice with broccoli." She turned and headed for the kitchen. She was limping slightly.

"I haven't, and bless you. But I can get it."

"I don't want you to get it." She paused, looking over her shoulder. "I don't know what happened to make Rule turn around and come back. He won't tell me. Oh, he says he got sick suddenly, but they don't get sick, do they? And Toby had that look he gets when he isn't supposed to tell me something." Her lips tightened. "They are so fond of *secrets*."

"They have reason," Lily said quietly, knowing that "they" meant lupi. She'd noticed that Mrs. Asteglio—whom she was now supposed to call Louise—seldom used the word. She'd thought it was lingering prejudice, but maybe not. Maybe the woman had trouble putting a name to something that would inevitably take Toby away from her. "That doesn't mean we have to like it, though, does it?"

"I don't expect he has many secrets from you. But never mind me—I'm gloomy tonight. Whatever is wrong, I think he needs you. He's watching those stupid news reports." She shook her head, baffled by such behavior. "Toby's asleep," she added, and flipped on the light in the kitchen.

Lily followed instructions and her heart. She went into the den.

Rule sprawled on the couch, staring at the television. A perky brunette anchor with a familiar face was solemnly informing viewers that tragedy had struck a small Southern town.

Lily slipped off her jacket and unbuckled her shoulder holster. It was as much a relief to take that off as it would be later when she removed her bra. She draped jacket and rig on the coffee table and curled up with Rule. He took her hand. Neither of them spoke.

Tension drained from her shoulders, her neck. The headache that had started that morning, which ibuprofen had dented without eliminating, slowly drew its talons out of the base of her skull. Almost dizzy with the sudden easing and exhaustion, she closed her eyes. The television switched to a commercial.

Rule would be feeling much the same things. The mate bond—infernal, even dangerous, as it could be—did pay its way. Most lovers instinctively reach for each other when life bitch-slaps them, but for the mate-bonded the comfort of touch was as heightened as it was inescapable.

Not that Lily wanted escape. At the moment all she wanted was right here—a comfortable couch, no need to move, and the feel of Rule, the subtle scent of him.

She noticed another scent just as the microwave dinged. One that made her stomach growl. A second commercial began, and Mrs. Asteglio—Louise—brought Lily a steaming plate. "I'm going on to bed now. You two don't stay up too late."

The older woman headed for the stairs. Lily turned to Rule. "What is it about her that makes me want to mind without tripping any of my mother switches?"

"Years of practice." His fingers toyed with her hair, but his gaze stayed fixed on the TV.

Lily watched, too, in between bites of chicken and rice.

First there was Rule saying, "You are here because of my son. So am I." The sheen in his eyes couldn't have been planned, Lily thought. Then there was a shot of all of them together on the porch swing. The brunette gave a brief voice-over about the child custody hearing of "lupus prince Rule Turner," then said, "but no one could have foreseen the tragic turn events would take" as the image of Rule sprang to his feet—leaped—and Changed.

The camera caught even less of the process than Lily's eyes. At the moment of Change, Rule seemed to burst into static, a second's frozen explosion of colorful confetti hanging in midair. Then he was wolf, landing on his feet and streaking through the crowd.

The cameraman had been blocked by that crowd, thank God. There were no shots of Rule knocking Hodge to the ground and lunging for his throat.

"Had Rule Turner not been present," the brunette was saying gravely, "and had he not acted with preternatural speed to subdue the shooter, casualties might have been much worse. As it was, two people died and three others were injured in this senseless shooting. One of those injured was Ed Eames, a reporter for the Associated Press."

The scene switched to a close-up of the AP reporter being questioned by the brunette. Looked like Ed wasn't going to be just a "treated and released" figure after all, Lily thought, turning her head to look at Rule. "This is the first time the Change has been caught on camera, isn't it?"

"Yes. They've shown that clip several times now." He didn't speak for a moment, then his mouth twitched. "My father isn't thrilled about it, but I think his chief regret is that Nokolai isn't earning anything from rights to the clip."

"Uh-oh. Does that mean he's going to want to film you Changing and sell it?"

He snorted. "He might like to, but no. This . . . allowing ourselves to be revealed so publicly during the Change . . . it's deeply against our instincts. Even those who live openly as lupi will be disquieted by such exposure."

Oh, yes, lupi were very fond of secrets. And not without reason. "Are you in trouble?"

He shrugged. "Not personally. With my mate and son in danger, I Changed. I doubt any will argue about such a need. But those who oppose integration with the human world can use this. If I weren't known to the media as the Nokolai prince, there would have been no press conference and no cameras."

Were they talking about lupus policies because they were afraid of bringing up the scary stuff, or was that just her? Lily didn't know how to ask about Toby, what his chances were, what could be done. She wasn't sure she *should* ask.

But she didn't think she could keep stepping around the

subject, either. She leaned forward, set her empty plate on the coffee table, and drained half the glass of tea Louise Asteglio had supplied along with dinner. Then she tiptoed closer to the scary stuff. "The mate bond screwed up your plans. You can't go to Leidolf's clanhome."

"No, they'll have to come to me."

Her eyes widened. "The whole clan?"

That brought a tired grin. "Mrs. Asteglio's hospitality would be sorely stretched. No, only the youths participating in the *gens compleo* need come, though I'm sure some of their families will attend, also. Normally the ritual is conducted at a clanhome because the youths must present themselves to their Rho, not the other way around. In this, I act as their Rho. I can require them to come to me."

"Can you require them not to bring too many people with them? We've got a situation here."

"I won't be holding the ritual in the backyard. Not in Halo at all, actually. There are miles of forest nearby. Of course, depending on what the mate bond is allowing, I may need you to attend, but it's a brief ritual."

"Damned tricky bond." She leaned back against his arm, unhappy. The sudden dizziness when he was driving . . . the damned bond could have killed him or Toby. Especially Toby, who didn't yet heal like a lupus. "How far out were you when it yanked?"

"Just under eight miles from this house." His fingertips played across her nape. "Don't fret about Leidolf. You've enough worrying you. My duties to that clan needn't be on your list."

Less than eight miles. That would really restrict them. Why now? Why had it suddenly tightened? "I'll take that off my list, then. What about the Leidolf Rhej? Have you summoned her, too?"

His fingers stilled. "No one summons a Rhej, and she can't leave Victor. Her skill is all that holds him to life. I did speak with her. I also spoke with Cullen."

"Oh?" She thought she did that well—just the right amount of interest. "What did he say?"

He tugged once—a little too hard—on her hair. "That you ordered him to call me."

She grimaced. *Call Rule re Toby,* she'd texted Cullen. *Urgent. Use tact.* "His notion of tact . . . never mind. I, ah, thought he might know something that would help." At some point in his checkered career, Cullen had attended medical school. Magic couldn't help lupi afflicted with the wild cancer; he'd hoped medical science might. He hadn't learned how to cure it, but maybe he knew something about this supposed connection to a boy's sensing of the Change.

Rule's voice softened. "You were right to call. I wasn't going to. You aren't aware of the reason Cullen sought so hard for a cure, so you wouldn't . . . You see, Etorri is much more subject to the cancer than the other clans. It killed his father."

The muscles in Lily's stomach clenched. Cullen had tried to save them. The father who'd turned his back on him, the clan that had kicked him out—he had tried to save them. "How old was he when he went to medical school?"

Rule understood what she was asking. "He was pre-med when Etorri made him a lone wolf. For a couple years directly afterward he was, ah . . . somewhat unstable, but after an adjustment period he was able to continue on to medical school. His father died before he completed it."

"*Did* he complete it?"

"No."

She rubbed her tense stomach, her fingers finding the burn scar. "He'd really hate it if he knew I was hurting for him."

Rule's smile was small, arriving mainly in his eyes. "That he would. Naturally he was annoyed with me for not calling him immediately about Toby. He disliked the notion that I was, as he put it, tiptoeing around his sensitive feelings, and told me I was panicking unnecessarily. He'll be here tomorrow."

She sat straight up. "What?"

Rule shrugged. "I was surprised, too. He wouldn't explain, but I am to stop listening to old wives' tales and use my head. Anecdotal evidence is often misleading, and I'm on a false trail. He also wished me to tell you three things. First, it's fortunate that you have some sense, because I obviously don't."

Lily felt a smile starting.

"Second, you're not to worry about the plane fare. He'll charge it to my credit card. He considers his previous methods for handling credit inappropriate now that he consults for the FBI."

That surprised a laugh out of her. It was so typically Cullen. VISA still didn't understand why its computers insisted on offering unlimited credit to an unemployed stripper. Lily didn't know how Cullen had done it, either. She'd probably have to arrest him if she ever found out. "And the third thing?"

"Cynna found the boy—frightened and injured, but alive."

Okay, that was good. Lily relaxed back against Rule's arm. She loved the feel of him, the leanness and the strength, the sheer maleness of the muscles she leaned against . . . muscles that were relaxed, not taut with worry. "You believe him, even without an explanation."

"Cullen might twist the truth or withhold it, but he wouldn't outright lie to me. Not about this."

But Lily thought he might very well do just that—if he thought it was what Rule needed. And then devote the next three or four years to finding a way to save Toby before First Change.

"Lily." Rule smiled and tickled the ends of her hair. "He's coming here. He can't lie to me in person."

"Oh, right. I guess you could ask as his Lu Nuncio, couldn't you?" One of the functions of a Lu Nuncio was to act as a prosecuting attorney within the clan—one to whom witnesses couldn't lie. Not successfully, anyway. Lupi couldn't always sniff out a lie, but supposedly the guilt of lying to their Lu Nuncio made it impossible for them to carry it off. "You think he's flying here to make sure you believe him?"

"No. There's something he won't say over the phone."

Paranoid of him, but Cullen combined normal lupus secrecy with a sorcerer's suspicion that everyone really was out to get him—or at least to steal his spells. "Maybe he'll be able to consult on my case while he's here."

"If you pay him, he probably will." He wound a strand of her hair around one finger.

"He's an approved consult." Rule kept touching her. That was his way, but those constant, light touches were replacing comfort with other feelings.

"You want to talk about the case?"

She met his eyes . . . and her heart ached at what she saw in his face.

He'd lied. It was his father's fault, she thought, in so many ways . . . but his own doing, too. Rule had learned early to project confidence, the kind of unworried air people—human or otherwise—crave in a leader. He could make his body lie for him, make it speak of control or power or ease, whatever was needed. And he'd needed to hide how much he still feared for his son. Maybe Cullen's words had helped, but they hadn't erased the fear.

But why hide it from her? No, she realized. No, he hadn't hidden it from her. He'd imposed ease on his body for his own reasons, not to keep her out. He'd left his eyes unshuttered, hadn't he? Let her see his need, the place that words couldn't touch.

Other things could, maybe. She'd try.

Lily touched his cheek gently. *I see you. I will be careful with the places that hurt.* "I don't think so."

"No?" He drifted a thumb across the line of her jaw.

"No. We're not in the driveway now, are we?"

He glanced around, eyebrows tilting in feigned surprise. "I believe you're right. We're on a couch, indoors . . ." He switched his attention to her mouth, and all he did was look at it . . . intently. Her lips tingled as if he'd touched them. "But hardly private. And you've had little sleep."

"True." She sighed, picked up the remote, and turned off the TV, dropping them into darkness. "And you've had even less. None, I think, which is a shame, because you're going to have to pay up anyway."

"Pay up?" Amusement warmed his voice. There was warmth, too, in the hand that clasped her waist.

"You're charged with inciting a cop, buddy, and the penalty's pretty steep." She moved deliberately to straddle his lap, placing her hands on his shoulders and bringing her mouth close to his. Close enough that he would feel her breath on his lips. "How do you plead?"

The lips she wasn't quite kissing curved up. Both of his hands now gripped her waist. "I get a chance to plead my case, do I?"

"Oh, yes." She skimmed her mouth over his. "Though I recommend we go straight to the plea bargain. Judge's chambers. Upstairs."

His hands slid lower to cup her ass. Rule had a thing for her ass. "Will the court entertain an insanity plea?"

"Mmm." She undulated gently against him—breasts, belly, groin. "You saying I make you crazy?"

"Guilty." His hands smoothed their way up—ass, back, shoulders, head. Which he pulled down, toward his.

She resisted briefly, smiling. "I'm pretty sure there were onions in that chicken and rice."

"I love onions." His tongue licked at her smile, asking. She answered by parting her lips and he dived in, his mouth suddenly hungry. His hands went back to her butt. And he stood up.

She made an undignified noise that in someone else she would have called a squeak, quickly hooking her legs around him. Not that she needed to worry. He supported her easily.

Rule leaned his forehead against hers. "Upstairs, I think. Quickly."

Oh, yeah. Lily agreed with her mouth, but in a way that didn't use words. Judging by the growl low in his throat, he appreciated her communication skills.

He started up the stairs, dimly illuminated by a night-light at the landing and one in the hall at the top. She stopped what she was doing to say, somewhat breathlessly, "I can walk."

"It's more fun if I carry you." His fingers did interesting things to demonstrate what he meant.

"We're not alone. Not alone *enough*. Mrs. Asteglio might wake up."

"I'd hear her before she . . . Lily, I won't notice a brass band following us up the stairs if you keep doing that."

She grinned, bringing her hand back up to his shoulder, and snuggled her nose into the curve of his throat, where she could breathe him in. "Maybe you should put me down, then. I'm not sure I can restrain myself."

Reluctantly he did. Not, she knew, because he was the least self-conscious about sexual play in public, but from courtesy. To a lupus, it was rude to indulge in front of someone who lacked a sexual partner. And Mrs. Asteglio really could wake up.

So they held hands for the last few steps, and they paused together at the door to Toby's room, left ajar. Lily had learned during Toby's visits to always leave his bedroom door cracked—and never to mention it. Like his father, Toby hated small, enclosed spaces. Like his father, he insisted they didn't bother him at all.

Rule pushed Toby's door wide open.

Lily glanced at him, puzzled.

In three quick steps Rule was at the twin bed, where a huddled form seemed to lie beneath the covers. One fling of the covers, and even in the darkness Lily could see that the huddled form was a pair of pillows.

After a moment's stretched silence, he moved to the window. It was open. She joined him, looking out at the slatted beams that covered the porch. It would be an easy exit for an athletic boy.

Rule sighed. "I'll go outside to Change. Too much of his smell here for me to track him in this form."

"I'll get my shoulder holster. Just in case."

FOR the fourth time in twenty-four hours—the third since the sun rose—Rule prepared to Change into wolf. He stood in the backyard with the dirt under his bare feet and the moon's lopsided grin over his shoulder. Lily waited, holding the clothes he'd removed.

It took more time than usual, long moments spent spinning through pain. When he finished, he let his head hang, catching his breath, already dreading the Change back to human. He was tired. He'd slept roughly one of those twenty-four hours, curled around his son in the late afternoon. A son who, at the moment, he'd very much like to nip.

Sorting out Toby's most recent trail wouldn't be easy, not with his scent everywhere. Rule trotted to the gate first . . . and paused, surprised.

Toby had marked the grass beside the gate—marked it as if he were wolf already, with a few drops of urine.

Alarm spiked. Until that moment, Rule had been annoyed, not worried. Boys will sneak out. Lupus boys in particular feel a need to taste the night, and at Clanhome that wasn't a problem. They were taught always to mark their trails in case they got in trouble. But why would Toby practice this in the midst of the human world?

Obviously he meant for Rule to follow. As to the why . . . Rule thought he knew, but had to be sure Toby hadn't been coerced somehow. He checked the grass again, sniffing up along the gate for the touch of hands other than Toby's.

Toby's trail was fresh, no more than a couple of hours old, and Rule didn't find any other traces as recent. He paused and, as he had in the woods something over twenty hours ago, he shifted something in his focus, bringing the mantles into the mix of sensory impressions.

Scents immediately sharpened. And no, Toby hadn't been afraid when he passed this way. So Toby wanted his father to find him; he wasn't afraid, yet he hadn't told Rule. Either he'd been sure Rule would forbid whatever action he'd taken, or he'd given his word not to tell.

Rule was betting on the latter. He lifted onto his rear legs, nosed the latch, and dropped back onto four feet as the gate swung open onto an unpaved alley. He picked up Toby's scent immediately and started west. Lily followed silently, carrying his clothes.

He'd nearly told her not to come.

The wolf snorted, disgusted. If his motives had been clear, he'd have nothing to condemn himself for. Lily was tired, too, her human system probably as wrung out as his by a day that had started at four A.M. and just kept going, a day spent wading through violence and bureaucracy. But his motives were murky as hell.

Well, to the man they had been. Considered from the vantage of a wolf's brain, his motives were as obvious as they were foolish. Rule found the next spot Toby had marked, glanced at Lily and nodded to let her know they were on Toby's trail, and trotted on down the alley.

When Lily said she was coming, Rule had noticed the dirty wash of resentment in time to stifle it. He'd nodded, accepting that of course Lily would go with him. It was practical, of course—there were many places a wolf couldn't go, and a naked man sometimes alarmed people more than a wolf, which they might take for a large dog. It was also typical of Lily. She'd already made room for Toby in her heart and was busily making room for him in her life.

All of which was what he'd wanted . . . and part of him resented her. Part of him—a thoroughly human part he'd tried to ignore into nonexistence—didn't want her intruding on his relationship with Toby.

The wolf thought this was very silly. But he supposed it wouldn't go away just because he had better sense in this form than in the other.

They reached a street empty of traffic and crossed quickly. A quick check confirmed Rule's first guess—Toby had proceeded down the alley. They did, too.

Rule knew where the resentment came from. Now that he'd recognized it, that was obvious. He'd been raised without a mother, hadn't he? Technically, at least. In practice he'd been mothered by virtually every woman living at Clanhome, dispersing the feminine ideal through a dozen loving lenses, leaving him with an idealized version of motherhood . . . soft-focus, unreal . . . too unreal, he saw now, to have come between him and his father. Or between him and his son.

Lily was extremely real. He stopped beside another gate and sighed. She would expect him to talk about this, and man and wolf both disliked that notion.

"Something wrong?" Lily whispered.

Nothing they could deal with now. He shook his head . . . and prepared to Change yet again.

NINETEEN

SOMETHING crawled across Toby's ankle—he noticed because he hadn't bothered with socks. He flicked it off with his finger. "I can't just stay here."

"I know, but . . . a little longer." Talia huddled her long, skinny arms closer around her knees. Talia was two years older than him and Justin, and four inches taller. Toby liked her pretty well, even if she had started painting her fingernails lately and worrying about her hair.

There was just enough breeze to keep the leaves whispering tree secrets to each other. That was good. Toby didn't like it when the tree house—which was just a platform, really, without any sides, but they all called it the tree house—got to swaying because the branches started moving.

Funny how steady trees looked from the ground, he thought. Get up in one and it was never entirely still.

"We've got to come up with a plan," Justin said firmly.

"Come up with a plan," Toby muttered. "Sure. You go first, since you don't like my ideas."

"We can't tell them!" Justin forgot and let his voice get a little loud, and Talia shushed him, looking back at the house. "Toby, you know what my folks are like."

"Yeah. They're nice. I like them."

"Well, duh! But they're just stupid about this sort of thing." Justin waved a hand in the general direction of his sister. "You know that. They're all creeped out about you now, too, since you've been on the news and all, and that makes it worse."

Shit. Toby tested the word in his mind, found he liked the weight of it, and tried it aloud. "Shit. They saw that stupid news deal about the custody hearing, huh?"

"Toby." Talia could put more frown into a whisper than anyone else Toby knew. "Don't you be cursing."

Justin broke off a little twig growing out from the trunk. "Everybody's seen it. Everybody in the whole country, I bet."

"You'd think they'd be paying attention to people getting shot, not to the stuff about me." Toby hadn't seen much when it happened because of the way his dad had pushed him down. He'd glimpsed Dad Changing in midair, heard the scary-big blast of the gun. The people screaming. Lily's voice all crisp and fierce telling him and Grammy to *stay down, don't move.*

He hadn't really seen much at all. So why did it stick with him so hard? Toby's stomach felt tight and unhappy. He swallowed.

Justin and Talia looked at each other.

"What?" Toby scowled when they didn't answer. "You'd better tell me."

"Nothin'." Justin gave all his attention to stripping the leaves off his twig.

"He might as well know." Talia eased her hunch. "Daddy thinks the shooting was about you. He says Mr. Hodge went crazy because he found out what you are and was trying to shoot you, or maybe your dad and you both, only he's a real bad shot."

Toby sat up straight. "That's not right. That's not right at all. Talia, you know better. You have to tell—"

"I can't! If they find out—"

"I'm afraid," said a deep, sympathetic voice from the ground below them, "you are going to have to tell."

Talia yipped as if she were the lupus. Justin shot to his feet so fast he hit his head on the branch over him. Toby turned and peered over the edge of the platform, feeling about a hundred pounds lighter. "Hi, Dad. That's my dad," he added to his friends. "I guess I'm in trouble?"

"Some," Dad said, keeping his voice low. "I think you should all climb down now. I could come up there, but I'm tired. And I don't think Lily is in the mood for tree-climbing."

Lily? He'd brought her along? Toby frowned, trying to see past all the leaves, not sure how he felt about Lily being here. Probably just as well, he decided. Lily was who Talia needed to talk to, anyway. "Okay."

Justin grabbed his arm. *"No."*

"What's the matter? You scared to go down there with the big, bad werewolf?"

Justin shook his head hard but said nothing. It was Talia who answered. "Well, I'm going down. I bet none of *them* will come around Toby's dad."

"Come on," Toby said to his best friend. "If we don't go down, he might think he has to tell your folks."

That persuaded Justin. A few moments later, Toby stood with Talia on one side, Justin on the other, facing his father and Lily. They did not look happy with him.

"I assume your friends asked you to give your word not to tell," Dad said in that quiet voice that might make some people think he wasn't mad, but Toby knew better.

"Yes, sir. Well, I gave my word about Talia's secret a long time—" Justin poked his side. Toby gave him an exasperated look. "He heard us talking. He knows there's something we aren't telling, so he knows there's a secret." He looked back at his dad. "But even though they don't have to keep my secret anymore, I still have to keep theirs. Because I promised."

Dad nodded, agreeing. Toby had known he would, about that part of it. "Yet that doesn't explain why you sneaked out of the house."

"That," Toby said, "was a judgment call."

Lily made a little choked sound but didn't say anything,

and Dad just waited, so Toby rushed ahead. "See, Justin's got a cell phone, but I don't, so I bought one of those phones where you buy minutes? So Justin could call me sometimes. And he called tonight and it was sort of an emergency, so I made a judgment to come like he asked. Only you can't tell if it was a good judgment or a bad one unless they say I can tell the secret, or if they tell you themselves. Which they ought to." He bent a frown on Justin and Talia.

Lily spoke in that quiet way she had that wasn't like Dad's quiet voice, but still made you want to listen, like what she said was probably important. "Maybe you could start by introducing us to your friends."

Toby flushed. Proper introductions were one thing lupi and Grammy agreed about, and he'd completely forgotten. "Oh, yeah. Dad, Lily, this is Justin and Talia Appleton. Justin and Talia, this is my dad, Rule Turner, and his mate, Lily Yu." Wait—was he supposed to say mate?

Toby frowned unhappily. He wasn't.

"Pleased to meet you, Talia, Justin." Dad glanced at Lily. "Perhaps we should sit down and discuss the situation."

Justin and his sister exchanged a disbelieving look. They weren't used to adults wanting to have a discussion when rules were broken. Mostly the adults they knew just ganged up together, and kids were not allowed to have secrets. "Okay. C'mon, sit down. He'll listen to you," Toby encouraged his friends.

"Does that mean you aren't going to tell my folks?" Talia said.

"I don't know yet. That's one of the things we must discuss."

So everyone sat in a circle on the grass, which was cool and damp and smelled great. There was plenty of light from the moon, almost overhead now and three-quarters full.

"First," Dad said, looking at Justin, "will your parents be upset if they find Toby here?"

Justin grimaced. "They'll be mad we were outside without permission. And that I called him. They . . ." He gave Toby a look, apologizing. "They're bent out of shape that he's, you know, lupus. They didn't know until it was on the news."

Dad nodded. "I assume they'd be even more upset if they found me here, so if they should come out, I'll leave before they see me. Now, Talia. You have a secret you're afraid to entrust to your parents."

She nodded warily.

"This secret made you want Toby to come over tonight without permission."

Another nod.

"Toby, does Talia's secret involve anything criminal or dangerous to herself or others?"

"Not criminal! But . . . well, there's a danger, but it isn't a life-and-death thing. It's . . ." He spread his hands. "It's about her."

Lily spoke quietly. "Talia has a Gift, doesn't she? One you believe your parents would disapprove of."

No one said anything for a minute. Then Talia sighed real big. "I guess I'd better tell you. *They* want me to, anyway."

"They?"

"The ghosts." Talia's long face seemed paler than normal in the moonlight, and tight, as if her muscles were trying to close her up. "They won't leave me alone lately. They keep after me and after me, and the newest ones . . ." She stopped, gulped.

"I see. You're a medium." Lily didn't look shocked, but Toby hadn't figured she would be. "That's a tricky Gift. And your parents don't approve?"

Justin broke in. "They don't know, and they're not going to! They've always been down on magic, see, but ever since the Turning . . . that Reverend Barnes is all the time preaching against it now. He says anyone who consorts with spirits is dealing with the devil, but it isn't like that! Talia can't help it!"

"No, she can't, not at her age and without any training. Talia, are these ghosts trying to, ah—to speak through you?"

"I don't *want* them to." Talia was near tears, which made

her sound mad. She hated to cry. "There's always been some of them around. I'd see them, or I'd hear them whispering in my mind, but it wasn't a big deal. But ever since the Turning there's been more, and now there's these new ones, and they're awful. They scream inside my mind and they won't go away. And I can't fix things for them, I can't! That's why I needed Toby to come over. They stay away when he's around."

Lily gave Dad a surprised look, her eyebrows lifted like "What?" Dad shook his head. "I don't know. I never heard of ghosts having an aversion for us."

"Hmm." Lily turned back to Talia. "I suspect you're seeing more ghosts since the Turning because your Gift is stronger now. That happened to some people once there was more magic around. Will you let me take your hand?" She smiled. "I'm a sensitive. I can make a guess about how strong your Gift is."

Talia scowled and looked down at her feet. She picked at one toenail, then another. At last she shrugged. "I guess it won't hurt." She held out her hand.

Lily clasped it. "Oh, yes, you have quite a strong Gift. No wonder those ghosts are driving you crazy. Are there any around now?"

"I told you—they don't show up when Toby's here. I guess Mr. Turner would keep them away, too."

"Okay." Lily released her hand. "But Toby can't be with you all the time, can he?"

"Maybe if I tell you what they want me to, they'll go away."

"They want you to tell me something? Me, specifically?"

"Well . . . he didn't describe you very politely, but I'm pretty sure he meant you. The tall man, I mean. He's the oldest ghost and he usually makes more sense than the others, but I think people talked a lot different back when he was alive." Her face tightened in a scowl. "At first he called me 'little darkie,' but I made him quit. I don't care if that's what everyone said back then. People kept slaves then, too, and that was wrong. Though he says he didn't have any slaves, but I think that's because he was poor, not because he knew it was wrong."

"He's been a ghost a long time," Lily murmured.

"Uh-huh. Now he calls me 'little 'un.' He can't say my name. I don't know if that's a rule or if they can't remember names, not even for a minute, but none of the ghosts ever say names. Anyway, he's the one who said I was to tell you."

"Okay. What do they want you to tell me?"

"About *him*. The one who . . . I guess he's the one killing people. They said he's making ghosts, and that's what they call him—the ghost-maker. So I guess they mean he's killing people. Only there's more than one killer, isn't there? So that doesn't make sense. Ghosts usually don't."

"Is that exactly what they said?" Lily's voice was soft, like Grammy's was when Toby had had a bad dream. "That this 'he' is making ghosts, not that he killed them?"

"Ghosts *won't* talk about death. Sometimes they'll say what happened to make them ghosts, sometimes they won't, but they won't ever say they died. They want you to stop him. The little girl says he's real cold, always cold. Her brother doesn't talk—he's really fuzzy—and she mostly cries, but she did say that. And their mom keeps saying, 'He doesn't know,' over and over, looking at me like it's important. I think I was supposed to tell you that. And the tall man . . . he said they're scared. They're all scared, not just the new ones."

"They?"

"The ghosts. They're scared of *him*, whoever he is."

"I understand that they can't or won't use names, but did they describe him in any way?"

Talia's mouth twisted. "I asked and asked, but ghosts are pretty stupid. They just keep telling me the same stuff again and again. And 'help me.'" Her eyes glistened, but her jaw set stubbornly. "They say that, too, and sometimes they cry. Not the tall man, but some of them cry a lot. I hate that. But the new ones . . . they're the worst. They started screaming in my head tonight, and it's like . . . like they're ripping at my brain. It's horrible."

Lily reached for Talia's hand. "I'm so sorry you've had to live with this. It's more than many adults could handle. Is this screaming a physical pain?"

"No, but—but it feels so awful."

Lily nodded. "Pain doesn't have to be physical to be real. These new ghosts . . . I need you to tell me how many there are, and what's different about them."

"Five. The boy and girl and their mom—they're the ones whose dad killed them. I'm pretty sure about that, though they won't say. And the two newest ones got shot today."

"I see. And they're different from the others?"

Talia nodded. "Usually it's the old ones who get all wispy, like crumpled tissues. They sort of wear out. Except the tall man—he's old, but he's still clear, and he makes more sense than most of them. I don't know why. But these . . . they're new, but they're fuzzy and tattered, as if they were real old. And they scream at me. The rest don't do that." Talia's mouth quivered into a smile. "You don't think I'm crazy? Or—or possessed, or making things up?"

"No. I can sense your Gift, remember?"

"Are you going to tell my parents?"

"I'm hoping you'll decide to do that. Wait, wait," Lily said when both Justin and Talia burst into words that tumbled over each other like upset puppies. "I know you believe they won't understand. You're afraid they'll think your Gift is evil. Some people do think that way, because magic can be scary, and they don't understand it. So you might be right. They might react badly. I don't know. But I'd like to tell you a story about me, if that's okay."

Talia and Justin looked at each other. Talia nodded.

"I'm a sensitive. I told you that. But for years and years—all my life up until about eight months ago—I wouldn't have told you. My family knew, and that's where I'm different from you. My family knew and they were okay about it, but I knew lots of other people wouldn't be. I wanted to be normal—what I thought was normal—and I didn't want to deal with the screwy ideas people have about sensitives. So I didn't tell anyone."

"But now you do."

Lily nodded. "Now I do. And you know what? It's better this way. Some people don't understand, and they're wrong in the things they think about me. Some people are rude, but most aren't. And I breathe better now that I'm not hiding my secret anymore. Have you ever had a broken bone?"

Talia blinked. "Yes, ma'am. My arm. Right here, see? It's fine now. I broke it in the third grade."

"You know how it felt right after the cast came off? The skin's really soft and tender, and your arm is weak because you haven't been using it. It feels like you still need to protect it, as if it could be hurt easily—but I bet you didn't want the cast back. Right? Well, that's how I felt when I stopped keeping my Gift a secret."

Talia considered that a moment, frowning. "But your family knew about it already. They were okay with your Gift."

Lily nodded. "And that's an important difference. But you've got family who know about your Gift and support you, too. Your brother's right here, and he doesn't think you're evil. Or no more than any brother thinks that about his big sister." She gave Justin a quick grin, and he grinned back. "What you don't have—what you need—is an adult who will stand by you while your parents get used to the idea. I don't think my mother would have accepted my being a sensitive very well if Grandmother hadn't been there telling her . . . Well, Grandmother is not always polite."

Toby chortled. "I wish you could meet her. Lily's grandmother is really something. She can make anyone do what she says. She made the pres—"

"We don't talk about that, Toby," Dad said quickly.

"Oh, yeah, that's right." Toby was still grinning, thinking of when he'd stood on the White House lawn near the president, because Grandmother insisted he be there when the dragons arrived. "But she really is something."

Lily smiled, but didn't look away from Talia. "Can you think of an adult relative who would be on your side?"

Justin answered promptly. "Aunt Sherri. No, really, " he said when Talia looked doubtful. "She's always telling Mom that Reverend Barnes is full of beans. Sometimes she doesn't say 'beans,' " he added, grinning.

"Mom doesn't listen to her—she just changes the subject."

"Mom doesn't want to listen 'cause of Daddy. She doesn't want to get in a fight, and Daddy thinks Reverend Barnes is Jesus's best friend. Like the two of them have sleepovers and play ball together all the time, so Reverend Barnes has the inside scoop about heaven and all." Justin paused, worry retaking his face. "Daddy's going to be a problem."

"*If* we tell." Talia obviously hadn't decided to.

"Maybe you could talk to your aunt Sherri about your Gift," Lily said. "See what she thinks about telling your parents."

"Yeah. Yeah!" Talia brightened. "I think she'd promise not to tell them something as long as it wasn't about drugs or sex or something bad like that."

"This still leaves us with a problem," Dad said quietly. "When Toby comes home with us, Talia has no way to keep the ghosts from bothering her."

"Can't he stay?" Justin said. "Just for tonight. They're worst at night. She's tried crosses and holding on to a Bible and everything, but nothing keeps them away except Toby."

"Not without your parents' knowledge and permission." Dad had a way of saying things in a way that made you know there was no point in arguing. "You need help managing your Gift, Talia. Neither Lily nor I can offer that, but for now . . . perhaps the ghosts are satisfied since you've passed on their messages. Why don't you go to the other side of the yard and see if they're still here? Would that be far enough?"

"Sure. I have to be real close to Toby to keep them away." Talia bit her lip, then nodded and scrambled to her feet. The rest of them stood up, too, and watched as she went to the old swing set on the south side of the yard. She waited there a few minutes, looking around. Then she nodded, said something too softly for Toby to hear, and came back.

Her face looked a lot calmer. "The tall man said they—the regular ghosts—he said they're circling the new ones to keep them from screaming at me. But they can't pay attention for long. None of them can. They'll forget why they're doing it and quit. He said you really need to stop the ghost-maker."

"I will," Lily said.

It sounded like a promise. Toby worried about that. Could she really promise to stop the ghost-maker? They didn't know who he was or how he was making people kill.

Dad did his thought-pulling thing, bending down to say softly, so only Toby would hear, "It's what she does, you know. Right now she isn't asking herself if she can stop the killing. She knows she will. She's worrying about when."

Toby swallowed. *When* made a difference, all right. "Okay. Only I can't help wondering . . ."

"Yes?"

"What would ghosts be scared of? They're already dead."

Dad squeezed his shoulder. "Good question."

TWENTY

WHAT would ghosts be scared of?

It was, Lily thought as she followed Rule and Toby through the gate, a very good question. Not the only one clogging up her pipes—her fingers itched for a notebook to jot some of them down—but maybe the most important one. If she could answer it, she'd go a long way to answering the rest.

The gate creaked as she closed it. Toby looked up at his dad. "I didn't even hear the gate when you came. I thought I was listening, but I didn't hear it."

"Lily and I came over the fence."

"Yeah?" Toby looked at Lily, then at the fence, obviously measuring their respective heights. Impressed, he said, "It's a pretty high fence."

She smiled. "Your dad gave me a boost once he was two-legged again."

"But you still did it real quietly," he said, determined to give her credit. "Uh . . . I'm sorry about calling you Dad's mate. I'm not supposed to say that, but I forgot. It's just that I don't have a word for you."

So she wasn't the only one. "I've been bothered by that,

too. I can say what you are to Rule, but I don't have a word for what you are to me. Though maybe I've found one."

"What's that?"

"Family."

Toby's face lit up like she'd plugged him in. Quickly he looked at his feet, as if he might need to keep an eye on what they were up to. "Cool," he said, in the way of a boy embarrassed by his emotions.

She wanted very much to hug him. "Of course, my family is kind of messed up."

He looked up, grinning. "Your grandmother's cool."

"That she is."

"Toby."

That's all Rule said, and in a mild voice, but the boy deflated. He sighed and scuffed his shoe in the dirt. "How much trouble am I in?" He looked up at his dad. "You figured out what I meant, right? When I made you a trail."

"I did." Rule stopped and put his hands on Toby's shoulders. "You handled a difficult situation with honor. Not perfectly, mind, but with honor. I'm proud of you."

The light came back in Toby's face. He all but glowed as he asked casually, "So what's my punishment?"

Lily's mouth opened. She closed it before she got her foot in, but a couple more questions joined the rest on her mental list.

"Well." Rule started walking again. "You did leave the house at night without permission. And this isn't Clanhome."

"I know." Toby paused, then said hopefully, "Laps?"

Dad chuckled. "Oh, that would be such a punishment. You love to run. No, I'm afraid it will be math. Three days, one page of fractions each day."

"Shit," Toby said. Then, more quietly, "Whoops."

Rule didn't quite smile, but Lily could see the effort it took. "An extra page the first day for disrespecting your grammy's rules about your language. Toby, I can tell Lily is puzzled by your punishment, since I said I was proud of you. Would you explain it to her, please?"

"Oh. Sure. See, I couldn't tell . . ." But he stopped as they reached the street, quickly checking for cars.

He always did that, she'd noticed. It seemed to be a lupus thing. He never lost track of his surroundings, even when he might have assumed adults were watching out for him.

His pause was brief. They stepped into the empty street together. "I couldn't tell Dad about the ghosts because I'd promised. It was an actual promise, so I couldn't just decide things had changed and I needed to tell, see? Like if I say, 'See you at school tomorrow,' that's not a promise. I could get sick or something. But if I promise to be at school tomorrow, I *have* to be there, even if my leg's broken or a tornado comes. There's no mitigating circumstances with a promise."

The "mitigating circumstances" almost made Lily smile. It was so Rule. But this was deadly serious for Toby. "Admirable, but a hard standard to live by. Is this a lupi thing? Or just Nokolai?"

"Lupi. Like Grandpa says, we're supposed to hoard our promises, or put limits on them, so maybe I shouldn't have promised Justin and Talia to keep her secret without, like, establishing some parameters. I was pretty little when I did it," he said from the lofty vantage point of his nine years. "I didn't know about parameters. Anyway, when Justin called and said Talia was in trouble from the ghosts, I couldn't tell anyone, but I needed Dad to know because Talia needed help. And you needed to know what the ghosts said. So I, uh, left a trail for Dad. I didn't break my word, but I found a way to do the right thing. But I did break the rules."

"By sneaking out."

"Yeah. Kids don't get to pick which rules we obey, just like clan don't get to choose when they'll obey the Rho. And sometimes there's a price for doing the right thing. I have to be willing to pay the price."

"I see," she said gravely. "Is math a high price to pay?"

"Well . . ." He darted a glance at his father. "Not real high. I don't like it much, but I can do fractions pretty fast, so it's not going to take me lots of time. Did it help, hearing what the ghosts said?"

"Yes, though I haven't sorted out what it means yet. Apparently the perp is male. That should help." She glanced at Rule. "I'm thinking it's lucky my boss is a precog."

His eyebrows shot up. "Ruben foresaw this?"

"No, but remember the investigative panel I told you about? The one he put together after that ghost disrupted Cynna's wedding?"

Toby immediately had to know about the ghost. Lily was happy to let Rule take over telling the tale while her own thoughts turned to ghosts . . . and memory.

After the incident at the wedding, Ruben's precognitive Gift had prodded him to find out more about ghosts. The Unit lacked a medium, so the experts he'd brought in had all been civilians—a varied crew, as it turned out, but they'd agreed on one crucial point: no one knew what caused ghosts.

Murder was certainly a factor, but not all violent deaths threw ghosts. The suddenness of death was a factor, too, but sometimes a lingering death resulted in a ghost. The old canard about the ghost needing to resolve something held true, yet any number of people died with serious issues left unresolved—and went on to the Big Whatever without leaving any ghostly residue behind.

Most ghosts didn't linger long. Some did. Most couldn't affect the physical world. Some could, using what might be telekinesis—doors slamming, knickknacks falling off shelves, that sort of thing. Many ghosts were sad or confused. A few were actively hostile.

None of the mediums had reported ghosts who screamed in their heads.

The experts didn't agree on what a ghost *was*. Some—those who didn't believe in an afterlife—insisted that ghosts were a sort of congealed energy that failed to dissipate when the person who'd generated it died. They were simply patterns, not people, lacking real cognition or sense of self. But to a woman—and for reasons no one understood, mediums were always female—the mediums disagreed.

Lily had to cast her vote with the woo-woo crowd on this

one. Something survived beyond the body. Might as well call it a soul.

What bugged Lily was that not all mediums were Gifted. At Ruben's request, she'd checked them out. Turned out that a few people were able to see ghosts without possessing a hint of magic. That had been confirmed in double-blind tests comparing their sightings with those of Gifted mediums. They couldn't interact consistently with the ghosts, though. Only those with a medium's Gift could.

This struck the dead-is-dead experts as proof that ghosts weren't people. They claimed that the medium fed the ghosts energy, giving them a semblance of life. The mediums had done some eye-rolling over that. Sure, the ghosts were using the medium's power to communicate, but even without that magical boost they were discrete entities. Maybe not the entire soul, but some part of it.

The part with the memories. Lily's heart bumped up a beat. That was the other thing everyone agreed on. When asked about this world or their current existence, ghosts' answers ranged from vague to nonsensical. But they remembered themselves and their lives. Clearly. Vividly.

As for names . . . there was something about names in the report. She couldn't quite remember . . .

"Penny for them," Rule said, taking her hand.

"Hmm." They'd almost reached the Asteglio back gate. Unlike the two males with her, she'd lost track of her surroundings. "Nothing coherent, I'm afraid. I wish I could have asked the ghosts some questions through Talia."

"Why didn't you?" Toby asked. "Talia would've done it, I bet, especially with me staying close enough to make them go away if they got mean."

"I'm not supposed to interview a minor without the knowledge and consent of her parents, much less encourage her to use her Gift for me. And it might not be safe for Talia. You can't be beside her every minute, and I don't know what to make of the new ones screaming at her."

"Huh." Toby thought that over as they passed back into his

yard. "Can you get an adult medium to come talk to the ghosts?"

"Maybe. There aren't any in the Unit." And she wasn't sure a medium could help. Ghosts were seriously unreliable witnesses, which was why Ruben hadn't made more of a push to recruit a medium for the Unit.

Toby wanted to know if Rule was going to tell Grammy about him sneaking out. Rule chuckled and said she might ask for an explanation when she saw Toby doing fractions on a sunny summer morning. "Morning?" Toby said—a little too loudly. Rule hushed him, and Toby launched a whispered campaign against morning math, as opposed to afternoon math, that carried the two of them up the stairs.

Lily stayed behind, clearing away the plate and glass she'd forgotten earlier. Before heading up, she grabbed her purse and dug out her phone; it was the quickest way to send an e-mail. She needed the report on ghosts that Ruben's panel had produced.

An hour ago, climbing the stairs had been foreplay. Now they were just stairs, the path she needed to take to reach the bed she was longing for . . . and for entirely different reasons. Somewhere between rinsing her plate and sending the e-mail, exhaustion had hit.

Rule was still in with Toby when she reached the top of the stairs. She headed straight for the bedroom.

Parents do this sort of thing all the time, she thought as she pulled off her jacket and unbuckled her shoulder holster. Coitus interruptus took on a whole new meaning with kids around. Maybe most parents didn't include the walking-a-wolf-down-the-alley bit, but kids climbed out windows. Kids did all sorts of crazy things, and parents had to sift the rights and wrongs and dangers of a situation, and somehow convey all that to their kids.

Preferably without yelling. She hung up the jacket, pulled off her T-shirt and bra, and dropped the last two on the closet floor, regretting the lack of a clothes hamper. Not that her mother had raised her voice, exactly. She'd turned shrill.

Sarcastic. If there was a way to show that you disapproved of an action without disapproving of the child, her mother had never found it.

As far as Lily could tell, she hadn't looked. Lily had quit listening long ago. *Didn't stop reacting to her, though, did I?* She sighed, turned off the bedside lamp, and slipped naked between the sheets, too tired to dig out a sleep shirt. Which she seldom bothered with at home, but she had intended to use here.

Wasn't Rule going awfully far to the other extreme, though? Sure, he'd disciplined Toby, but first he'd said he was proud of the boy. Talk about mixed messages.

Sneaking out of the house was serious. Even in Halo, bad things happened to kids on the streets at night. And right now there was something or someone who could make people kill.

She didn't hear Rule come in, but she felt him. Eyes closed, she listened to the rustling sound of him undressing, and she smiled. Oh, yeah, she was stupid in love with the man. She knew his clothes would go on the floor, not out of sight in the closet, and still she smiled.

He'd probably pick them up in the morning. He knew disorder bothered her, so he usually remembered. Maybe, she thought sleepily, it worked out better for kids if their parents—the ones they started out with, or the ones they collected along the way—didn't agree about everything. Might as well hope that was true, because that's what most kids got.

The mattress dipped. Automatically she rolled onto her side so Rule could curve his body around hers. He kissed her ear, sighed, and sank onto the pillow, lazily draping one arm over her waist to cup her breast. "We missed our moment, didn't we?"

She nodded without opening her eyes.

"Not going to tell me I was wrong about Toby?" he murmured.

"Nope. Too tired." Though she couldn't resist adding, "I don't think this is the first time he's slipped out."

"I'm sure it isn't. We're looser about some rules than you're used to, in part because our children can't lie to us. We don't allow disobedience about the important things."

She suspected they defined "important things" differently. "You would have been a lot more upset if he'd broken his word."

"Yes." He nuzzled her hair. "He's my only son, *nadia*. He will almost certainly be Rho someday. His word will bind the entire clan, and lupi will die to uphold it if necessary. He must understand the weight of his promises."

It was a cold, scary ideal to impose on a boy, but he was talking about himself as much as his son. And, she realized, his father. She had a glimmering of what it meant to be Rho. The head of a clan was, in an essential way, separate from the rest, set apart by a responsibility the others couldn't share.

Did Isen, in holding the clan's mantle, enjoy the comfort of it that the rest of the clan shared? Or was it another burden? Or some combination of the two?

Mantles . . . something she was going to ask . . . but sleep dragged at her. As her mind shut down, she snuggled closer to Rule so he would know he wasn't alone. But her last thoughts, oddly, were about his father.

She had no doubt Isen Turner could have sex as often as he wished. But did anyone simply sleep with him? Or was he alone in that way, too?

TWENTY-ONE

RULE slept in the next morning, which annoyed him. Normally he needed no more than five hours of sleep, but he'd done without entirely the night before. It was just past six thirty when Lily slipped out of bed, waking him—and spoiling his plan for how to wake her. She was in a hurry, unfortunately. She'd called a briefing for seven thirty.

Ah, well. One of the pleasures of their bond was knowing there would be other mornings. He spoke firmly to himself about the value of delayed gratification as he showered, having seen Lily off with a decent kiss, followed by a mug of decent coffee to take with her.

He finished his own coffee while shaving, then headed downstairs, carrying his laptop and the empty mug. His business wasn't as urgent as Lily's, but still needed tending. Financial matters, mostly—he handled the investments for the clan—plus some details concerning the All-Clan. Plus he needed to speak with the Leidolf Lu Nuncio again about the *gens compleo*.

Toby was still asleep, but his grandmother wasn't. He exchanged "good mornings" with her while refilling his mug. She'd applied her makeup already, as was her habit, which he took as a good sign. Yesterday's violence had been hard on her. "You slept well?"

"Surprisingly so." She took down a large mixing bowl. "I'm making pancakes this morning. How many will you want?"

"Pancakes." He smiled with pleasure. "I'll take as many as you care to offer. I'm good with eggs, but have never mastered pancakes. May I help?"

"You can get the eggs and buttermilk out. Lily doesn't make pancakes?"

"Lily butters a mean slice of toast."

She chuckled. "Toby told me you do almost all of the cooking. I must say, I was surprised. I'd imagined you with an endless stream of women cooking for you."

"Mrs. Asteglio, I haven't—"

"Louise. I should have asked you to call me Louise years ago. And I know you haven't exposed Toby to that endless stream I imagined flowing through your . . . kitchen."

Surprised, amused, he acted instinctively, bending to kiss her cheek. "Thank you. Does this mean I'm no longer Mr. Turner?"

Her cheeks pinked. "Of course."

"Are you all right this morning?" he asked softly. "Yesterday was . . . difficult."

"It reminded me of why I never worked in the ER. Blood doesn't bother me, but violence . . ." Trouble overtook her eyes, and bafflement. She shook her head sharply. "Never mind. I deal best by staying busy. You can separate out the whites, if you like, and whip them—soft peaks. The mixer's in the second drawer by the sink."

He retrieved the mixer. "You trust me to know about soft peaks?"

"I expect you've the sense to ask if you don't. It's good for Toby to see that men can be handy in the kitchen."

"Lily's learning. It offends her sense of fair play for me to do all the cooking, so she's—" The doorbell rang. Rule didn't allow himself to frown, but it wasn't likely to be good news. Not at seven fifteen in the morning.

Perhaps Cullen had caught an earlier flight? "I'll get it."

"No, you won't." Mrs. Asteglio set down the bowl and
started for the door. "My house, my door. You mean well, but
I don't need to be shielded."

He considered not following her, which he thought she'd
prefer. But not for long, so he was only a few paces behind her
when she opened the door—without using the peephole he'd
had installed years ago, dammit. She just swung the door open
to whoever was there.

And said not a word.

Into the silence came another voice, one Rule hadn't heard
in person in nine years. "Hi, Mom. I'm not sure if I'm the bad
penny turning up or the prodigal daughter to be welcomed
with . . . Oh, hell, that's cloying. Never mind. May I come in?"

LILY briefed her four borrowed agents along with the sheriff,
the chief of police, and a couple of local detectives with homicide experience. She gave them both outline and details,
omitting the source when she said there was "reason to think"
the perp was male. "Not necessarily a human male," she added.
"As I said earlier, my consultant thinks it could be some creature accidentally blown here at the Turning."

"Your consultant." The chief of police had a good sneer
going in his voice, though he kept his face bland. "Would that
be someone who turns hairy once a month and howls at the
moon?"

She'd already realized the chief was going to be a pain.
Idiots usually were. He'd glared at her throughout the briefing, asking the occasional dumb-ass question, implying that
anyone who claimed to possess magic was by definition stupid, untrustworthy, and probably evil.

This time she just looked at him a second, then went on as
if he hadn't spoken. He wanted to make her angry. She wouldn't
give him the satisfaction. "I'm hoping that the sheriff's department and the city police will concentrate on learning everything there is to know about Meacham and Hodge. We have
to figure out what they have in common. Why those two men

instead of two others? This is your town, your people. You're the best ones to handle that end."

"Yeah, but is that going to tell us anything about who or what is doing this?" Deacon asked bluntly. "Seems like we need someone who can figure out the magic end of things."

That would be nice. "My boss has experts looking into the possibilities, but the more information we can give them, the more help they can give us."

"And what will your people be doing?"

"Visiting veterinarians." Her people looked surprised by that. At least, three of them did. Nothing dented Brown's doughy cynicism. "Human practitioners work up to human sacrifice. We need to know if animals have gone missing or been found mutilated or dead of unexplained causes. There's also the possibility our perp isn't human and came through at the Turning. If so, what has he been doing the last seven months? Again, there could be a connection with missing or dead animals."

"Miss Yu." The chief was one of those people with features too small for his face. He had narrow eyes, a dainty little nose, and a small mouth just made for pursing in disapproval, all crowded into the bottom half of his face and overwhelmed by the expanse of freshly shaved pink skin. "You talked about wanting our input, so here's mine. You've built a whole huge hullabaloo out of nothing. These murders aren't related. Meacham went nuts and killed his family. Hodge hated weers—"

"You have evidence of that?" she asked sharply.

"Not yet, but I'm betting we can confirm it pretty easy. It's obvious, isn't it? He went after your lover and maybe his boy."

"There are no reports from witnesses at yesterday's shooting to suggest Hodge aimed at Rule Turner or his son. I'm one of those witnesses. In addition, physical evidence confirms that the victims were not in a line of sight between Hodge and Turner. There is nothing to suggest that he was the intended target."

"The old man could be senile, could be using, could be just plain nuts. You never know. But the plain fact is, there's nothing to say these two killers are connected, nothing to say they were under some weird-ass compulsion, and nothing to prove there's death magic involved." Such a little mouth made for tight smiles, one of which he offered now. "If death magic even exists. I'm thinking it's as much hogwash as demonic possession."

Lily nodded. "I see. We'll skip the part about demonic possession being hogwash, save to mention that the Catholic Church, several Protestant denominations, the FBI, the Secret Service, Congress, and the President of the United States disagree. Otherwise, you might have a workable theory—if I were willing to stipulate that I'm a liar."

"Well, now, I didn't say that. Anyone can make a mistake. All this magic stuff—people make mistakes with that all the time."

She leaned forward, looking him right in the eye. "I'm telling you that I've touched death magic. I know what it feels like, and there is no possibility of a mistake. Those bodies have death magic on them. So does Meacham. So does Hodge. So did the damned dogs that attacked me and Sheriff Deacon. Am I lying?"

Apparently he was unwilling to commit to that. He fell back on glaring.

"Is your department going to cooperate with this investigation?"

"Cooperate! You call this cooperation? You're just telling us what's what while you ignore what we say."

"When you disagree with the evidence of my senses, I do. I hope the police department will participate in the investigation. We could use the manpower. But if not, Sheriff Deacon has good people."

He was silent, fuming.

Nathan Brown stirred. "Horace—it is Horace, right? I nearly forgot to give you a message. I was talkin' to Marianne Potter over in Charlotte just last night. She said to tell you hello. Asked after that pretty little wife of yours."

Half the color drained out of the chief's face, leaving it blotchy. "You—you—"

Brown had a particularly nasty smile. He used it now. "Now, Horace, I know what you're thinkin'. Agent Yu isn't one of us. She'll head back off to D.C. or the West Coast or somewhere. But I won't. I'll still be in Charlotte, less than a hundred miles from here. You might want to think about stayin' on good terms with your local FBI office."

Ten minutes later, the door closed behind the chief and his detectives—who hadn't been precisely thrilled to learn that Brown would be handling the coordination of city, county, and federal officers.

Deacon paused on his way out. "You think that's a good idea, putting him in charge?" A jerk of his chin indicated Brown, still seated at the conference table.

"Agent Brown assures me he's good at working with the locals. Though I'll admit," she said with a glance his way, "at the time I made the decision I hadn't realized he was referring to the use of blackmail."

Brown actually had a real smile. His lips curved up and his eyes lit with amusement. "Don't know what you're talking about."

"Marianne Potter?" Deacon cocked an inquisitive eyebrow.

Brown waggled a hand. "Friend of a friend."

"Your friend is a friend of the owner of a, ah, real well-known escort service?"

At this interesting point Lily's phone buzzed. That meant a call forwarded from her official number. She grabbed it. "Yu here."

"I sure am," a cheery male voice said. "How'd you guess?" A chuckle. "I suppose you've heard that before. My sense of humor is, alas, very basic. Oh, this is Dr. Alderson. I conducted the autopsy on your dogs."

"Right. Thanks for calling, Doctor." She glanced at her watch. "You've learned something? Given the way magic screws up lab results, I wasn't sure how much you'd be able to find out."

"Your dogs weren't intrinsically magic, so the magic still present doesn't seem to be interfering with tests. And of course the visual exam is unaffected."

"But you did treat the bodies as biohazards?"

"Oh, yes. Quite a nuisance, but I don't want to catch whatever those poor beasts had. I'll skip the gross physical findings for now, save to confirm that they had indeed ingested human remains prior to death. Oh, and there was a chip in one animal—the Doberman—so we were able to get a name and address for the owner, or at least the person who owned him at one time. Do you want that now?"

Hot damn. "Absolutely." Lily grabbed a pad and pen. "Shoot."

He gave her the name and address—a Halo address—then said, "The part I thought you might find interesting concerns the brain damage."

"Brain damage."

"Oh, yes. There's significant generalized damage superficially similar to that caused by encephalitis, most extensive in key structures—the hippocampus, the prefrontal lobe, the frontal and temporal cortexes, with lesser damage to the amygdala. Specimens from those regions exhibit intrusions strikingly similar to Negri bodies, though the dFA was negative, precluding rabies."

She understood the last two words. "So it wasn't rabies."

"That's what I said. We've just begun the lab work, but there seems to be significant alteration in rostral linear nuclei and in periaqueductal gray neurons. Also, there is a notable loss of Purkinje cells—a condition that, in humans, is associated with ocular motor apraxia."

"You do realize I have no idea what you're saying, right? Except the ocular part. That means eyes."

"Oh, dear." He chuckled. "The layman's version, then. I found extensive inflammation of the brain which was particularly severe in the regions associated with memory and emotional control. I understand the dogs attacked you? Poor things had no choice. They would have been flooded with rage."

"And the part about the eyes?"

"There's damage in the area of the brain that controls movement of the eyes."

"Blinking?" she said, suddenly urgent. "Could it cause someone to blink a lot, or not at all?"

"Hmm." He was silent a moment. "Possibly. One study suggested that synaptic plasticity occurring in Purkinje cells might be involved in—oh, dear, I'm descending into technobabble again. Suffice it to say that we don't know enough about the brain and blinking to be sure, so my answer must be 'possibly.' I'm sorry I can't be more definite," he said, his relentless good humor momentarily eclipsed by apology. "I was reluctant to call with such a preliminary report, but your Mr. Brooks assured me you'd want to know."

"My Mr. Brooks was right." Ruben usually was. "You've already told him about this?"

"Yes, and faxed a copy of—oh, that's right. He wanted me to tell you he'd see that Georgetown University Hospital received a copy of my preliminary report. He assumed you would know what that meant."

"Yeah, the obvious is finally biting me in the ass. Give me a minute to think this through." She tapped her fingers on her thigh, scowling, as she did just that. "Okay. One more thing I need you to do," she said. And told him.

He agreed, asked a couple of questions, and refined her original suggestion. Lily disconnected.

"That's just gross."

The agent who'd spoken was almost as short as Lily and ten years older, with fluffy blond hair and twenty extra pounds. She was also named Brown—Mirabelle Brown—and the others called her Brown Two.

"It is," Lily agreed. "But it's the surest way to find out if my initial assumption about those dogs was wrong."

Brown Two's nose wrinkled. "And feeding bits of them to some other poor animal will tell you what, exactly?"

"Whether the death magic can be ingested along with the flesh." She glanced at Deacon, who still hovered near the door, determined to hear whatever she'd learned. Looked like she owed him one. "I assumed that's what happened to the dogs."

"I recall that," he said levelly.

"Unfortunately, we all know what 'assume' makes of 'u' and 'me.' The vet who autopsied them is going to—"

At that moment the fax machine began chattering.

"The vet is quick," she said wryly. "Very briefly, Dr. Alderson found a pathology in the dogs' brains that relates to symptoms exhibited by Roy Don Meacham. I want to know where those dogs came from."

"Oh, sure," Brown Two said dryly. "Two of them had collars, but no tags. Be a cinch to find out who owned dogs that lack tags."

Lily mentally gave the woman points for attention to detail—and verbally gave her another assignment. "No tags when we found them doesn't mean their owners didn't register them. That's why you're going to talk to Animal Control. Get a list of all the registered dogs in the area and start tracking owners of those particular breeds. But first, talk with these people."

She handed Brown Two the name and address Dr. Alderson had given her. "They owned the Doberman at one time. Had a microchip in him. The rest of you . . ." She gave them a quick scan. "Even untagged pets can be loved and missed, so I want all of you to ask about animals matching the descriptions of these dogs when you ask about missing pets. You're also going to share Dr. Alderson's report with the other vets and ask about animal attacks on humans or on other animals, particularly where one animal killed another."

No one said anything for a moment. Then Deacon did, softly. "Shit."

The obvious had just taken a chunk out of his ass, too. Lily gave him a level look. "Pretty much, yeah."

"I'm not following you," said the youngest agent—a man who, thank God, was *not* named Brown.

"If you've read my report about finding the first bodies, you know Rule Turner was attacked, but not killed, near the bodies."

"Yeah," Brown One said, the usual grumpy expression on his plump face. "Doesn't fit. Why was the perp even there?"

"Exactly. My consultant suggested some kind of spell-trap near the bodies, but that's not a very satisfying explanation. Why didn't the dogs spring it? Why even have a trap? But if we toss out some assumptions, it starts making sense. Maybe the perp was there because that's where he hangs when he's between murders. Maybe he made Turner for lupus after initiating the attack and decided to go after something easier to kill, like me and Deacon."

Brown's mustache twitched with what might have been excitement. Or it could have been the urge to sneeze. "The dogs. You think the perp was possessing or controlling the dogs, and he wanted them to kill you and the sheriff."

"Yeah, I do."

"All of them at once?" Brown Two was skeptical. "You think we have multiple perps possessing animals?"

"Maybe. Or we may have someone who can control or possess more than one animal at a time. And yes, that's supposed to be impossible, but this case is just crammed with impossibilities."

"So how do we decide what to pursue?" Brown Two said, frustrated. "If everything's equally impossible . . ."

"That's why it's such fun working on Unit cases. We get to make it up as we go along." Lily sent her gaze around the room. "For now, we're focusing on the animal vics. Those dogs tried to kill me and Deacon for the same reason Meacham bludgeoned his family and Hodge decided to blast away at neighbors and strangers—because they were possessed by something that feeds off death. Which means that people in this community may be in danger from the family pet."

TWENTY-TWO

A shower had swept in, washing the air with the best smells in the world. Toby sat in his bed with the window open, which Grammy wouldn't like because the covers might get wet.

He didn't care. He didn't care what she liked or what anyone else liked or didn't like. They could all just leave him alone.

Especially *her*. She'd never had a problem doing that before.

He'd heard her. He'd been about to come downstairs and get some breakfast and see if Dad wanted to do something, maybe kick the ball around or go to the park so he could practice corner kicks. Then he heard her talking to Dad. His stomach had seized up and his throat had closed, almost as if he were scared.

He wasn't, dammit. He tried the word out in a whisper. "Dammit." It didn't make his stomach feel any better.

His door opened. Toby looked around, scowling. It was Dad, and he hadn't even knocked. "You're supposed to knock."

"Knocking implies I'd go away if you didn't give me permission to enter. I'm not waiting on permission. I'm not Grammy."

A worm of guilt squirmed around in Toby's gut. He'd yelled at Grammy to go away when she knocked. *Tough on her. She always takes Mom's side.* "I don't want to talk to her or you or—or anyone."

"Anyone meaning your mother, I take it." Dad came over and sat on Toby's bed—again without waiting to be asked. "You will apologize to Grammy."

Toby just scowled. He probably would. Just not yet. "You're gonna make me go down and be nice to Mom."

Dad shook his head. "No, I'm going to make you apologize to Grammy."

Surprise wiggled in so fast he couldn't stop it. "So it's okay if I don't want to talk to Mom?"

"I don't tell you what to want or not want. I sometimes tell you what you must do or not do. I've decided this one is your choice."

Curiosity made it hard to keep his anger hot, so he scowled extra. "How come?"

"More or less the same reason I allowed you to choose to speak with the press. If it's a mistake, it's one you can learn from."

"I hate her." His stomach roiled unhappily. "I'm pretty sure I do. What does she want, anyway?"

"She wants to talk with you. That's all I know."

"It's about the hearing, I bet. She didn't tell you why she's here?"

"She won't speak of her intentions until you come down."

And they needed to know. They needed to know why she was here, if she'd changed her mind about custody, what she was going to do. Toby's chin set stubbornly. "You could make her tell."

Dad's face turned hard, as if Toby had insulted him. "I do not *make* women do things against their will."

Shame added itself to the unhappy mix in his stomach. "You think she'll go away if I stay up here? Or come up and knock on my door and . . ." And that's who he'd wanted to yell at, he realized. Not Grammy. He'd wanted Mom to come to the door so he could yell at her to *go away.*

"I don't know. My guess is that she isn't leaving without speaking to you, but you can wait here and see." Rule paused. "I assume you've thought about the consequences of this choice."

He hadn't. He didn't want to think about her at all, but he couldn't make himself stop. "I don't want her here. I don't want to talk to her or look at her or—or anything." He wanted to keep hating her, but he might not. If he saw her, he might not hate her enough to . . . to keep from feeling other things.

"You're very angry with her. She hasn't put your needs first. But she's given you the chance to have those needs met by others, especially Grammy. She's spent time with you, but she's never stayed with you. She's let you down."

She hadn't come for Christmas. Toby swallowed and looked away.

He didn't need her to live here with him and Grammy, not all the time, but she hadn't come home for Christmas. That had been the one thing he could count on her for—that she'd be here, and she'd bring presents, and they'd eat turkey and dressing together, and she'd stay a few days. For a few days they'd all be a family like they were supposed to be.

Last Christmas, she hadn't come. She'd gotten a fancy new position with the AP on the other side of the world, and she hadn't come. And for all the months since Christmas, she hadn't come. When Grammy broke her leg, Dad and Lily had come and helped. Uncle Mark and Aunt Deirdre had, too. Mom had called, sure, but she hadn't come.

Now she had.

Toby looked down at his feet, which were up on the bed with the rest of him, on covers that were, maybe, a little damp. His stomach hurt. He couldn't think of what to say.

"You're in a place where none of your choices feel good, aren't you?" Dad had sympathy in his voice. Not pity, not poor-little-boy stuff. Just sympathy.

That sympathy unwound him and *stuff* burst out. "I just feel so much! It's too much! I don't know what to do with it all, and it's all mixed up! I wish I could shut it off, or barf it all up and get it out of me!"

Dad nodded as if that made sense, but he didn't answer. Instead, he pulled Toby close against him and sat still. Not talking, not holding on tight. Just being there with his whole body.

Toby leaned his head on Dad's chest and listened to his heartbeat, and after a while he felt a little better. Not a lot, but some. He sighed. "We need to know what she wants. Why she's here."

"It would help."

"I don't know what to do. I guess I should go down there, but I don't know what to do when I see her." He might start yelling at her, which would upset Grammy. But if he didn't yell . . . What if he cried? He blinked fast. He was *not* going to cry. "Dammit," he whispered, his head still on Dad's chest.

"Would you like a suggestion?"

"I guess." Dad must have heard the "dammit," but he hadn't said anything. For some reason that made it okay to straighten himself up and look at Dad, full on, for the first time since Dad came in.

Dad's eyes were real serious, not angry or worried or disappointed in him. "Don't plan out how you need to act when you see her. Plans like that come undone when the other person doesn't behave the way we'd pictured them behaving. And they usually don't."

That made sense. "Okay." Toby nodded and said it again. "Okay, let's go see what she wants." But he reached for Dad's hand so it would be *them* going downstairs, not just him.

She looked the same. That was all the think Toby could manage when he went into the den, where she'd been sitting on the couch beside Grammy. She'd stood up when he came in with Dad and now she stood there, smiling at him, but like it was hard to smile.

Maybe her hair was shorter than the last time he'd seen her. She had real dark hair, almost black. A lot darker than his. Dad's hair was dark, too. Grammy said Toby's hair probably came from her because she'd had light brown hair before it turned gray, so her genes had mixed in and lightened up

Toby's hair. Mom had dark eyes, too, and was taller than
Grammy or Lily. She was a pretty woman.

Her eyes were shiny and damp. "Hello, Toby."

Her voice made something inside him shaky. "Don't you
cry." His own voice came out gruff. "You'd better not start
crying."

"No promises." She laughed, but not like she thought she
was funny. "Not that you'd believe me if I did promise, I suppose. I understand that you're angry with me about Christmas."

That made him mad. She didn't *deserve* to understand
him. He tried to make his face stony, the way Dad did sometimes, though hardly ever at him.

"Well." She smoothed down her shirt, which was made of
something stretchy the color of tomatoes. "Maybe we should
sit down, then. I have some news," she added, doing what
she'd said and sitting on the couch.

Toby went to sit on the hearth, which was low and had
some pillows in Grammy's favorite colors—blue and green—
and faced the couch. Dad sat beside him and spoke in that
polite way he used when he was determined not to be mad.
"I'm certainly interested in your news, Alicia. Is it about the
custody hearing?"

"In a way." She rubbed her hands on her skirt this time, as
if her palms were damp. But it was Grammy she looked at,
not him and Dad.

"Then maybe you'll stop dragging this out." Grammy's
voice was crisp as a potato chip. Salty like one, too. "We haven't
even had breakfast yet."

Hurt flashed over Mom's face. Maybe she didn't like it that
Grammy hadn't asked her to eat with them. She smiled
brightly. "I think I'm allowed to make this particular announce-
ment my own way."

Dad said, "Does it have something to do with that gold
ring on your left hand?"

"Why, yes." Mom's smile was too big, too bright, like she
wanted to smile the rest of them into happiness. Or maybe she
wanted to make herself happy, as if her feelings might catch

up with her face if she smiled hard enough. "I got married last month, and my husband and I want Toby to live with us."

LILY wasn't sure why she was on Sherwood Lane. She'd had a surprisingly useful interview with the conspiracy nut, who'd gotten excited about being part of an investigation once she convinced him she wasn't hauling him off to some secret location. He'd given her a tentative ID on one of the dogs and was calling around, compiling a list of other missing pets

Now she had to build on that. Sherwood Lane wasn't exactly out of her way, but there was no reason for her to be here . . . no reason except Rule.

If this was the damned mate bond tugging at her . . . Almost, she turned around and headed back to the main drive.

But it didn't feel like the mate bond. She knew how that felt pretty well now, and it was a physical tug, not this . . . this emotional static. Like she wasn't thinking straight and wouldn't until she saw Rule.

Maybe she'd turned psychic. Cullen was due in sometime today, and she did need to talk to him. Maybe she'd psychically picked up on his arrival.

Lily snorted. More likely, she admitted, she was being stubborn. Uwharrie National Forest butted up against the woods where Rule had found the bodies. She wanted to talk to the ranger there about any unusual increase in the number of dead animals—but the ranger's station was over ten miles away. The mate bond wouldn't let her go that far, so she'd either have to send one of the other agents or get Rule to come with her.

It pissed her off. She . . . Hey, look at that! There was a white Taurus pulled up behind Rule's Mercedes. Automatically she took note of the plates. A rental? Cullen would be renting a car in Charlotte and driving in.

Huh. Maybe she *was* psychic.

Lily parked along the curb in front of the Asteglio house and got out.

The front door opened. A tall, dark-haired woman with

blunt, sensual features stepped out, saying something over her shoulder to Louise, who followed. Louise didn't look happy. The two of them were so involved in their conversation—which involved dinner plans and someone named James—that they didn't notice Lily until they were about six feet away.

The dark-haired woman finally saw her and jerked to a stop. Louise did, too. Her hand fluttered to her chest. "Oh—Lily. I wasn't expecting you at this hour."

"Lily?" The other woman's full lips curved up. "I see. You're short, aren't you? Much shorter than I'd imagined."

"And you're more rude than I'd imagined, given my acquaintance with your mother. You are Alicia Asteglio, right?"

Dark eyebrows lifted. "I was."

"Alicia," Louise chided, "you're beginning this poorly."

Alicia shrugged. "I do everything badly, according to you." She left it at that, stalking off to her car, where she paused. Her eyes were intent, but her voice was soft, the tone somewhere between coaxing and pleading. "I'm trying to make things right, Mama. Believe it or not, I am. You'll call about the time?"

Louise nodded once, tight-lipped.

Her daughter got in her car, slammed the door, and backed out quickly.

"You're upset," Lily said carefully.

"Upset?" Louise made a noise that was not a laugh, though maybe she'd meant it to be. "She got married. She got married last month and didn't tell me, didn't want me there . . . Yes, I'm upset. She thinks I should be happy for her. I suppose I am, but . . ." She shook her head.

Sounded like everything was all about Alicia. Her feelings counted. Her mother's didn't. Lily experienced a distinct twinge. She didn't do that to her own mother, did she? "Was this a sudden thing?"

"Sudden for me. I don't know about her. She's been living with James for the past six months, in Beirut." Abruptly Louise started for the house. "I've never met him. Spoken to him on the phone a few times, and he was pleasant enough, but what does that mean? Oh, never mind me. It's Toby I'm worried about."

Worry put a hitch in Lily's breath. "Is she going to oppose Rule's custody?"

"It's complicated. Everything to do with Alicia is complicated. Do come in, dear. Have you eaten?"

Lily assured her she didn't need to be fed, though she did check out the coffeepot as they passed the kitchen. Empty. Oh, well.

Rule and Toby were in the den—Rule on the phone, Toby sitting beside him, arms crossed, staring at the floor. Rule had his expression shut down. Toby had storms all over his.

Toby looked up as Lily entered behind Louise. "I'm not going to stay with her."

"She has legal custody of you still," his grandmother said wearily.

"Didn't say I wouldn't go. I said I wouldn't *stay.*"

Rule broke off his conversation. "You'll stay," he said tersely. "If you do go with your mother, you will not run away."

Toby's expression left that somewhat in doubt—especially considering he'd run away to his father once already. Lily looked at Louise, her eyebrows asking the question for her.

"Alicia has decided she wants Toby. She says she'll let him decide, however—if he comes to stay with her and her new husband first, for six months."

Lily's eyebrows shot back up. "Is she still living in Beirut?"

Louise shook her head. "She's in D.C. again. It's technically a demotion, because she'll be at a lower salary grade, but James—James French is her new husband—was transferred there by the agency he works for, and she wanted to come back to the U.S. with him."

Eight months ago Alicia had chosen her career over her son when she moved to Beirut. Apparently a lover rated more sacrifice. Lily did her best to keep her distaste from showing. "And getting married makes her want to be a full-time parent?"

"I'm surprised," Louise admitted, her voice low. "She wants this chance, for both her sake and Toby's, but she'll abide by Toby's wishes if he ends up choosing his father."

Lily looked at Rule. "Get it in writing."

Rule nodded, but his attention was clearly with whoever was on the other end of the line.

Louise sighed again. "He's talking to his attorney now."

"I'm not going to stay with her," Toby repeated.

Lily went to sit next to him on the couch. "Why not?"

He frowned, obviously thinking she was being stupid. "Because I want to live with Dad and you."

"And we want you to. Six months is a long time."

"Yeah! And she could have talked about it with me. She could have told me she was getting married to this James guy and asked if I wanted to live with them, but she didn't. She just up and says we've got to do things her way, or else."

"'Or else' meaning she'll fight Rule's custody suit?"

"She said she won't pull any punches, that it will all come out, and she made her face look like this"—his expression mimicked a fox, sly and knowing—"as if she knows secrets. But she doesn't. I never tell her any Nokolai stuff."

That didn't mean Alicia couldn't find out, figure out, or make up something. "It sounds like a choice between two things you really, really don't like—either stay with your mom for six months, or have a knock-down, drag-out battle for custody."

"Dad *won't*." Toby's eyes glistened. "He says six months isn't forever, and that I don't understand how bad it would be if we had a big fight in court."

"Well, he's probably right about that. What doesn't he understand?"

Toby blinked, then frowned slightly, thinking that over.

Louise stroked Toby's hair, but spoke to Lily. "Rule has been very restrained, but he's upset, of course. I'm upset. Toby's upset . . . I suppose Alicia is, too, though I wish she'd talked to me about her plans. I wish . . . I don't think she's doing the wrong thing, necessarily. But she's going about it the wrong way."

Lily kept her voice mild. "You think it would be good for Toby to live with her?"

"Not permanently, no. If I could say . . ." She sighed. "Well, I can't. But I think Toby should have a chance to mend things with her. She'll continue to be his mother no matter who he lives with."

Rule disconnected. His eyes went straight to Lily. "You didn't stop here to see if we were having a crisis."

"I thought you might be able to go see a forest ranger with me." She spread her hands. "Obviously not a good idea right now. What did your lawyer say?"

"He advises me to take what she's offering, but to go through the judge so it's binding. We'll suggest a shorter period than six months, too." He gave Toby a nod. "There's no saying we'll get it, but we'll try. He's going to find out what he can about James French."

Louise gave Rule a chiding look. "I'm sure that's not necessary. They're coming to dinner tonight. We'll get to know him then."

Tonight? Oh, the fun just kept on coming. Lily stood and said to Louise, "Look at it this way. If we have some of the facts about French's background, we won't be grilling him over the pot roast." Lily gave Rule a glance. "I might be able to help with that."

He gave her the ghost of a grin. "I hope you don't mean the pot roast."

"No." Louise shook her head. "It will not be pot roast. We just had pot roast. And James," she added grimly, "is vegan."

Toby frowned. "What's vegan? Is that where he's from?"

"It means he doesn't eat meat. No beef, chicken, or fish."

Toby's mouth fell. "Not at all?"

"No," Lily answered when a glance at Louise showed her to be preoccupied. "Not if he's a practicing vegan. He also won't wear leather or eat eggs or dairy products. Nothing that comes from an animal."

"Lasagna," Louise muttered. "No, no, can't make lasagna without cheese. I'd better check my cookbooks." She started for the kitchen.

"There will be vegan recipes online," Lily called after her.

"I can look them up for you," Toby said, shoving to his feet. He glanced at his father and whispered quite audibly, "It's not like I care about this stupid James guy, but Grammy hates it if she doesn't have the right stuff for guests."

Rule laid a hand on Toby's head. "It's all right if you like Mr. French, Toby. That takes nothing from me. At Clanhome you care about and are cared for by many people, not just me."

"But Mr. French isn't clan."

"No, but as your mother's husband, he's family. We don't always like everyone in our family, but it's perfectly acceptable to do so."

"Is it okay if I don't like him?"

"As long as you're polite, yes. But I hope you'll give him a chance."

Toby looked scornful. "He doesn't eat meat."

"He's not lupus, so we shouldn't require him to live as we do. Though we'll have to make sure your mother understands that your dietary needs do include meat, if you end up staying with her for a time. Now, I could use a run. What about you?"

Toby brightened. "Yeah! Maybe we could run over to the park and practice corner kicks? And if Justin and Talia could come—"

The doorbell rang.

Lily glanced that way. "I'll get it."

Louise had pulled a thick cookbook out of a cabinet. She tucked it under one arm. "No, dear. I prefer to answer my own door."

Lily followed. Not that she thought someone was going to jump Louise, but—okay, she did think that. "Use the spyhole, okay? I don't want—"

Too late. Louise had already swung the door open. Her hand fluttered to her chest and her words came out in a whisper. "Oh, my sweet Jesus."

TWENTY-THREE

THE man on the porch had eyes the unlikely blue of the Aegean Sea. His hair was cinnamon and spice, his features a marvel of symmetry, with the sensual mouth balanced by a jaw firm enough to keep all that beauty from leaning toward the feminine. As for his body . . . well, most women would agree it deserved an hour or two of study, like any work of art.

Of course, the perfect jaw was stubbled, the spicy hair hadn't been combed, and the flawless body was clad in jeans worn to threads in spots and a T-shirt that supported people's right to arm bears. His athletic shoes were almost new, however—and muddy. No socks.

He hadn't worn socks on his wedding day, either. Or shoes. Or a shirt.

The ocean eyes were amused. "Hello, love. If you're not going to shoot me today, would you mind putting your gun away?"

Lily slid her weapon back in place without apologizing and stepped aside. "Good to see you, too. Louise, this is Cullen Seabourne. Cullen, this is—"

"Cullen's here!" Toby cried. "Hey, Dad, Cullen's here!" The

thud of running feet proved that not all lupi moved as quietly as drifting snow. Toby darted around Grammy and Lily to hurl himself at the scruffy demigod on the porch.

Cullen caught him and swung him up to ride on his shoulders. "You've grown again. Just keep doing that, don't you?"

Toby grinned. "It's my habit. I like growing. Maybe I'll be taller than you when I'm finished. Did you bring Cynna?" He peered around, as if Cullen might have stashed Cynna someplace close by. "Where's Cynna?"

"In San Diego by now, if her flight wasn't delayed."

Toby twisted to say seriously to his grandmother, "Cynna's cool. She's having Cullen's baby in a couple or three months—I forget when, exactly. She an' Cullen went to Edge, then when they came back they got married, only I couldn't go to the wedding, so I missed seeing the dragon. Some people in the clans are mad about him getting married, but I'm not. Dad's not, either, but Cullen says Dad's jealous 'cause he'd like to get married to Lily, too, only he can't because he's Lu Nuncio and all, but I don't—hey!"

Cullen had turned Toby upside down and was holding him by the ankles, shaking him gently. "Way too much information, short stuff."

Toby giggled and tried to climb up his own body to right himself.

"I see." Louise's response, delivered in a faint voice, said she didn't see at all. "Well, it's a pleasure to meet you, Mr. Seabourne. Rule told me you were coming, but in all the confusion I'd quite forgotten. Do come in."

"Take off those shoes first," Lily said. "Did you walk here in the rain or something?"

Cullen glanced down at his shoes as if he'd forgotten he was wearing them. "Hmm. No, I made a stop along the way. Down, sport," he said, depositing Toby on the porch. He bent to untie his shoes.

"We're gonna go run, then kick the ball around some," Toby said excitedly. "Maybe Justin and Talia can come, too. They're my friends. Maybe you can come with us."

Cullen glanced up from wet, knotted shoestrings, smiling. "Not right away, I'm afraid. I need to talk to your father about some clan business, and I suspect Lily means to snag me for some assistance with her case."

"Now?" Toby's face fell. He looked at his father. "Do you have to do clan business now?"

Rule hesitated only a second. "It can wait until after lunch," he said as easily as if he weren't desperate to hear what Cullen had flown here to tell him. "But I don't think Lily can postpone her business as easily as I can. We'd better let her have first shot at him."

"Hey," Cullen said. "No shooting."

That made Toby giggle.

"Go," Rule said. "Call your friends, see if they can join us. Whether they can or not, we're headed for the park. Oh, and bring me my shoes, please."

"Okay." Toby took off for the stairs.

Cullen gave Rule a thoughtful glance. "You don't mind waiting on our business?"

There was a longish pause, and Lily saw Rule's lips quiver once, ever so slightly, before he said, "He needs to run."

That telltale quiver meant he'd been subvocalizing. It was the way lupi communicated when they didn't want others to hear, speaking softer than a whisper without moving their lips. For a brief period several months ago, Lily had been able to hear subvocalizations, too, but it hadn't lasted. *The mate bond giveth and the mate bond taketh away.* Capriciously.

Rule smiled at Louise. "I'll order pizza for lunch. If Toby's friends wish to join us—"

"By all means," Louise said. "Justin and Talia are always welcome."

Cullen had finally gotten his shoes off. He set them neatly beside the door and padded inside barefoot. "Mrs. Asteglio." He gave her the kind of smile guaranteed to melt anyone equipped with a double-X set of chromosomes. "I'm glad to have this chance to meet you."

Louise pinked up again. "It's my pleasure. You're quite a

favorite of Toby's, you know. Do come sit down and let me know what I can get you. There's some carrot cake left, and I can put on some coffee. Or would you prefer iced tea? It will take a few minutes to brew, but I refuse to use that nasty instant."

"I never turn down cake, with or without tea. However . . ." He sent Lily a glance. "I'm afraid I have to be terribly rude and speak privately with Lily about her case first."

"Of course. I'll get the tea started."

"In here," Lily said to Cullen, gesturing at the living room. Louise wouldn't intentionally eavesdrop, but the open arrangement of den and kitchen would make it hard not to overhear.

Rule put a hand on her arm and spoke quietly. "Cullen called me from the airport. I told him about the situation with Alicia and about Talia's ghosts."

She glanced at Cullen. "Did you—"

She was stopped by the herd of elephants on the stairs combined with Toby hollering out the great news that his friends would join them at the park, and here were his dad's shoes, and could they go now?

Rule thanked him, slipped on the shoes and tied them, and looked at Lily. "You can have Cullen until lunch. I need him back then." He said that lightly enough, but she had some idea of what it cost him to wait.

Lily put her hand on his cheek, rubbing the freshly shaved skin with her thumb. "Until lunch."

He bent and gave her a quick, hard kiss. A moment later the door closed behind him and Toby, and Lily clicked back into cop mode. She looked at Cullen, who was no longer smiling. Somehow that confirmed what she'd suspected. "You have something for me."

"I think so. I'll need to see the last man who was possessed—he's in the hospital, right?—and his house."

"Hodge is getting his pacemaker replaced this morning, so that'll have to wait, but I can get you into his house. It's on the corner." She pulled out her phone. "Go eat cake and flirt with Louise. I'm going to rearrange my morning." She'd take Brown's advice and delegate.

* * *

FOR once Cullen did as he was told. They left Louise smiling and telling him to be sure to join the rest of them for dinner that night. "Come at six thirty. We'll eat around seven."

Cullen thanked her and accepted before Lily could find a subtle way to warn him about the undertow he'd be wading into. Not that Cullen minded a little conflict, armed or otherwise.

Stepping outside was like walking into the bathroom after someone had taken a hot shower. The brief spat of rain hadn't done much to clear the air of either heat or humidity. "That invitation you just accepted," she said quietly to Cullen. "Alicia and her new husband are coming to dinner. He's vegan, so it will be meatless."

"I'd better eat well earlier, then," he said. "Wouldn't miss this chance to meet the new hubby. Alicia's never shown an interest in day-to-day parenting—swooping in for the occasional weekend suited her fine, I'd say. I'm wondering if this sudden uptick in motherliness is due to him. Perhaps it's his idea entirely."

That seemed possible. "Did you bring any real clothes? Louise will be insulted if you show up in that T-shirt."

He glanced down at her, amused. "Really, Lily, you don't have to explain women's expectations to me. I could demonstrate, if you wish, what I know about female . . . expectations." He lingered on the last word with just the right hint of lasciviousness.

She knew he did that to annoy her. And dammit, it worked. "Tacky, Cullen."

"No, it would be tacky if I groped you. I can't flirt with most women anymore. They have a lamentable tendency to hope I mean it. And since I'm fast enough to dodge if you decide to belt me, I . . . Hold on a minute." He interrupted himself as they reached his rental car. "I need to get something."

"Cullen." She chewed it over with her conscience while he opened the car door and delved inside. It was okay to ask, she decided. "What are you going to tell Rule about Toby?"

"Can't tell you."

She stiffened. "I know he deserves to learn it first, but he's not here and I'm involved, too."

"I meant exactly what I said," he explained—patiently, for him, since he snapped out the words without burning anything. He straightened, holding a small brown paper bag in one hand and his backpack in the other, and slammed the car door. "I *can't* tell you. I'm not supposed to tell Rule, either, but I will—if he promises not to repeat it to his father."

She blinked. "You want him to keep secrets from his Rho? Is that allowed?"

"Of course not. Tell me about these ghosts the little girl has seen. Rule said they screamed at her."

"That's the way Talia put it." They fell into step together, heading for Hodge's house. "The screaming is distressing or painful for her. What's in the bag?"

"Grave dirt. She said the other ghosts were frightened?"

"Yes—at least, her main contact among them told her that. The one she calls the tall man. What in the world do you need grave dirt for?"

"A spell. Like I said, I stopped off on the way here. And let me tell you, it was not easy to find dry grave dirt. This child—Talia—said the ghosts call him a ghost-maker?"

"Yes."

He frowned. "I need to talk to her."

"If Rule's able to bring them back to Mrs. Asteglio's for pizza, you'll have a chance to do that. Though I don't know that the parents will agree. They're not fans of lupi, from what the kids said last night."

"Oh, Rule will probably talk to them himself. I told him I need to see the girl. Not only will he sound utterly trustworthy—"

"He *is* utterly trustworthy."

"Which makes it easier for him," Cullen agreed cheerfully. "I have to work much harder at it, and usually have to settle for appearing harmless. No one mistakes Rule for harmless, but he has that whole prince-of-my-people thing going for him."

True. "Cullen, Talia said Toby keeps the ghosts away. Rule had never heard of ghosts being repelled by lupi."

"Oh, that." He tossed one hand, flinging away a foolish notion. "No, they aren't repelled by us, but our innate magic suppresses the type of magic used by mediums. I'm not sure of the mechanism, but the Etorri Rhej . . ." He glanced at her, smiling. "You've met her."

"Oh, yes." Lily smiled in spite of herself, thinking of that wedding.

"She says the effect is heavily localized. She has to move only a few feet away from one of us for her Gift to function. Of course, she's an extremely strong medium, so Talia's Gift may be tamped down at a greater distance. But that's what the girl is experiencing—a dampening of her Gift, not a repulsion of ghosts."

A repulsion of ghosts. Was that like a gaggle of geese or an exaltation of larks? Lily noticed that her smile had lingered. Funny how Cullen could have that effect when he wasn't making her want to punch him. "Is there any way you can make a shield for her, or something along those lines? I'm worried about those mind-ripping screams."

"A shield, no. I haven't deciphered the ones I was given enough to re-create them. But didn't you say the sheriff here has a spell that damps down his Gift?"

"I don't know if he'll share it. He doesn't want anyone to know about his Gift, so he won't be happy I told you. Can ghosts do real damage to Talia?"

"Normally, no." Cullen turned grim. "But these aren't normal ghosts."

"I seldom hear 'normal' and 'ghosts' used together. What's different with these?"

"You're going to have to wait until I confirm something. Is that the house?"

"Yes. You see something funny about it?" Cullen was like her, in a way. She touched magic. He saw it.

He gave a noncommittal hum and strode for the front door.

"Let me get the key." She dug into her purse.

"Not necessary." He wiggled his fingers at the knob—reached for it, turned it, and opened the door.

She huffed out a breath. "You did that to annoy me."

"Certainly, but I also hate to pass up a chance to show off. No, don't come in. Stay on the threshold for now. You don't soak up magic like a dragon would, but you might have an effect on a spell this delicate."

Startled, she stopped. "You think I can affect spells?"

"Undetermined," he murmured, kneeling in the center of the living room with his little bag of dirt. He pulled a candle stub out of his backpack. "But possible, especially with spells that depend more on finesse than power. I'd like to do some tests, but . . ." He sighed as he drew out a square sheet of brown paper covered with arcane symbols, spreading it on the floor in front of him. "Not the time for that, is it? There's never enough time."

"You aren't setting a circle."

"Circles keep things out or in. That's not the goal here." He placed the candle stub dead center on the paper, frowned, and moved it an imperceptible fraction closer. "Now hush."

She hushed. He began chanting, his voice soft, the words utterly alien. It was only a few phrases, she realized, repeated over and over. He did that awhile, then waved at the candle stub. It lit.

Still chanting quietly, he dug into the bag, then held his fist over the candle flame and cried out sharply. "*Ka!*"

He flung the dirt up. The candle flame sputtered—and sprinkled itself over the paper like burning dust. And the dirt he'd tossed hung, suspended, in the air. As Lily stared, it began moving, churning in a slow circle, as if stirred by an invisible finger.

Then it exploded in a single, soundless burst.

So did the bits of fire.

"Holy hell." Cullen sat back on his heels. "It worked."

TWENTY-FOUR

"**YOU** didn't think it would?" Lily snapped. She darted inside to slap at Hodge's recliner, where several of the bits of splashed fire had landed. "Dammit, Cullen, get some water or something."

"Oh. Sorry, I forgot." He held out both hands. All the baby flames leaped toward him, banging together to make a single large flame that danced a few inches above his raised palms . . . then faded away.

Lily quit slapping at the upholstery. "You're showing off again, but at least this time it was effective. What did this spell do? Other than sling fire and dirt around Hodge's living room, that is."

"It's a Finding spell, of sorts." Cullen rose, dusting off his jeans. "One I adapted from a couple of Cynna's *kielezo*. I've used it to find haunts, but couldn't be sure it would react to traces of the scattered dead." He frowned. "I expected the dust to go flying. I wonder why the fire did, too."

"Figure it out later." The scattered dead: that had an ominous ring. "Are you telling me we're after a ghost?"

"Yes and no. He's more of a ghost-maker, like the ghosts said. But he's definitely dead. Well, mostly dead."

"Mostly?" This was one of the want-to-punch him times. "I'm sure that means something."

"I'm afraid this is one of those good news, bad news deals, love. The good news is that I can tell you what has been possessing people."

"And that would be?"

"A wraith."

She frowned, trying to match the word with anything she'd heard or read. "Doesn't that just mean ghost?"

He shook his head. "Ghosts occur naturally from time to time, and are almost always harmless. Wraiths are far from harmless. And far from natural."

"Keep talking."

"They . . ." He ran a hand over his head, spiking his hair. "I'm laying this out poorly. I'll start with the historical record. Wraiths existed in the past, but there hasn't been a confirmed account of the creation of a wraith—"

"Creation?"

"Yes, they're made, and yes, that means you have a human practitioner to look for. Don't interrupt," he said, scowling. "Let your questions pile up while I lay out what little I know, which is . . . ambiguous, unsteady, unreliable.

"As I was saying," he continued, beginning to pace, "I'm unaware of any confirmed accounts of a wraith for perhaps two hundred years. I have reason to think their absence is mostly due to a lack of available power, not the eradication of spells to create one. Because the accounts are so old, most of what I tell you is anecdotal at best. The stories often contradict each other . . . but there are stories of wraiths in almost every culture. Hungry ghosts, they're sometimes called, or the scattered dead. They both create and consume death magic."

"How—"

He stopped, fixing her with a firm stare. "Hush. There are a few, very few, mentions of possession by wraiths. I would have called those bits highly apocryphal, but it looks like they were accurate. I need my references." He brooded on that briefly, then resumed his restless motion. "Almost all of my texts and scraps of texts are back home. Cynna's going to check them for me."

"You talked to her about it?"

"Yes. She has a Vodun acquaintance, a *mambo*—that's a female priest—who has told her a few things about wraiths. They could be complete fabrications, made up to frighten or impress. The woman is not exactly reliable. But Vodun deals with spirits, so its practitioners are probably the best contemporary source on the subject."

He paused again, his expression intent. "I'll give you a summary of the things that hold true in most of the stories, both those I've heard about or read and what Cynna's contact told her. First, wraiths are created by a practitioner delving into forbidden arts. That part's solid. To create one, the practitioner must blend magic and spirit in a—call it an unholy manner. It may be an attempt to create a soul-slave. That's not solid, but it has a good probability."

"What's a—"

"Save it. Second, wraiths may or may not be able to kill directly—that's one of those areas where the stories contradict each other—but they can certainly hasten death for the ill or infirm. They feed off the act of dying, the transition from mortal to something else. In feeding, they create damaged ghosts. And no, we don't know why. Normal ghosts fear the damaged ones and the wraiths who make them. That's what tipped me off that you had a wraith here.

"Also, I have reason to believe it would take either enormous power or skill on a level of an adept to create a wraith. There aren't any adepts around, so I believe yours was made during the power winds of the Turning. That's the only time there would have been enough free magic available. All right." He gave her a single nod. "Ask your questions."

"Why do you think it would take so much power?"

Magnificent blue eyes narrowed in irritation. "I should have known. How is it you're able to zero in on the one thing I don't want to talk about?"

"Sheer, mind-boggling talent. Usually the things people don't want to tell me are exactly what I need to know. So talk."

"All right, all right. It won't help you, but I don't want you wasting your delightful obsessiveness on a distraction. I once saw a spell intended to create a wraith."

She took a quick step closer. "You saw it? But of course that helps. If you know how they're made—"

"I don't. I burned it."

Lily stared. "You burned it." She shook her head. "I would have voted you the man least likely to destroy any spell, no matter how icky."

His face was tight. "Icky. That's one word for it. There was a . . . miasma about the very parchment it was written on. A foulness. Two layers of reality, and the one underneath was . . ." He lifted both hands. "I can't describe it to one who doesn't see what I do, but that spell was abomination."

"If you burned it, how do you know it would take so much power?"

"I read part of it before I realized what it was."

"So what do you remember about it?"

"I don't," he said curtly. "I have been careful not to remember. There was this compulsion . . . Mind you, this was before I had my shields. Years before. I think the spell may have drawn me to it."

Her eyebrows shot up. "A sentient spell."

"Hardly. But there was something about it, something that could crawl inside you . . . Evil accumulates, just as holiness can." He shrugged. Cullen was as uncomfortable discussing religion and spirituality as she was. "The point is, I saw enough to understand that there were two ways to implement the spell. One required great knowledge; the other, great power."

She took a moment to order her questions. "What's a soul-slave?"

"Probably impossible, but during the Purge some sorcerers were accused of trying to create one by binding a soul after death." He shrugged. "I've never put much store in those accusations. Sorcerers were also accused of eating babies and drinking the blood of virgins—anything to whip up enough hysteria to do the job, which was killing, maiming, and blinding people like me. Some of whom, admittedly, were not nice folks, but the wholesale butchery . . . Well, that's not today's subject, is it?"

"Okay, You said wraiths hasten death. Hospitals have dying people. What can we do to protect them?"

"I have no idea."

"Cullen—"

"A really strong protective circle might work. I could make one that would, but I can't make one that strong that's larger than about ten feet. And I can't spend all my time at the hospital, holding a circle around one or two patients."

She took a breath, let it out slowly. She'd come back to that later. "Next question. If the spell was cast at the Turning . . . that's nearly seven months ago, but it gives me a place to start. Are there likely to be any unusual ingredients? Stuff I could trace?"

"Blood and death. The practitioner needed blood from someone who was dying. Then he needed their death. It takes a death to make a wraith."

Of course. Of course. Lily tapped her fingers on her thigh. "Then I need to find out who died at the Turning. Someone in Halo or nearby, right? If a wraith is like a ghost that way, I mean. Ghosts are bound to a place or, more rarely, an object."

His eyebrows lifted. "You've done some homework."

She waved that away. "Ruben had this panel about it. Is a wraith like a ghost? Bound to a certain area?"

"Most likely, yes. If the stories are true."

Progress. "I'm looking for a violent death, right? Death magic requires violence."

"A wraith creates and consumes death magic, but the spell to create one—damn, how to put this? The spell is just that, a spell. A relatively simple working, not a ritual. I suspect any death could be used, but the spell caster would have to be present at that death."

"So I've got two perps, and one of them, the spell caster, is human enough to arrest." That pleased her on several levels. "He or she would have been present when someone died at the Turning. That gives me something solid to look for. When we find him or her . . ." Lily frowned, turning it over in her mind and not liking what she came up with. "I guess we get the human perp to stop the inhuman one."

He sighed. "You'll remember I said this was a good news, bad news deal. We've arrived at the bad news."

"Persuading the perp won't be easy. The law wasn't designed to cover this sort of situation, but maybe with the promise of a reduced sentence—not that the bastard deserves it, but . . ." Cullen was shaking his head. "What?"

"The stories about wraiths are consistent about a few things. The practitioner who creates one must feed it to maintain control. A wraith who feeds on its own has broken free of its creator."

She absorbed that. "You think this wraith is no longer controlled by its creator?"

"It's possible, even probable, given the sudden change in its feeding pattern. And if so, I have no idea how to stop it."

"Mage fire burns anything. You've always said that."

"Lily, even mage fire won't kill someone who's already dead."

TWENTY-FIVE

LUNCH was lively. As Rule expected, Lily didn't join them—
he gave her some pizza to eat while she worked—but Toby's
friends did. So did Louise's neighbor. Connie Milligan was a
short, merry woman about Louise's age with unlikely brown
hair and a sly sense of humor. She and Cullen hit it off.

"Uh-oh," Toby said when Louise invited her friend to join
them for dinner.

Rule leaned closer and murmured, "I thought you liked
Mrs. Milligan."

"I do," Toby whispered back, "but it's growing. It started
out just a dinner, and now it's turning into a dinner *party*."

"That's a problem?"

Toby looked as if his faith in his father's wisdom had been
shaken. "I guess you haven't ever seen Grammy when she has
a party. She frenzies. We're gonna clean *everything*."

"Hmm." Rule nodded knowingly. "Worse than Lily was at
Christmas when her parents were coming?"

"Well . . . close. But Lily had decorating stuff to do, too,"
Toby said in a fair-minded way, "only she didn't have time
because of all her work, so probably that was worse. Except

that we did have a couple days for that cleaning, and now we've just got this afternoon."

When the pizza was gone, Rule said he and Cullen would walk Justin and Talia home "as soon as we all clean up." This prompted protests from Louise, who insisted on tidying up, and startled looks from Justin and Talia, who doubtless thought themselves able to walk the short distance on their own. Toby whispered something to Justin, who whispered to Talia, and both children looked at Cullen with questions in their eyes.

And Toby, of course, wanted to go along, so Rule reminded him of math. He grimaced, but accepted the necessity. Finally they set off.

Walking the children home was both necessary and useful. Obviously Rule couldn't let them go alone, not with every person they saw a potential killer. Also, Cullen needed to help Talia gain some protection. Rule wasn't entirely sure what a wraith was—Cullen's description had been brief when they spoke on the phone, in part because Rule's focus was fragmented. No doubt Lily had pulled more details from him. But the danger was obvious, after what happened yesterday.

And once they dropped the children off, he and Cullen would be able to talk where Toby couldn't overhear.

Oh, God. Oh, Lady, let him say there is no chance of Toby developing the wild cancer.

As soon as Rule thought that, he knew it was foolish. There was always a chance. But the cancer was rare in Nokolai, very rare, and had barely crossed Rule's mind before. Now it was lodged right in front, a sullen lump poisoning every other thought.

The air was sweating under a sullen sky hazed by clouds. Once more they took the alley, needing its relative privacy. They stayed on the grassy edges—the red clay was slick and full of puddles.

They were a few steps from the gate when Justin said, excited, "Toby says you can help Talia, Mr. Seabourne."

"It's more that I hope to show her how to help herself." He

smiled at Talia. "I understand that you're a pretty good medium, but you have no control of your Gift."

Talia's eyes were large. "Are you a medium, too?"

"No, my skills lie in other areas. I can't teach you specifics about controlling your Gift, but I can show you how to raise a protective circle."

"That's magic, right?" Talia exchanged a glance with her brother. "Daddy wouldn't like it if I did magic. He thinks magic is wicked."

"Normally I wouldn't encourage a child to go against her parents' wishes, but this is not a normal situation. You may be in danger."

"What kind of danger?" Talia whispered.

"To your mind. I don't know enough about how your Gift functions to say for certain, but those screaming ghosts worry me. I want you to have a way of protecting yourself from them, if necessary."

Justin frowned. "We're all in danger, aren't we? Something is making people kill people. That's a lot bigger danger than ghosts. Ghosts don't hurt people. Will your circle protect her from whatever wants people to kill?"

"Hmm. How to put this? You two are good at keeping secrets, I'm told." They both nodded seriously. "Well, for now this part has to be secret. The thing that's making some people kill is called a wraith. When this wraith possesses someone, it takes over the body and uses that body to kill. A circle won't protect you from bullets."

Justin's eyes were large. "Can this wraith possess *anyone*?"

"We don't know yet. Probably not, but we don't know the parameters it operates under. Talia, you have an advantage the rest of us lack. You'd be able to see the wraith. If you see something that . . . hmm. Tell me what ghosts look like to you."

"Like people, only not as solid. You can kind of see through them even when they're real present. They're not all bloody or scary or anything. The older they get, the more bleached-out and wispy-looking, and finally they just fade away. Except for the tall man. He's wispy sometimes; almost solid, others. I think it's up to him how solid he looks." She frowned unhappily. "But the newest ones, the ones this wraith made, they're all wispy like they're really old."

"Do these new ghosts look exactly like the old, wispy ones? Think about it a minute. This may be important."

She did as he asked, looking at her feet as they walked along the dirt and ruts of the alley. "They've got holes in them," she said after a moment's contemplation. "Or not holes, exactly, but they aren't the same see-through everywhere. Parts of them are a lot thinner than others."

"That helps. Thank you. Well, this wraith probably won't look like a person. It will be see-through the way ghosts are, but it might be just a blob, or a mixed-up version of a person, or something that isn't shaped like a human at all. I suspect it will be dark and murky, not pale, and it may be thinner in places, the way the damaged ghosts are. If you see something like that, Talia, I want you to get away quick. As fast as you can."

"You don't think I should make a circle?"

"No. If you see the wraith, you run. Period. If you get away and can't see it anymore, you call Lily and let her know where you saw it. The circle is to protect you from the screaming ghosts."

Talia sighed heavily. "I don't like this. I don't like it at all."

"Well, duh," said her sympathetic brother. "At least you'll see this wraith if it comes around."

Cullen switched his focus to the boy, his voice and smile light. "One thing that may help the rest of us is that this wraith is not good at acting like a person. If someone you know acts a little bit funny, well, he's probably okay. If he were possessed, he'd be acting a whole *bunch* funny."

The kids giggled, as much from pent-up feelings as humor. Cullen began describing the casting of a circle to Talia. And Rule's thoughts went back to the sodden lump of fear squatting at the front of his mind.

He'd had time to think . . . or perhaps had at last begun to think instead of obsessing over the lump or denying it existed. Cullen had assured him that the anecdotal evidence of a link between a too-young sensing of the Change and the wild cancer was highly exaggerated. Very well. But Rule could see no connection between that assurance and Cullen's sudden need to fly here and speak to him in person.

Unless Cullen could *see* the early appearance of the cancer. That was possible. The cancer was magically wrought. Cullen saw magic. Maybe the assurances he'd offered were true, but he still wanted to check Toby out.

Wouldn't he have told Rule that, though? Why would he—

"Mr. Turner?"

Rule dragged himself back to the present. They'd reached the gate to Justin and Talia's yard, and it was just as well his protection hadn't been needed. He'd been too deep in thought-circles to notice anything less than a machine gun fusillade.

At the moment Cullen was handing Talia a piece of chalk and talking about the need for a physical component. Rule looked down at her brother's worried face. "Yes?"

"Do you believe in God?"

Oh, God, Rule thought—and noticed the irony of his irreverence, but didn't smile. "Yes." Probably not the humanlike deity the boy had been taught to believe in, but there was certainly a Source.

"Why does He let bad things happen? I asked Mom and she said everything happens by His will, but I don't see why He'd want those people to get killed or Mr. Hodge to get possessed. Daddy said we're not supposed to question, but have faith, but that doesn't *help*."

"Well." If there was a God—the sort of personal, got-a-plan-for-you God so many people believed in—Rule felt sure She was having a good laugh at him right now. "As I said, I believe in God. I don't try to define Her."

"Her?" Justin was shocked.

"A personal bias," Rule explained. "I tend to think of deity in the feminine, which I'm sure is no more accurate than defining deity in the masculine."

"I have no idea what you just said."

Rule grinned and tousled the boy's hair. "I used fancy words to say that I don't know why bad things happen."

"Oh. Me, neither. Do you believe in prayer?"

"Ah . . ."

"Daddy says God always answers prayers, but sometimes the answer is 'no.' I think," Justin confided, "the answer is mostly no, 'cause God hardly ever does what I ask Him to. But Mr. Seabourne told Talia to pray when she sets her circle. He said God always helps if you ask Him to when you're making a circle."

Rule managed not to shoot Cullen a startled look, but it was a near thing. "I wouldn't turn to Cullen for spiritual advice, but he knows magic. If he says prayer will help her, it will."

"Oh. Okay." Frown and worry faded. "I didn't know if he— wow!"

Cullen was turning in a quick circle, pointing at the ground—and drawing a thin ring of fire with that pointing finger. "There. Come closer, and don't be distracted by the fire—that's just the quickest way for me to set a circle. Concentrate on the air around me. What's different about it?"

Talia squinted at what looked like perfectly ordinary air to Rule. "I don't see anything," she said, disappointed.

"Different Gifts respond to a circle different ways. You might hear it, or feel warmth or discomfort, or just sense a different energy."

"Oh—you mean that humming? I can barely hear it. That's your circle?"

"Yes. Now put your hand through the air above the circle."

She stretched out a tentative hand. The fire vanished. "It's gone!"

"Very few circles can withstand anything physical, and once something crosses a circle, the magic dissipates. But now you know how to tell when you've set your circle correctly. That's your goal—to set a circle that hums to you."

She looked dubious. "Okay."

"You won't set your circle the way I did. I draw on Fire.

Your element is spirit." He smiled. "I want you to try it now. Draw your circle . . . Wait." He grabbed a stick from the ground and handed it to her. "Use this. Draw your circle, sit in its center, close your eyes, and ask for help. Then imagine that humming sound coming from you, surrounding you, protecting you."

Talia did as he said, scraping the outline of a circle in the dirt, then folding thin, caramel-colored legs to sit tailor-fashion in the red dirt. She closed her eyes. To Rule's vision, absolutely nothing happened.

Justin frowned, fidgeted, and said, "What's she doing?"

"Hey!" Talia's eyes snapped open. "You ruined it. I had it—at least, I think I did . . ." Her voice trailed off.

"You cast a circle." Cullen was as certain as the girl wasn't. Of course, he'd have seen it. "It was thin and dissipated quickly, but to get one on the first try is excellent. Now all it takes is practice."

"Why do I need to practice if God's helping me?"

"Didn't say God would do it for you, did I? Do you know how to ride a bicycle?"

"Of course I can!"

"You weren't born knowing, though. I'll bet someone taught you, helped you. Your mom? Your dad?" She nodded to the second guess. "He didn't help by hopping on your bike and riding it himself. What did he do?"

"Ran along behind me and pushed until I could balance and pedal at the same time." Her eyebrows squinched down. "You mean that's how God will help, too. I have to get on the bike—I mean, cast the circle—myself, but He'll push."

"More or less. For now, I want you to work on balance, not worry about pedaling." He gave her the easy smile that charmed females of every age. "The good news is that it doesn't take much pedaling to keep out a ghost. They're weak."

"Even the screaming ones?"

"Even them. I told you, Talia, the ghosts are using *your* Gift to speak to you—even when they scream instead of talking. With a circle you deny them access to your Gift. Without it, they can't do much."

She got up, dusting off the seat of her shorts—a useless effort, since the damp red clay stuck like glue. "I can do this."

"Certainly. You started up a circle right away. You're a natural." He bent and whispered something in her ear. She grinned.

Rule watched his friend talk with the girl. He'd made her comfortable with her Gift, comfortable enough to cast a spell she'd need for protection. He would, Rule thought, make a good father when the time came. With children, the notoriously impatient sorcerer had endless patience.

Normally Rule did, too. Today he wanted to drag Cullen away. The girl needed instruction, but it could wait until after Rule spoke to Cullen and heard . . . whatever it was he had to hear.

He didn't grimace. The habit of concealment went deep enough to prevent that, but he gave himself a mental bitch-slap. Sure, Talia could wait, and Cullen could come back here later . . . knock on her parents' door and explain that he needed to see their eleven-year-old daughter alone for a while. Yes, that would work.

Rule took a slow breath. And waited.

At last Cullen told the kids to go in before their parents wondered what was keeping them. The second the gate closed behind them, Rule strode down the alley, heading away from the Appletons' house.

He knew he couldn't run away, not figuratively or literally, but movement helped. Still, the first question he asked was, "You didn't want the girl to try casting a circle to protect her from the wraith. Would it be capable of crossing circles, then?"

"Any she could cast, yes. I could set one it couldn't cross, but to be sure of that, I'd want prep time. Spur-of-the-moment circles wouldn't be strong enough." He glanced at Rule, easily keeping up. "Are we going somewhere in particular?"

"No. You told Talia to pray before setting her circle."

"Certainly. First, it helps her accept that her Gift isn't evil, and neither is the circle she'll cast. Second, there's my original training. Wiccans believe mediumship is a Gift connected to the spirit element, so prayer should help her connect with her Gift. Third, with a new practitioner, confidence is half the battle. If she believes God is helping her set her circle, she's a lot more likely to do it."

"Did you lie to me about the risk to Toby?"

"More or less."

Rule stopped and swung. Cullen—damn him—ducked and danced back, ending up several feet away. Rule stood, chest heaving, hands clenched.

Cullen's face was as carefully blank as his voice. "You need to scrap a bit before we can talk?"

"No." It took another minute, though, to fight back the need to attack something. Anything. "Maybe afterward. It's a good thing you're fast."

"I think so, too. Are you able to listen?"

Rule nodded once.

"First, the part I lied about. Lupus boys who feel the pull of the Change well before puberty do have a much greater chance of incurring the cancer when they reach First Change."

Rule's lips were numb. "How much greater?"

Cullen shook his head. "Insufficient data. Back when I was researching the cancer, I did find two adult lupi from different clans who'd experienced an early pull but did not go on to develop the cancer. No doubt there are others I didn't find, but there's no way of telling how many. But among the young lupi who did develop the cancer, the correlation seems to be one to one. I spoke with the families of thirty youngsters who developed the cancer. All of them said the boy had experienced an early pull."

He paused. "You know that Etorri are especially prone to the wild cancer, but the bump in occurrence at adolescence is very small."

Rule nodded. It was all he could manage.

"There's a reason for that. Before I tell you, I'll have your promise not to repeat this to anyone. That includes Isen."

"What?!" Rule stared at his friend. Cullen's face was stony. He meant it, meant that he'd go no further without Rule's word to keep this from their Rho. Why would . . .

Because it was an Etorri secret, of course. A secret that Cullen had kept all these years, even as a lone wolf rejected by the clan. "Does Isen know you've held back Etorri secrets from him?"

Cullen nodded stiffly. "Before the *gens amplexi*, I told him there was an Etorri matter I was honor-pledged to withhold from him, but that it posed no threat or trouble to Nokolai. He allowed it." A very small smile. "He did ask me not to go out of my way to reassure Etorri. He was amused by the notion they would be wondering if their secret was out."

That sounded like his father. "Very well."

"You promise not to repeat what I'm about to reveal about Etorri?"

"I do."

"Etorri has a way of reducing—almost eliminating—the incidence of the cancer at First Change."

"They *what*?" Etorri the honorable—the most revered clan, the most trusted. "They can keep it from happening and *they haven't told anyone*?"

"Their method is not available to anyone except Etorri. You know what the Lady promised Etorri after Liguri's sacrifice at the end of the Great War."

"That his clan wouldn't die." And it hadn't. Liguri—the single Etorri who'd survived that conflict—had been altered in ways that set him and his descendants apart; the magic was too wild in them, leaving them even less fertile than other lupi. In the long centuries since, the clan had nearly winked out of existence more than once. Yet Etorri persisted. It remained by far the smallest clan, yet it never died out.

An idea hit so hard that Rule felt it in his chest, stealing his breath. "Are you saying . . . Liguri of the Three Mantles? He's the only lupus to have carried more than one, and he— his descendants—have suffered greatly from the cancer. Is Toby in danger because I'm carrying more than one—"

"No. Listen. Listen to me. After Liguri's sacrifice, the Lady altered Etorri's mantle. Among other things, this alteration makes it possible for them to save those of their youth who might otherwise succumb to the cancer at First Change."

He drew a breath. "The Etorri Rho holds about half the clan's mantle. The rest is held by all adult male Etorri."

For a moment Rule couldn't take it in. If Cullen had said, "All adult Etorri are female," it would have made about as much sense. Women couldn't Change. Mantles couldn't be held by anyone except the Rho and his heir. "You mean it's held by them?" he said at last, speaking carefully. "Not that they are part of the mantle. That they *hold* part of the mantle."

"That's right. At First Change, the mantle is . . ." He paused, scrubbing a hand over the top of his head. "Words don't fit well, do they? But as I understand it, in other clans a youth at First Change is exposed to the mantle by being surrounded by clan. With Etorri, the mantle is actively shared. That's what keeps the cancer away, Rule. Holding a bit of mantle."

Rule was still trying to get his mind around the impossible. It wasn't just that he'd been told it was impossible, though he had. As one who carried parts of two mantles, he *knew* it was impossible. "Mantles despise division. They are . . . Their very nature is to unite."

"I told you," Cullen said, "the Lady altered Etorri's mantle. Ah . . . it may ease your conscience about keeping this from your father to know that the Rhejes are aware of the nature of Etorri's mantle. That part's in the memories."

"I don't see how it could be altered so much it accepts division. I don't see how the clan functions when members don't have their places clearly set by the mantle."

"But they do. Everyone holds part of it, but not equally. The mantle itself decides how much each one will hold."

Rule shook his head. "I don't disbelieve you, but I don't . . ." Realization hit. "Good God. You carried a portion of the mantle, then. When you were kicked out of Etorri—"

Cullen had gone white around the jaw and eyes. "Yes. Until then, I held part of the Etorri mantle." His smile held nothing resembling humor. "Actually, I was third in line for the Rho's job, based on how much I held. That's one of the reasons they were so strongly disinclined to allow me to remain clan. Can't have a sorcerous Rho."

Rule struggled to understand. How could they have done

that to Cullen? To make him outcast was terrible enough. To take away the portion of mantle he'd *held* . . . "Just how different is the Etorri mantle?"

Cullen's shrug lacked its usual fluidity. "Put it this way— the mantle was willing for me to remain Etorri. Never mind that." His quick gesture banished the past. "The point is, Rule, Toby needs to be given a portion of mantle to hold at his First Change. The mantle will reinforce his pattern, not allowing the cancer to get a start."

"Holding a Rho's portion didn't reinforce the pattern for Victor Frey." Frey was dying of the wild cancer even as they spoke—slowly, yes, sustained by the Leidolf Rhej's healing Gift, but dying.

"Victor is 160 years old. I'd say the mantle did a pretty good job for the first 159 years of his life."

Rule took in a slow breath. Released it just as slowly. "Very well, then. The Nokolai mantle won't accept splitting the way Etorri's does. My father will have to be persuaded to make Toby his heir instead of me. It's a break with tradition, naming an heir too young to function as Lu Nuncio, but—"

"Rule." Cullen shook his head, sighing as if Rule were a slow pupil. "You have two heirs' portions. By the time Toby hits First Change, Victor will be long dead. If you're Leidolf Rho, you can give Toby the heir's portion of that mantle."

TWENTY-SIX

AT two o'clock, Cullen sauntered into Lily's temporary field office in the sheriff's building. Two of her people were there—Brown and Brown Two—and a couple of deputies. She'd just finished briefing them on their new hunt: for a death. One that occurred on the day of the Turning.

Deacon, who'd been out of his office since before lunch, escorted Cullen in. "Ran into this guy downstairs. He claims he's one of your people."

"He is. I told you to expect him. Everyone, this is Cullen Seabourne. He's consulting for me."

"Yeah?" Deacon gave Cullen a head-to-toe look-over. "Looks like a Hollywood type, not a cop. An actor, maybe."

Cullen smiled sweetly. "No, I'm a stripper."

Lily rolled her eyes. Cullen never tired of his favorite punch line. "Retired stripper, and currently a consultant for the Unit, Sheriff. Like I told you." She felt like the kid who'd been followed home by a disreputable mutt.

Not that Cullen resembled a mutt, but he had the disreputable part down.

"Christ, woman, would you close your mouth?" the male

Brown said to the female Brown. "You're getting drool on your chin."

Brown Two shot him a venomous look—but she did take up the slack in her jaw.

"Okay, could we talk about the case for an eensy moment here?" Lily said. "Cullen's going to brief you on wraiths." She'd skimmed that explanation earlier, waiting for the expert.

The expressions on her team's faces ranged from skeptical to incredulous. Except for Brown, of course, who remained as generically disgusted as ever. "Never thought I'd be taking ghost lessons from a goddammed stripper," he said, stuffing another piece of gum in his mouth.

Cullen beamed at him. "Nonsense. I'm officially undamned, and I've got the holy water to prove it. My wife insists I keep some with me, just in case. Never know when you might trip over a demon, right? The briefing's in just a sec, kiddies." He turned to Lily. "I've got a—"

"You're *married*?" Deacon exclaimed. "I thought you were a w—uh, a lupus."

"Oh, I am. I'm also a newlywed. Ring's still shiny." Cullen held out his hand, ostentatiously admiring the gold band.

Lily said dryly, "Cullen's goal in life is to be the exception to every rule." In this case, he claimed that the Turning provided the exception. There was some reason to think the influx of magic since the Turning would improve fertility for his people, so the ban on marriage could be dropped. Maybe he'd be proved right . . . eventually. So far the birth rate hadn't changed. "You can congratulate him later. I'd like to get some work done."

"So driven. So masterful." Cullen offered her a sly grin, and the rest of them a little bow. "I need a moment to confer with your fearsome leader. Then I'll tell you my ghost stories."

He dug in his pocket as he crossed to Lily. "You need to have a word with the Etorri Rhej," he said much more quietly, handing her a wrinkled scrap of paper with a phone number scrawled on it. "I called ahead and arranged it. She agreed, but you need to call now. She's got an appointment in thirty minutes."

"Thanks. Could you try to act like a grownup for a while? I'd like them to take this seriously."

"I'll use visual aids. Everyone loves visual aids." He turned to grin at the others. "As I was saying, children—the first thing you need to accept is that I do know what I'm talking about. So gather round the campfire, now . . ."

Lily gave up on making him behave and made the phone call. The line was still ringing when he showed what he meant by visual aids. A small blaze sprang up in his palm. It was a pretty little fire, crackling merrily, though unusual—and not just because it was cupped in a man's hand. It was green. Bright, springtime green.

"Show-off," she muttered.

"Not usually," said an amused feminine voice in her ear.

Lily winced. "Ah—Serra." That was the honorific for a Rhej; they were never addressed by name. "This is Lily Yu. I was watching Cullen play with fire."

"I see." The woman chuckled. "He does enjoy that. Now, I hate to rush you, but I have an appointment. Cullen said you're dealing with one of the scattered dead."

"That's one of the terms he used for it. Mostly he calls it a wraith."

"The memories refer to wraiths as the scattered dead. I'm afraid I have very little for you, but that's one small point—the name for these creatures in the memories. They're scattered, not whole. That, and the fact that they eat deaths."

"Is eating death the same as death magic?"

"Similar, but . . . I suppose it's like the difference between a farseeing spell and a farseeing Gift. Both a wraith and death magic make use of death as a transition, the power involved when we cross to the next state. A wraith consumes that power, leaving the souls unable to transition fully."

"Creating damaged ghosts?" With half an ear Lily kept track of what Cullen was telling the others. So far, it was the same as what he'd told her. The two Browns and the deputies seemed to be paying attention.

"Yes. Normal death magic . . . good God, that sounds awful. As if it could ever be normal! I mean that death magic generated through ritual uses a relatively small portion of the energy released by a dying. Such magic is ugly and horrible, but the souls involved are usually able to move on."

"The wraith is more efficient, I take it. It uses—eats—most of the power released by death."

"That's pretty much it, yes."

"Can these damaged ghosts hurt regular ghosts? The, uh, young medium I spoke to . . . I think Cullen was going to put her in touch with you."

"Talia, he said. Yes, I'll be calling her after I get back from the job interview."

Job interview? Wasn't being a Rhej enough of a job? Lily banked that question for later. "She said the other ghosts were afraid of the damaged ones. What could harm a ghost?"

"Frankly, I don't see how a ghost could be harmed, but there's a great deal I don't know. They may simply be afraid of what, to them, is a terrifying condition. Those souls are truly trapped."

"I thought that was true of all ghosts."

She chuckled. "No, most of them are merely stubborn. The ones who linger, that is. Ghosts are actually common as dirt—"

"Yeah? That's not quite what the other mediums said."

"Not many mediums are as good as I am," she said without a trace of brag in her voice. "Though it may also be a matter of language. Some mediums consider the newly dead to be distinctly different from ghosts. I disagree, but whatever you call them, most of the newly dead move on within an hour of crossing, often within seconds. Those who don't move on fast enough harden into ghosts. I think of ghosts as souls with memory problems."

"Memory problems?"

"Sure. They may be fixated on one particular memory, often of their own death. Sometimes they're hung up on the memory of a wrong they did someone—that was the problem of the haunt at Cullen's wedding, you'll remember. Or they may be suppressing a memory, sometimes of dying, sometimes of something else, and they can't move on until they allow themselves to experience that memory."

Souls with memory problems. Lily shivered. Was that what would happen when she died? Would she become a ghost? Most of the time she couldn't remember what the other-her had experienced. "Will destroying the wraith give those damaged ghosts back whatever was taken from them?"

"I don't know. I pray that it does."

Now for the big question. "Do you know how to destroy the wraith, or stop it?"

"No. I wish I did. Whoever created it has trapped it in a terrible state. It must be suffering greatly."

"Hmm." Lily couldn't summon much sympathy for the wraith, but maybe that's because she couldn't imagine what it *was*. Did it think, feel?

At that moment Cullen stopped talking to glance at his hip. "Just a moment. I'd better see . . ." He pulled his phone out of his pocket. It was a snug fit. "I need to take this call. Hey, gorgeous." Then: "You're *what*? Dammit, you were headed home! You said . . . All right, you didn't explicitly say, but you let me think . . . That's not the point, dammit!"

Lily grinned. That had to be Cynna calling. Which brought up another, unrelated question . . . "May I ask you something off-topic, Serra?"

"Sure, if it'll take five minutes or less."

Cullen was scrubbing his hand through his hair, scowling as he listened to whatever Cynna had to say. Lily watched him as she asked, "Why did you go to Cullen and Cynna's wedding?"

"You know, you're the first to ask me quite so directly. Most clan treat us so . . . carefully." She was amused. "Of course, we're careful, too. We almost never offer advice unless we're asked, and not always then. The Lady doesn't want us directing the clans, so we're cautious with what we say."

Cullen strode over and thrust his phone at her. "Here. The crazy woman wants to talk to you."

"Just a sec. Serra? That didn't quite answer my question."

"I suppose not. The realms have shifted, though, haven't they? The world is changing. It's possible the clans will decide to change, too. And now I'm going to break my rule and offer one bit of advice. You know that the Lady rarely speaks to us directly."

By "us," she meant Rhejes. "Yes."

"She occasionally gives guidance in one other way— through a mate bond. So that's my bit of unsought advice. Listen to whatever the mate bond is telling you. And now I'm afraid I have to go. I've got your number. I'll call if I come up with anything that might help."

The mate bond was telling her something? Not in English, Lily thought as she disconnected and took Cullen's phone. Or even Chinese.

It had forced the two of them to stay close, though. And the wraith had attacked Rule once, out in the woods. Was the mate bond telling her Rule needed her protection?

She set that aside for later and took Cullen's phone. "Hi, Cynna. I take it you're the crazy woman Cullen referred to."

"Hah! As if he has any room to talk. Did you know there's a television show about pregnant women?"

"Uh—yes, I think I've heard of it."

"I was channel surfing last night and saw those big bellies. Hooked me right in. Those women had every kind of complication—preeclampsia, prediabetes, pre-I-don't-know-what-all. I am never watching that show again. You wouldn't believe what I dreamed."

"I'm kind of hoping you won't tell me right now. Middle of a case, cops standing around listening . . . you know."

"Sorry. Pregnancy hormones have scattered my brain to hell and gone. I only hope I get some of the pieces back after the little rider pops out. Anyway, I just finished talking to that Vodun priestess I told you about."

"I thought she won't tell you anything over the phone."

"Or without an infusion of cash, which is why I flew to D.C.—and flew first class, too, thanks to the upgrade Ruben okayed because of me being pregnant, so there's no reason for Cullen to be in such a snit. It's not like I have any edema. But

he thinks I'm going to disintegrate or something if I go anywhere without him." Her voice softened. "It's kind of sweet."

Lily studied the pacing sorcerer—who wasn't burning
anything, but he didn't look close to "sweet." Not unless you
got mushy about explosions. Okay, really sexy explosions.

He was muttering something under his breath . . . cigars?
He was muttering about cigars? Lily shook her head. "So
what did the priestess tell you?"

"It's what the Baron said through one of the congregants at
the service. She had to hold a service, see, to give the Loa a
chance to come through, and the one who showed up was the
Baron. Ah, Baron Samedi is one of the Ghede Loa, or maybe
the father of them. His favorite offerings are cigars, rum, and
sex."

"Cigars? What could an immaterial spirit—" Lily shook
her head. "Never mind. What's a Loa?"

"The major spirits who act as intermediaries between us
and God. According to Vodun, anyway—I don't agree, but
then, I'm Catholic. But the Loa are real, whether you invest
them with religious purpose or not. This Baron Samedi is in
charge of graves and death, and boy, is he pissed. He did not
like it that someone made a wraith. He said you have to get
the wraith's name. Well, actually, he said that if you don't get
the name, you're in deep shit."

"Good to know," Lily said dryly. "He couldn't help out a
little more? Like, for example, by telling you the name."

"Either he doesn't know it or he can't tell. He did have
some advice, though I think he considered it orders, not
advice. Some of the Loa are pretty bossy. He said to salt the
grave once you find it, and when you have the living one who
made the abomination—he meant the wraith—you should
salt her palms."

Lily felt questions piling up. "Her?"

"Yes, he said the practitioner who made the wraith is a
medium. He used another word for it, but Thérèse says that's
what it means—spirit-talker or medium."

Thérèse, Lily assumed, was the priestess. The *mambo.*
"What does the salt do? Will it kill the wraith or stop it?"

"Actually, it's supposed to help the wraith hold together."

"Not a priority of mine," Lily said dryly.

"I think you should do it, Lily. This Baron is no one to mess with, and he was clear about the salt."

"You think it's better if the wraith is, ah, more together?"

"Maybe it'll be less likely to kill. I don't know, but in magic, dry salt is often used as a fixative. Not salt water, mind—that has different properties. But you can use salt to fix in place a circle or a spell. So I'm guessing that maybe the salt will 'fix' the wraith to its grave, but I don't know. It might do something else entirely."

Great. "I'm supposed to send cops and federal agents out to find graves, armed with saltshakers?"

"It'll take more than a saltshaker, I think," Cynna said apologetically. "I'd guess a couple handfuls of salt per grave. Cullen can explain about that. Listen, Lily, the Baron said he's coming down there to help."

Lily wasn't entirely sure what this Baron guy was, but she didn't think she wanted him hanging around. "You have any idea what that means?" she asked cautiously.

"Not really. Thérèse just laughed and shook her head and said, 'That Baron, he's something, isn't he?' She's got a weird sense of humor. Well, she did say something about you having sex at midnight near an open grave, but that's just her trying to get white folks to do stupid stuff so she can laugh about it."

"White folks? You tell her my last name? Never mind." Lily rubbed her face. "Do you think this Baron shares her sense of humor?"

"Well . . . some of the Loa are kind of twisty, but he was straight about catching the wraith. It's his province, after all—graves and death. He takes this shit seriously."

"You think I should take what he said seriously, too, then."

"Yeah, I do. Sorry. I know it won't be fun persuading some judge to let you salt graves."

Lily had to laugh. "Fun isn't the word I'd use, no. I need to go, Cynna. You want to talk to Cullen some more?"

"Has he stopped pacing yet?"

Lily smiled. Cynna knew her man pretty well. "He's slowed down."

"Close enough. Hand me over. Bet I can have him grinning in under a minute."

"You're on." Lily crossed to Cullen, told him the crazy woman wanted another word with him, handed him back his phone—and turned when someone cleared his throat.

Deacon stood there, looking grim. "Seabourne says we'll be looking at people who died on the Turning. That this wraith was created from a death then."

"That's right." A quick glance told her Cullen was still scowling.

"My grandfather died that day. Right when it hit. He was in the hospital, waiting on a heart bypass operation."

That got her attention, but she shook her head. "If you're thinking you're under suspicion, Sheriff, you don't have to worry about it." A sharp crack of laughter from Cullen made her glance at him. Sure enough, he was grinning. "I just got some new information. Our perp is probably a medium."

That drew Deacon's face in even grimmer lines. "My granny's a medium."

DEACON'S granny lived with his parents in a small frame house on the east end of town. His folks were both at work. His granny was tucked up in a hospital bed in the living room, the TV remote in her hand and a troop of kittens clambering around on her.

Marjorie Abigail Deacon was a wrinkled little raisin of a woman with a sweet, toothless smile—her dentures were on the table by the bed—and milky cataracts. She was delighted to see Deacon, and Lily, too, though she thought Lily was someone named Sherry.

Lily was introduced to each of the four kittens and to Harold, Marjorie's husband . . . the one who died seven months ago. Of course, it was possible that Mrs. Deacon really did see Harold. Her wits might be wandering, but Lily confirmed with a touch that she retained her Gift.

She spoke happily about the garden she'd planted and about her children, who were sometimes grown, sometimes still small and "full of mischief." Twice she called Deacon by his father's name. She was obviously too far gone to be capable of the kind of spellwork that might create a wraith, but seven months ago she'd been much keener, Deacon said.

It didn't matter. She'd been bedridden for the past year, and Lily very much doubted someone that frail could have handled the kind of power needed to create a wraith. She'd check that with Cullen to be sure, but for now she wasn't putting Mrs. Deacon on her suspect list.

When Lily got up to leave, Mrs. Deacon spoke to the air on her left. "What's that? Oh, yes." She turned that sweet smile on Lily. "Harold wants you to tell your wolf he's got a might pretty lady. Oh, and he's to trust her, no matter what, and pull on that robe of his hard as he can."

TWENTY-SEVEN

IT was a long, muddled afternoon for Rule.

Cullen left as soon as they returned to the house. Lily needed him for the investigation, and it was just as well. Rule needed time to absorb what Cullen had told him, time without his brain hopping on the hamster wheel and spinning, spinning, without going any-damned-where.

He kept busy. He checked Toby's math, made phone calls and received one, even got some work done. There was solace in the simplicity of numbers, so he focused on the proposal for a company that a clan member wanted to start, with Nokolai's backing. He also went to the grocery store for Louise, who didn't keep tofu, soy milk, or fresh basil around. He must have behaved correctly, because Louise didn't seem to notice anything wrong.

Rule assured her he didn't mind the grocery run. He didn't. It gave him a chance to grab a double-meat hamburger. The spinach and tofu quiche she was planning would doubtless be delicious, but tofu was not meat.

But always, always, the question beat against his mind. Could he abandon honor for the sake of his son? Of course, when he tossed the question on its head, the answer seemed obvious: Could he abandon his son for the sake of honor?

No, no, and no. But it wasn't that simple.

He desperately wanted to talk to Lily about it. And couldn't. He'd given his word. And perhaps it was just as well, for she was stretched to the limit with her investigation, and she wouldn't understand, would she? She wouldn't grasp the repercussions of his assuming leadership of Leidolf permanently. Or of his making Toby heir of that clan.

Leidolf would try to kill Rule, of course. Not immediately; they couldn't act until Rule had an heir, or the mantle would be lost, and with it, the clan. There would be a period of a few years when Leidolf would protect their new Rho zealously.

Once he made Toby heir, that would change. Some in Leidolf would Challenge; others wouldn't bother with anything so formal, opting for assassination. It was possible the other clans would Challenge, too, which could drag Nokolai into outright clan war.

War was the worst-case scenario. Best case left Rule distrusted and dishonored. Leidolf, the other clans, even his own clan—all would consider it a blatant power grab. Rule could live with that. He could live with Challenges or assassination attempts. But the possibility that some in Leidolf might target his son . . . Oh, yes, that could happen. There was a certain cold logic to it.

Kill the man who was their Rho, and Leidolf's entire mantle would go to a boy not yet old enough to control his wolf. They might do that, counting on being able to force Toby to give up the mantle to one of their choosing. But it was risky. No one could say whether a boy so young would be able to hold an entire mantle. It had never happened.

Kill the boy, though, then try to force Rule to choose an heir from within Leidolf . . . Yes, some would see that as safer for the clan. Those who underestimated the power of the mantle—and Rule.

Cullen understood these possibilities. He'd still urged Rule to do it. "You'll just have to change Leidolf's mind about you. You'll have three or four years to do that."

Change Leidolf's mind about him. Rule smiled grimly, shut down his computer, and headed downstairs. Oh, yes, after centuries of ill feeling between Nokolai and Leidolf, all he had to do was persuade them that the heir to Nokolai could lead their clan well.

Assuming, that was, his father let him remain Nokolai's heir.

Rule set that issue aside. He'd learned not to waste time and energy trying to guess which way Isen would jump, or what his plans truly included. If Rule became Leidolf Rho, his father might cackle with glee, having intended that result all along. He might revoke Rule's heirship. He might kick Rule out of the clan.

Isen would do what he thought best for Nokolai, and Rule would accept that.

Toby was vacuuming the living room when Rule reached the first floor. In the kitchen, Louise was in full war mode. She pulled a pie shell out of the oven just as Rule entered. "Beautiful," he told her. "And the smell is delightful."

"Thank you. I have never used tofu. The recipe said to drain it, but . . . does this look right?" She'd put the tofu on a cutting board lined with paper towels and placed a heavy pot on top.

"I think so," he said gravely. The paper towels were damp, so they must be soaking up the extra moisture. "What can I do to help?"

"Connie is bringing her fruit salad, so that's covered. For a side dish, I was going to fix glazed carrots. I wasn't thinking. That takes butter, and you said the store didn't have any vegan butter—whatever in the world *that* is. I suspect it isn't butter at all. Probably one more way to make tofu pretend it's something else." She glared at her pie shell. "Steamed carrots are so bland."

"Why not roast them? All it takes is carrots, olive oil, and a little salt. The high heat caramelizes the sugars. Delicious."

"Have you done that?" she demanded. When he admitted he had, she asked, "How long does it take? The quiche will be in the oven."

"About twenty minutes, but they can go on the bottom rack while the quiche bakes above."

She sighed in relief. "You're in charge of carrots, then. Here." She pulled two pounds of carrots from the refrigerator. "The quiche takes fifty minutes."

Toby finished vacuuming and was immediately put to work setting the table. Rule was scraping carrots when his phone beeped. "Toby, would you answer that for me, please? My hands are messy."

His phone was in its holster, hung from his belt. Toby retrieved it. "Hello, this is Toby Asteglio. My dad's peeling carrots." He listened a moment. "Okay. Dad, it's Alex Thibideux. He wants to know if he should call back later."

"No, I'll take it." Quickly Rule rinsed his hands. He gave Toby a smile. "Alex is the Leidolf Lu Nuncio. I am always available to him."

Toby didn't say anything, but the face he made when Rule said "Leidolf" spoke for him. It was a prejudice he needed to put a stop to—now more than ever. "You'd like Alex," he said casually, drying his hands. "He's an honorable man and an excellent fighter. Your uncle Benedict considers him one of the few who can make him work for a win."

Toby perked up slightly. "Yeah?"

Rule nodded. "He probably saved my life during the, ah, commotion following the Turning. Thank you," he added, taking the phone. "Yes?"

Alex's gravelly voice greeted him. "What's this 'probably,' Nokolai whelp?"

Rule grinned. He and Alex got along well these days. Odd as it seemed, they might be on their way to real friendship. "*Probably*, Leidolf runt," he repeated. The "runt" was carefully chosen. When on two legs, Alex was six feet and well over two hundred pounds, all of it muscle. His wolf was equally outsize. "I wasn't, perhaps, in the best shape at the time—"

Alex snorted.

"—but my *nadia* was present. She might well have retrieved one of those rifles before Brady finished me."

"She doesn't lack guts, I'll give you that. Here's the deal. I drove up so I could look over the area you've proposed for the *gens compleo*. Been in those woods before, but it's been years. Thought I could give you a hand selecting the spot."

"I'd appreciate that. You're in Halo now? Where are you staying?"

That's when Rule lost control of the situation. He couldn't say later how it happened, except that Louise overheard and would not hear of Rule's friend eating in "some burger joint," especially when he would make their numbers right. They'd sit eight at the table if he joined them, she said, as if that were the clincher.

When Rule gently pointed out that Alex would make them nine at table, not eight, she immediately switched course and nine was the magic number; and besides, her table had two leaves, so there was plenty of room, and she'd already decided to make two quiches. So Rule ended up inviting the Leidolf Lu Nuncio to dinner with his son, his friend, his mate, his son's mother, his son's mother's new husband, his son's grandmother, and his son's grandmother's neighbor.

He began to see what Toby meant about his grandmother and parties.

"Rule, do vegans drink wine?" Louise called from the pantry.

"As far as I know."

"Vegans," Alex repeated, his voice lacking all inflection. He would, of course, have heard Louise—who probably didn't realize that.

"Yes, Louise's new son-in-law is vegan. She's making a wonderful spinach and tofu quiche that should work for him."

Alex was silent a moment. "Thanks, Turner. I'll be sure to eat a couple burgers first." He disconnected.

So did Rule. If he became Alex's Rho permanently, there would be no chance of friendship between them. Alex would despise him. Rule regretted that possible loss keenly.

"The spoons go with the knives, right?" Toby called from the dining room.

"Yes. The blade should face the plate, not out." But that regret was nothing, nothing at all, compared to what he felt as he watched his son align knives and spoons carefully on the wrong side of each plate.

LILY blasted through the door at six twenty. Connie Milligan was in the kitchen with Louise; the other guests hadn't arrived yet. Rule had just come upstairs to shrug into his suit jacket, so he heard her rapid-fire apology to Louise as she streaked for the stairs. Apparently she believed six thirty meant six fifteen at the latest.

He met her at the head of the stairs. She handed him a folder. "Here. It's incomplete. Ruben had one of his hunches."

He looked inside. His eyebrows lifted. "You asked Ruben to run the check on James French?"

"Not exactly. Like I said, he had one of his hunches. I'll explain later. I've got to get ready." She cast a regretful look at the door to the bathroom. "Not enough time for a shower."

"We don't have to be down at the stroke of six thirty."

"Yes, we do. In my mother's eyes, tardiness for a family dinner is a decapitation offense."

He ran his hand along her neck. "Hmm. Still attached."

"My father routinely commutes the sentence." She laid her hand over his. Her eyes darkened with feeling, but her voice was quiet. "Rule? Did Cullen . . . What did he say?"

He jerked his head, indicating their room. She followed him in; he shut the door. And she put her arms around him, bringing him the rightness of her scent, the living heat of her body. She didn't speak. She just held him.

And undid him. A slow tsunami shuddered up his spine, all the crammed feelings unwinding in a mudslide of fear and fury, razors and sludge. All, all at once, rolling up through him so that all he could do was hold on. Hold on.

He wrapped himself around her and inhaled hard, bringing the citrus of her shampoo inside him, the musk of her skin, the slight tang of cinnamon from her breath . . . *red hots. She loves those cinnamon red hots.* The thought was absurdly comforting, unleashing another flood, this one of fondness for all the small pieces of her he'd picked up along the way, like shells washed ashore by the ocean.

He rubbed his cheek against her hair, resting in her, man and wolf leaning into love as if it were a pillow, a bed, a stream he could float on.

Overload, then release. It was no wonder his eyes filled. That was all right. He was safe here. He didn't have to hide.

Except that he did. Not the feelings, but some of the facts. Some, he realized, not all. And there can be enough space between *some* and *all* to wedge in some truth.

Hadn't Toby done the same thing? "*Nadia,*" he murmured to her hair, then straightened so he could see her face. Worry, fear—he saw those plainly. She'd held them close, held herself silent, so she could give him what he needed.

He touched her cheek. "I've convinced you Cullen's news was bad. It wasn't, not wholly, but it was difficult. It brings me a choice that's all edges, and—Lily, I'm sorry, but I can't tell you what he said. He needed my word not to repeat him, and I gave it."

A carefully chosen promise, he understood now, and wanted to hug Cullen—and slap himself for not catching on earlier. Cullen had steered the conversation so that Rule promised specifically not to repeat Etorri's secret. He hadn't promised to *keep* that secret. Keeping it would mean safeguarding it, doing all he reasonably could to be sure no one learned of it through him.

Learned of it—or figured it out. He stroked his thumb along the curve of Lily's cheekbone. "I can't repeat what he said, but because of it, I may choose to retain Leidolf's mantle when Victor dies."

She stared. Frowned. "You don't want to be Leidolf Rho."

"No."

"But you might retain their mantle, because of what Cullen told you about Toby."

He nodded.

Her breath gusted out. "Huh. That would cause problems, wouldn't it?"

And this he could certainly tell her, so he did. Briefly, because six thirty must surely be upon them, but even a brief telling of the possible consequences was grim.

"So your choice," she said, "is to do nothing and hope Toby doesn't contract the cancer, but the odds aren't good. Or you can accept leadership of Leidolf for reasons you can't tell me. The latter could cause trouble and turmoil, possibly even including some kind of war between the clans, and could well endanger Toby. Yet you consider it a valid option. Obviously, keeping the mantle somehow guarantees that Toby won't get the cancer."

He did appreciate her mind. "I cannot confirm or deny what you've said."

"Hmm." That came out almost amused. "You sure you aren't a lawyer? Never mind. Are you honestly thinking you haven't made the decision yet? Because I know which you'll pick."

His eyebrows shot up. "Do you?"

"Sure. You'll go for Door Number Two. It gives you some control, some options. If you can get Leidolf to stop hating you, for instance—"

"Cullen's suggestion," he murmured. "Not that he knows how I might stop generations of distrust and hatred."

"As to that—"

The doorbell rang.

"Damn." She pulled out of his arms and dashed to the closet. "How much money have you made Nokolai over the years?" She grabbed another of her pretty jackets, this one yellow, and a black silk camisole.

"I do a good job with our finances, but—well, to put it bluntly, lupi are not humans. We don't base our loyalty on money."

"Humor me. How much?" She slipped out of the black jacket she'd been wearing and unbuckled her shoulder holster.

"We did well in the boom. I suppose that, allowing for inflation, Nokolai's assets have roughly tripled since I began handling the majority of our financial matters. Certainly we need less *drei* than Leidolf does."

"*Drei*? Oh, yeah, I remember. That's your head tax. Now, Leidolf's relatively poor, though it's a bigger clan than Nokolai, right?" She tugged off her tee.

This distracted him, naturally, but after a moment's silent appreciation, he said, "That's right. Leidolf is the largest clan."

Cami in place, she grabbed her ankle holster and strapped it on. "I need more clothes," she muttered. "I didn't pack for this."

He considered asking if she meant to shoot Alicia, but decided she wouldn't appreciate the humor right now. "I'll take some things to the cleaners tomorrow, if you like."

"That would be a help." With her backup weapon hidden beneath the full leg of her black slacks, she added the yellow jacket to her outfit. "I know you're not exactly human. I know that, but you're awash in our culture, and your people are very conscious of power. I can't believe lupi are oblivious to the power and security money represents. I know your father isn't."

Rule shrugged. "That's one of the ways Isen differs from many of the Rhos."

"Money makes Nokolai more secure. It can do that for Leidolf, too. Add increased security to the fact that you aren't crazy and mean like Victor . . . plus the Leidolf Rhej likes you. Her opinion carries weight."

"She won't like me if I break honor and . . ." Wait. Cullen had told him the Rhejes knew about the way the Etorri mantle was shared. The Leidolf Rhej might guess what he was doing—especially if he did exactly what he'd already planned to do: have her examine Toby for any trace of the cancer.

The doorbell rang again.

"Shit." Lily glared through the floor at whoever had arrived. "Why is there never enough time?"

"We have to make time for the important things. Like this." He took her shoulders and kissed her as thoroughly as he thought she'd allow, given the guests accumulating downstairs. Long enough for her to soften against him and his own body to ready itself for something that, unfortunately, was not happening.

Not happening yet, he promised himself. Not yet, but soon.

He lifted his head, smiling and tasting cinnamon. "You make me clear to myself." Because she was entirely right. He'd choose the option that gave him options, however difficult, rather than surrender his son to fate.

She smoothed her hands down his shirt. "I could use some clarity, so I'm hoping you can return the favor later. I, uh— sorry, but I'll have to go back to work after dinner. Maybe I can bring you up-to-date, get your input. Not now, though. Now we have other dragons to face." She grimaced and ran a hand through her hair. "Lip gloss. I don't have time to redo my makeup, but lip gloss, at least."

He handed her purse to her. She delved inside. "Oh, one more thing. You have to start saying 'we' instead of 'they' when you speak of Leidolf. They're your clan, too."

"It doesn't work that way. Even if I wanted to—to be Leidolf . . ." And oh, but saying that left a sourness in his gut that warned him of just how much would have to change. "I underwent *gens compleo* with Nokolai, not Leidolf."

"That's when you're accepted into the clan, right?" Her lips now shiny, she capped the gloss. "Which is accomplished when the mantle recognizes you, or something like that. Well, I'd say the Leidolf mantle recognizes you now."

"Holding part of a mantle isn't the same as being held by the mantle."

"Is it a difference in degree, or kind?"

He opened his mouth . . . and shut it again. There was a flaw in her reasoning. Somewhere. There had to be. "I . . . There is a difference." But was it a difference that mattered as far as clan membership went? If Etorri had, for centuries, been recognizing its members by investing them with a portion of the mantle . . .

"Rule." She slid the tube back in her purse and looked at him. "I admit I don't understand about mantles, and I know you're mostly Nokolai and are accustomed to tracing your descent through the male line. That makes sense, since only males are lupus. But your great-grandmother was Leidolf.

That's why Victor was able to force the mantle on you. Which means you've always been part Leidolf, by blood. Now that you've got both the blood and the mantle, you're Leidolf as well as Nokolai. It's time you accepted that."

TWENTY-EIGHT

DINNER could have been worse. Lily pointed that out to herself more than once as the meal progressed. The wraith could have shown up, for example, and a possessed Alicia might have stabbed Lily in the back literally instead of settling for verbal jabs. That would have been worse.

But easier to defend against. Alicia was smart enough to keep her digs under the radar—more like sprinkling too much salt than openly dumping poison. Lily didn't think any of the others noticed. Normally Rule would have, but beneath his impeccable manners, Rule was distracted. Shaken, she suspected. Probably she'd picked a bad time to point out that he had two clans.

Fortunately, Lily was a side dish for Alicia, who focused most of her attention on her son.

Lily was seated close enough to eavesdrop. At first Toby was stiff, resentful. Alicia kept asking questions, teasing gently until she got him talking about soccer, *The Simpsons*, and his desperate need for a puppy, which his dad had promised to take care of when he moved to Clanhome. Lily was aware of the promise, having been in on the negotiations.

The promised puppy was announced with a stubborn tilt

to his chin. After a moment, Alicia asked what kind of dog he wanted, and they discussed beagles and Great Danes, both of which, it seemed, were acceptable to Toby. All in all, Alicia was patient, observant, and interested. Not exactly maternal, maybe—more like a big sister or favorite aunt. But she did okay. She did fine, really.

So where was the CEO of Narcissists R Us whom Lily had encountered earlier?

Lily went back to being a good guest. Alex, seated on her left, was one of those men who acted like he'd been issued a certain number of words at birth and didn't want to run out. It took a little effort to get him talking, but a mention of his new SIG Sauer did the trick. Like most lupi, he had an aversion to firearms—but he'd decided to overcome that after the events of last December.

Cullen stayed busy charming everyone, including the new husband. They got into quite a discussion of jackals—which apparently were close relatives of wolves—and the merits of tryptophan in the *Canis* diet.

James French puzzled Lily. He was so . . . bland. The only thing that stood out about him physically was his tan, which she learned came from spending as much time as possible observing Lebanon's fauna. An economist by training and profession, he was an enthusiastic amateur naturalist. He was a thin man, maybe five-eight, with soft brown eyes behind gold-framed glasses. Lily wasn't sure she'd ever met a more innocuous person.

Even without Ruben's hunch, she would have found all that blandness suspicious.

Finally it was time for dairy-free brownies in the living room. Chocolate and coffee were always a good idea, though it would have been better if the coffee weren't decaf. Tasted pretty good, though Lily noticed that Rule barely sipped his.

He insisted caffeine couldn't affect him. She had her doubts.

Rule, Alex, and Lily sat on one couch facing Alicia, James, and Toby on the other. Louise had brought in two chairs from the den. Cullen sat in one by the piano, and Louise sat in its mate near the window. Connie had excused herself right after the meal, claiming she couldn't sleep if she ate chocolate. Lily figured she was tactfully clearing the way for a family discussion.

Toby wolfed down his brownies and bounced up from the couch. "I guess I should get my stuff now. I'm going to spend the night with Justin, Mom," he added. "You remember Justin."

Alicia, startled and not pleased, shot her mother a look. "I didn't know Toby was going somewhere tonight."

"However things turn out," Louise said quietly, "Toby has a parting coming up. Of course I allowed him to spend time with his friends now, while he can."

"Still, I think I should have been asked." Alicia looked at Toby. "You need to ask my permission, too."

Toby's jaw set. He didn't respond.

Louise's expression never changed as she said to her daughter, "Do you really wish to challenge my authority at this time, dear?"

"Your authority? *I* have custody of my son."

James French leaned forward, placing one hand on Alicia's knee. "Licia," he said firmly.

She turned a stormy face to him. Their eyes met. Gradually the storm faded to a rueful expression. "Wrong battle?"

He nodded, smiling faintly. "Also the wrong time and place."

She rolled her eyes. "Okay. Toby, I shouldn't interfere with your grammy's arrangements. But when you're living with me, I'll expect a different attitude from you."

The storm that had left Alicia's face landed in Toby's. He opened his mouth.

"Toby," Rule said.

This time father and son locked gazes. After a moment Toby sighed. "Yes, ma'am. *If* I go live with you, I'll have to mind."

Before Alicia could argue about the qualifier Toby had appended, Rule said, "Alex has agreed to drive you over to Jus-

tin's. That's nonnegotiable," he added as Toby's mouth opened
once more.

Toby gathered himself up and gave Alex a dignified nod.
"Thank you. I don't think it's necessary, but thanks."

When Toby hit the stairs, James started talking to Alex,
using that reliable source for male bonding—football. Lily
took advantage of the moment to lean closer to Rule and whisper, "Justin's parents aren't afraid that Toby will contaminate
him?"

"I had a chat with Mr. Appleton after my grocery store
run," he said softly. "I was able to allay some of his concerns
by, ah, allowing him to lay hands on me and pray."

Oh, my. Lily's lips twitched. "Mistook you for a demon,
did he?"

"Behave." But Rule's lips tilted up, too. "Toby needed to
be there tonight. Cullen's concerned about Talia. She's learning quickly, but she doesn't know how to set a permanent
circle, so she'll be vulnerable when she sleeps."

Toby came hurtling down the stairs, backpack slung over
one shoulder. "'Bye, Grammy! 'Bye, Dad! 'Bye, everyone!
Alex, are you ready?"

There was a small delay while Louise made Toby come
into the room to say goodbye properly and informed him that
he was to address Alex as Mr. Thibideux. Alex took his leave
with grave formality. As the door closed behind them, Toby
was asking Alex if he was really "almost as good as Uncle
Benedict."

Alicia looked at Rule and said dubiously, "You're sure
about this Alex Thibideux?"

Lily didn't know if Alicia was bothered because she didn't
know the man, or if old-fashioned prejudice was rearing its
head. Alex must be mixed race—Leidolf was originally a
Germanic clan, so his father would have been white—but he
didn't look it. He was very large and very dark. Lily happened
to know he had a degree in sociology, but that, like his father's heritage, didn't show on his face.

"Quite sure. He would die before allowing harm to come

to Toby." Rule smiled slowly, allowing a hint of the wolf to show. "And Alex is hard to kill."

"That he is," Cullen said cheerfully. "Do you want me to head out now, too? I hope not. I think we're about to get to the interesting part of the program."

Alicia looked at Rule and sighed faintly. "I suppose you arranged for Toby to be gone so we could talk."

"In part, yes. We need to discuss your sudden change of mind about custody."

"There's little to discuss. Look, Rule." She leaned forward, hands clasped on her knees. Since she'd worn a killer little green-and-white print dress with a scoop neckline, this gave him a good view of her breasts. "I've loved Toby from the moment I saw his wrinkled, red little face, but I'll admit I've been slow to take responsibility. Mother's injury earlier this year was a wake-up call for me."

Rule's face lacked expression. "Love him? No. You're very fond of him, but you've never allowed that fondness to interfere with your life."

"Don't tell me what I feel! You disapprove of my choices. Fine. We can talk about that, but—"

Lily's phone sounded the first bars of "The Star-Spangled Banner." "Sorry," she said, rising and pulling the phone from her jacket pocket. "I have to take this." As she headed for the hall, she heard Alicia angrily disputing Rule's claim that there was anything lesser about her love for Toby.

The caller was Ruben, as she'd known from the ring tone. She didn't have to ask any questions; Ruben covered everything clearly and concisely. "Damn," she said softly. "No, I agree. Not yet, anyway. Thanks, Ruben." She disconnected, then took a moment to order her thoughts.

When she reentered the room, Alicia was talking about the possibility of joint custody ". . . on an informal basis. There's no need to put Toby through the difficulty of a custody hearing if you and I can come to an agreement."

"If our agreement is in writing and approved by a judge," Rule said politely, "that might be possible—if Toby agrees."

She tossed back her hair. "He's nine years old. It's wrong to put that kind of responsibility on him."

"I have a question," Lily said mildly.

Alicia looked surprised, rather as if a chair had spoken. "What?"

"Do you still despise lupi?"

"I never said—"

"Alicia," her mother said gently, "you may not have used that word, but you've said often enough how little you trust Rule and his people."

Lily nodded thoughtfully. "You know, it doesn't strike me as healthy for Toby to be raised by someone who detests what he is."

"He's a little boy," Alicia said hotly. "Maybe he'll be lupus one day, but—"

"No," Rule said. "He is lupus *now*. He can't Change yet, but he's lupus."

Alicia's gaze darted to James, who met her eyes. It was quick, over in a second—but Lily caught the flash of something like triumph in Alicia's eyes.

Shit. "I really hoped you didn't know," she said softly.

Alicia flicked her an annoyed glance. "Are you playing the mysterious Oriental, or is that supposed to mean something?"

"You think you can keep Toby from becoming lupus by not allowing him to Change. Ever."

Alicia was good. She leaned back with nothing more than annoyance showing on her lush and lovely face. James wasn't so good. Guilt chased excitement across his oh-so-ordinary features before he settled on looking puzzled.

"Lily?" Rule said quietly. Just that.

She looked at him, aching. He'd guessed what she meant. By the tautness in his face, by the restrained fury in his eyes, she could tell he'd guessed. "Ruben's hunch played out the way most of them do. Let me handle it, okay?" *I know how to take a suspect down. I can do this.*

He held her eyes for a long moment, and maybe he read her determination. He nodded.

"There is," Cullen said slowly, "only one way to prevent the Change."

"That's right. Gado, it's called, from gadolinium, the rare earth element that's used to make the drug. The government developed the formula for gado back when it was forcibly registering lupi, but the use and manufacture of gado is now illegal—since lupi who are kept too long from the Change tend to go insane."

"Nonsense," Alicia snapped. "I know they claim that, but it simply isn't true."

"Actually, Alicia, that's what the FBI says. It was the FBI's Magical Crimes Division that used to trap lupi and administer the drug, and their records are pretty clear, though the government has not released them to the public in spite of filings under the Freedom of Information Act. But I've seen them. Half of the lupi kept on gado for more than a year committed suicide. Of the remaining half, thirty percent suffered psychotic breaks and most of the rest became catatonic."

"Good God," James said. "Alicia—"

"She's lying." Alicia was scornful. "She's so besotted by him she'll say anything. She admits these alleged records aren't available to the public, so she can make up any statistics that suit her."

Tempting as it was to slap the certainty right out of the bitch, Lily knew where the weak link was. She focused on James. "You're probably aware that the formula itself is protected by law. You may not have realized that purchases of gadolinium are tracked."

He flapped a hand. "Is that what this is about? You're jumping to conclusions. I bought a bit of gadolinium, sure. It's used in several other applications, you know, like MRI imaging. It has some intriguing paramagnetic properties, and I'm curious about how—"

"No, James. Whatever story you've concocted isn't going to fly. Agents have already spoken with your friend—the one who retired from the CDC." She glanced briefly at Louise. "The Center for Disease Control handled the manufacture of gado, back in the bad old days when lycanthropy was considered a disease with public health implications. James's friend must have given him the formula for gado."

James was still trying to tough it out. "I won't implicate John."

"Fine. There are agents at your house right now. They've found the wolfsbane."

Rule growled. It was not a human sound. But it was Cullen whose control snapped—and Cullen was fast, even for a lupus.

TWENTY-NINE

CULLEN damn near got to James. He would have, if he hadn't had to go past Rule to reach his target, but Rule was almost as quick as Cullen. He was on his feet before Lily could react, grabbing Cullen's arm, spinning him around.

James squeaked like a mouse stooped on by a hawk.

The two lupi locked gazes. Cullen's face was set, intent, but his eyes blazed as if the fire he could call was very near the surface. After one frozen second, Cullen jerked out a single nod, pulled his arm away from Rule—and left.

A second later, the front door slammed behind him.

Lily understood. Cullen had spent too many years as a lone wolf, and still had some anger-control issues. When fury flared too high, too fast, he got out.

"I don't understand." Louise's voice quavered.

"Don't you?" That was Alicia, her voice sharp with rising fury. And fear, Lily saw when she turned. The woman was terrified of lupi. "After watching that—watching them—he wanted to kill James! Didn't you see that? Don't you see what they're like? An inch away from violence, always. I won't let them make Toby like them! I won't!"

Lily ignored her to explain to Louise. "Cullen understood when I mentioned wolfsbane. It's the other key ingredient in gado. Wolfsbane is an herb with magical properties that interfere with a lupus's healing. Without it in the gado, they'd heal before the drug could have much effect." She paused. "It's also known as monkshood or aconite, and it's a deadly poison."

"Not to lupi!" James protested. "To humans, yes, but lupi—"

"To lupi, also." The growl wasn't quite gone from Rule's voice.

"It's a quick-acting neurotoxin for humans," Lily said. "A slow-acting poison for lupi. Even with the addition of the wolfsbane, they eventually throw off the effects of gado if it isn't readministered. At least . . . the adults do."

Her meaning sank in fast. James paled. "No. No, you must be mistaken."

Alicia jumped up from the couch. "They lie! Can't you see that? They'll say anything to make sure Toby turns out like *them*—"

"Shut up." Lily spun to face the other woman. "Shut the hell up, Alicia. Your hysterical determination to turn Toby into a human would have killed him. You were planning to poison your son—who will *not be able to heal major damage* until after the Change that the drug you fed him would have prevented!"

"Dear God," James whispered.

"It's not true." Tears began to gather in Alicia's large, dark eyes. "Mama, James—it's not true. You believe me, don't you? I'd never hurt Toby. He starts healing fast well before First Change. He *told* me so. That's one of the signs that the Change is nearly on him."

"Slightly faster, yes." Rule's voice was human once more, but flat. Utterly flat. "If you gave him gado now, he'd die in under a minute. Give it to him just before First Change, and it might take ten minutes or so to kill him."

In the silence that fell, Lily could hear the clock in the hall ticking. A car passed on the street. She could hear the *shush* of its tires clearly. She watched Alicia, watched as the woman's insane certainty began to crack.

It was James who broke the silence, though, his voice matter-of-fact. "Am I under arrest?"

Lily studied him. Beneath the outdoorsman's tan he was pale, his shock visible in the whiteness around his eyes. She shook her head. "Not at this time. The DEA will want to speak with you, but they're a busy bunch. I doubt they'll prosecute . . . unless someone pressures them to."

Alicia gasped. "That's a threat. You're threatening James."

"That would be an abuse of my authority." Lily had herself back under control. "But I strongly urge you to grant Rule full custody of Toby, as you agreed earlier. It would be awkward for you and James both if this all came out in court and became part of the public record, wouldn't it? The DEA might feel compelled to do something about a public violation of the law."

"Mama," Alicia said. "Mama, you heard her threaten me. You'll testify that she abused her authority, threatening to arrest James if I don't give in."

Louise's eyes were swimming, but her voice was clear. "Alicia, you concocted this reckless scheme without knowing what the consequences might be. Without even trying to find out. I don't know how you persuaded James—"

"She said it had been done to other young lupi." He stared down at his feet. "That if—if we could prevent First Change from occurring, the boy would never turn wolf. She . . . We wanted to save him from violence and ostracism. I . . ." His voice broke. "I thought she *knew*! I thought she must know about lupi, about . . ." He stopped, clamping his lips together.

Rule looked at him with the oddest expression, almost as if he pitied the man. "The only way to prevent First Change is to kill the youth undergoing it."

"I don't believe you," Alicia said. But her lip trembled.

Louise spoke. "Alicia, you didn't know what the effect of this drug would be. You assumed it would give you what you wanted, just as you always assume you can bludgeon reality into the shape you want. No, I will not testify for you. I will not allow Toby to live with you—not for six months, not for six weeks. At the moment, I'm not sure I'd trust you with him overnight."

"Mama." Tears clogged Alicia's voice. "Mama, don't."

Hurt swam in Louise's eyes, the kind of deep hurt that doesn't happen all at once. This had been building for years. "You don't know your son. You don't know him, not really, because you refuse to see the parts of him that scare you. Even if you'd been right about this gado drug, what you planned was wrong, terribly wrong. It would be like—like planning to lobotomize him."

"I want to save him!" Alicia cried. "You used to agree with me. You didn't trust *them* any more than I do."

"I used to fear what I didn't understand." Louise paused to give Rule a quick, apologetic glance. "Maybe I still do, a little. But at least I want to understand. You don't. You just want to make that part of Toby go away."

At this critical moment, Lily's pocket rang out with "The Star-Spangled Banner" again. She grimaced and gave Rule a look of apology. He squeezed her hand, telling her it was okay. She hurried to the hall.

This time Ruben's news had nothing to do with the drama being played out in the living room. After she disconnected, she had to make a couple of calls. She was speaking to Sheriff Deacon when James and Alicia left.

Lily stepped back, giving them as much privacy as possible. It didn't matter. Neither of them saw her. Alicia was crying quietly. James had his arm around her, his expression bewildered. He'd meant everything for the best, hadn't he? How could everything have gone so wrong?

Lily had put away more than one perp who'd meant everything for the best. Sometimes she'd felt sorry for them. Not this time.

In the living room, Rule was comforting a woman she did feel sorry for. Lily slipped her phone in her pocket, took a breath, and went back in.

"No." Louise shook her head. Rule had an arm around her

shoulders. "No, don't call. I don't need Connie or my son right now. I'd have to talk to them, and—" She drew a shaky breath. "I'm pretty much talked out for now."

She looked so tired. Lily had seen her looking her age before—when her leg was broken, and yesterday, after the shooting. This was different. "Mrs. Asteglio, I'm so sorry. If you—"

"Louise," the woman corrected her tartly. "It's Louise still, and don't you go thinking any of this was your fault, or that I hold any blame for you in it. You handled it as well as it could be handled. As well as she'd let you handle it," she added with some bitterness. "I imagine you'll search back over your conscience later, no matter what I say, because you're the type to worry that way. So am I. I'll spend time wondering how I could have blinded myself to just how far sunk Alicia was in her—her hatred for Toby's heritage, and what I should have done differently with her over the years. But not tonight."

She pulled back, away from Rule—and patted his cheek. "That's about as much hugging as I can manage. I'm not as comfortable with it as you are, and never will be, but I appreciate your caring. I'm going to bed now. It's early, but I . . . the dishes." She cast a glance at her kitchen, obviously second-guessing her decision. "Well, it won't take that long."

"We'll clean up the kitchen," Lily assured her. "I think I know where things go."

"Thank you. And that," she said with a faint smile, "is quite a compliment, if you don't know it. There aren't many I'd trust in my kitchen, but I know you'll clean it properly. Good night."

At the doorway, she paused and looked back at Rule. "You're wrong about one thing, you know. She does love Toby. It's a wrongheaded love that can't wrap itself around the whole of what he is, just the human part, and it's a selfish love in some ways, but it's there. So's the fear, but it isn't only fear of what he'll become. All his life she's been too afraid of losing him to let herself stay with him much. Toby knows that, in his heart if not his head. You need to know it, too, or you'll step wrong with him."

"Well," Lily said when she was gone. "How did a woman like Louise end up with a daughter like Alicia?"

"We've all got fault lines that our parents aren't responsible for." With a gust of a sigh he slid both arms around her, holding her as if that was all he needed in the world. Then stood utterly still, as if movement and words were both beyond him for the moment. His breath stirred her hair.

After a moment he spoke quietly, in a voice husky with emotion. "Toby's mine now."

Lily blinked suddenly damp eyes, but felt obliged to say, "Alicia could change her mind again."

"She won't." He stroked her hair. "Not this time. Not when it would mean James's arrest on drug charges." He straightened, and now, amazingly, he was grinning. "Was that a bluff, that you'd put pressure on the DEA to make the arrest?"

"The DEA doesn't much care which cases I want them to prosecute," she said dryly. "But we could certainly bring some of it up in court and, uh, leak it to the press. The publicity might force them to act." She hesitated. "You feel sorry for James, don't you?"

"You gave me the luxury of pity," he said, and dropped another kiss, this one on her forehead. "You stopped them."

"Ruben did it, really."

"Ah, yes. His hunch. How did he happen to have a hunch about a man he'd never heard of?"

"I told you I was going to do a run on James? Well, I asked Ida to do it—just a basic run, you understand, nothing fancy. She said she was ready to e-mail me the results when Ruben came out of his office, looking puzzled. He asked her why she'd run a Level Three search for me. She said she hadn't, of course. I don't have the authority for a Level Three—it involves so many agencies outside the Bureau. So Ruben said to her, 'Ah, I see. But it's supposed to be Level Three. Let Lily know I authorized it, will you? And find out if she knows why.' Then he went back into his office."

"He didn't know why he authorized it." Rule shook his head in a marveling way.

"Neither of us did until we saw the report from the agency

that tracks sales of gadolinium." She sighed. "I was hoping it was the wrong James French. That happens sometimes, though the social security number was a match. But I should have told you. There was so much going on, and we were late, but . . . I should have told you." He'd have kept an eye on Cullen if he'd had more warning. As it was . . . "Would Cullen have killed French if you hadn't stopped him?"

"He loves Toby, and he had an unpleasant experience with gado many years ago."

Which did not answer her question . . . or maybe it did.

He hugged her closer for a moment. "About those dishes. You had another phone call from Ruben. I can handle the cleanup, if you need to go."

She shook her head, a leaden feeling in her stomach. "I'm not needed. I already notified Deacon and the hospital. Ruben's sending a Medevac chopper to pick up Hodges. He needs more expert care than he can get here."

"Why?"

"Roy Don Meacham died a couple hours ago. Progressive neurological damage, they said. Just like the dogs."

DARKNESS and light are the same to one without eyes, yet it remembered night. It remembered so much more than it had before—not what it needed most to remember, but other things. Things like night, street, boy . . . when the boy left with the other warmth, it had almost followed. It had been excited because it remembered *boy* and had wanted to see what a boy did. There had been something about the other warmth, too . . . something *familiar*.

That was it, yes. It hadn't remembered, but for a moment it had seemed there was something to remember. But it wasn't drawn to that warmth the way it was to the man. The one who knew it.

It had formed a plan. It would stay near the house until the man came out. Somehow it would speak to the man. If it could hang on to words long enough to speak to the man, maybe it would know what to ask.

So it stayed outside the house. It knew walls once more, but that wasn't why it didn't enter, for it also remembered sliding through walls. This puzzled it—why did it remember walls as a barrier? But this house would not admit it, not through walls or doors or windows. It didn't know why.

Perhaps the man had forbidden it to enter.

It cringed back upon itself. Yes, that might be. It didn't remember a forbidding, but it forgot so much, so much. Still, it remembered attacking the man. While in the old man's warmth, it had tried to kill the man. The horror of that moment made its pieces clatter together, a harsh and painful dissonance.

In its misery, it had allowed The Voice to call it back. But The Voice fed it poorly, with such small lives—sparks only, little sparks that flared for a second, then were gone, swallowed by the cold.

It had left The Voice, searching until it found the house once more, the house where the man was.

The man had nearly killed it. It shuddered, remembering that as well. It had bared its throat—the warmth's throat—and tried to hold itself still for that terrible judgment, which was the man's right.

It had failed, and fled.

Coward.

That word it didn't want to remember, but it did. Yes, the man had probably forbidden it entry to the house, and it had to obey the man. It deserved no better. But it was cold, so cold again . . . always cold, unless it was in a warmth. Even feeding well didn't warm it for long. But the right warmths were so hard to find . . .

Hunger and cold and a longing so keen it drowned the rest drew it closer to the house whose walls wouldn't allow it in. It could feel the warmths inside, several large warmths other than the man. They didn't interest it until one warmth shifted, moving its thoughts or its self in a strange way. Opening . . . For a second it saw a way in.

Then it was gone. A door had opened in that warmth, then shut. It hung there, astonished, as still as it could be with its crashing, disintegrating pieces.

The door didn't open again.

Disappointment crushed it. It needed to feed. It needed to feed and be warm—oh, how it needed that, before it began losing *night* and *street* and *boy* and all that it had remembered.

It was afraid to enter the small warmths the way it had before. They lacked words. Maybe that was why it had lost words for so long: it spent too much time in the small warmths. But it couldn't hold itself together much longer. It needed . . . needed . . .

The Voice was calling. It heard, and all its pieces vibrated with hate. Not yet. It wasn't going back yet to the thin meals and commands and—and something it couldn't remember, but that it hated above all the rest. It had a plan. It hadn't followed the boy because . . . because . . .

Why hadn't it followed the boy? It couldn't remember. It had had a plan, but it couldn't remember.

Screaming in silent rage and despair, it lost its hold on where it was and began drifting. The Voice was calling, tugging at it. It gave up and allowed this. The Voice would feed it.

Maybe this time it would find a way to make The Voice feed it properly. Maybe if it fed enough, it could kill The Voice. That felt right. Important. Kill The Voice, and it would regain . . . something. Something it needed so much.

The comfort of this new plan eased the pain of losing the other one. Something involving the boy . . . It did remember the boy.

Maybe, once it fed, it would remember what it needed from the boy.

THIRTY

THE next morning was Saturday. In July, the sun sticks his head over the horizon around six twenty. Rule dragged Lily out for a run at six.

Since he'd woken her even earlier for another sort of exercise, she didn't complain as much as she might have—especially when he was right. She needed a good run to clear her head.

It was almost cool at that hour. The air was thick, the ozone warning high, but the mercury had dipped below seventy by at least a degree. Maybe even two.

She didn't push herself until the last mile, so was able to fill Rule in on where the investigation was headed. Laying it out for him cleared her head, too. By the time she was in the shower, washing off the sweat, she'd figured out what the next step needed to be.

They'd soon have a list of graves to be salted. Headquarters was working on it. That was one great thing about turning fed—she could get information a helluva lot faster, even when she needed data from several jurisdictions.

The hundred-mile radius around Halo included multiple North Carolina counties as well as parts of South Carolina and Virginia. That was the problem, Lily thought, with these dinky little eastern states. A hundred miles this way or that, and you ran right out of state. Plus they needed to sort by sex—the ghosts were consistent about calling the wraith "he"—and time of death. The major power wind of the Turning had hit at 2:53 EST, so they were excluding deaths after four P.M. that day.

They'd received the first list well before Lily left for dinner: eighty-two deaths that might have produced the wraith. Unfortunately, it turned out to be incomplete. After a great deal of thinking, pacing—and the occasional sketching of arcane symbols in the air, which worried the cops in the room no end—Cullen had declared that the spell casting could have taken place up to two days after the death. Blood retained a magical connection to the deceased for that long. He thought it likely the spell had been cast very soon after death, but they had to look at deaths over a period of two and a half days.

Lily had had to call headquarters and get them to start over. With luck, though, the expanded list would be waiting for her when she booted up.

Narrowing that list was going to be a lot harder. "Get the name," Cynna had said. She was trying.

They had no criteria for eliminating any of the male decedents over that three-day period, so they had to go after the human end, the practitioner who'd created the wraith. That practitioner, according to this Baron spirit, was a medium. A woman.

Next step, then, was hunting a medium among all the people who'd had contact with one of the deceased at or near the time of death. That was going to take a while. Lily could tell by touch if someone was a medium. Cullen could see a person's magic, but couldn't always tell what their Gift was. Sometimes, yes, but not always. This morning on her run, she'd figured out how to use him anyway.

And the press would help.

She got to her temporary field office at 7:10, booted up her laptop, and got to work. The list was there—and hallelujah, it was sortable. It made sense to start with the deaths on the day of the Turning and those in or very near Halo.

When Brown—the older, grumpier Brown—arrived at seven thirty with Jacobs—white, male, ten years with the Bureau, seldom spoke—she had a lot of white thumbtacks stuck into the map they'd pinned to the wall. That map already had red and green pins in it, showing where dead animals had been found.

The dead animals were noticeably clustered on the west side of town.

"Whatcha got?" Brown asked, sipping from an oversize foam cup of coffee.

"The list of deaths. We've got more animal deaths on the west side of town." She gestured at the map. "We'll focus on deaths on that side first."

"Hospital's on the west side."

Which meant it included the majority of deaths. "We'll need to check hospital personnel anyway. Here's the plan. You know we're looking for a medium, which means we're looking for a woman."

Brown grunted. Jacobs actually spoke. "Problem is, you're the only one can tell."

"That's right. And I can't testify about what I learn, but we'll jump that hurdle later. For now we just need to find her."

"You're buying all that voodoo stuff?" Brown said.

"I trust the agent who collected the information, so—yes. We'll assume for now it's accurate, so we're looking for a woman who had access to the body. She needed blood for the spell. Brown, you'll divvy up the list of decedents and make the assignments. I want to know everyone who had access to these people just before, after, or when they died."

"Male and female both?"

"Yeah, get both. We'll look at females first, but we might need the others as witsnesses. I'll be visiting funeral homes and the hospital."

Brown nodded glumly. "Better look at paramedics, too. Ambulance drivers. Cops."

He caught on quick. Emergency personnel, like hospital workers and morticians, had plenty of access to the dying and the dead. "Good point." She grinned. "Careful, Brown. I might start liking you."

He managed to control his enthusiasm.

"When you're divvying up the deaths to investigate, leave yourself out. I'm going to give a press conference."

"Shit. You're not asking me to—"

"No, I'll talk to the reporters. Locals only, emphasis on TV and radio. I'll ask that anyone who knows someone who died on the day of the Turning come to the sheriff's office and speak with us. You'll interview those who turn up. You and Seabourne."

Now he looked horrified. "You're pairing me with that—that—"

"I am. You'll take names and addresses, relationship to the deceased, and ask who else was around at the pertinent period. He'll spot any who have Gifts. He may be able to tell if one is a medium."

"Somehow I don't think our perp will trot herself down here to chat."

"If she doesn't, we'll still have more information than we do now. We'll be able to cross off some of those connected to the deaths on our list because they lack Gifts."

He sighed heavily. "Putting her on notice, are you?"

"Yeah. Yeah, I am. Might shake her up a bit." She grinned at him, her blood fizzing. She had a line on the human perp now, and a way of hauling in that line. It was just a matter of time.

THE next two and a half days were as frustrating as any Lily could remember. The high point hit Saturday afternoon when she found a medium who worked for one of the mortuaries. Sandy Kaufman dressed the hair of the dead and she was very, very blond—in every sense of the word. Her lights were several bulbs short of a string, in Lily's opinion—but she was a fairly strong medium.

Unfortunately, she hadn't dressed the hair of any of the dead from the Turning. She'd been in Hawaii, basking on the beach with her boyfriend, her mother, her mother's boyfriend, and her mother's boyfriend's mother.

Lily heard from Dr. Alderson on Sunday. The rats they'd fed the contaminated meat to were doing fine. No detectable brain damage.

On Monday at four thirty she was alone in the conference room. In the last three days she'd checked out every person who worked at the town's two mortuaries and all but two of the EMTs, paramedics, and ambulance drivers; those two were on vacation out of the state. She was about a third of the way through the hospital personnel who might have had contact with any of the dead.

In addition, seventy-two people had come forward in response to her press conference. Cullen had spotted four Gifted women, three of whom Lily would need to check. The fourth had an obvious Fire Gift, he said.

Takes one to know one, she supposed.

It was a good thing she was patient. You had to be, if you worked in law enforcement. There was so damned much waiting involved, so many wrong turns, dead ends, false trails. They had the names and locations of 181 graves that might or might not hold the remains of one of the scattered dead. They did not have permission to pour salt on those graves.

Judges were not known for consulting with spirits. They were also not keen on anything that smacked of the desecration of graves. The U.S. attorney Lily had contacted had passed the job to an assistant, who'd been dragging his feet. Lily couldn't really blame him, but she'd sicced Ruben's secretary, Ida, on him anyway. No one withstood Ida for long.

At the moment she was going over the reports on Hodge and Meacham one more time while she waited for her phone to ring. Rule, Alicia, Toby, and Louise should be in the judge's chambers by now, with their attendant lawyers.

Lily had offered to go, in spite of the case; Rule told her she wouldn't be needed. This meeting with the judge was a formality. He and Alicia had already drawn up and signed a custody agreement giving Rule sole custody of his son. The judge simply had to approve it.

She hoped he was right. Of course he was right. There was no reason to deny the change of custody other than the most blatant prejudice against lupi, and judges were generally sensible, levelheaded people.

Except for the few who were complete bobble-heads. She'd run into a few so persuaded of their judicial invincibility—and for so little reason—that they'd rule against Mother Teresa if they were in the mood . . .

Focus, she told herself, and returned to her reading.

She was going over everything they had on Meacham's and Hodge's backgrounds one more time. There had to be something the two men had in common other than a Y-chromosome. Something that had caused them, rather than two others, to be possessed by the wraith.

She finished the physical findings and set them aside. Nothing helpful there. Meacham had AB positive blood; Hodge had O negative. One drank; the other was a teetotaler. One was of European extraction; the other, African American. Neither smoked, but that was true of too many others to be useful.

Moving on to the statements from friends and relatives, she found that Meacham had spoken of being allergic to cats. Nothing about any allergies in Hodge's records, but she made a note to find out. Unlike Meacham, Hodge was still alive, so they could just ask him.

Though he was showing signs of neurological damage—slight, but it was there. Just like Meacham. Just like the dogs.

She started slogging through a long account by a woman who'd known Meacham since he was a kid and had felt compelled to share everything from the third grade on up. Meacham hadn't gone to the same school as Hodge, not until high school, but the town had only one high school, so that wasn't significant.

Sounded like Roy Don had been something of a hell-raiser . . . several tickets for speeding, and the woman said he'd totaled his car when he was seventeen, and . . . wait. Wait. Might be something here.

Quickly she shuffled back through the official medical reports. Yes, there it was—a record of the emergency room treatment he'd received. It took her a moment to translate the doctorese, but it sounded as if the impact of the steering wheel had bruised his heart, causing fluid to build up. His heart had stopped beating briefly.

Hodge's heart had stopped, too. Wasn't that what the chatty Dr. Patel had said? Last year Hodge had a heart attack on his way to the operating room, and his heart had stopped beating.

Check it, check it. She dived into another stack of papers, rummaging for the medical report on Hodge.

Her phone rang in her jacket pocket. Beethoven's Fifth. She grabbed it. "Yes?"

"He's mine." The relief and joy in Rule's voice jigged her heart into a quick flip. "The judge signed off on our custody arrangement. Toby is fully mine now."

Yes! No bobble-heads in that courtroom! "We're celebrating, right?"

"With dinner out. I know it's hard for you to get time clear right now—"

"I'll be there. Unless someone else gets killed, I will absolutely be there. Um . . . there's that Leidolf deal tonight." The secrecy bug was catching. Even though no one was in the room, she avoided saying anything specific about clan stuff. "Maybe we could have dinner a little late and go directly there after?"

Rule suggested seven thirty. The door opened and Brown Two marched in, brimming with purpose and urgency.

Lily said a quick goodbye and disconnected. "What?"

"One of the graves on the list has been disturbed," Brown Two said crisply. "The groundskeeper notified the local police, who are out there now."

THIRTY-ONE

"So it was just kids doing a little freelance gardening?" Rule asked.

"Yeah." Lily sighed. "They messed with several graves, not just the one that's on our list. That's the problem with going to the public for help. Before you know it, a few enterprising teens decide we've got a zombie outbreak on our hands and they'd better plant garlic on graves at midnight. Garlic." She was disgusted. "They couldn't even get their myths right. That's for vampires, who also don't exist."

"Zombies aren't a myth," Cullen said from the driver's seat of Rule's Mercedes. "They aren't affected by garlic, but they aren't a myth."

Lily stared at the back of his head. "You've got to be kidding."

Rule sat in the backseat with Lily. It wasn't his preferred spot, though being able to put his arm around his *nadia* was welcome. But the dignity of his role tonight required some touches of pomp.

Cullen was acting as chauffeur, Alex as bodyguard. Normally Cullen would have been seriously unwelcome at a Leidolf ceremony, but with the Rhej unable to attend, the families had been glad of Cullen's offer to provide the *ardor iunctio*. The magical fire wasn't essential, but it was traditional.

"No one makes zombies," Cullen was saying, "because they're entirely too much trouble. It takes an ungodly amount of power and the spell's a son of a bitch, and what do you get? A shambling corpse that stinks to high heaven, loses fingers and toes, and doesn't come with a remote control. What good is that?"

"You haven't. Tell me you haven't tried."

Cullen snorted. "Am I an idiot? Of course not. Like I said, too much power, time, and trouble for very little results. What would I do with a zombie once I raised one?"

"What would anyone do with one?" Alex asked. "Someone must have thought they'd be useful. They created a spell for it."

"People keep trying to use magic to skip over death the way you can skip commercials with TiVo. It keeps not working. Whoever created the first zombie-raising spell back in the pre-Purge days wasn't trying to raise a corpse to make it walk. They wanted to bring the dead to life." He shrugged. "Not all sorcerers were as sane and sensible as yours truly."

Rule grinned. "Everything's relative. Turn's coming up on the right."

They were winding along a narrow gravel road, headed for a parking area near a campsite. The others would already be there.

They'd celebrated Rule's custody victory at the local pizza place, an incredibly noisy place with arcade games and truly wretched salads. Toby's choice, obviously. Alicia had behaved with great dignity in the judge's chambers; afterward she'd asked to spend some time with Toby before she headed back to Washington. Of course Rule had agreed. Toby wanted his mother to be part of his life. He needed that.

Tonight, though, Toby was home with Louise. Children did not attend a *gens compleo*.

It would be held inside the Uwharrie National Forest in a picnic area where hikers were allowed by day. Technically the area was closed at night, but one of Leidolf's members was a senior ranger. They wouldn't be bothered.

Not that Rule had explained this in detail to Lily. The informality of their arrangements—which hadn't included applying for permission—might worry her.

"You're jazzed about this ceremony, aren't you?" Lily asked softly.

He had one arm around her, the better to play with her hair when the mood struck. So he did. "The *gens compleo* is a joyous occasion. I've performed it once before, standing in for my father when he was healing. Ah, not the most recent healing, when we met." Which had been the result of an attempted assassination by Leidolf. "This was years ago."

"And it's joyous even when it's Leidolf."

He knew the point she wanted to make. "I haven't rearranged my thinking yet, but it is . . . changing. And the mantle is in no doubt. It rejoices."

"You make it sound sentient. Like it knows about the ceremony."

"It isn't sentient, but it isn't precisely not sentient, either." As usual when trying to describe a mantle, he ran out of words. "It . . . recognizes what is to happen. Lily, I haven't thanked you for making time for this tonight. I know it wasn't easy."

"No, it wasn't, but this is what we came here for. This and Toby." She gripped his hand and squeezed once. "Who is now ours."

"Another place where I must rearrange my thinking," he murmured. "When I called you, I said Toby was mine."

"According to the court, he is."

"But I like the sound of *ours* better."

"Well." Her voice went low and quiet. "So do I."

The car slowed and pulled into a small, bare-ground parking area. It was full except for the section reserved for Rule's vehicle. Two men waited there, dressed in the preferred lupus style—jeans, no shirt. Cullen kept the motor running while Alex got out and spoke briefly to the men, then motioned for Cullen to park.

"More guards?" Lily said, eyebrows lifting. "I thought you were safe."

"I am. No lupus, Leidolf or otherwise, would attack a Rho—and for tonight, I stand in place of a Rho—at a *gens compleo*." Rule waited for Alex to open his door. "It would be deeply insulting if I appeared without guards, however."

Cullen opened Lily's door and bowed—overdoing it, of course. Alex opened Rule's door without flourishes.

"The guards are ceremonial, then?" Lily asked when he joined her. "A way of marking the importance of the ceremony?"

"In part. More, though, to appear without them would be like saying I didn't think any of them could pose a threat."

"But they aren't a threat. You just said they wouldn't attack."

"There's a difference between wouldn't and couldn't. The presence of guards acknowledges that they *could*."

"Lupus psychology," she muttered. "Is there any part of it that isn't based on who can beat up who?"

Cullen grinned. "There's also sex. Can't leave that out."

Lily rolled her eyes.

Silent for the moment, they walked along the path to the picnic spot—Alex in front, then Rule with Lily, followed first by Cullen, then by the two guards. The air was warm, silky, rich with scent. In Rule's gut the mantles coiled and stirred, awake to the possibilities of the night.

Rule was amused by the relationship that had developed between his *nadia* and his closest friend. From the first, Lily had opted to treat Cullen like a younger brother—annoying, uncouth, but hers to put up with. That was funny for so many reasons, not least that Cullen was over thirty years older than Lily.

The role had amused Cullen, too, at first, but Rule suspected he'd grown to cherish it far more than he'd admit. Now it was habit, one they both enjoyed.

Sometimes Rule wondered how conscious Lily's initial choice to make a brother of Cullen had been. Did she know she'd done it to guard herself from Cullen's potent sexuality?

She would have believed it terribly wrong to sleep with Rule's friend, or even to lust after him.

And now . . . and now, Rule was uneasily aware, he felt the same way. It would tear something in him if she were to be with another man.

Jealousy was a monster that destroyed the joy men and women could make together. He knew that, and yet . . . Lily was his mate. He was incapable of being with another woman; perhaps it wasn't so terrible to want to be the only one she lay with.

Lily spoke, her voice thoughtful. "Rule, you can tell what clan a lupus belongs to by smell."

"That's right. It's subtle, but unmistakable."

"So which clan do you smell like?"

Must she push about this every moment? "Nokolai."

"Mostly," Cullen said.

"Mostly?" Astonished, Rule turned to stare at his friend.

Cullen shrugged. "Lately there's a whiff of Leidolf, too. There wasn't at first, but there is now. Interesting, isn't it?"

"You didn't know?" Alex asked softly.

Rule had himself back under control. He turned around. "No." One didn't smell oneself, after all. Nor had he been through the blooding ceremony by which a lupus was adopted into another clan.

Nor, dammit, had anyone *told* him. "You smell it, too?"

Alex nodded.

He considered a moment, then said, "Good. I won't smell entirely strange to the youths I bring into the mantle."

Alex's smile was small and brief, but Rule felt he'd passed some test. How annoying. He didn't care for tests—or for having everyone else be aware of something as basic as a change in his scent. Why hadn't they told him?

Lily leaned closer to whisper, "Pissed about me being right, aren't you?"

"Yes." After a moment he added, "More that I didn't guess. Cullen smells like Nokolai now, after all. It should have occurred to me. But you can't smell the difference."

"No, of course not."

Yet she'd guessed. He couldn't decide how he felt about that. He knew how he felt about no one telling him, though. Annoyed.

He'd been hearing the crowd ahead for some time—laughter, talk, a couple of violins that couldn't settle on a song to share. Apparently it was loud enough now for Lily's ears, too, for she said, "Sounds like everyone's excited."

Her words and voice were matter-of-fact. He wasn't sure how he knew she was tense, but he did, and took her hand. "They'll welcome you," he said gently.

"I don't see why they should. I'm not Leidolf, and I'm the reason they couldn't hold their ceremony at their clanhome."

Unexpectedly, Alex stopped and looked at her. "No! This—this alteration is not because of you, but because the Lady wished it so. They understand that. You're a Chosen. It doesn't matter what clan . . . Well, it doesn't matter greatly. A Chosen must be welcome, just as a Rhej would be."

For Alex, that was a long speech.

Lily blinked once—a slow blink, a cat's acknowledgment. "Thank you for telling me that, Alex."

Alex nodded, turned, and resumed walking. A few moments later they reached the clearing.

There were coolers scattered around the perimeter, and lanterns—the old-fashioned kind, burning lamp oil. The scents were rich, from that of the burning oil to that of the people, perhaps thirty of them, young and old, male and female. Everyone was two-footed still. No children. Children attended most ceremonies, but not the *gens compleo*, which marked the turning from child to adult. Almost everyone wore jeans or cutoffs, the men without shirts.

The two notable exceptions were young, male, and naked.

Rule waited. Lantern light flickered on smiling faces that, a few at a time, turned toward him. As they saw him, they fell silent.

He touched Lily's arm and nodded at the nearest cluster of people. She nodded and moved away.

When everyone was still, Rule walked alone to the fire pit in the center of the clearing, where neatly stacked logs waited.

Quite a large pile, he noted, holding his face appropriately stern. They were taking advantage of having a sorcerer here to handle the *ardor iunctio.*

He nodded at Alex and Cullen. They moved to their positions—Alex at his right hand, Cullen at his left. The two guards took up positions at his back.

Rule took a deep breath—and called up the newer mantle.

They both came, a rush of power fizzing in his blood, flooding his muscles. He'd expected that. He took a second breath and carefully tucked the Nokolai mantle back down. It didn't want to go, but slowly he eased it into its coil in his belly.

And spoke. "Leidolf!"

Voices answered, not in unison: "We listen!" mingled with the more formal, *"Nos audio!"*

"We are here to admit two of ours into Leidolf as adults. I call the *gens compleo.*" He paused while they cheered. "David Alan Auckley. Jeffrey Merrick Lane. Come forward."

Two naked, healthy young men stepped out of the crowd. One was typical Leidolf—very northern European with pale skin and wheat blond hair, a lean young animal proud of his body and his place tonight. The other was ruddier, burlier, with longish brown hair and a gleam in his eyes that suggested he took very little seriously.

Each dropped to one knee in front of Rule.

Rule had never met either youth, but he'd been told their names and which was the elder by a few days, and so would go first. He looked the blond boy in the eye. The mantle knew him. "David."

Immediately David ducked his head, baring his nape.

Rule looked at the other one. Again the sense of recognition from the mantle as their eyes met. "Jeffrey."

Jeffrey dropped his head.

He said their names again, putting more power into his voice. This time they prostrated themselves, lying flat, facedown, in the dirt.

He knelt then at their heads, laying a hand on each young,

strong neck, curving his fingers until he found the vein he needed.

He dug in his thumbnails, scraping across both veins.

This was the part he'd been unsure of. Nokolai used a blade fixed to a thumb brace to open the vein. Leidolf used the traditional method. Rule had filed his thumbnails to as sharp a point as he could.

It worked. Blood trickled down each neck.

The next words were not Latin. They came from an older language, one lost to all except the Rhejes, who must have such words in the oldest memories. He spoke them softly, making each sound distinct: *"Nera ék amat."* He had no idea what the words meant.

It didn't matter. The mantles knew. They leaped to his call, sliding down his arms like water, rushing along his hands, tasting the blood there. The two young men jolted as if he'd shocked them with an electric current, but he knew it was bliss, not pain, that shuddered through them.

The mantles, never quite separate from him, returned. The sense of them was subtly different, enlivened by the richness of youth. He straightened.

Only then did he realize what had happened. What he'd done. He'd successfully sent the mantles into both young men, and drawn part of them into the mantles.

Both mantles.

David and Jeffrey were now fully Leidolf . . . and fully Nokolai.

THIRTY-TWO

LILY watched as Rule stood. According to what he had told her earlier, the actual *gens compleo* was finished now. The rest of the ceremony was more symbolic, and mostly for the families.

He said something in that bastardized Latin they used. The two young men rose to face their families, neither of them bothered one whit by full-frontal, public nudity. Lily couldn't say the same for herself, but she was adapting as best she could to lupus ways. And the view was . . . interesting.

Rule stepped back, exchanging one long glance with Cullen. Neither man's expression changed. Then Rule gestured at the waiting logs.

This time, Cullen was *supposed* to show off.

Lily suspected he would have relished a robe with long sleeves that could sway dramatically, but he made do just fine in his ragged jeans. He stepped close to the fire pit, lifting both arms and chanting softly—and, she suspected, unnecessarily. Cullen could call fire with the flick of his hand.

He shook his hands over the logs as if dashing water from them, and fire fell as if it were, indeed, flung water drops. The logs burst into flame all at once, with an enthusiastic *whoosh*.

Normal flames at first. Gradually they changed, turning the bright green of a Granny Smith apple. The same green as the baby fire he'd played with in the conference room, she realized. He looked at Rule and nodded.

"Leidolf," Rule said, "come share in the *ardor iunctio.*"

That meant "joining fire." Lily had been learning a few bits of Latin, those that any clan member was expected to know.

Solemnly, in twos and threes, the clan members approached the fire. The woman next to Lily—an older woman, gray-haired, with glasses and a fair amount of pudge poured into her jeans—said, "Come on," and took Lily's hand.

"But I'm not—"

"You're welcome to the *ardor,*" the woman said, and tugged again on Lily's hand.

So Lily, too, moved up to the joining fire.

Rule went first. He plunged his hands into that spooky green fire, up to the elbows. And smiled. This, he'd told Lily earlier, was when he let a trickle of the mantle free, just a drop, joining it to the flames.

He stepped back, and those closest to the fire moved up, thrusting in their hands, some scooping up handfuls of flame—and it clung to them for several seconds, dancing merrily on flesh.

After a few moments, and with a few sighs of regret, the first group moved back and others moved forward eagerly, reaching for apple green fire. As they touched it, they grinned. Some of the women giggled. One man laughed out loud. His fire had scampered up his arm and kissed his cheek.

The others laughed, too. Lily looked at Cullen, who grinned. A curl of flame swam up a young woman's arm to lick at her lips. She laughed, delighted.

Oh, yes, Cullen was showing off, and enjoying it immensely.

It was Lily's turn. Green fire, she told herself firmly, was nothing like mage fire or regular fire. She'd seen how little hurt anyone took from it. So she held her breath and sank her hands into the blaze.

It tickled. It was warm and dry and merry in a way her skin understood, if her head didn't. There was magic in it. And the magic tickled.

Everything tight and worried eased out of her as she watched the wonder of green flames dance cheerfully on her skin. Then a bright, mischievous thread darted up her arm—and jumped onto her breast. She yelped. "Cullen! Behave!"

He laughed. Everyone laughed. And then it was time for her to reluctantly step back, time to allow the rest their turn to safely play with fire.

When they had, and had stepped back, Rule spoke softly, in a rhythmic cadence that suggested the words were part of the ritual, though this time they were English words. "We are the fire."

"We are the fire," everyone repeated, not quite solemn anymore.

"Safe in joining, safe together. We are clan."

"We are clan," the others echoed.

Rule grinned. "Let's eat. And then we play."

Cullen snapped his fingers. Yellow and orange flames ate up the green, returning the bonfire to a normal sort of cheer— hot and happy and dangerous.

Lily made her way over to Rule. She leaned in to hug him—and whispered in his ear. "What's wrong?"

Because something wasn't as it should be. That glance he'd exchanged with Cullen . . . She knew both men too well. Their faces hadn't revealed a damned thing, which was what had tipped her off.

He nuzzled her ear. "I'll tell you later. It won't matter right away."

Well, that was interesting.

Interesting, too, was the next part, which was very much a party. The coolers held beer and soft drinks—the beer being for those women who wanted to indulge, since lupi didn't bother with alcohol. Their bodies purged it too quickly. There were cupcakes, too, and brownies, and cookies, all home-made.

Rule stayed with her at first, introducing her and learning names. After the first few minutes, she relaxed and enjoyed herself. The only other time she'd hung out with Leidolf had involved guns and threats. This was much nicer.

Unlike Nokolai, Leidolf had a lamentable tendency to divide up into male and female clusters. She was chatting with one of the female clusters when one of them said to another in a low, gossipy voice, "Thank goodness Crystal didn't come."

"Now, Rachel, don't you start."

"No, really. You've got to admit it's better this way. She kept insisting she would come. I really thought she would, too."

"She and David are close, after all," put in another woman.

"Well, fuck-friends aren't normally asked to a *gens compleo*, are they?"

"Rachel," one of the older woman said sharply, "that's enough. If Crystal had wanted to come, we would have welcomed her. That's tradition. This would have been Charley's night, so his family had the right to attend if they wished."

Rachel tossed her head. "I don't care what you say. I think she showed good sense by staying home. It would've been painful for her and just drained the joy right out of things for everyone else."

"Crystal Kessenblaum?" Lily asked, curious.

"Yes, do you know her?"

"As a matter of fact, yes. At least we've met. I had no idea she was Leidolf."

"Oh, no, she's not clan," the older woman assured her. "She and Charley shared a mother, not a father. But traditionally, even out-clan family are welcome at the *gens compleo* if they wish to come. Rachel here is out-clan herself." She gave Rachel a pointed glance, then sighed. "Poor Charley. Such a tragedy when they die so young."

At that point Rule gave a low whistle. Everyone turned toward him.

"Anyone up to a chase?" he asked, grinning.

A couple of the younger men whooped. Every man there immediately shucked what little clothing he'd bothered with. The women laughed, some shouting catcalls or ribald suggestions. The older woman who'd told Lily she was welcome to the fire went up to the burly, brown-haired youth, now a young adult in his clan's eyes, and hugged him hard. The blond youth had a few hugs to give and receive, too, but quickly.

The men were eager for the chase. Lily was not.

Rule and Alex had discussed this at length. It was common for an older Rho to let his Lu Nuncio lead the chase—but until now, the Lu Nuncio had always also been the heir.

Alex was Lu Nuncio. Rule was heir. It would have been acceptable for Rule to give Alex the role, but in the end Rule had decided he would take the Rho's part fully. He was young enough, fit enough, to give the rest a good run. To give the role to Alex said that either he considered himself less fit, or that he didn't trust the Leidolf wolves to honor the chase.

Which meant that in a moment, Rule would Change and race off into the night. Alex was supposed to count off twenty seconds' head start—but, Rule had told her, grinning, it was almost never the full twenty seconds. Somewhere around fifteen, Alex would release the other wolves to the chase.

It was all in fun, and yet it wasn't. The chase game was a way of reinforcing the Rho's dominance. A Rho or his Lu Nuncio was supposed to outrun or outfox the lupi on his tail and return to the bonfire without being tagged. Tagging meant a touch solid enough to leave some of Rule's scent on the other wolf. A bit of blood was allowed, but not encouraged, since there wasn't supposed to be any combat. A Rho's prowess was judged on both his canniness and his athleticism—and on how long he kept the others running after him.

Alex would remain behind, as would Cullen, who had no part in a Leidolf chase. And so, dammit, would the two guards.

Lily had argued when she learned about that, but Rule would not be budged. A Rho did not take guards on a chase game. Ever. So he'd be running from a dozen lupi who might or might not want his blood.

They wouldn't kill him, he'd assured her calmly. They wouldn't endanger the mantle that way. At worst, if he was clumsy enough to be trapped by a few Leidolf willing to break the rules of the chase, they'd bloody him. Or try to. He seemed entirely too sure of his ability to bloody them worse.

Rule had stripped down as enthusiastically as any of them. He winked at her, grinning. She wanted to punch him. Then he looked around, a gleam in his eye that made her think of Cullen—or of Toby. Pure mischief, that gleam.

And he Changed.

Not quite as instantly as when he'd pulled himself through that door in midair, but still too fast for her eyes to track. One moment he stood there, naked and grinning. The next he stood there four-footed and grinning. And her heart just turned over.

That's how I remember him . . .

The thought ghosted across her mind even as the love welled up, a butterfly kiss from her other self, who'd known him only as wolf. Even as, she realized, a dozen other lupi Changed—unexpectedly, pulled into it by the sudden, imperative Change of their leader. Even Cullen. The sorcerer gave one surprised yelp before being dragged into the Change willy-nilly.

Oh, he'd tricked them, hadn't he? Given himself a good head start. Lily grinned as Rule raced off into the night.

THE door! The door was open!

They had come. The warmths had all come to it, even the man, and it had thrilled. Surely this was meant. But when it tried to rush in close, it couldn't. It had watched and wept pieces of itself, longing with everything it was to go up to the fire, to join in the fire sharing. And it couldn't. Though they had come to it, it was blocked. Blocked, it understood dimly, by the one it most needed to get close to. By the man—or by the magic the man held within him.

But its waiting paid off, for the man Changed himself and rushed off—and when he did, the other warmth opened the door to itself once again. This time the door hung open slightly, beckoning.

Desperate, elated, it rushed in.

RULE ran full-out, rejoicing in the speed, the sheer physical effort of the chase. It had been too long, much too long, since he'd played with other wolves, and he knew now that all his solid, logical reasons for taking this role were only part of the story.

He wanted them to chase him. He wanted to outrun them, trick them, fool them, and win. He grinned at the night air rushing past his face as he leaped a fallen log.

And felt Lily die.

THIRTY-THREE

COLD. Freezing cold, the most terrible cold Lily had ever known, swarmed into her like a living force. And with it, death magic—flooding her from the inside, unspeakably foul, choking her—breaking her, some part of her, something she grabbed after even as the cold swallowed it, leaving her alone. Unbearably alone.

You came to me, something crooned. *You came.*

What—?

All of you came to me. This is meant to be. The fire. Walk to the fire now.

The words were like ice chips cutting into her brain. It hurt. Her leg started to move. No! No, she wouldn't; she . . . That voice in her mind. That was the wraith. Could it be anything else? She wouldn't move, wouldn't let it make her kill.

Walk to the fire, the voice repeated.

Ice, slicing into her brain—she tried to scream. And couldn't. But . . . "No." It was a whisper, a breath, all she could manage. Her lips barely moved—but her legs moved not at all.

You can talk to me!

She felt its astonishment, a blizzard of surprise, ice floes shifting in a glacial sea. "Get . . . out . . . of me."

You don't move when I say. How . . . oh, no! Its wail sliced at her. *There are two of you! I got in through one door, but I can't get all the way in. Only one of you died, and I can't get all the way in!*

Maybe she could shove it out, then. She tried, pushing at the smeared foulness inside her. But her head hurt bad, so bad . . .

Still, you can hear me, it said, apparently not even noticing her efforts. *You can tell the man . . . ask the man. There is something I must ask him. I don't remember. Help me. I must remember so I can ask him . . .*

"Ask . . . who?"

He knows me. We will kill, it crooned. *Together we will kill, then I will remember.*

"No," she whispered. "Together . . . we will . . . die. Look." And she managed to pull her gaze to the left.

A red wolf with eyes a bright, unlikely blue crouched ten feet away, snarling. Cullen's sorcerous vision worked in either form, and he did not like what he saw.

He leaped, crashing into her, knocking her to the ground— she glimpsed slashing teeth, his muzzle reaching for her throat—

She convulsed.

RULE ran faster than he ever had in his life—as if he could outrun death, race backward in time, find Lily safe and alive and laughing at him.

Three of the Leidolf lupi had Changed quickly enough to be on his trail. He barreled straight at them, the growl rising from his chest and breaking free in a maddened howl. They scattered.

He leaped over the next one. Then he'd reached the clearing and saw Lily's body crumpled on the ground, and Cullen— Cullen!—crouched over her, teeth bared.

He slammed into his friend's red-furred body, getting him

off her, off Lily, twisting in midair to go for the throat, needing blood, blood, oceans of blood—

Cullen ducked his head and Rule got mostly fur in his mouth. The two of them landed hard and tangled, rolling, bones jarred by the force of Rule's charge. Rule snapped at the paw nearest his teeth. Missed.

Around them, women's screams. Other wolves gathering, growling. Other wolves . . . In the madness of grief, Rule hadn't thought, wasn't thinking much now, but—Cullen? No, Cullen wouldn't kill Lily. Maybe he'd been standing guard over her body . . .

Her body. Rule raised his nose and howled.

Cullen Changed. Then stood there on two legs, hands on his thighs, head hanging, blood dripping from a slash on his shoulder near the neck. "Rule, she's alive. Lily's alive. The mate bond . . ." He gulped, as if he were holding back tears. "The mate bond is gone, but Lily's alive."

"I hate hospitals," Lily muttered from her perch on the exam table.

"I know." Rule leaned his forehead against hers.

She could feel his warmth, his skin. She couldn't feel *him*. Not anymore. If she didn't see him or touch him, she didn't know where he was.

It was a small loss, she assured herself. The mate bond hadn't given her access to his thoughts or feelings. Just a sense of where he was, physically. "I'm not hurt." Except maybe in her brain, but that damage wouldn't show up right away. And the wraith hadn't been in her long—hadn't been able to move her, control her. Maybe there wouldn't be any damage.

She tried not to remember the sharp edges of the ice. She tried not to blink too much.

"I know." Rule kissed her cheek and straightened. "But you'll indulge me and allow the doctors to finish looking you over."

"They've checked every inch of me, and their evil cohorts have drained me of blood." Some of the results of the blood tests wouldn't be back for a while, but that wasn't what they were waiting on. Halo's hospital didn't usually run MRIs at night. They'd had to be persuaded to get their MRI tech out of bed.

Ruben had accomplished that with a phone call. Got to have a good look at her brain, after all. So they'd know if it started going wonky.

"Nettie will check you out tomorrow," Rule said.

"Nettie? But she . . . Rule, you didn't ask her to fly across the country."

"Of course I did." He was still speaking in that utterly calm voice, the one he'd used since she came to after her seizure. "I spoke to the Rhej, also."

"Which one?"

His smile was as beautiful as ever, and as dear. It was the calm voice that made her want to hit him. "The Nokolai Rhej. What happened was impossible. I asked her how the impossible could occur."

"And—?"

His smile died. "She said the mate bond is dissolved by death. Somehow the wraith pulled the bond inside it. And the wraith is dead."

Lots of impossible happening lately. Like a wraith sliding in past her Gift as if it didn't exist. It seemed she had a back door. "Now we know who is susceptible to the wraith," she said wearily. "That's something."

"You said something about that earlier." Rule slid up to sit on the exam table beside her. "Things were somewhat confused at the time, but you said you thought you knew how it . . ." His voice trailed off as if he found the reality too hard to speak.

"How it got in me," she finished grimly for him. "Yes, I think so. Earlier today I learned that Meacham and Hodge had one thing in common. They both died for a few minutes. Cardiac arrest, no heartbeat. I need to talk to Brown about that, get him checking hospital records. We need to warn anyone who's been clinically dead for a little while."

He didn't speak. She turned and saw that he was gripping

the table so hard his knuckles were white. He stared straight ahead.

"Rule." She put a hand on his shoulder. "Unpack it, whatever it is."

"My fault," he gritted. "I . . . What you did in Dis, that was because of me. You died. Part of you died. It's my fault that abomination got in you."

Aw, shit. She twisted so she could grip his shoulders, making him look at her. He allowed that. The bleakness in his eyes hurt her all the way down. "All of me would have died in Dis if part of me hadn't." That came out jumbled, but he knew what she meant. If war was hell, war in hell was a double-dip of deadly. If the other-Lily hadn't made that sacrifice, they wouldn't have lasted long.

"And since none of me died for good, it wasn't a bad deal."

A shudder traveled up him, and suddenly he grabbed her, holding on tight. He rubbed his cheek along hers, then buried his face in her hair and sucked in air, shuddering again. "This time, I thought you were all the way dead," he whispered.

For long moments she said nothing, just held him. She needed this, too. Funny. Even without the mate bond, she needed this. Finally she pulled back enough to brush his hair back and look at him. His eyes were damp.

She tried a smile. "You thought Cullen did it. You ass!"

"He was standing over you."

"You know why."

"I do now."

Cullen had seen the ugly smear of death magic covering Lily. He'd read the desperation in her eyes, and he'd guessed what had her. He'd done the only thing he could—scared the hell out of her in order to persuade the wraith it would die if it stayed inside her.

It had worked. When the wraith left, she'd convulsed. Just like Hodge. Unlike Hodge, though, it had left no smear of death magic on her. Once the wraith was gone, her Gift rid her of that.

She'd made Cullen check. Just to be sure. "Did you ask

Nettie about my theory?" Cullen couldn't see the wraith. Her own Gift couldn't stop it. That told her the wraith might use death magic, might eat it the way the Etorri Rhej had said, but its basic self was something other than magic.

Spirit, in other words. Her Gift didn't protect her from spiritual stuff.

"I did. She agrees with you."

"The wraith wanted to talk to someone there at the *gens compleo*. Ask him something. I think it wanted you."

Rule stared. "You heard it?"

"Yes." The others hadn't, but it never got all the way inside Lily. Maybe that's why she'd been able to hear it, because they'd shared her body rather than her being shoved completely into the backseat.

There's two of you . . .

She shivered at the memory. "It wanted me to go to the fire. I could understand why. Ice . . . doesn't begin to describe that kind of cold."

This time when he put his arms around her, it was to comfort her, not himself. "Warm now?"

Lily nodded, but it was a lie. She was physically warm again, but inside she was still shaking, still cold. Afraid.

And alone. Rule held her. She felt his breath on her hair, the heat from his body, yet she felt alone in her body in a way she hadn't for nine months.

Damned mate bond, she thought. And wept.

"**OUT.** Out. Get out."

"Shh, baby, it's okay. You're okay. It's gone."

Yes, the wraith was gone. A dream. That's all it had been, just a dream. Lily blinked her eyes open, aware of Rule's body curved around hers, his hand stroking her hair. The smutty air of predawn told her it was early, but no longer night.

She'd dreamed the wraith was still in her, that it had hidden so well it had fooled everyone. And Rule . . . Rule had left her. The mate bond was gone, so he'd left her.

Her damned subconscious didn't bother with subtlety, did

it? Hit her over the head with her worst fear when she was already hurting. Stupid subconscious. She sat up, shoving back her hair. "I need to get to work."

"It's early yet. You don't have to—"

"No. No, listen. In the dream, it kept telling me how glad it was I'd come to see it. But that happened for real, too. It did say something like that. It said that I—that we—came to it."

He said nothing for a moment, then spoke slowly. "It was already there, in the forest."

She nodded. "I need to look at the map."

RULE went with her. She could have stopped him, probably—if she'd had every available deputy at the sheriff's office man the doors, ready to shoot. He'd know if the wraith got into her again, he said. He'd smell it. When it was in a body, he could smell the death magic.

"Then what?" she asked sourly. "You going to make scary faces at me until it leaves?"

His smile had been faint. Distant.

But he was right, and though she tried not to notice too much, it comforted her to have him with her. Maybe he wouldn't be with her that much longer.

Shut up, she told herself. Rule hadn't stopped loving her when the mate bond snapped. They'd adjust. They'd be okay.

Assuming her brain didn't fry. Was she blinking more than usual, or just noticing it more?

"Here's the spot where you found the bodies." Lily pointed at three red pins. "Here's where Deacon and I shot the dogs." Those pins were blue, and almost on top of the first three. "Last night we were . . ."

"Here." Rule tapped a spot a few inches away. "The blue pins are animal deaths?"

She nodded and stuck in a white pin, then used her finger to estimate the distance. "That's only about five miles between the bodies and the picnic site. The way the roads curve around, it seemed farther."

"What's this?" Rule tapped another white pin.

"Meacham's house. It's not far from the woods. Well, we knew that, but we were thinking in terms of how easy it was for him to take the bodies there, not—"

The door opened. "How come I always have to get my own donuts?"

It was Brown, disgruntled as ever. And holding a white box with the Dunkin' Donuts logo. "Here," he said, thrusting the box at her. "You might as well eat some, since I damned near had to draw on that deputy to get past without him mooching. And don't give me any crap about your diet." He glared. "Someone who's been in the ER needs sugar."

It was a get-well gift, Brown-style. "Thank you." And bless him, there was a chocolate cake donut with chocolate icing. She snagged it.

"What are you doing here?" Brown asked Rule with no more belligerence than usual as he helped himself to one of the donuts. "And where's the other one, the pretty guy?"

Lily had to smile at that description, but with her mouth full of donut, she let Rule answer.

"Cullen's holed up at his hotel. His wife couriered him some of his materials. He hopes to find out more about wraiths. And I'm watching out for Lily," Rule finished levelly. "I can smell death magic."

"Oh. Good idea." Brown chewed as he talked. "If that wraith gets in her again, you'll know, huh? Not sure what you can do about it, but at least you can warn the rest of us. What?" he said when Rule narrowed his eyes. "It's not a great idea to have the lead on an investigation under the control of a crazy spook. She's armed, for Christ's sake. I'd appreciate a little warning."

"I'll do my best," Rule said dryly.

"I'll be having frequent MRIs," Lily told Brown. "To make sure my brain's functioning normally. For now, I'm clear of crazy spooks and my brain's working as well as it ever does. Which isn't all that great, but I finally noticed something."

She pointed at the map. "Here's Meacham's place, where the wraith entered a human for the first time. Here's where the dogs were, the ones it had been riding. We think the wraith was in one of those dogs when it attacked Rule near the grave site, right here. And here"—she tapped the map—"is where it was last night. It told me . . . It said we had come to it. It was there already."

"You think that's where it's hanging out? In the woods?" Brown came closer. "Reasonable, but over here's Hodge's place, nowhere near the other spots."

Lily exchanged a glance with Rule. "It may have followed me or Rule into town when we discovered the bodies. It . . . wants to talk to someone, possibly Rule."

"The crazy killer spook wants a conversation?" Brown shook his head and grabbed another donut. "So you figure its grave is out in those woods?" When they stared, he waved the donut in his hand, looking almost embarrassed. "I just thought—you know. Graves. Spooks. Seem to go together."

"Maybe the death wasn't reported," Lily said slowly. "If it wasn't, the woman, the practitioner who created it, had a body to dispose of. And maybe"—she looked at Rule—"Meacham didn't bury those bodies. The wraith did, while still in Meacham's body. It had some sense that bodies should be buried, and it took them to the place it knew."

"Not quite the same place," Rule said. "I would have smelled another body if it were close."

"A seven-month-old body?"

He considered that a moment, then nodded. "I think so, yes. I'd have to be close, but the soil smells different when there's a body beneath it."

"So you could do it now. You could find it." A body would mean an ID. A name.

"I can try."

"Let's go."

"Lily." Rule gripped her arm, stopping her. "You're the last person who needs to go looking for the wraith's grave. You're too vulnerable."

She kept herself steady. Inside she wasn't, but she kept her outside steady, and she was proud of that. "You're going to go sniffing without me?" She shook her head. "It may not be there. It could be right in this room now. We don't know—"

"It's more likely to be there than anywhere else."

"I think I know how to keep it out."

"That's not good enough."

She lowered her voice, hoping to keep Brown from hearing. "It came in through . . . the other-Lily. You know what I mean. It came in when I'd just felt her memories brush against me. If I close her out, it can't get in." Maybe. She swallowed. "I need to know, Rule. I need to know I can keep it out."

When he let go of her arm, it wasn't really acceptance. His eyes were too flat and closed to call it that. But at least he wasn't fighting her.

Okay. Get moving. Lily grabbed the other chocolate donut and shoved the box at Brown. "You're going to need these. You've got that list from the hospital?" The list of those who had, temporarily, died.

"Yeah."

"Bribe some cops. You'll want help finding and notifying the people on that list that they're in danger." She looked at Rule. "Let's move."

They did.

Lily had a hunch. The wraith was cold, unbearably so. That's almost all she'd noticed at the time because it hurt her with its iciness.

But she'd also felt alone, horribly alone. And in her dream . . . in her dream, she hadn't been the only one who'd lost someone, who was left alone.

Maybe she was projecting her own fears onto her memory of the wraith, but she didn't think so. Beneath the wraith's freezing cold—in addition to it, or maybe causing it—was a vast and terrible loneliness.

Had it brought the bodies of those it killed near its own, trying to find some company in death?

THIRTY-FOUR

THE woods were so different in the day. Sun streamed through green, spotting the ground with freckles of light. Lily walked along a route she'd walked before, in the dark.

So far, so good. No deadly ice creeping in. "It's all so innocent now. You wouldn't think there were bodies here, would you?"

Rule glanced at her. "You see innocence. I see a pleasant hunting ground."

"Feeling wolfish today, aren't you?" Or focusing too much on their differences. The loss of the mate bond had to affect him, she told herself. That didn't mean he wanted to leave her. "Should we have brought Cullen to help? Or another lupus—Alex, maybe? Cullen's probably best left to do what he's doing."

"If I can't find the scent, none of the others could."

That calm voice was getting on her nerves. "Both wolfish and arrogant."

"The others," he said imperturbably, "do not have mantles to help them."

"I thought you weren't supposed to use them."

"I used them last night."

"Them?" She stopped and looked at him.

He grimaced. "Unfortunately, yes. I had the Nokolai mantle tucked away, but when I used the words of invocation"—he gestured widely—"it decided to join the party, too."

"So are David and Jeffrey Nokolai or Leidolf?"

"Yes."

Oh, shit. "That's going to cause all kinds of trouble."

"I'm aware of that. It's tomorrow's problem, however. Today we have other things to deal with. We need to talk, Lily."

Oh, God, she was so not having that kind of conversation. Not now. She resumed walking. "Not a good time for it. I need to stay focused."

"I can talk and walk at the same time." He proved that by striding along beside her. "Lily—"

"Look, let's just see if I'm going to survive first, okay?"

He stopped—and grabbed her arms, forcing her to stop, too. "You will live." All that horrible calm was gone. His voice was low and fierce, and the dark slashes of his brows were drawn in a scowl over darkly burning eyes. "That is not in question. If there is any damage, Nettie will heal it. The mate bond will help."

"Ah . . . the mate bond."

"It must be restored, of course."

"Your Lady hasn't been in a rush to do that."

"She's leaving it up to us, as she usually does. We will catch the wraith and force it to give back what it took."

"Give it back?" She stared, unable to believe what he was saying. He had to know better. The bond was *dissolved* by death, not stored on some shelf inside the wraith. "Even if we could, what's this about it healing me?"

"Have you had a cold since we met? A stomach bug?"

She frowned. "I must have."

"You haven't. Nor any cavities, I think. None of the usual small ills."

"I don't heal the way you do. I'd have noticed." She'd had enough assorted knocks and burns and cuts since they met to be sure of that.

"You don't get sick, though. The mate bond increases your

resistance to illness. It will help your body heal, if healing is needed."

"Maybe, but . . ." She shook her head. If Rule needed to believe they could regain the mate bond and it would make everything all better, why argue? Reality would make itself known without her help. Personally, she was pinning her hopes on the fact that the wraith hadn't been in her nearly as long as it had been in Meacham or Hodge. "Could be. I guess we'll find out."

"You're humoring me."

"Pretty much, yeah. But that means you get to say a big, fat 'I told you so' if you turn out to be right." She knew why he wanted so badly to believe the mate bond could be restored. And couldn't bear to think about it—so she wouldn't. She started walking again. "We must be nearly there by now."

He fell into step beside her. "The Lady tightened the bond earlier. She wanted us to remain close—and not so that an abomination could destroy it."

"Could be."

"It's a good thing I don't believe in violence toward women," he said, falling back into that übercalm voice, "or I'd give in to the urge to shake you."

She managed to grin, just as if everything were all right between them.

"If I'm wrong, and we can't restore the mate bond—"

"Isn't that the spot up ahead?"

"Dammit, Lily!" He grabbed her again and spun her around, his fingers digging into her shoulders. "We *will* talk about this!"

She jerked back. He didn't let go. "You want me to tell you it's all right if you go back to catting around? Well, it isn't! Without the bond you're able to go plant your seed in as many wombs as possible, and I will not—"

He smashed his mouth down on hers.

She shoved on his chest, turning her face away. Panting. "You can't kiss me into agreeing. I won't share you. I don't care what your people believe."

"Bugger my people."

That shocked her into holding still. Rule had told her once that his people considered "fuck" a lovely word describing a lovely activity, and he refused to use it for cursing. "Bugger" was about as vicious a curse as he ever used.

His mouth turned soft, pressing kisses along her cheek, her jaw. Gentle, courting kisses. He spoke softly against her flesh. "Lily. We are idiots."

Her body was kindling, her brain going fuzzy. She wanted to cry. She wanted to grab him and kiss him back. "We are?"

"Mmm-hmm." He trailed kisses down her throat. "I've been frantic. Knowing how you felt about the mate bond, I thought . . . I feared . . . I'm afraid I had as little trust in us as you do."

"I . . . It's not that. I know what you believe—that the survival of your people depends on—on—"

"Planting my seed in many wombs?" He straightened, cupping her face, smiling down at her. "You'll forgive me, I hope, if I say, 'Been there, done that.' I don't want to do it anymore. Only you, Lily. I want only you."

Her heart turned over. She could swear it just inverted itself in that moment, opening up wider, bigger. She slid her hands up to his shoulders. "They'll put pressure on you."

He cocked one eyebrow. "You believe I succumb to peer pressure?"

"Father pressure," she said. "Rho pressure."

"He'll learn to accept my decision. Or not." His thumbs stroked the sides of her face. "I was going to inform you that you were not free. That I was not letting you go, no matter what. I had quite the little speech ready, but you wouldn't let me use it."

Easy, so easy, to smile at him now. "I was too busy keeping you from telling me that, however regretfully, you were going to have to go on that seed-planting mission from time to time."

"Idiots," he said again, his eyes smiling . . . and his hands moving. Warming her breasts. "Both of us."

"Uh, Rule, this isn't the time or place—"

"We're alone." He pressed a kiss to her collarbone, then

flicked it with his tongue. The warmth of his hands lingered on her breasts as they moved again, sliding down to her rump, then up again.

"That's a point."

"And I want you."

"Mmm." Heat arrived, a languorous, swelling heat, making her stretch like a cat beneath his stroking hands. "I might be persuadable."

"Let's see."

This kiss was as soft as the first had been hard. He licked her lip, then sucked gently on it. She did the same with his tongue. Their mouths parted and joined, first from this angle, then that. The climb into desire was easy, slow, and mutual.

He wore jeans, like her, with his shirt untucked. She slid her hands beneath the warm cotton of his shirt, needing the feel of his skin. His arms tightened. Her breath caught. He cupped her.

Between one breath and the next, the easy climb was over.

Need had teeth. They sank into her, pumping in lust like a venom, hot and swirling. She gasped, her fingers digging into his muscles as she rocked against his hand. "Rule."

"Jeans," he said, and tugged at her zipper. "I hate jeans."

She nearly strangled on a laugh. "Harder on me than you, since we can just unzip yours and there you are. Here, let me . . ." She helped him tug her jeans and panties down, but they caught on her shoes. One ungraceful hop and a tug, and she had one leg free.

That was all he required, apparently. He swept her up, taking her to the ground with him on the bottom. She swung her bare leg over his hip, looking down at his flushed skin, at his dark eyes looking up at her.

He cupped her face. "I thought I lost you."

"You didn't. I'm here. I want you in me."

He agreed—wordlessly, urgently, freeing himself from his jeans.

She slid down over him, moving as slowly as she could make herself go. Wanting to memorize every sensation. Looking into his eyes the whole time.

He gasped. "Lily—"

"Almost," she whispered. "Almost . . ." Then she was fully seated. She bent to kiss him slowly, lingeringly. Let their lips separate, just barely, and whispered against his mouth, "Okay. Okay, no more slow."

"Thank God."

From that moment on, their loving wasn't entirely mutual. Lily was strong and agile and quick, but she wasn't anywhere near as quick as Rule was when he got in a hurry. And he clearly wanted speed. He gripped her hips and pumped fast, then faster, and the raw bolts of feeling tore a cry from her throat, ripping through her so hard and fast she couldn't keep up, couldn't—

And then she did, convulsing from the inside out. One blind second later, she felt him empty himself into her. She collapsed on top of him.

After a moment, she felt him stroking her hair. She smiled and considered opening her eyes. "Mmm. That answers one question."

"What's that?"

"It wasn't just the mate bond that had us yanking each other's clothes off all the time, was it?"

"There was some question about that?"

He'd put just enough offended hauteur into that question to make her smile widen. "I love you."

"I love you." He paused. "We're okay, then?"

The question was flavored with just enough uncertainty to make her prop herself up so she could look at him. "We're okay. Not dignified," she added, looking at the jeans and panties still wrapped around her left leg. "But very much okay."

RULE found the body in a tiny clearing just before eleven.

Lily could hardly believe he'd done it. He'd coursed in wolf-form, naturally, slowly covering a fifty-yard swath along the route between the bodies and the picnic area where the wraith had appeared last night.

Such an arbitrary number, fifty yards. If the body had been buried another ten yards away, he wouldn't have found it.

She'd sent for the ERT—and then she'd poured the salt she'd brought on the grave.

Rule had cocked an eyebrow at her. "You're planning to remove the body."

"The Baron didn't say to salt the body. He said to salt the grave, and this is it." Probably. It was worth trying, anyway, and not just because the Baron said to. She remembered that cold . . . Was that how the wraith felt all the time?

And then they waited. If the wraith was around, she never felt it.

Rule was positive a body lay beneath the soil. He couldn't be sure it had been human. After so long, there was no way to tell by smell alone. It was just possible someone had buried Fido way out here. But not, Lily thought, very likely.

It was also possible they'd found another victim of the wraith, rather than the wraith's mortal remains. Lily didn't know how they'd be able to tell. Signs of a violent death wouldn't be enough. The wraith could be the product of murder. Such a secret grave suggested as much.

When the ERT arrived, she advised them of the salt. She got some looks for that, but no one protested.

Whoever had handled the burial had worked hard. The ERT was nearly four feet down and still digging—slowly, carefully—when Lily appointed herself gofer. She couldn't help with the excavation. She wasn't qualified. So she headed back to their vehicle, which was parked as close as they could get it, about half a mile away. They had a cooler with soft drinks there.

When she got back, the chief tech was wiping his arm across his sweaty forehead. He looked up as she approached and accepted the Coke she held out. "Looks like someone, somewhere, gave Fido a really decent burial."

"You're kidding." She put down the cooler and came closer to the grave.

Rule stood at its edge, staring down. "Not a dog," he said quietly. "A wolf."

"Don't see how you can tell." The man squinted at Rule dubiously. "Sure, there's some fur left, and it could belong to a wolf. Could belong to a husky, too, or a plain old mutt. We'll have to send the bones off to be sure."

"It's the way he's buried." Rule held one arm out and curved it in a half circle. "Nose to tail. That's the traditional burial position when one of my people dies in wolf-form. We don't put our dead in boxes."

Lily touched his arm. "He's lupus?"

Rule nodded. He was wearing his blank face, the one he donned when there was way too much going on inside. "I think . . ." He drew in a breath suddenly, as if he'd been forgetting about air. "Beneath him you should find some clothing, possibly even identification. When one of us dies as wolf, we include his human side by burying human things with him." He looked at her. "That's why the burial was secret, why the death won't be on your lists. When one of us dies as wolf, he doesn't end up in a human cemetery."

"But . . . here?" She gestured at the forest around them. "If he's Leidolf, wouldn't he be buried at Leidolf Clanhome?"

"Maybe he loved to run here and requested this as his burial spot. Maybe he's not Leidolf and was killed by them, so they buried him decently." He sighed, and what she saw now was sadness. "It might not be your wraith, Lily. We may have disturbed this one's rest for nothing. I'll call Alex. He'll know of any burials here."

Alex didn't answer his phone, and it took another forty minutes to remove the bones. Underneath, as Rule had said, were the rotted remains of clothing. Jeans, maybe, though it was hard to say. The boots were filthy, but almost intact.

One thing was entirely intact, because it had been sealed in a plastic bag—the see-through kind with a zipper, like you'd use to save leftovers in the freezer. Lily rubbed dirt off the bag to get a better look. "Oh, Jesus," she whispered as the puzzle pieces suddenly fell in place

It was a baby blanket. Blue and green, faded from pastel to ice colors. Crocheted by loving hands, not bought at some superstore. And sealed up against decay. "Rule." She showed him the bag. "Is this unusual? Sealing it up this way?"

"It's not our practice. What we bury with the dead we expect to go to earth with them."

"But she was human," Lily murmured, turning the bag over in her gloved hands. "She wasn't clan. And she loved him so very much." Only a mother would bury her son with his baby blanket. One she'd made for him. One she refused to allow to decompose gracefully into the earth.

She looked up. "Call Cullen for me."

"Agent Yu," one of the techs called. "Got something here you want."

Oh, yes, he did. A wallet.

The leather was badly rotted, much worse than the boots. Pieces crumbled off despite her care, but she got it open. The driver's license inside was plastic and intact. She pulled it out and rubbed the dirt off with her thumb to reveal a small photo of a smiling, red-haired young man.

Charles Arthur Kessenblaum.

THEY were nearly back to town when Rule's phone chimed. Lily was on her third call, this one from Deacon.

She'd notified Brown and asked Deacon to send someone to pick up Crystal Kessenblaum—not as a suspect, but as a witness. Crystal wasn't a medium. Her first call had been to Marcia Farquhar, but the blasted woman was in court. But surely the woman who'd been godmother to one of Mrs. Kessenblaum's children would know about the other. Hadn't Louise told her best friend the truth about Toby, right from the first?

They'd drifted apart, Farquhar had said, over the years. But not completely. Surely not so much that she wouldn't know about Charles Arthur.

Charley. That's what the women at the *gens compleo* had called him. He'd been twenty-three when he died. Last night would have been his coming-of-age party.

It was the mother. Lily knew that in her gut and her bone, and Cullen had agreed it was possible. Mrs. Kessenblaum created an abomination not because she wanted a soul-slave, but because she wanted her son. She'd tried to bring him back to life, or keep him with her as a spirit. Like those foolish bygone sorcerers who'd made zombies, she'd refused to accede to death.

"Crystal's not at her apartment," Deacon said. "She's not at work, either. Hasn't been in for days."

Shit. Preoccupied, Lily barely glanced at Rule when his phone rang and he answered. But some instinct made her look again.

She told Deacon to hold on a moment and put her palm over the phone's mic. "What is it?"

Rule shook his head at her, listening intently. "You're sure? Yes, of course you are. I don't . . . Just a minute." He looked at Lily. "Toby went with his mother this morning."

She nodded. They were going to the miniature golf place, then Alicia was going pick up Louise and they'd all go to lunch together.

"He—they—haven't come back. And Alicia isn't answering her phone."

THIRTY-FIVE

LILY was certain Alicia had snatched Toby. Rule didn't believe it. Alicia had concocted a crazy plan, true, but she wasn't a lawbreaker by nature. She wasn't a woman who would throw away her entire life in order to steal her son from the father she'd agreed, after all these years, could have him.

And it didn't matter which of them was right, not immediately. Lily had done what was needed. She'd gotten Deacon to put out an APB for Alicia's car—having memorized the make, model, and even the license tags. Rule wanted to kiss her for that.

Probably, he told himself, Alicia's car had broken down and she'd left her phone somewhere, or forgotten to charge it. That happened. She'd feel foolish when some officer saw the car and pulled over, but she'd get the help she needed.

There was no reason to panic.

"**I'VE** got to go," Lily said, holding both of Rule's hands in hers.

They were at Louise's house. He'd had to come here, of course, to be with Louise . . . to be here when Toby and Alicia arrived. But Lily couldn't stay. He understood that. Finding the wraith's creator had to be her priority. "Of course. I'll call you when Toby turns up."

She thought he was deluding himself. He saw that clearly in her face, however cop-blank she made it.

"Alicia wouldn't kidnap him," he said again. "I don't know what's wrong, but she wouldn't do that. Her career means too much. Her new husband matters, too. She's not the type to go on the run."

Louise came in. "Of course not. I just can't understand where she *is*." Her voice was calm, but her eyes were frightened.

Lily squeezed Rule's hand, then let go and went to Louise. "There haven't been any auto accidents that could have involved her. Sheriff Deacon checked for us."

"I know. I'm just being a mother and worrying." Her smile wobbled. "Goes with the territory."

The doorbell rang. Louise rushed to answer, with Rule and Lily right behind. Though why would Alicia and Toby ring the bell? Surely Toby had a key, even if Alicia didn't.

And he didn't hear Toby. There were undoubtedly moments when Toby didn't chatter, but coming back from an outing with his mother . . .

Of course Louise flung open the door without checking first. "Oh. Oh, come in."

The disappointment in her voice stopped Rule cold. He closed his eyes. He would not panic.

"Cynna's flying out," Cullen said briskly. "She managed to snag a seat on the same flight as Nettie, in fact. With the time difference, that has her getting into Charlotte about midnight."

Rule opened his eyes and saw his friend in front of him, holding his ratty backpack by one strap. "Cynna's coming."

"Yep. I've got a couple of Find spells, and I'll try them, but they're nothing compared to what she can do." He grinned. "I admit it even when she isn't here, ready to thunk me."

Midnight. Rule wanted to believe Cynna wouldn't be needed. Surely they'd find Toby long before midnight. But if they didn't . . . if they didn't, Cynna would. She was the best, quite literally the best, at what she did. So good she'd been involuntarily recruited by agents of another realm for a while.

She was also about five months pregnant. It should have been seven months, but the time she'd spent in Edge had passed differently from here on Earth.

Rule swallowed. "Thank you."

Lily glanced at Cullen and got a nod. "I'm off," she said.

"I'll keep reading," he assured her.

Rule frowned. "Wait a minute. Cullen, Lily will need you. You're going with her."

"No, I'm not."

"I do not need a babysitter."

"Shut up, Rule," Cullen said gently. "I'm not much help, I know, but you're stuck with me."

Lily put it another way. She came up to him, kissed his cheek, and said, "Not a babysitter. A friend. He wouldn't be much help for me anyway, not until he figures out how to stop a wraith."

"Like I said"—Cullen jiggled his backpack—"I'll keep reading."

Lily reached for the door—and Rule spun the other way. He'd heard the back gate—and now footsteps in the yard. Running. Someone light or small. Child-size. He was at the back door by the time a small fist started pounding on it.

He jerked it open. "Talia!"

The girl turned a frantic, teary face up toward him. "She's got Toby! The bad one, the one who made th-the wraith. The Baron told me."

Lily came up behind him. "The Baron?"

She nodded jerkily. "Yes, h-he's not a ghost. Well, he sorta is, only he's different, and he understands things here more than ghosts usually do, and he's really clear, not wispy at all. But only part of what he said made sense."

"What did he look like, Talia?" Cullen asked.

"Tall, with a funny black hat and black clothes. His skin was real dark, darker than mine, but his face was white. Truly white, not just pale. Sometimes," she said, her voice dropping, "it was almost like there was just a skull, not a face at all. That was scary."

"That's the Baron, all right."

"Come in." Rule moved aside and, as soon as she'd entered, went down on one knee in front of her. "What did he say, Talia?"

She scrunched up her face. "This is what I'm supposed to tell you. *She's* got Toby. He said you knew who she was, that she made the wraith. She's gonna do a big spell with Toby, but the Baron said she's got it all wrong. Th-that's when his face looked like a skull, and he wasn't laughing. He looked . . ." She shuddered.

Rule put an arm around her. "We'll stop her, Talia."

"Yes! But you have to stop the wraith, too, Mr. Turner," Talia said, her eyes huge. "You and Agent Yu. He said you have to do it together."

Lily squeezed Rule's shoulder. "He give any hint how?"

Talia shook her head, her eyes tearing up. "He wouldn't answer my questions. I asked, but he laughed like it was all one big joke, and he made me memorize this next part. It doesn't make sense, but he made me memorize it. It goes like this: 'It wasn't midnight, but the performance was lovely and the grave was indeed open. Empty now, but open.' And he said you owe him some cigars."

CHARLES Arthur Kessenblaum had died on the day of the Turning. He'd been driving his car when the power wind hit and, like every lupus on the planet, the enormous surge of power had forced him to Change. The car had been traveling at highway speed. He'd been killed almost instantly, with no time to heal the wounds.

His mother's name was Mandy Ann. Mandy Ann Kessenblaum. If her daughter was, as Lily had said, a hippie wannabe, Mandy Ann was the real thing—a flower child who dropped out and never came back. Though she'd had two children, she'd never married. She lived alone in a one-room log cabin on a few acres and sold some of the organic vegetables she grew at a roadside stand, augmenting that income by cleaning houses and selling handmade quilts.

She didn't sound evil.

The information about the cabin and Mandy Ann came from Alex and Marcia Farquhar, who'd called Rule and Lily back within minutes of Talia's delivery of the Baron's message.

Sheriff Deacon had delivered his message in person. One of his cruisers had found Alicia, unconscious and bloodied, next to her car. It looked like she'd put up a fight, he said. She was being rushed to the hospital.

They'd left Louise to go to the hospital alone—and wait. She had the hardest job, Rule thought.

MANDY Ann's cabin lay a short distance from the place Rule had found the first bodies—less than three miles, but on the other side of the highway. It was roughly the same distance from the wraith's grave.

No, from Charley's grave. He had a name, Rule reminded himself. Whatever he was now, he'd once been lupus and young. So very young. He'd died before being acknowledged as an adult of the clan, before being entered into the mantle.

It took fifteen minutes to reach the spot where they left their cars. An ambulance was following and would park out of sight of the cabin.

Rule was careful not to think about the ambulance.

There was a long dirt road that led to the cabin, but of course they couldn't take that. So the sheriff led them a roundabout way from the highway.

It was small team Lily had assembled. Most of them were, in Rule's opinion, superfluous. Deacon was there to get them to the cabin. Brown had tagged along when Deacon came to deliver the news about Alicia, so Lily brought him, too. But they'd stay behind. Getting into the cabin fell to Rule and Cullen.

Since Rule would have gone regardless of what Lily decided, it was fortunate she agreed with him. He could move faster than any human and absorb more damage without being stopped. Marcia Farquhar said Mandy Ann had a shotgun, so that was a factor. And he was trained in stealth by his brother Benedict. He'd be quick and he'd be quiet.

Cullen wasn't trained, but he was even faster than Rule and almost as quiet. He was also the only one who might be able to deal with whatever spell Mandy Ann was casting or planning to cast.

The others would wait for Rule to give the signal to come in. Lily had wanted to wire him for sound, but it would have taken too long.

He used the short walk from the cars to ready himself. He sank into the physical, aware of his breathing, of the clever flex and shove of his muscles and the strength they held, waiting for the moment he would draw upon them. His heartbeat slowed. Neither fear nor anxiety was real now—only this, the sunshine and heat, the motion, Lily beside him. Though he still used only two feet, he now walked like the wolf.

They stopped in a woody area. He could just glimpse the cabin through the trees. A small field separated the woods from the cabin.

"Be careful," Lily told him tersely. "Grabbing Toby may be a way of drawing you to her. The wraith seems to have an interest in you."

That seemed obvious now. "He's drawn to the mantles."

"There's power in them, if he can get it," she agreed. "Remember that Mandy Ann has at least one gun, and she may have help—or an additional hostage. Crystal hasn't been seen for days."

He nodded, collected Cullen with a glance, and set off.

His planned approach was simple enough. There were windows on three of the cabin's walls; none on the north, where a large stone chimney was the only break in the log wall. On the west side was a chicken coop. They would avoid that. Chickens made a fuss if you came close. Though he couldn't see it from here, he'd been told there was a diesel-powered generator, the only source of electricity for the cabin.

He and Cullen circled slightly to approach from the north.

Rule paused at the edge of the woods. The field here was grass for about twenty yards, and cultivated closer to the house. The furrows would slow them down, but the soft earth would be quiet beneath their feet if they avoided the plants.

They didn't know if Mandy Ann had a dog. She used to, according to Marcia Farquhar, but that old hound had died a couple years ago. She might have gotten another one. Dogs were noisy and hard to sneak up on.

Rule inhaled deeply. There was very little breeze, and it blew from the east—little help.

He smelled chickens. Something with tomatoes and spices was cooking nearby. Compost . . . yes, there was her compost pile, neatly penned. And the faint, pervasive scent of human. Someone human walked these woods often. "No dogs," he murmured to Cullen.

Cullen gave a single nod, a sharp-edged smile.

"You remember the signals?" Rule subvocalized this time.

Cullen nodded.

"Follow at whatever pace is quietest." And he set off.

The grass was knee-high. No way to move through it in complete silence, but Rule trusted in the poor hearing of humans and eased through it slowly.

Luck smiled on him. Halfway through the grassy area, the diesel generator kicked in, making enough racket to drown out a dozen men rushing the cabin. He broke into a lope.

He'd reached the furrows when the smell hit him. Corruption, faint but unmistakable. His calm faltered—but no, it could not be Toby. Toby had been alive only hours ago.

He was still alive. He had to be.

Then Cullen's whistle—a single high note—brought his head around. That was the signal for abandoning caution and charging. Rule didn't know the reason, but he didn't hesitate. He covered the last twenty feet in an all-out run, racing around the corner of the cabin, where the door—good gods—stood open.

Without hesitation or caution, he dashed inside.

"Stop!"

He did. Partly blinded by the change in light, he still saw enough to freeze.

The woman had long hair worn in braids that reached to her waist. She was short, muscular, chubby. There was a raw scrape or scratch along one of her plump cheeks. She wore a man's blue work shirt tied at the waist with the sleeves rolled up, and a full skirt in faded tie-dye swirls.

The skirt was spread out around her on a big, pillowy bed covered in a lovely old-fashioned quilt. She held Toby's limp body propped up against her with one sun-browned arm.

Her other hand held a knife to Toby's throat. A butcher knife, large and efficient.

But he breathed. After a few seconds, Rule's eyes adjusted enough to be sure of that. His son's chest rose and fell steadily.

"Come in," Mandy Ann said in a high, chirpy voice. "Oh, you already did!" She giggled. "But don't come any closer. I don't want to damage my boy's new body."

Cullen skidded to a stop beside Rule. "A ward," he whispered. "There was a damned ward laid right into the earth. I didn't see it until you crossed it and it flared, and too late then. She'd been warned."

"Oh, aren't you the pretty one. Pity I can't use you." Mandy Ann shook her head. "But Charley wants the boy. He told me so."

"What's wrong with Toby?" Rule did his best to keep the growl out of his voice. He didn't entirely succeed. "What have you done to my son?"

"Is he your boy? Nothing at all. I gave him a bit of my special tea so he'd sleep. I wouldn't want to scare the poor boy."

Rule's eyes had adjusted fully to the dim light inside the cabin. It was hot in there. He could feel his shirt sticking to his back. All the windows were open to catch what breeze they could, but the curtains were drawn. They barely swayed, listless.

The cabin was one large room, as he'd been told. Mandy Ann and the big, cozy bed occupied a prominent place on the south wall to his left. Opposite her were the living area and kitchen. There was a big wooden table in the kitchen that held an odd-looking piece of equipment. It reminded Rule of the paddles they use on those medical shows on TV when they yell, "Clear!" and try to jolt someone's heart back to life.

A young woman with red hair and a galaxy of freckles sat at that table—in a manner of speaking. She was tied to one of the chairs. Her head hung limply. Her eyes were open and staring, and a fly crawled idly across one madly freckled cheek.

THE second Lily saw Rule and Cullen take off at that impossible speed, she knew the situation had gone south.

The hell with waiting on permission. Either Rule and Cullen would deal with what they found immediately, or they'd need backup. "Brown, come in from the west, get to the window on that side. Deacon, take the south window. Weapons drawn, but hold your fire unless I give the order, or if you can see there's immediate danger of casualties. Use your judgment." She hoped to God they had judgment. "I'm assuming a hostage situation."

Deacon didn't argue about jurisdiction or who could give orders to whom. He just unsnapped his holster, withdrawing a nice Glock. Brown drew his .38 from his shoulder holster—an old-fashioned guy, apparently.

"You two good shots?"

"Middlin', with a handgun," Deacon said. "Better with a rifle, but it's a small cabin. At that range I'll be okay."

"And I," Brown said, "am goddamned good. You're taking the front, then. You going in quiet or loud?"

"Friendly. I'm going in real friendly."

I'M going to have to ask you to tie each other up," Mandy Ann said apologetically. "Oh—you can't quite do that, can you?" She giggled again. "But you—you're this one's dad?— you can tie up your friend. I'm not sure what I'll do with you, but we'll start by you tying up your friend. Go on, now." She shifted, pulling Toby with her as she scooted farther into the middle of the bed. She nodded at the big kitchen table with its three unoccupied chairs. "Sit yourself down next to Crystal."

"I can't think of why I'd do that," Cullen said. Not arguing, exactly. Just making an observation.

"Because I'll hurt the boy if you don't, of course. I don't want to." She clucked her tongue. "Poor mite. I'd rather not hurt him at all, but I will if I have to. It won't matter in the end, because once my boy's in there with him, he'll heal up whatever I had to do." Her eyes gleamed merrily. "Keep that in mind, and behave. I can hurt him quite a bit if I have to."

"I hope you won't have to," Lily said from the doorway.

Rule jolted. He hadn't known she was there.

"Another one of you?" Mandy Ann's eyes opened wide in amazement. "My, my. At least I know who's going to tie up the big one, here. And I do have four chairs, don't I?" She giggled.

That giggle was getting to Rule. Or maybe it was the corpse of the woman's daughter, held upright by the ropes around her.

"What's the plan, Mandy Ann?" Lily asked coolly. "How is this helping Charley?"

"You know about Charley? I guess you must, or you wouldn't be here." She cocked her head, smiling at Rule. "You mustn't worry about your boy. He may not like it at first, but all children have to learn to share."

"You want to put your dead son into my living son," he said. "I'd call that hurting him."

"Charley's not dead." For the first time the merriness slipped, letting out something barbed and frightened and quite mad. "And it won't hurt, not a bit. Just ask Crystal. I thought he could use her, you see," she confided. "But she's so selfish. She didn't want to share. It wasn't wasted, though, all the time I spent learning how much current to use. Now I can do it right."

The apparatus on the table that looked like an electrical

paddle . . . That's what it was. That's why she'd started the generator, Rule realized with sick horror. But she didn't want to start a heart with it. She meant to stop one.

Toby's.

Lily said, "Mandy Ann, we can't ask Crystal anything. We aren't mediums, and Crystal is dead."

"Don't be silly." But her hand tightened on the knife. "She's sulking. She didn't like it when I . . . when I . . . But I saved him. I saved my Charley. I didn't understand at first . . ." Confusion clouded her eyes. "I did the spell right, but it didn't tell me I had to find him a body. I thought he did that on his own. But he told me." She straightened, giving a satisfied nod. "He told me he needs the boy. A lupus boy."

"Did he?" Lily asked softly. "I don't think he can talk to you, Mandy Ann. If he were a ghost, he could. But he isn't exactly a ghost, is he?"

"Of course not. He's not dead."

"He talked to me."

That got her attention. "When? What did he say?"

"When he possessed me, I could hear him. I could feel some of what he feels. He's suffering terribly, Mandy Ann. He's so very cold."

"He is not suffering!" The chirpy voice turned shrill. "You're lying. He didn't talk to you at all."

"Is he here? I bet you can see him, even if you can't hear him very well. If he's here, I could let him into me again, and he could tell you himself."

"Lily—" Rule started to move, maybe to shake some sense into her. Mandy Ann jerked when he did, and a thin trickle of blood started down Toby's throat.

"Now look what you made me do." She sounded like she'd accidentally dropped an egg on the floor. "You all get over there now. Over to the table. Scoot, scoot."

"All right," Lily said easily, and started moving—and as she passed Rule she subvocalized quite audibly, *"Sharpshooters at windows. Leave a clear field."*

Rule followed her, but kept it slow. Cullen matched his

pace. The more Mandy Ann had to work to keep track of all of them, the better. As long as they seemed to be obeying, she wouldn't hurt Toby.

Please, Lady, don't let her hurt Toby.

"I asked you before, Mandy Ann," Lily said as she arrived at the table—took a quick look at Crystal, and jerked her gaze away. "What's your plan? Charley can't get into anyone who hasn't been technically dead at some point."

"That's what the paddles are for, of course. That's why I gave the boy some of my tea. That part isn't very pleasant, and I don't want him to suffer. But he'll be fine. His heart only needs to stop for such a little while."

"That's what I thought." Lily glanced around casually—taking note of where Rule and Cullen were, Rule thought. And said, quite offhandedly, "If you have a clear shot, take it."

The explosion of sound as the gun went off rattled the plates on the shelves.

The woman sitting on the bed jolted as if startled by the noise—and slumped, her lax hand releasing the knife as she sank onto the big, cozy bed, her eyes as open and staring as her daughter's.

Before his ears stopped ringing, Rule had snatched Toby off the bed with its old-fashioned quilt, now spattered with blood and brains. He held his sleeping son close and rocked him, rocked him.

Lily came to him and curled her hand around his arm, but her eyes were on the bed. She sighed. "You're right, Brown," she said to the man climbing in the window. "You're a god-damned good shot."

THIRTY-SIX

DEACON radioed the ambulance. Rule carried Toby outside to wait for it away from blood and death. Lily stayed in the cabin to do her job—first by summoning the ERT to yet another crime scene.

She felt weak. Shaky. Slightly sick to her stomach. *Adrenaline aftermath,* she told herself. *Keep moving and it will go away.* She looked at Deacon. "Would you call the hospital, have someone talk to Louise, let her know Toby's okay? I don't have that number in my phone."

"Sure."

Cullen was standing in the middle of the room, turning in a slow circle, his gaze slowly lowering to the floor.

"What are you doing?" she asked.

"Her grimoire. I need it to figure out how to stop the wraith. I need to find the spell she used."

The wraith. Unbelievably, she'd almost forgotten about it. She put a hand to her temple, rubbing it and wishing she could sit down for a minute. The nausea kept trying to rise. "Charley. His name is Charley."

"Right." He stopped. "Root cellar! Of course. But where's the entrance?" He frowned at the floor.

Was he not making any sense, or was it just her?

Brown stumped up to her. "Why the hell aren't you out there with that boy and your man?"

"I—"

"You think I can't keep an eye on a crime scene until the techs get here?" He shook his head, disgusted as ever. "Go out there. Hug your man. Hug that boy you saved. It'll make some of this"—he nodded at the body on the bed—"go away. Not all of it, but enough."

Gratitude caught her by the throat and squeezed. For one terrible second she thought she might cry—which would have horrified Brown even more than her. "Thanks," she managed.

"You'll go with him to the hospital," he told her. "Don't give me any shit about that."

She found she could smile. Not very big, but that's what it was. "I will," she said, and headed for the door.

Deacon spoke as she was leaving, but not to her. "There's a cellar entrance outside, if that's what you're looking for. It's by the back door if you want to . . ."

He didn't bother to finish; Cullen was already dashing for the back door.

LILY stepped into sunshine, blinking at the brightness.

Rule sat at a picnic table several paces away, cradling Toby, whose legs dangled to the ground, his head bent as he watched his son breathe.

"His color's good," Lily said as she approached.

Rule looked up. He had a smile for her. "So are his breathing and his heartbeat. He's pretty deeply sedated, though. Hasn't stirred at all. I can't help wondering if there's a magical component to that tea she gave him."

"Bet I can answer that." She came close, bent, and put her hand on Toby's cheek. "No magic," she said softly, knowing Rule was remembering another time when his son had slept, unable to wake. That had been due to demon magic.

He sighed hugely in relief. "*Nadia . . .*" He broke off, unhappiness crossing his face.

She wasn't his *nadia* anymore. *Nadia* meant knot, bond, tie . . . "Do you violate some code if you call me that when we aren't mate-bonded?"

"Perhaps not. Are you all right?"

She took a moment, checking her insides. "I will be. Brown sent me out here." She grimaced. "He pulled the trigger, but I'm the one with the shakes."

"You gave the order. I understand the need, and the price, for such orders. When it troubles you—and it will, at times— ask yourself if Mandy Ann would have been better off alive. She would have been ruled insane, surely. What if doctors had somehow been able to return her to reality, and she knew she'd electrocuted her daughter and condemned her son to an endless, living death?"

"Yeah." Lily gusted out a breath. "Yeah." She looked past him at the road, where an ambulance was bumping its way along the ruts. "Good. Here they come."

They were loading Toby into the ambulance when Cullen came hurrying around the corner of the house, carrying a plain spiral notebook in one hand and a Mason jar in the other. "I found it."

"That's a grimoire?" Lily shook her head. "Never mind. What's in the jar?"

"Blood."

"Cullen, we can't take evidence away without—"

"Charley's blood," he said grimly. "And to hell with the evidence chain. We're going to need it."

THEY would let only one person ride in the ambulance with Toby, so Lily walked back to the car with Cullen. By the time they reached it, she was still tired, but the shakes and nausea were gone.

Cullen buckled up and spoke not a word for the first ten minutes of the drive into Halo, studying Mandy Ann's spiral grimoire. The word he used to break the silence was "Shit."

"You don't know how to stop it?"

"I do, but I don't like it. You're not going to like it. And Rule is going to hate it."

Already he was right about her reaction, and he hadn't told her anything. "And the answer is—?"

"The only one who can kill the wraith is Charley."

"Charley *is* the wraith."

"Bingo."

ONE thing about going to the ER in an ambulance—they saw you right away. Which was just how Rule wanted it. By the time Lily and Cullen arrived, the doctor had already checked out Toby and left to deal with patients "who actually need me. This boy of yours will wake up with a bit of a headache, if that."

"Toby's okay," he told them. "They want to keep him here for a couple hours for observation, but he's fine. The doctor managed to rouse him briefly, so this isn't like the other time." He smiled ruefully at Lily. "I know you already checked, and I believed you, but . . . it was good to see his eyes open for a moment."

Lily's face softened. She walked to the bed where Toby lay, covered by one of those paltry blankets the ER used, and touched his cheek. "He looks fine. He looks wonderful. Have you had time to see Louise?"

"She came down here after we arrived. Someone let her know we were here. She says Alicia has a concussion and a fractured shoulder blade. They think she'll be okay, though they're keeping her overnight for observation. But she's woken, too. She was . . . When she first woke, she was frantic about Toby."

He stopped, remembering how sure he'd been that Alicia didn't really care about her son. Yet she'd fought for him.

"Does she remember the attack?" Lily asked.

"Most of it. She'd stopped for gas. It was one of those automated places, with no attendants. A friendly woman dressed like an aging hippie was the only other customer. She asked

Alicia for help. She was having car trouble. She thought it was the battery."

"Mandy Ann."

"Yes. Alicia remembers peering into the rear-mounted engine of the woman's old VW bug when something struck her hard on her shoulders. She fell to the pavement—her shoulder blade was broken by the blow, though she didn't know it—and saw that harmless old hippie woman with a baseball bat in her hands. The woman grabbed Toby's arm and yanked him toward her car, and Alicia got up and fought for her son."

Rule swallowed. He'd seen the scratches on Mandy Ann's face, hadn't he? "She doesn't remember being hit a second time, but Mandy Ann must have swung that bat again, this time giving her a concussion."

Lily put her arm around Rule and leaned into him. His arm naturally circled her. "Weird, isn't it?" she said. "I guess people love the way that they love. It isn't always the best way, or the way we want them to, but love happens."

Love happens. He smiled. "It does." They stood for a moment in silence. *This is still comfort,* he thought. Still necessary, even without the mate bond.

Cullen sighed. "The good news isn't universal. We still have a wraith to deal with, you know. Can we talk about it outside?"

Rule shook his head. "I don't want to leave Toby. He could wake again at any time and be confused."

"All right, then. First, you need to know what she did to Charley, in the name of love. She took the still-living blood from his body before he'd finished cooling. She'd been experimenting with blood magic for some time."

"Blood magic isn't always necessarily evil," Rule said. "You told me that yourself."

"Some of it's neutral, some's gray, and some . . ." Cullen's mouth twisted. "I saw what she'd been dabbling in, and she'd left gray behind."

Lily cocked an eyebrow. "You're saying she'd already gone over to the Dark Side when her son died?"

"Put it how you like—her mind had been twisted by what she'd been practicing."

"Charley died suddenly," Rule said. "There was a ghost?"

"Good guess. Yes, he'd been on his way to see her, but only his ghost arrived. Came as quite a shock." Cullen shifted as if wanting to pace, but there was no room for it in the tiny room where Rule's son slept. "She was brilliant, really. She had an old runic spell, very old, that she'd been studying. She'd worked out some possible variations already. The amount of improvisation she did on the spot . . . brilliant. Pity she was batty."

"Yes," Rule said dryly, "I think her son and daughter would agree."

"So she saw Charley's ghost," Lily prompted, "and went out and did her spell?"

Cullen nodded. "She raced to the crash site and collected his blood, then used it to write the runes. The power wind was still blowing—you remember how long that final wind lasted. She used it, too. She ripped his spirit apart. He lost his name, his past, the memory of having been lupus, even his memory of her. She sank the memories into his blood, which she enspelled against decay. Ever since, she's used that blood to call him back to her, over and over, and feed what's left of him on death."

"Sweet Lady." Rule shook his head, shaken. "Did she understand what she did to him? How could she do that to her son?"

"She convinced herself she was saving him," Lily said quietly.

He looked at her, and thought of Alicia and of what Mandy Ann had planned for Toby. And shuddered.

Lily's arm tightened around him. "She thought she could get him a new body, didn't she?"

"At first she expected him to take care of that himself. When he didn't, she decided to help him out by making his sister, ah, susceptible to his possession."

Rule felt sick. Sick and unbearably sad. "Crystal didn't know what her mother had done, did she?"

"No. We have to stop the wraith, Rule."

"You don't usually bother to point out the obvious."

Then Cullen told him what they had to do to stop the wraith.

Rule heard him out, fury gathering in his belly. When he finished, Rule had two words for the idea. "Absolutely not."

"Rule." Lily looked sad—and, damn her, determined. If he hadn't known for a fact there was no blood bond between her and Toby, he'd have sworn he recognized the tilt to her chin. "Only part of it is up to you. The part that's mine, I'll do. Whether you agree or not."

"I'll stop you." He said that as certainly as if it were possible.

"How?" She held his gaze steadily. "If it's the only way to keep the wraith from killing again and again, then it has to be done. And if it's the only way to . . . to free Charley, then that needs doing, too."

He couldn't stop her. He knew that, in spite of his foolish words. All he could do was fall in with his friend's damnable plan—and make it work. He looked at Cullen, the mantles stirring uneasily in his gut. "The wraith must be compelled, you said."

"You've got the mantles. That's compulsion—or will be, after you do the first part."

"I have the heirs' portions. This will require a Rho's authority."

Cullen caught on quickly. "Shit. Oh, shit."

Rule smiled coldly. "You advised me to become Leidolf Rho, didn't you? It seems I'll be assuming the position ahead of schedule."

"What do you mean?" Lily asked. "If you plan to go to Leidolf Clanhome and kill Victor—"

"I don't have to go there to do it." Cullen knew. He'd carried a bit of mantle. He knew what the answer was.

Cullen sighed and looked at Lily. "He's going to take the mantle from Victor. He's got a larger than usual heir's portion already, and a mantle . . . uh, usually it wants to be with the strongest, most capable leader. Victor's in a coma. Rule's betting the mantle won't resist much. If Rule pulls it away from Victor, Victor dies."

"No," she said. "No, Rule. It isn't necessary. Leidolf will never forgive you, and the other clans . . . God, it might technically be murder. No."

"Are you going to arrest me?" His lips still curved up, but he wasn't smiling. "Only part of this is up to you. The part that's mine," he said, giving her back her own words, "I'll do."

THIRTY-SEVEN

THEY took Toby home late in the afternoon. He was still very sleepy and didn't object to going up to bed—though he did get the ban on television in the bedroom lifted temporarily. Grammy brought in what she called the "sick set," an old TV that she hooked up when Toby was ill.

Alicia had continued to improve, and her husband was with her. Louise planned to go back to the hospital tomorrow, but she, too, needed a rest. When Toby fell asleep watching cartoons, she decided to lie down and "rest my eyes a minute."

She dozed off almost as fast as her grandson.

It was twilight when Rule, Lily, and Cullen went into the backyard with the jar of blood. Twilight, the between time, with dusky air flooding the senses with honeysuckle and fresh-cut grass, with hints and possibilities.

A good time to deal with the unnamed place that lies between life and death, Cullen said.

The first part was simple enough, no magic or ritual required. All Lily had to do was remember.

She settled cross-legged in the grass, closed her eyes, and thought about running. Running all-out for the edge of a cliff, the acrid air of Dis burning her lungs, everything she loved left behind.

No cold stole into her.

She tried other memories . . . bicycles. She remembered how delighted part of her, the hidden part, had been when she remembered riding a bike as a child, and the other-her shared that memory. The other-Lily had had no memories to sustain her in hell. *Like the wraith,* she thought. Like Charley.

But she'd had Rule. She hadn't had her name, but she'd remembered grass and sunlight and stars. She hadn't known if she'd ever ridden a bicycle, but she'd remembered bikes. She'd had her body, and she'd had Rule. He'd been wolf . . .

"That's funny," she said, sniffing. "Do you smell cigar smoke?" And just like that, she fell into ice.

Or was shoved.

It was, impossibly, even colder than the first time, or maybe it was impossible to recall such cold, a fierce cold that stole her breath, shutting down her muscles so that she swayed and would have toppled over. But Rule was there. His face was a mask of intensity as he steadied her and looked into her eyes.

"I know you," he said, his voice seeming to resonate from deep within. "Leidolf's mantle knows you."

And the icy voice spoke, painful shards cutting and shifting in a way that was almost hope. *Leidolf?*

"Use . . . my mouth," she told it, barely able to breathe the words. "I give . . . permission."

It flooded into the warmth, almost all the way in this time! It didn't have the use of the legs, but it didn't need legs. It had words still. It had hung on to words, waiting and waiting, and that had been hard, but now it could ask the man . . . It couldn't quite remember. "So hungry," it whispered with those strange lips. "Feed me. Feed me so I can remember." It felt its warmth's face twisting, and didn't know which of them did that. "Hurts. Hurts."

But it was the other warmth who acted, not the man, unfastening something . . . *a jar* . . . and dipping his finger in. He held out a wet, glistening finger. It closed those borrowed lips around the finger . . .

Warmth? Yes. No. A different kind of not-cold than it felt from its warmth. Just a flicker of it, but sweet. So sweet. "More."

"Listen," the man said. "Listen to me, Charles."

Charles . . . ?

Another glistening fingertip. It fastened on that finger eagerly, feeling its pieces shifting, scraping . . .

"Take your name, Charles Arthur Kessenblaum."

The heat! It hurt, it hurt—its pieces were whirling too fast, too much! Panting, it tried to shove the man away, but these arms didn't listen to it. "Hurts!" it screamed.

The man gripped the warmth's face and stared into the eyes. "Charles Arthur Kessenblaum, you will heed me. Leidolf knows you."

Leidolf, it panted. It almost remembered Leidolf, and the word was so dear it needed to say it over and over. *Leidolf, Leidolf, Leidolf.*

"You will kneel. Today is your *gens compleo,* Charles. You will kneel."

It trembled with a feeling it had no word for—a terrible, wonderful feeling. But the legs, the legs didn't listen . . . *"Use the legs," its warmth said. "Use my arms, and kneel. I give permission."*

And then it could move. Eagerly, clumsily, it knelt, staring at the man, the man it didn't know, yet the man knew it. The man held everything it needed.

The man looked him in the eyes and said, "Charley."

It screamed as the world broke. The world broke and broke, and with it all his pieces, but they broke *perfectly*—a sweet, perfect fracturing, as if they danced instead of clashing, a beautiful explosion that made the pieces . . . fall . . . back . . . together.

"I," he whispered. "I. Am. Charley."

The man agreed. He said it again. "Charley."

Suddenly he knew. He knew everything he needed to know. This was it, his *gens compleo,* and he was staring at—good Lord, could he get it any more wrong? Quickly he ducked his head, baring his nape.

"Charley," the man said one more time.

Eagerly he prostrated himself in the grass. It smelled wonderful. He hadn't smelled anything so wonderful in . . . But there was something terrible at the end of that thought, so he shut it away.

A hand, warm and male, rested on his neck. He trembled with readiness.

But nothing pierced his skin. Puzzled, he waited . . . Then he felt wetness there, and he smelled blood, but it was as if someone had painted it on instead of finding it beneath his skin.

And then it didn't matter. He felt the mantle race through him. Joy beyond words shook his body. *I will never be alone again.*

But that thought, too, made him tremble, as if it pulled on the other thought he didn't dare finish. He was confused. The dizzy rush of the mantle retreated, a tide from an ocean that wasn't his—but the ocean held him now. He both was and wasn't with the mantle, and it was right.

"Charley," the man's voice said, and it was different this time. Sad. "You died seven months ago."

Died? But no, that was foolish. He lay here in this wonderful grass, smelling it, feeling the soothing pleasure of the mantle connecting him.

"Sit up."

All right. He sat, but he was oddly clumsy.

"Look at the body you're in."

No. No, he wouldn't. Fear so vast it could swallow him whole froze him. He couldn't look.

But that left him looking into the man's eyes, and they were dark and almost as terrible as the fear. "Bad things happened to you after you died, very bad things. They weren't your fault, Charley, but they caused you to take things that you should never have touched. Now you have to give everything back. Give back all that you've taken wrongly."

He licked his lips. They felt . . . strange. Wrong. "I don't know what you mean."

"Give me your hands."

When he did, the man did a very odd thing. He rubbed something into them. Something gritty that smelled like . . . salt? It . . . it burned. Burned, and ripped at him—he was in pieces again. Pieces, shards, horrible memories slashing him everywhere—his car smashing into a tree, the pain! The steering wheel crushed him, crushed his chest, oh, God, *Mommy* . . . and his mother, weeping and weeping, doing something with his body—dear God, his wolf body, he'd Changed and he'd died, but his mother . . .

Cold. Vast, unstoppable, horrible cold.

Fast now the fragments flew through him. He was in a dog's body, not a wolf's. He caught and killed, but he didn't eat the flesh of the raccoon. He ate . . .

Charley retched, but this body—whatever body he was in—didn't bring anything up. The man held him, his hands gentle, while he tried to purge himself of things this body had never done.

"There was a gun," Charley whispered. "I remember . . . an old man and a gun. He cried."

"That wasn't you," the man said. "That was the wraith."

"But I remember . . ." Then he understood. "The wraith didn't have self." It had never thought "I," denied even that much of a center, its fragments held together by the darkest of magic. And by suffering. The wraith hadn't known it was an "I," but it had known it suffered.

"Now you know what you must give back. And you can, Charley. You attacked me once. When you realized I held part of a mantle—part of Leidolf—you pulled back every bit of the death magic you'd used. Even in your sundered state, you knew how to do that."

Charley remembered that—and quickly shoved the memory away. "I won't do those things anymore," he said, pleading. What he'd taken—what he'd eaten—that was wrong, so horribly wrong. But if he gave it all back, he would be dead. He didn't want to be dead. "I know better now. I remember. I won't do those things."

The man gripped Charley's face in both hands. "Give it back."

"I won't!" he screamed.

The dark eyes closed. The man's face—who was he?—went still, as if he were thinking hard, or praying. But his fingers tightened on Charley's face. His breath started coming faster—fast like Charley's now. And Charley's heart was pounding hard, but oh, it was so good to have a heartbeat again! He wanted to keep it. He *would* keep it.

Suddenly the man gasped. He swayed, but his hands never left Charley's face. His eyes opened, and it seemed they were even darker than before. He said Charley's name once more, then spoke slowly, as one who must be obeyed. "You will give it all back. You will release everything you took."

Oh, Charley thought, staring into those eyes. This wasn't some man. This was his Rho. His Rho commanded him.

So Charley wept. Tears poured down, but he wasn't ashamed. His Rho was asking him to give his life, and there was honor in that. "Yes," he whispered. "I will do . . . as you say. But please . . . the fire? If this is my *gens compleo* . . . please may I have the joining fire first?"

The other man—the one Charley had thought of as a warmth, something to be used or killed—made a fire. Right in the middle of the green grass that smelled so sweet, he tossed a fire down as easily as someone else might sprinkle fertilizer. It was small, but that was all right. It was also green, a lighter, brighter green than the grass. And when Charley put his hand into it, it scampered up his arm. It rolled all over him, tickling.

It was while the fire played with him that he began to let go. It was easy, really. Just as the wraith had instinctively known how to eat, Charley knew how to let go of what he'd taken. It was only energy now.

When he was finished, though, there was still something left. Something very powerful, and . . . shaped. Not just energy. Something incredibly lovely.

"Ready to go?" someone asked.

He looked up as the last of the green fire flickered on his hands and died. A black dude with a paper white face and a top hat stood a few feet away, grinning. He looked odd, but right. Somehow he looked right.

"Who are you?"

The black dude doffed his hat with a little bow. "Think of me as the taxi driver. I'm here to pick you up."

"But what do I do with this?" He indicated in a way he couldn't describe the shaped power that still rested inside him. "Everything else is gone, but this didn't leave."

"It's not going anywhere. You are. Just leave it where you found it." The man held out his hand.

Charley took it.

Lily felt him leave. And she felt what he'd left behind—right where he found it. "Rule," she said, flooded with wonder. "Rule, the mate bond is—"

But she couldn't say anything more, because her lover, her mate, her Rule was holding her too tightly for words, and laughing. Laughing as he covered her mouth with his.

THE day after Charley died for the second and final time, Rule sat in the porch swing with his son. No reporters today, thank God. The grass was wet from a shower last night and the sky was a solid sheet of gray, promising more rain to come. This time, the rain had managed to dial down the thermometer; it was twenty degrees cooler than it had been this time yesterday.

Nettie and Cynna had arrived at Charlotte's airport late last night. Cullen had picked them up and brought them to Halo, going straight to the hospital, where a grouchy Lily was being kept while experts argued about whether she should be released. Her MRI scan didn't show any problems—but everyone who'd been possessed by the wraith had ended up suffering brain damage.

Ruben had given Nettie a security clearance that allowed her full access to all test results from both Meacham and Hodge. She'd studied those as well as Lily's test results. She'd also examined Lily directly, using whatever means healers used to sense the body. In the end, she'd arrived at a theory that the other experts agreed with: possession triggered changes in the brain's chemistry—changes that initially were minor, but which caused a cascade effect if left unchecked, resulting in irreversible damage.

But Lily hadn't reached that point. There were signs of what Nettie called instabilities, but the mate bond seemed to have put a stop to the chemical cascade. Nettie had still ordered Lily to bed—an edict Lily tried to appeal, but no one, not even Rule's father, won that sort of argument with Nettie. Lily was upstairs in bed now, probably asleep.

Nettie's healing Gift couldn't work on Lily directly. A sensitive could not be affected by magic, even if she wanted to be. Yet Nettie could put Lily *in* sleep, a trancelike state that heightened her body's innate healing. Nettie said this was because, as a shaman, she could call on spiritual aid, and Lily's Gift wasn't proof against the spiritual.

The wraith had certainly proven that.

The whole business annoyed Lily no end—for the same reason, Rule suspected, that she was unsettled by the mate bond, the same reason she was baffled by religion. None of them were quantifiable. None offered clear, consistent answers to her questions.

A pale green sedan cruised past. On the sidewalk, a middle-aged woman and her large, happy Labrador retriever trotted past, ignoring the imminent rain. The woman smiled and nodded. The Lab looked astonished.

Caught a whiff of Rule's scent, probably. "What about a Lab?" he said. "They're athletic dogs and are happy with low status as long as they're fed and loved." Since every lupus the dog met would outrank him or her, this was a factor. A few breeds were too innately dominant to thrive at Clanhome.

"Maybe." Toby watched the dog, which stopped twice to look over his shoulder at them. He giggled. "Can't believe his nose, can he?"

Alicia was still hospitalized. She'd done something to her shoulder—Rule was unclear on the specifics—that made her doctor decide to keep her an extra day. Tomorrow she and

James would drive up to D.C. Rule had offered to move to a hotel with Lily so Alicia could recuperate at her mother's home, but Alicia hadn't wanted to.

Perhaps that was for the best. Toby had become upset at the idea of his father staying elsewhere. Rule should stay here, "to protect Grammy."

Clearly Grammy wasn't the only one Toby felt needed protection. He didn't feel safe anymore in the house where he'd grown up, not unless his father was present. It ached Rule's heart.

Not that Toby clung in an obvious way. Once he'd thrown off the effects of the drug last night, he'd asked a lot of questions. Was his mother okay? Why had that woman stolen him? What happened to her? What happened to the wraith she made? Was it okay to kill a woman if she wanted to kill you?

That last question had stalled Rule out. He could discuss killing with his son, but killing a woman . . . Lily had been there, though, and she hadn't hesitated. "Killing someone is never a good choice," she'd said. "But sometimes we don't have any good choices. Is it okay to kill a dog?"

"No!" Toby had exclaimed, frowning in disbelief at the question.

"I had to shoot two dogs that attacked me. They were sick and possessed by the wraith, but even though that wasn't their fault, I had to kill them so they wouldn't kill me. I didn't have time to find another choice. They attacked too fast. Was that okay?"

Toby had thought that over. "Maybe it's a little okay, but mostly it's sad." He thought some more, then asked, "Was the woman who stole me sick like the dogs?"

"Not the same sickness, but yes, she was ill. She'd made some bad choices, and by the time she took you, she didn't know what she was doing anymore."

"Then I guess that's mostly just sad, too."

There on the porch swing, Rule smiled. His *nadia* was wise. His son was, too. They both asked good questions.

The green sedan went by a second time.

"Dad?"

"Yes?"

"Did you know that someone stole Lily, too, when she was about my age?"

Rule looked at Toby, startled. "Yes, I did. She told you about it?"

"Uh-huh. She said a man stole her an' her friend, and the police came and saved her, but they were too late to save her friend. She said sometimes bad stuff happens that isn't our fault, but we can't help thinking about how maybe we could have made it not happen, and I should talk to you when I get to thinking like that."

"Are you thinking like that now?"

"Sorta." Toby fidgeted, then said, "I keep thinking that if I hadn't wanted to play miniature golf, Mom wouldn't have been at that gas station and then she wouldn't have been hurt and I wouldn't have gotten stolen and Lily wouldn't have had to kill the sick woman."

"Maybe. Or maybe the sick woman would have tried to steal you somewhere else, and even more people would have been hurt." Rule squeezed Toby's shoulder. "There's a difference between learning from our mistakes and thinking that everything depends on our choices, as if other people's choices don't count, too. You aren't responsible for what other people did."

"Yes, but . . . but then it seems like we can't ever be sure. We can't know how to act or what to do so we're safe."

"Life isn't safe." It was a hard lesson, but one that lupi believed children must learn. "The best we can get is 'safe enough for now.' "

"I know, but . . ." Toby's voice trailed off unhappily.

"But knowing that in your head is different from knowing it in your gut."

"Yeah."

"Hmm." It wasn't quite raining. It wasn't not raining, either. The air was filling with a fine mizzle that turned it as gray as the sky.

Children weren't good with shades of gray. Rule hunted

for a way to make Toby understand "safe enough." "Your wolf is probably too deeply asleep to counsel you, but perhaps you could imagine what he would say about fear and safety."

"If I could Change," Toby began, then stopped, scowling. "I was gonna say that my wolf wouldn't be afraid, but wolves can get hurt, too, so that doesn't make sense. Does your wolf know he can be hurt?"

"Oh, yes."

"But he isn't afraid about it?"

Rule bit back the need to tell Toby the answer he wanted the boy to find. Some answers had to come from inside. "Wolves feel fear. What do you imagine your wolf would be afraid of?"

"Guns, maybe. Bigger wolves, especially if they're mad at him. Things that could blow him up." Toby thought a moment, his eyes unfocused, as if he might be consulting the sleeping wolf. "Oh. That's all *now* stuff, isn't it? Not maybe stuff."

Rule smiled. "That's right. Wolves fear immediate threats, not the possible threats the mind conjures."

"So is the wolf right? We shouldn't be afraid of stuff that isn't happening now?"

"Mostly right. The world is complex, and wolves aren't good at abstract risks or multiple contingencies, so the wolf may counsel the man on the present, but the man must counsel the wolf on the future. The wolf needs the man just as the man needs the wolf."

Toby said glumly, "I'm not a man yet, and my wolf is asleep. I don't know what's a real threat and what isn't."

"Your job is to learn. My job is to protect you . . ." Rule's voice drifted off as the green sedan approached again. "To protect you while you learn."

Toby looked at the car, too, this time. "That's Alex. How come he isn't stopping? Is he a threat now, because of you taking the whole Leidolf mantle and all?"

Rule knew his body had announced his alertness, and Toby had noticed. "He may be angry, but he won't hurt me or attempt to. I'm his Rho. However, he could be a future threat to me or mine or to plans I've made." He stood, glancing at his son. "I need you to go inside now. Not because there's danger, but because Alex is waiting for that. It's a matter of respect." He paused and smiled in spite of himself. "And tell Lily she may as well come out. As a Chosen, her presence won't signal disrespect."

"Okay, but Nettie's not gonna like it if Lily gets out of bed."

"She's already up, I'm afraid."

The front door opened. "I may not have your hearing, but I'm not deaf," Lily said.

"Also, you opened the window earlier."

"Well, yes. I saw Alex circling the block." She came out on the porch—barefoot, wearing an old T-shirt and jeans . . . with nothing beneath the shirt. She hadn't taken time for a bra. His body signaled strong approval for her haste.

She looked good. She looked wonderful, but then she always did. More important, she smelled healthy. But she wasn't supposed to be up.

"So how come she doesn't show disrespect and I do?" Toby asked as he moved reluctantly toward the door.

"Later." Alex had pulled up to the curb. Rule heard the silence when the engine shut off. "I'll explain later, but basically it's because she's a Chosen. Lily, you should sit down."

Toby sighed and closed the door behind him. Lily moved up beside Rule. "I'm so rested I could scream," she said. "That won't keep Nettie from putting me back in sleep once she finishes yelling at me for getting up, but I'm okay. You can prop me up if you want to," she added in the way of one making a concession.

A wave of feeling rose up, cresting tsunami-high and breaking over him in a wash of love. It had never and would never occur to her to obey him. She did what she did out of choice, and his Chosen chose him over and over.

He accepted her suggestion, sliding an arm around her waist to support her as much as she'd allow . . . while she supported him.

Equals. It wasn't a concept that came readily to a lupus,

but with her, he dealt always with a sovereign power, one that would neither bow to him nor insist on his submission. She was a gift freely given.

A thought floated in as he watched Alex start across the lawn. It wasn't the first time this thought had come to him, though originally it had been so alien he'd given it little heed. But more and more the idea compelled him, drawing him with its rightness. So strange, yet so right.

So difficult, too, he acknowledged wryly, brushing lips across Lily's hair. He strongly suspected his *nadia* would be among the difficulties. But what was life without difficulties?

He turned his full attention to the one who approached.

In the gray drizzle, Alex's damp skin gleamed like melted chocolate. He wasn't a tall man—Rule had three inches on him—but he was broad, and every bit of that breadth was muscle.

Rule had seen Alex fight. He was trained, strong, and quick, a formidable opponent in either form. Rule had spoken truly when he told Toby that Benedict thought highly of Alex's skill.

Rule was trained, strong, and quick too, however. And he had one advantage Alex lacked: he'd been trained by Benedict.

"What are we expecting?" Lily murmured very low.

"To learn in what manner he acknowledges his Rho." A Challenge, most likely. There were other ways to formally recognize a new Rho, but Rule accepted that he'd forfeited the more peaceable options when he killed Victor Frey.

From this man, at least. Rule wouldn't tolerate Challenges from other Leidolf. But Alex had been Frey's Lu Nuncio, and was entitled to express his outrage, so Rule would accept without using the mantle. Better to allow the man to express his anger honorably . . . though Rule had best win the Challenge.

Alex stopped at the foot of the porch steps. He tilted his head the exact fraction necessary to meet Rule's eyes. Leidolf's mantle stirred in Rule's gut, edgy, wanting to answer the implicit challenge in that steady gaze.

Rule restrained it. Neither man spoke.

Alex broke the silence with four terse words. "I greet my Rho." Abruptly he dropped to his knees—then lowered himself awkwardly to his stomach. He lay flat, fully prostrated, on the damp grass.

Astonishment gripped Rule so hard it took him a moment to respond. He stepped off the porch, bent, and touched Alex's nape. "Rise," he said softly.

Alex rose to his feet more gracefully than he'd lowered himself. His mouth moved the fraction that stood for a smile with this deeply taciturn man. "Your face looks funny."

"I am . . ." Flabbergasted. "Seldom as wrong as I was about this. You don't object to my being Rho? Or to the way I assumed the mantle?"

Alex snorted. "Took you long enough."

THIRTY-EIGHT

EVENING dawdled in the summer in North Carolina. At seven thirty, sunshine still slanted brightly through the banked clouds Lily saw out the bedroom window. Those mounds of bruise-colored clouds suggested the rain wasn't through with them yet, but for now the air was clear and almost cool.

Lily had looked up from her laptop, appreciating that dramatic sky, when a female voice said, "That doesn't look like bed rest to me."

"I'm in bed, aren't I?" Lily turned her head, pleased by the company. "And Ruben needs my report. Two birds, one stone."

Cynna Weaver leaned against the doorway frame, arms crossed. She was a tall woman with a butch-crop of blond hair, highly decorated skin, and—at the moment—a sly smile. "I don't think Nettie would see it that way."

"She's not here. She checked me over and didn't, for once, put me back in sleep, so . . ." Lily's voice trailed off. She frowned. "Why are you looking so sneaky and smug?"

"Me? You're imagining things." Cynna straightened, still looking like she ought to have canary feathers on her face. "Pretty nice work clothes."

Lily smiled. "Rule's notion of a bribe. I, uh, got up for a bit earlier, so he shows up with a silk nightgown. I think he thinks I won't go wandering around if I'm wearing it. So are you joining us for supper?"

"Not you. Cullen and I are taking Toby and his grandmother out for pizza."

"Oh. Good. It will be good for him to get out of the house." But that was not what had Cynna smiling that way. Lily couldn't find a clue to the mystery on her friend's face, but maybe that was a clue coming up the stairs. "Sounds like Rule and I are eating by ourselves."

Cynna nodded, trying to keep her face solemn, but whatever secret she was sitting on had her all but wiggling like an excited puppy. She turned her head, grinning. "Hey, Rule," she said to the man coming up behind her. "My, you do clean up pretty."

She shoved away from the door. "Guess I'd better be going." She slid Lily a last wicked grin, waved, and moved aside, letting Lily see that Rule had, indeed, cleaned up. Into a tux.

Every man alive looked better in a tuxedo than just about anything else. Rule in a tux . . . a little curl of lust tightened down low. *Sex and danger,* Lily thought, *sleeked over with a civilized gloss.* A really gorgeous civilized gloss. And under that . . . Lily knew the lean body beneath the beautiful clothing. She knew the sharp, clean bones of his face and the drowning black of his eyes when the wolf wanted out. She knew the strength and the taste of him.

She wanted a taste now. Her eyebrows lifted. "You didn't pack a tuxedo."

"Rented, I'm afraid." He cast one perfectly tailored sleeve a disparaging glance.

"I'm feeling underdressed. I guess we aren't having pizza?"

"Good guess. I hope you've saved whatever you were working on, in defiance of orders."

"Nettie said I should stay in bed, not that—hey!"

He'd set her computer aside and scooped her up in his arms. "Hungry?" he asked softly, nuzzling her ear.

"Getting that way." She traced the quick arch line of his eyebrow with her finger. He was fond of toting her around. At the moment she was inclined to let him get away with that. There were things to do in a bed that didn't involve a laptop, things that might not strike some as restful, but she was sure she'd rest much better afterward. Her current position made it easier to argue her point. "Have I mentioned that you have the sexiest eyebrows I've ever seen?"

The brow in question lifted slightly. "Ah . . . you like my eyebrows?"

"They're one of the first things I noticed about you."

"Pickles and eyebrows," he said obscurely, but he smiled as if whatever connection he'd made pleased him. He started for the hall. "We're dining al fresco."

"Outside? Rule, I'm wearing a nightgown!"

"It's silk. One can't be underdressed in silk, and the others have left." He paused at the top of the stairs, aiming a smile at her. "Indulge me?"

"You're in a funny mood," she murmured. But why not? She was sure sick of the bedroom. "Okay. Dining al fresco in my nightgown. I can handle that. So what," she said as he started down the stairs, "did Alex say when I left you two to your clan talk?"

"Clan secrets," he said promptly.

"Rule—"

He chuckled. "Most of it involved the logistics of bringing as many Leidolf as possible to their clanhome as soon as possible. We'll hold the *gens subicio* next week. Not all will be able to attend, but most will."

"This *gens subicio*—it's when the clan acknowledges you as Rho?"

"The other way around, actually. I hold the mantle. I must recognize them." He cast her an apologetic glance as he started down the stairs. "I realize you hadn't arranged to be away for so long. If necessary, we can fly back to San Diego and wait there until the clan is assembled."

"A week won't matter. I've been put on sick leave." Lily heard the pout in her voice, but couldn't seem to get rid of it.

"No one listens to me. I'm fine. If Nettie didn't keep putting me in sleep, I probably wouldn't even be tired." She didn't stay in sleep long, but she stayed sleepy, dammit.

"I listen to Nettie, who says you don't have to stay in bed after today, but you do need to rest and sleep much more than usual."

Ruben listened to Nettie, too, dammit. That's why she was on sick leave. "She also said I'm healing just fine."

"I wonder . . . could that be because she keeps putting you in sleep and making you rest?"

Lily frowned. "I'm better at sarcasm than you are. Did Alex explain why he was okay with you being Rho?"

"After chiding me for being dense enough to believe he'd disapprove, he pointed out that a live Rho—even one who still smells halfway of Nokolai—is better than an all-but-dead Rho. Especially one who was crazy before he went into coma. He couldn't indicate that to me before, of course. He's an honorable man."

Lily picked out the significant part. "Halfway?"

"Apparently I smell about half Nokolai now and half Leidolf."

"You okay with that?"

He was silent a moment. "Historically, women were sometimes wed to their families' enemies to foster peace. They gave up their names and their homes, yet some of them remained close to their original family. It's possible to find a balance."

He meant he wasn't one hundred percent okay, but he intended to get there. How like him, she thought, to find the example he needed in women's lives. She touched his cheek. "You don't have a problem using a feminine role model?"

"My people have always revered the strength of women."

"Not Leidolf."

"I am Rho now. Leidolf will change." He said that with a certainty verging on arrogance. "Now, if you'd get the door?"

They'd reached the glass sliders. She reached for the handle and pulled. "I want them to change, too, but I don't want you to get yourself killed trying to . . . oh. Oh, wow."

The little gazebo in the center of the yard had been draped

with tied-back white sheers and about a thousand twinkle lights. The dusty lawn furniture was gone; instead a round table wearing floor-length white and two chairs occupied the concrete floor . . . which had been covered with a plush white rug.

There were candles. Flowers floating in a shallow white bowl. China so delicate it was almost transparent. And everything was white, a white brightened by the brilliance of blade and leaf, bush and tree surrounding the little gazebo. Even the towering clouds gleamed white at their crests before tumbling down through silver, gray, rose, and lavender.

"It's so perfect," she whispered. "How could you make it so perfect?"

"God helped. The background was Her idea."

She shot him a startled look, then laughed. "Okay, so what are we celebrating? You can put me down now."

He didn't, crossing the lawn with her still in his arms. "We might be celebrating your managing to stay in bed for nearly the entire day."

"Almost worth it," she decided as he at last set her on her feet next to one of the glossy white chairs.

There was champagne chilling in a bucket. Rule reached beneath the draped table and pulled out an ordinary ice chest—but the contents were anything but ordinary. Grapes, three kinds of cheese, apple blini with sour cream—who in Halo knew how to make blini?—and cold roast duck.

Also pickles. Five kinds of pickles. Lily nearly teared up over the pickles.

"In memory of our first meal together," he murmured. "You piled half a jar's worth of pickles on your burger."

"And you piled half a cow's worth of patties on yours. Rare." She smiled—and, dammit, she was tearing up. "Now look what you've done. I . . . What, there's more?"

He'd bent to retrieve one more thing from beneath the table—a lily. Or rather a cluster of lilies on a single long stem, lilies the color of flame, with big brown freckles like sunspots on their tightly curled petals.

Lilium lancifolium. The Oriental tiger lily.

"How in the world did you find tiger lilies? I've tried—for Grandmother, you know—but florists never carry them. They fade too quickly."

"It . . ." Rule stopped. Swallowed. "Toby. He went around on his bike, found someone who grew them. I . . ." Mutely he held out the bright flowers.

She took the stalk, but her attention was for Rule, not his offering. He was . . . tongue-tied? Nervous, definitely, and she's never seen that in him.

"The ribbon," he said, his voice tight, as if his throat were closing up on him. "The ribbon."

Oh. She hadn't noticed, but yes, there was a green ribbon tied in an awkward bow at the center of the stalk, half-hidden by one of the blooms. Did he want her to untie it? Puzzled, she moved the bloom aside . . .

And shoved to her feet, her heart pounding like a mad thing, her eyes wide and fixed on the orange flowers she'd dropped, such a bright orange against the white china plate. Flowers tied with a green ribbon. A ribbon threaded through a ring.

A ring with a single diamond.

"It's not a snake," Rule said dryly.

"It's a ring. An engagement ring." Now she looked at him, her voice rising. "You can't give me that. You can't."

"I can. I have. The question is whether you'll accept it." He pushed back his chair, stood, and ran a hand over his hair. "I had this speech worked out. I thought it was good, but I can't remember it. I can't remember a single word. I got everything else right, but the words . . . I wanted it to be right."

She spoke slowly, as if he might need time to absorb each word. "You can't get married. You can't marry, so you can't give me an engagement ring."

"Marry me."

That's when she lost words.

He'd found them again. "I'm pretty sure that was part of the speech, though I hope I worked it in more gracefully. Marry me, Lily."

"You think I'd do that?" she demanded, suddenly fierce.

"You think I'd agree to cut you off from your people, force you into something you believe is wrong, in order to please myself or to satisfy some—some bunch of whoevers who know nothing about us?"

"No. Marry me because I ask." He rounded the table and gripped her arms just above the elbows. "Not to satisfy anyone else, though other people *do* matter, Lily. Your family matters. All the people who deride you for associating with me—their barbs can hurt. And they make trouble for you. You know they do."

"No biggie. I can handle that sort—who wouldn't stop being assholes if I wore a ring, you know."

"They aren't all assholes. Take Sheriff Deacon. He made your job harder because of me. He's not a bad person—bigoted, or he was, but that's ignorance. He's basically an honorable man, and he couldn't see you clearly because of me. Because he believed I treated you dishonorably."

"So to make my life a little easier I'm supposed to ruin yours? Rule, I may not have grown up in the clans, but I *know* how they'd react. How your father would react."

"I can handle it. Handle him."

"Some of them are shunning Cullen. Did you know that? You must. He shrugs it off, but he's used to being an outsider. You—"

"He was right. He said I was jealous, and he was right. I want this for *me*. You'll have to decide if it's right for you, but . . ." His expression hardened. "I warn you, if you say no, I won't give up. I'll keep asking."

Reality had turned fizzy. Or maybe that was her blood bubbling in her veins. Her head felt light, floaty, as if she'd already downed that bottle of champagne. "That's not exactly fair, is it? I can't leave if you—if you keep bugging me."

"You'll have to deal with that."

Oh, there was that arrogance again, but with it, beneath it, he was grim. Her heart fluttered. "Why?" she whispered. "Why do you want this? I love you. We're bonded for life. Marriage won't . . ." Her voice trailed off. She swallowed. "Why?"

"I want to plight you my troth." His voice was soft now. Quiet. "It's a lovely old word, isn't it? Troth. It means loyalty, the pledge of fidelity. It comes from an Old English word meaning truth. You are my truth, Lily."

This man, she thought. This was the man, the only man, her Rule, her mate, the one she loved in both his selves, wolf and human . . . Loved his mysteries, his beauty, his quirks, and his arrogance. Loved his slanted eyebrows and the way he listened and the way he gave and gave and gave. She loved him. *Loved* him.

And he said it again. "Marry me."

Like suddenly starred ice, she cracked—the fissures spreading, breaking up into giggling shots of fizz—a cork-popping, fiercely bubbling, frost-and-fire effervescence that had her laughing, throwing her arms around him and laughing as she held on, held on to him as she said it: "Yes."

AUTHOR'S NOTE

I hope you enjoyed *Mortal Sins*. If you've been following the series, you know that sometimes worlds collide literally in my books. In *Blood Lines*, the worlds involved were more personal. Every time two people fall in love, there's a collision—the need to blend furniture, jobs, beliefs . . . and families. A permanent bond between a couple means their families are joined, too, for better or worse.

If you're new to the series, you may have questions about the history of these people and their world. There's a list of previous books in the front pages of this one, but I'll add a few details here. In *Blood Lines*, worlds collided literally—the realms shifted, bumping together, and magic leaked back into our world. After a centuries long exile, dragons returned to Earth. This time, they were welcome. Magic and technology don't play well together, and the increased level of magic since the Turning has played havoc with computers and other technology. Dragons are natural magic sponges—they soak it up like kitty litter absorbs liquid.

Lily Yu played a part in that. But before the Turning and the return of dragons, she'd encountered them in Dis, a realm also known as hell. That's when her soul was ripped in two, leaving her vulnerable to the wraith in *Mortal Sins*. If you want to know more, I hope you'll check out *Mortal Danger*.

Before *Mortal Danger* came *Tempting Danger*, where

the orignal head-on collision—the mate bond—occurred. *Tempting Danger* also introduced Cullen, who suffered his own world-twisting bump when Cynna turned up in *Mortal Danger*. Cullen and Cynna fought and eventually fit; their story is told most fully in *Night Season*. There's also a free short story about them on my website: www. eileenwilks.com. You'll find a link to the story on the *Night Season* page.

Collisions continue in the next book in the series, *Blood Magic*. Lily is coming to terms with the consequences of saying "yes" to marriage when the past smashes into the present. An old enemy of the family will stop at nothing to achieve revenge, littering San Diego with nightmares and death.

Turn the page for a preview
of the next lupi novel

BLOOD MAGIC

Coming soon from Berkley Sensation!

THE mountains east of San Diego were almost always hotter than the city. Their higher elevation didn't make up for losing the cooling power of the ocean. But the sun was down now, and in the small valley that held the village at the heart of Nokolai Clanhome, the temperature had dropped to a balmy seventy-six.

The moon wasn't yet up, but Lily kept track of that sort of thing these days. She knew it would rise half-full in about two hours. The clan's meeting field was alive with song, laughter, and people—far more people than actually lived there—and Lily was relieved bordering on smug.

The baby shower had gone off without a hitch, and the meeting ground was so full she had to thread her way through the crowd. Many of them didn't live at Clanhome, so she didn't know them. They all knew who she was, though—a bit disconcerting, that, but she smiled and nodded when strangers greeted her.

There were a lot of kids. They raced through the crowd in shoals like minnows swimming a living current. Toby was one of them, but she hadn't seen him since he finished bolting his food.

So far, becoming a parent to Rule's son was almost too easy. The only hard part was prying the boy loose from the rest of the clan. Lupi adored babies and children of all ages, and they saw no reason Toby shouldn't spend all his time at Clanhome.

Most of the adults were male, and most of them weren't wearing much. Among adults, male clan outnumbered female about three to one, and lupi possessed no body modesty whatsoever. Every man in Lily's sight was bare-chested, barefoot, and barely covered between the navel and the knees. Cut-offs were the most popular choice.

Lily enjoyed the view. What woman wouldn't? Even the chests with grizzled gray hair were worth a second glance. There was no such thing as a fat, sloppy, out-of-shape lupi. Everyone knew that. Just like everyone knew that the lupus ability to turn furry was inherited, not contagious. And that they were always male. And that they didn't marry. Ever.

Lily rubbed her thumb over the ring she'd slipped onto her finger for the party. Everyone could be wrong, it seemed. Including her.

Rule was beside her, talking investments with her brother-in-law, Paul—not a subject that held much interest for her. Lily let her attention drift away, looking for Benedict or Cullen. She wanted a word with the former, and she needed to give Cullen the . . . Wait. Was that who Beth had seen earlier?

But how could Beth have mistaken that man for their cousin? The man she'd glimpsed was certainly Asian, but he didn't look like Freddie. About the same height, maybe, but his nose was different, and she thought he was older. Plus he'd been wearing a T-shirt and ball cap. Stuffy Freddie didn't own a ball cap. She wasn't sure he owned a T-shirt.

She touched Rule's arm. "I need to find Cullen and give him his present."

He gave her the kind of smile he ought to reserve for when they were alone, brought her hand to his lips, and kissed it. "You'll save me a dance."

"Maybe two." One dance here. One when they were alone.

Lily smiled at that thought and went looking—and not just for Cullen.

The fiddlers launched into a lively song and people were making room for dancing ... square dancing, maybe, from the sound of the music. So far no one was calling, though, so maybe it would be Western swing this time.

That was another thing about lupus gatherings—there was always music and usually dancing, but you never knew what kind. It depended on who showed up and what they wanted to play.

Lily knew one of the men fiddling for them tonight. In his other life, he was first violinist at the San Diego Symphony—and no one he worked with knew he was lupus, which was reason enough to track down Benedict. Nokolai might have gone public, but some of its members hadn't. With the Species Citizenship Bill still bogged down in committee, some couldn't afford to. It was legal to fire a lupus for being a lupus, and plenty of places would do just that.

Ten minutes later she gave up on finding the Asian man. She couldn't even find anyone who'd seen him. In this sea of Caucasian faces and bare chests, he ought to stand out, dammit. Any human male ought to stand out here, but the few who'd noticed an Asian man apparently meant Paul, based on what they remembered about height and clothing. No one remembered seeing anyone in a ball cap.

Of course, that proved nothing. Lily had interviewed too many witnesses to have much confidence in human memory and attention to detail, and she had no reason to think lupi did any better.

But some of them did. Some, she realized, would have been paying attention. She nodded to herself and started looking for a man no one would overlook.

Sure enough, Benedict was easy to find.

Benedict was at the north end of the field near the tubs of drinks, talking to a man she didn't know. They spoke briefly, then Benedict moved on. Lily raised her voice slightly. "Benedict."

He turned and waited, giving her a nod when she reached

him. Benedict was in charge of Clanhome's security. Now that the training dance was over, he'd added some of his usual accessories to his cut-offs—a large sword sheathed on his back, a holstered .357 at his hip, and an ear bud. His phone was fastened to his belt opposite the .357.

The combination of low-tech and high-tech weaponry, bare skin, and impressive musculature gave him the look of an animated gaming character, with a whiff of Secret Service from the ear bud. She had to smile. "No machine gun?"

"No. I'm not expecting trouble."

He was serious. At least she thought he was—with Benedict it was hard to tell. "That dance was really something. I've never seen anything like it."

He nodded, agreeing. Maybe pleased.

"Does it mean—"

"I won't discuss my relationship with my brother with you."

Her eyebrows climbed. Good guess, even if he was wrong about the outcome. Sooner or later, they would discuss that. "I'll table that for now. I have a security concern."

He didn't move. His expression didn't change. Yet everything about him sharpened. "Yes?"

"I've seen an Asian man here I can't account for. Not Paul— you've seen Paul Liu, my brother-in-law? This man is shorter than Paul and possibly older. I only got one glimpse, so I can't give much of a description, but he was wearing a dark ball cap and a pale shirt with short sleeves. Probably a T-shirt."

"I haven't seen him or received a report of him, and my people are tracking all the *ospi* currently at Clanhome."

Lily blinked. *Ospi* meant out-clan guest. "My sisters? You're tracking my sisters?"

His smiled slightly. "I keep track of any out-clan who enter Clanhome."

Had she been mistaken? Lily drummed her fingers on her thigh. No, she decided. She hadn't. "There aren't any Asian Nokolai, are there?"

"Two," Benedict said promptly. "Half-Asian, of course. One has a Korean mother and lives in Los Angeles. He's ten years old. The other is an adult whose mother was Japaense. John Ino is fifty-seven and lives in Seattle, and I doubt he's here today. But it's possible."

"Find out. I saw an Asian man in a ball cap. He's not a guest, and it sounds like he isn't Nokolai." Maybe he'd only worn the cap for a short time. Maybe he'd seen her looking for him and faded away from the crowd. Maybe he'd left altogether, in which case they were too late, but it was worth finding out. "This party would be one hell of an opportunity for a paparazzi, and they make cameras really small these days."

Benedict considered her for a moment, then nodded. "All right. Whoever he is, this man didn't come in either of the gates. It's possible to enter elsewhere, but only on foot. Which means he's left a scent trail." He pulled out his phone and hit a number. "Saul. I need you. I'm by the soft drinks."

He put up the phone. "Saul's got the best nose of any of my people. He'll Change and you'll show him where you saw the man. With so many trampling over the ground, he may not be able to pick up the scent there, but it's a place to start."

"Good. Why did you participate in the dance tonight?"

"To impress the youngsters so they'll try harder."

"That's not the only reason. Rule danced, too, and neither of you usually does."

His mouth curved up a fraction. "You're perceptive. It's annoying at times. Very well. I also sent a message. I'm not speaking to my brother, but I fully support my Lu Nuncio. It was best that everyone understand that."

So his problem with Rule was personal, not a "good of the clan" thing. "You think they'll get that message from the dance?"

His eyebrows lifted about a millimeter. "Of course."

Hmm. "Well, it made for a fantastic show. But how in the world did you end it that way? Even if you're strong enough to just stop him one-handed, it seems like you'd break a few bones—his, yours, both."

"Seabourne's good. Quick. When he—" His head whipped up. Without a gesture or word or a single damned clue what was wrong, he took off running.

EILEEN WILKS

USA Today Bestselling Author of
Mortal Danger **and** *Blood Lines*

NIGHT SEASON

Pregnancy has turned FBI Agent Cynna Weaver's whole life upside down. Lupus sorcerer Cullen Seabourne is thrilled to be the father, but what does Cynna know about kids? Her mother was a drunk. Her father abandoned them. Or so she's always believed.

As Cynna is trying to wrap her head around this problem, a new one pops up, in the form of a delegation from another realm. They want to take Cynna and Cullen back with them—to meet her long-lost father and find a mysterious medallion. But when these two born cynics land in a world where magic is commonplace and night never ends, their only way home lies in tracking down the missing medallion—one also sought by powerful beings who will do anything to claim it...

penguin.com

Discover Romance

berkleyjoveauthors.com

See what's coming
up next from your
favorite romance
authors and
explore all
the latest
Berkley,
Jove, and
Sensation
selections.

Fall in love

- See what's new
- Find author appearances
- Win fantastic prizes
- Get reading recommendations
- Chat with authors and other fans
- Read interviews with authors you love

berkleyjoveauthors.com

M1G0907